WHERE SEAGULLS DARE

MARK FARRER

ISBN: 1 534 82425 1
ISBN-13: 978-1534824256

To Katie B.
for giving me permission.

PART 1

Start where you are

1

Georgi watched in disbelief as the sniper zoomed away in his little boat. He looked down at his leg, bleeding heavily, as his *Everything Is Awesome* ringtone echoed across the still water.

Stupefied, he unscrewed the lid from the bottle, poured some vodka down his throat and a good slug onto his leg. He almost blacked out from the pain and screamed angrily as his phone rang again. He pulled it from his pocket and hit the green symbol with his thumb to hear Tony's voice:

"Georgi, it's Tony. How did it go?"

Tony's Russian was practically non-existent but he guessed by the volume and stream of hard consonants that the translation of Georgi's reply was probably along the lines of "not very well". Georgi hung up and Tony decided he might wait a while before calling him again.

Viktor had dropped Georgi off at Stornoway Harbour two days earlier. He had immediately high-tailed it out of town and holed up at the Butt Of Lewis lighthouse. The tourist leaflets described the Outer Hebrides as a haven for wildlife, a tranquil landscape of unspoilt beaches, rolling farmland and hidden coves. A chance to slow down and sample life at a more natural pace, where the air was fresh, the sky was wide and blue, and the welcome was as warm as the people.

Georgi thought the place was a fucking dump.

His first issue was that he couldn't find anywhere open after 11pm where he could buy some booze. Everywhere seemed shut. If this was Stornoway on a Saturday night he didn't want to experience it on a Sunday.

The next morning he realised the full gravity of this statement - there would have been more open facilities in a Siberian gulag, abandoned to the permafrost, alone on the steppes, that was closed on Sundays. He had managed to arm wrestle a petrol station attendant to turn his back for five minutes while he smashed the locked roll-down screen behind the counter and swiped a few bottles of brandy and some cigars. But here on the floor of the lighthouse storeroom, two bottles and half the cigars later, the empties rolled and clinked with the draught under the door and the cigars had been no substitute for a solid meal. His guts complained and he farted noisily.

He also stank, but this was nothing unusual. For the past five years Georgi had lived his life rolling from one midden to another, barely ever coherent or sober, infrequently presentable, usually on the verge of being violent, sick or violently sick. In any award ceremony involving entrance into the pantheon of infamous Russian drunks throughout the ages, he would have certainly have been among the nominations - some achievement considering the quality of the competition. He didn't celebrate this fact, nor bother himself with it. He was what he was and anyone who didn't like it had better get used to it or get out of his face before he got off his.

He stood, scratched his bare arse and considered the view from the small sash window above the sink. What had Viktor said again? "Stick to instructions. Move round, stay low, do damage. Pickup in two weeks." Never one for chitchat, that Viktor. But, usefully, he did speak some English whereas Georgi himself could barely make himself understood in any language other than grunts and facial expressions. He relied heavily on the universal sign language for "No", "Fuck off" and "Now".

He unrolled an Ordnance Survey map from a stained and battered duffel bag and spread it on the unvarnished table. It was heavily annotated with Cyrillic characters in different colours of vibrant highlighter pen, mostly around the coast - scruffy trails of Barbie pink and viscous yellow, lime green and vivid orange across the Minches and North Atlantic. To the uninitiated it would have meant little; Georgi counted himself amongst that number. Whatever Viktor had told him about it had completely gone from his mind. Fortunately this did not dishearten him in anyway - he was used to working blind and having to vaguely recall instructions previously given. It hadn't held him back in discharging his duties thus far. The impact on his superiors, however, was another matter but certainly not one Georgi concerned himself with. For now, he had more immediate concerns - like where was he going to get more brandy now that he had finished his last bottle?

That Monday morning, he had tried to keep the clinking vodka bottles silent in his duffel bag as he *shhh*-ed himself out of the van and tumbled unevenly to the tarmac. It was still dark and there was no-one around the salmon farm this early but he was being extra careful in the way that only drunken men trying to be extra careful can be. The front bumper had picked up some hedgerow and assorted foliage from his wayward journey to the site and there were a couple of front gardens on the route out from Stornoway which would find they had been visited by a random topiarist fairy when their owners looked out at first light.

His exertions last night had taken their toll - the police would later identify an aggravated assault, theft of a vehicle, theft from a vehicle and an attempted ram-raid on a licensed corner shop. Four separate crimes in one two-hour window representing their peak crime period on the island for the last eleven years. He had finished off the first bottle while driving clear of the town boundary, pulled over in Tarbert to pack the canvas sacks into the back of the van, and then slept off the worst of his endeavours in a lay-by on the way down through Harris.

The shore-base for the farm was sited in the middle of a sweeping bay scolded by low hills. A promontory at each end acted as a natural tidal break from the Minch, which ran from the bay across to the west mainland of Scotland. Dotted across the bay were three separate farm sites, each with eight round cages arranged in pairs along a central spine of pipework and walkways which led from a floating barge anchored in place. Perhaps a mile apart from each other, one was only about 200m from the shore and this was the one Georgi set his sights on - he wasn't a good swimmer and didn't fancy the thought of sailing alone when over a mile from shore.

He parked up by the shore-base and found a small, untended flat-bottomed motorboat tied up next to the jetty. He opened the van doors at the rear and transferred the sacks to the boat two at a time. It was heavy work and he was soon sweating even though it was still very cold in the gathering dawn. When he was done he shambled over to the main building and put his fist through the small window next to a side door. The window mechanism was painted over and wouldn't budge but when he gave the door a shove he realised it was unlocked and it flew open. In a small room just inside the door he found a rack of survival suits, galoshes, gloves, and life jackets. He took off his coat, boots and duffel bag and suited up. Putting one vodka bottle in a large outside pocket, he emerged into the burgeoning light and walked down to the motorboat, swigging from his other bottle as he went.

He made it to the first barge with surprising ease and congratulated himself on his newfound seamanship. He climbed out of the boat and onto the deck, lugging the sacks out after him. Christ they were heavy. He didn't know what was in them - Viktor hadn't told him (because Viktor didn't know either) - but it felt like they were full of rock salt. Damp, sandy, heavy sacks he had to lug into the van, out of the van into the boat, out of the boat onto the barge and then down into the barge itself.

Georgi looked around and wondered why this was called a barge. It wasn't his idea of one. It was more like a floating cube of concrete with railings around it and a small cabin on the top with a door which disappeared down into the cube's interior via a set of alarmingly steep steps. One at a time, crouching under the weight of each sack, he hunkered over to the doorway like a sou'westered chimp off to a bring-a-bottle party. He used one of the sacks to prop the door open and then threw the others down the steps. He threw the door jamb sack down last and then finished off the bottle of vodka, throwing it into the sea. It bobbed and drifted in the calm water.

He slid himself down the steps and began the process of emptying the sacks into the shiny feed silos in the belly of the barge. On the wall was a complicated control panel with lots of red and green buttons and silver pipes leading up from the hoppers out of sight through the ceiling. He vaguely remembered now a diagram that Tony had shown him illustrating the way these salmon farms worked: attached to each barge were a number of cages filled with salmon; pipes and hoses led to each cage and the fish food pellets in these silos were pumped up from inside the barge, along the tubes and then fired out over the surface of each cage, sinking as they went before being snatched by the greedy fish. He remembered particularly because Tony's diagram had a very funny (funny because it was so poorly drawn) drawing of a feeding salmon. Out of proportion to the barge, it looked like an angry sea monster from an old pirate map.

Georgi grinned to himself as, at last, he felt the sweet release as the weight of each sack disappeared with the "rock salt" as it emptied into the silos. It looked like rock salt as well. Job done, he sat on the floor surrounded by the empty sacks, lit himself a victory cigar and opened his last bottle of vodka.

When he woke, he didn't know how long he'd been out. His cigar had burnt out in his fingers but he still had tight hold of the bottle which was now half-empty. Stirring himself he got to his feet and clambered inelegantly back up the barge steps. He emerged into the daylight to the sound of shots being fired. What the fuck? Georgi ducked down behind the swinging door and listened carefully. A rifle, not automatic. One weapon only, no more. Firing from away to his left, he felt certain. He must have presented a pretty good target in this light, all clad in dayglo yellow. He took another swig trying to force his brain into some kind of forward gear. He didn't know what the fuck was going on but he had decided that, now that he'd dealt with the fish, he was going to deal with the bastard with the gun.

For Stanley it had all happened a bit fast. An hour ago he had left home as usual and headed for his first assignment. He'd arrived at the shore base in his 4x4, slung his rifle over his shoulder and headed down the jetty to the skiff moored there. Nothing unusual about there being no-one around. He'd dealt with seals here several times before and it made sense to do the shooting when there were no staff around, reduce the chance of someone being accidentally shot.

He piloted the skiff towards the nearest barge and checked out the water with his binoculars in one hand as he steered with the other hand. He killed the engine about a hundred yards from the cages as he thought he saw a disturbance in the leftmost cage. He crouched low in the boat and scanned the cage through his binoculars more carefully. After a minute he saw what he was looking for: the shiny head and mottled body of an adult seal, about two metres long, sliding through the water, nostrils flaring. Then it dived and disappeared from view.

Then he saw another. And another.

Grey seals are very partial to salmon. When one of their favourite foods is kept *en masse* in cages holding several thousand fish - each three or more kilos of tasty treat, packed tightly together - it is a smorgasbord for any seal. Not only can an adult seal eat its way through several hundred salmon, it can also damage the nets holding the fish. This damage can both let in other seals and allow the valuable cargo to escape. Whichever way you looked at it, seals were bad news for the salmon business, so snipers like Stanley were much in demand for their services in keeping the seal population under control.

He let the skiff drift gently into the barge and moored it against a service ladder onto the deck. He tied the rifle strap round his arm to steady it and lent carefully on the edge of the deck trying to get the seal in his sights. When the first seal reappeared he squeezed off a shot, and then another, unsure if he had hit it. He quickly scanned again with his binoculars and then raised the rifle back against his shoulder.

Poised, still, waiting for his target to reappear, Stanley suddenly heard the theme tune from *The Lego Movi*e cut through the morning air. Turning in the direction of the sound he saw a large bull of a man in a yellow survival suit, rampaging towards him. He was carrying a clear glass bottle in one hand and shouting "Fuck! Fuck! Fuck!" loudly as he swatted the pocket holding his phone with his other hand, presumably trying to silence it. He was perhaps twenty yards away and gaining rapidly.

The sniper turned smoothly, rifle still levelled at his shoulder and fired once. The man went down like a felled wildebeeste and writhed on the deck clutching his leg. He tried to get up but couldn't quite seem to catch his balance.

Stanley didn't hang around. He threw the safety on his rifle, slung it back over his shoulder, fired the skiff motor up and steered it quickly away back to shore. He was breathing hard and didn't dare look back. Internally he was already rehearsing his story for the police and reminding himself to add on a significant "danger money" premium when he later submitted his invoice.

2

The previous evening and a hundred miles away, Tony had had his own problems. He was sitting stunned and bleeding in the passenger seat while Viktor, the taciturn Russian, had put his foot down and steered the BMW efficiently through the rain.

The road was little more than an unlit dirt track, twisting and turning up the hill away from the hatchery. Behind them a small burst of flame licked out from a window in the portakabin, the largest of the buildings clustered together at the foot of the hill. A small explosion, silent now from this distance, saw the roof of the portakabin collapse and the fire spread to two of the other outbuildings nearby.

Once it reached the sacks of feed stockpiled in the storage warehouse the whole place would go up like tinder. Salmon feed contained a large percentage of fish oil - in this case, Tony knew, 52.8% exactly - and when that caught fire you'd know about it. And, if they had been sentient at this point, so would the millions of fish within this hatchery. Enough junior salmon to stock most of Lochs Carron and Kishorn for the next two years.

"Jesus titty-fucking Christ! What the fuck did you do that for?" Tony took his shirt off and tried wiping the blood and dirt from his face.

"Was necessary." Viktor couldn't have registered less emotion if he tried,

"No it fucking wasn't necessary. It was totally un-fucking-necessary!"

"Fire needed to start so I started fire."

"I had it in hand. I explained to you about the alarm system. I told you it would start to heat the tanks once the sensors were recalibrated."

"Was taking too long."

"No it fucking wasn't. You fucking red Russki retard!"

Viktor drove in silence, taken aback by the ferocity of Tony's alliteration

"Christ on a bike! You are packing some serious weapons-grade fuckupery, my friend."

"Is OK. Farm is now on fire."

"Yes, but don't you get it? When they come and investigate they'll see that it was started deliberately! They'll know it was sabotage. This is a total and complete clusterfuck."

Viktor barely shrugged.

"Don't you care or don't you get it?"

"Is not problem."

"It is a fucking problem, numb-nuts!"

"Is not a problem."

"Jesus. I don't know what your problem is, Viktor, but I bet it's fucking hard to pronounce."

Viktor looked across unperplexed. "You swear too much."

Davy Jackson was nursing a half when his mobile vibrated on the bar. The caller id showed it was the hatchery's alarm and he flew out of the pub and into his car, grinding the gears as he raced down the main road. The alarm system monitored the temperature of the different tanks and incubators. If any tolerance was breached the system would automatically dial the phone number of whoever was on out-of-hours call duty at the time. If the call wasn't acknowledged it would go through a list of backup phone numbers in turn until one picked up. If the temperature breaches were sufficient large it would also call the landline number at the Kyle fire station.

Davy was a mile from the hatchery when he saw the flames. He pulled over and dialled 999. When he reached the site he could see a number of the outbuildings ablaze but the main infrastructure looked still largely untouched. The major fire was near the feed store over by the main gate. He stood and watched for a few seconds and then dashed over to the main entrance and fiddled with his keys to get into the premises. The lights on the alarm control console were winking amber and red for six of the 24 tanks on screen. The fire station was over 20 miles away and he reckoned the fire brigade wouldn't be there for at least half an hour, assuming the crew were all within easy reach of the station. He kept watch out of the window as lights seven and eight winked amber and then red.

Viktor dropped Tony at the small Lochcarron View hotel, barely bringing the car to a stop before skidding and fishtailing off into the night. Tony had wrapped the blood-soaked shirt into a ball, stashed it in his rucksack and then pulled on a sweatshirt which he'd left on the backseat. He didn't look laundry fresh but he'd pass muster at a glance from a bored and sleepy clerk at the front desk.

His room was small and smelled of damp. It held an old double bed covered with a faded pink candle-wicked counterpane up against a wall with the only window. Along the opposite wall was an equally old mahogany wardrobe with one handle missing and a large scratch on one door. To the side of this was the door to the en-suite which, matching the bedroom, was small and equally malodorous.

Tony pulled the cord for the shaving light above the sink so he could examine his face properly. In the mirror he could see it was really only a cut about two inches long above his left eyebrow which ran up beyond his hairline. The bleeding had stopped so he ran the shower for a minute or two to get the temperature right, peeled off his clothes and jumped in. The water stung his head but he kept himself under for as long as he could bear.

He would kill that Viktor next time he saw him. The cut was all his fault and if they hadn't needed to get away so quickly before the fire caught, the pair of them would have been having a fistfight when the fire engines turned up. Tony had told Viktor not to do anything which might arouse suspicion. He'd done his research and spent a lot of time thinking and planning this through - far too many pains taken to have this clumsy Russian fuck it up at the eleventh hour.

What the fuck was Krupchenko going to say? Wait - no need for him to know right? The job had been done and Krupchenko would be back in Russia before any of this broke. This was just a small story in a remote part of Scotland - it wasn't going to make a national news bulletin or anything. Probably the stupid local fire service wouldn't even notice that an incendiary had been used to start the fire. Chill, Tony told himself. Chill.

Tony had been born and raised in La Jolla, California. His father had tenure and lectured in Life Sciences at UCSD, his mother had been a victim of the LSD counterculture of the 60's and thought she'd had a past life as an orange. Growing up in southern California, the son of wealthy parents, his youth had been an ideal mixture of sun, surfing and teenage sex. By the time he was eighteen he was 6' 2", 220 lbs of all-American beefcake - good hair, teeth, skin, genes. An absolute babe magnet.

His success with girls was, however, not quite the success Tony considered it to be. The endless procession of beach bunnies he paraded on his arm and in his car, spoke more to the disappointment each girl felt after a short period of time in his company than his own prowess in the sack. None of them, it seemed, loved him as much as he did. None of them were enamoured with his enormous sense of entitlement and his less than enormous male appendage.

His impenetrable veneer of self-belief, though, was never shattered. The fact that the arrival of his next conquest always seemed to coincide with the discrete departure of his current one, never occurred to him. If asked to vote, his ex-girlfriends would all have agreed that his principal failings centred on the endless monologues about himself he assumed others found fascinating, and the annoying habit he had of referring to his penis either in the third person or by unamusing euphemisms.

Led by Lil' Tony, his sticky grenade, his undercover brother, Tony considered himself to be the best pork swordsman in The Golden State. Without exception, however, his sexual partners felt both sorry for him and immensely grateful for their own narrow escape.

Thusly, Tony pursued his High School and College years. Never focussing, never settling, never concentrating. Carefree and benefitting from a distinct lack of close parenting he had inherited his mother's languid grace and athleticism rather than his father's intelligence and this, inevitably, led him to become a sports major with an effortless sense of superiority.

Until he was bitten by the eco-bug.

He could remember it clearly - although, more accurately, it was a memory of not being bitten. Another warm and sunny SoCal day, he'd been down at Black's Beach with some friends experimenting with a new surfboard and the concept of nude surfing. Not as painful as it sounded but, then again, not something he wanted to repeat on a regular basis. He had swum out to catch one last roller as the lazy afternoon started to drag when he caught sight of an upturned surfboard floating loose away to his right. He hadn't seen anyone else swim out this way but the current was strong in certain places. He looked again, though, as it dropped like a silent elevator and he felt his stomach do the same as he realised it wasn't a surfboard, but a shark.

Using what nerve remained, he pulled himself up onto his floating board and tried to lay still while he watched for the killer shape to reappear. The next wave came upon him and he clung to his board, his fingers white with grip, as the shark rolled stealthily beneath him. Piss trickled down his legs. Tony flailed his head all around, crying with fear, and saw nothing until away to his left he noticed a growing darkness beneath the surface rifling towards him. Fast. Deadly. True. As it neared Tony could see a huge black eye and then a flash of smooth flank as the shape leapt from the water and was met by another rising from the sea barely ten feet in front of him. There was an almighty wet smack and when the spray subsided he could see a great white shark with a bloody sea lion embedded in its mouth.

When he later looked back on it he would reassemble the jigsaw of what he had seen and arrange it into a comprehensible, if unbelievable, sequence of events. Either the shark had been in pursuit of the sea lion all along and Tony had been an unwilling witness, or - more incredibly - the shark had been on the point of eating him when the sea lion had given its all for humanity and committed a suicide leap into the mouth of the shark as it shaped to pounce.

The shark thrashed and jawed trying to free its throat but the sea lion had driven itself like a dart straight down it's gullet, past the rows of savage teeth, There was nothing to chew on and the speed and accuracy with which it had launched itself into the shark had either damaged some of the large fish's internal organs or acted as some kind of blockage to its gills as the disabled shark pitched and yawed with increasing violence and distress as it tried to dislodge the sea lion from its maw.

Gradually the shark tired and stilled and the slowly heaving waves gently rolled the carcass towards the shore. Tony followed at a distance, staying flat on his board, pulling himself through the water with his arms until he could stand in the shallows and see for himself the distended shape of the shark and the dead soulless eyes of this killing machine brought to its demise by one of its major food groups.

The event made the papers and a 30-second spot on the local news bulletin that evening - once Tony and his friends had put their clothes back on and called the coastguard. But it left Tony with a lingering awe and gratitude for nature's richness and variety and its recognition, to his mind, of humanity's more elevated position in the branches of the evolutionary tree. He had been privileged to witness, at first hand, the sacrifice of one mammal for another and it was a sign - confirmed by his mother when he spoke to her afterwards - a sign that he was being called to play a new role in life: to repay the favour, and spread the word that all living things were connected, interdependent. One.

Three life-changing decisions followed:

The following fall, he enrolled himself at UCSD to study Environmentalism.

He never surfed again and, in fact, sold his surfboards - along with many other belongings - to help fund his way through college.

Lil' Tony gained a host of new animal-based epithets, starting with the Slippery Sea Lion.

The morning Georgi had hung up on him in angry Russian, Tony looked at himself in the mirror. There was dried blood on his pillow from the gash to his temple and his head hurt like hell. He showered gingerly and tried to dress his cut with some gauze and tape as best he could.

It was fair to say that he wasn't too impressed with the room - or the hotel. He'd come to expect better than this since Vasilij had started what Tony liked to think of as his patronage. He may have spent years on the road campaigning against salmon farming, environmental damage and the eco-fallout from industrialised aquaculture, but this usually involved buffet dinners and stays in 4-star hotels. He'd spoken at conferences in Buenos Aires, Hong Kong, and Copenhagen; given seminars on cruise ships through the Arctic. This place didn't just fail to meet his standards, it lacked even the aspiration to reach them. Just the level of cleanliness was beyond a joke - so far beyond a joke, Tony thought, that light from a joke would take more than a year to reach it.

He turned on the TV and kept the sound down while he shaved, waiting for the local news at the end of the news bulletin. Eventually a cut to a distinctly down-at-heel, garishly lit studio and somewhat plain-looking newsreader mouthing from the autocue caused him to raise the volume:

"There was a fire at the Aquamarine Seafarms salmon hatchery at Lochcarron last night. Firefighters fought the blaze for over an hour before managing to bring it under control. A spokesman for Aquamarine said that several of the spawning and incubation tanks had been destroyed but the majority of the fish stocks had been saved. Police are working with the fire service to determine the source of the blaze which, this morning, is still unknown although police are not at this stage ruling out foul play. Sport now, and in Inverness…"

Tony's shoulders sank as he glared at the screen.

"Shit."

After breakfast he checked out, threw his luggage onto the backseat of his souped-up Subaru and sat in the driver's seat consulting his AA map book of Scotland. Mulling things over after Viktor's stupidity he made a decision. From here in Lochcarron he would now head south down towards Loch Fyne, a journey of about four hours, where he had scheduled his next act of destruction. After that, he would stow the remaining IEDs in his locker in Glasgow, out of harm's way, where the crazy Russian couldn't get them.

He imagined grabbing Viktor by the throat and pushing the tip of a sharp blade into one cheek just below the eye socket, letting it rest at the point of piercing the skin, willing Viktor to move or speak or give him any excuse to push the knife home and wound him for good. One way or the other, Tony was going to make sure the bastard would get his comeuppance soon.

On the drive South, the mid-morning sun was burnishing his windscreen when Kim called.

"Hey. It's me!" Her singsong voice trilled out from the car speakers.

"Hey. How's it goin'?"

"Aw, missing you loads. I'm stuck here manning the stall at this damned convention when I could be wrapping my legs around you!"

He put on his WC Fields voice: "Frankly my dear, the feeling is mutual." He redoubled his effort to focus on the road as the Tuna Torpedo in his trousers decided to put on a growth spurt.

"It was ok for the first couple of days but it's all gone a bit Antiques Roadshow. I don't know where they find this many old folk - it's like Edinburgh has an endless supply of them! All wheeling tartan trolleys behind them or zimmers in front of them. There's more metal in here than inside AP McCoy! God knows how the security men are handling it. Their scanners must be going off like Blackpool illuminations"

Antiques Roadshow? AP McCoy? Blackpool illuminations? Sometimes he had absolutely no idea what she was talking about. Although after a week on the road he had to admit it was good to hear her voice. His groin tightened just a little further as he tried to interrupt her flow - never easy at the best of times.

"Kimmy?"

"Yes? Oh, hang on a mo, Tony"

There was some unclear chatter in the background before she came back on.

"Sorry, roly-poly asking for a freebie. Goodness but there are some chubsters here. You can see why they have double-doors at MacDonalds can't you? Some women, I mean, really - they reach a certain age and just pull the ripcord, you know?"

"Yes. Kim?"

"Uh-huh, what is it sweetie?"

"Look, I'm driving. Is it ok if I call you back later? Five-ish maybe?"

"Ok! Er no, wait. Hang on. I need to start packing up then so we can get out on time for the presentations tonight. Shit. Sorry Tony, I'm run ragged at the mo. Dashing here, there, everywhere. I'm sweating like a footballer in a spelling test."

"Ok, well don't worry. I'll try calling later tonight - or, actually, why don't you call me when you're free? I'll be off the road after 5pm, and I'm just kicking my heels tonight so call-"

"Right, wilco!"

"- or sext!" He added hopefully.

She'd hung up.

While he drove he could picture Kim as he'd first met her - at a New Year's Eve dinner dance at the hotel in Gleneagles. The meal had been cleared away and the tables mostly abandoned, some folk heading for the bar, some for the dance floor. She had been slumped at an otherwise empty table wearing a strapless orange taffeta ballgown, high heels hanging off the back of her chair, her dirty blonde hair piled up on top of her head with drunken wisps cascading down a beautiful neck. Clearly drunk but attractive all the same, an expensive-looking purse lay open on the table. Sensing an opportunity, he had sat down next to her and put his hand gently on her shoulder to see if she would stir. She had surprised him by shooting bolt upright at his touch and he had then put on his helping-damsels-in-distress act. They had just clicked.

That had been ten months ago now. Ten months, his first long-term relationship. He hadn't stopped to think about it - that was Kim's job - and as long as his very own Pulsating Python had continued to find a home with her that was fine with him. Kim didn't seem to object to the constant demands of his Wizard Lizard and they had been hot for each other all through the rest of the winter and up to Easter. Even as summer came on and Tony got himself embroiled in Vasilij's schemes, he and Kim had still seen each other regularly. He still wanted to wrestle in the sheets and play hide the Cobra Commander. She appeared confident that this relationship had legs and cool that there was no urgent need to "talk about us" or what lay ahead for them.

Just as well, really, because if she knew he'd been stealing thousands from her trust account Tony was pretty sure she would not just kick him to the kerb but would make sure there was a hungry bull mastiff waiting for Mighty Monkey and the Juice Crew when he got there. Right now, of course, she didn't know but she wouldn't be able miss the steadily decreasing balance on her account for ever. When that happened, he would just have to disappear without explanation or looking back which, now he actually thought about it, would hurt.

But not as much as not having the money.

He turned on his indicator as he saw the signs for Local Services, pulled into the largely empty car park and went in search of an ATM.

3

"They'll be waiting for you so be ready."

Harvey had explained the way he had drip-fed the British press the information so that she would get maximum exposure. All she had to do was look surprised, wear an outfit as revealing as possible without risking arrest on arrival, and pout. Of course, pout. All she ever had to do was pout. Well, pout and thrust her chest out. Harvey had told her the British had an old expression in showbiz: *tits and teeth*. Advice given to showgirls about to go on stage. Smile ladies! Chest out. Come on, tits and teeth, loves, tits and teeth! What was the US equivalent she wondered? For her it would probably be *lips and nip slips*. Being papped getting out of cars, judging on talent shows, competing in Dancing With The Stars, appearing on Letterman or Ellen. Life was an endless round of lips and nip slips for her. And here we go again.

She had been met on the jet way by a couple of frankly puny security men, a woman with a wheelchair and a shawl and a plainclothes policeman with a curly wire in his ear. The wheelchair and shawl were to be a disguise, apparently, to allow her to slip through Glasgow airport and into a waiting taxi without notice. Blysse had declined, realising that Harvey's plans for a press conference would be nixed if she didn't even appear to have arrived. The police officer talked into his sleeve and eventually the two puny security men were replaced by larger ones, the woman with the wheelchair went away to serve someone who might actually require assistance, and Blysse was left to walk through the terminal behind the security detail until she reached Arrivals. It was at this point that approximately all hell broke loose.

On the other side of the customs hall she could see an impressive throng of photographers and cameramen, journalists with microphones and curious members of the public, all jostling for a view, noses up against glass.

"Blysse! Blysse!"

"How does it feel to be in the UK?"

"Blysse, are you looking forward to a Scottish Christmas? Any plans for a sexy holiday getaway somewhere in the Highlands?"

"Blysse, over here!"

The security men did their best to shield her through the scrum and she somehow managed to get to the limousine at the kerbside and into the car without doing anything more than pouting, smiling, waving and tottering on her heels. Harvey's instructions had been quite clear: *nothing* until the press conference.

Blysse lay back on the bed in her hotel room and waited for the knock of the door which would signal her departure for the press conference. She was feeling jet-lagged and numb, wondering what the hell she had let herself get roped into. This was all Harvey's idea. These things usually were. But then that's what she paid him for. She paid him to make money for her so she could pay him to make money for her.

She looked down at herself as she lay horizontally on the bed, which wasn't easy: the mounds of silicon obscured most of her view. She'd had three sets of implants over the years: the first put her in the frame for roles. If you didn't have cleavage you weren't going to get hired. Rule #1. Didn't matter how pretty you were, what contacts you had, how much you were willing to put out. No tits, no shows. Simple.

Second set had been a subtle but significant enlargement. She'd had this done at the height of her then fame and no-one had noticed - the surgeon had been so good, the job so beautiful. The results merely served to confirm to everyone who loved her and thought she was justifiably successful why she was lovable and successful in the first place. There had been some minor mutterings on some of those before/after websites but Harvey had jumped on them like a shot and got the stories withdrawn, the accusations retracted.

The third and final operation had been pre-emptive and reductive. Pushing forty, her first implants were threatening to leak (so her surgeon told her) and it was better to correct now than wait and suffer the consequences if they actually did leak. In the process they could be adjusted slightly so that her chest didn't look quite so pronounced. As the years ticked by and the elasticity of her skin reduced it would become more and more obvious that her breasts were substantially fake. Her success lay in the fact that her admirers might wonder if she was fake, might even assume they were fake, but they looked so damn good that no-one wanted to believe it and the longer she could pull that off the better it would be for her career and reputation.

In short, she had the best tits in Hollywood. No question. As Harvey had once put it: *Her tits were the business, and her business was her tits*. But this was no longer the case: her tits had not waned but business had. Harvey had been insightful in his analysis:

"Sweetie, we need to get your tits out front again. They can still knock 'em dead, we just need to find the right vehicle."

"So, like, a Camaro or something?"

"No honey, a media vehicle. A TV show, game show, movie - something that'll remind people you still got it."

"But I already did Dancing With The Stars?"

"Yeah, I know. But that's old hat these days. Ya gotta look to the UK - the TV people over there they know where it's at. They got all kinds of celebrity formats which get you back in the public eye. Front and centre. They got Big Brother, they got Jungle, they got Splash! Dive! Jeez, we gotta get you on one of those shows! You in a swimsuit? Hubba hubba!"

But Harvey's wheeze hadn't worked out. No-one had been interested. They wanted soap stars, jilted celebrity spouses, scandal-hit has-beens looking for the comeback trail. For whatever reason, right now, Blysse couldn't get herself arrested. Harvey though, bless him, kept looking. Plugging away through his contacts trying to find a way in, to get her chest the attention it deserved and, by doing so, getting her back on the casting list for bigger and brighter opportunities. Blysse had stayed home by the pool, sipping pink champagne and fawning over her Shih-poo, Hoffy. Harvey kept at it, day and night he'd told her, until one morning he called with news.

"Honey, sweetie. I got it! We got you a starring role in the UK. Just what we wanted!" That sounded perfect.

"Oh, Harve! Great, what is it?"

"It's the lead in a panto!". Silence for a moment.

"A what?"

"A panto?"

"What the hell's a panto?"

"It's a UK stage play. A Christmas comedy. It's called Babes In The Wood."

"A stage play? Like, in a theatre?" Not sounding so perfect now.

"Exactly!"

"Uh, like in front of people and that? Live?" Sliding down the perfection scale, at some speed.

"You betcha! And it's the lead!"

"The leading babe?"

"Huh?"

"Babe. In the wood?"

"Oh, no sweetie. It's called Babes In The Wood but there ain't no babes in it."

"Is there a wood?"

"What? Yeah, I guess. But the lead! Whaddyathink?"

"Lead is good." She mulled it over for a few seconds. "What part do I play?"

"Robin Hood."

"Huh?"

"Robin Hood. You know, and his Merry Men?"

"I thought you said it was called Babes In The Wood?"

"Yeah, it is."

"Not Babes In The Hood?"

"No. Wood, definitely." The sound of papers being shuffled and flicked. "Definitely wood."

"So what's Robin Hood got to do with it?"

"Sweetie, I don't know ok? I haven't seen the script yet. But trust me, this is sublime! The Brits go nuts for Panto, it's a Christmas tradition for them. Men dress up as women, women dress up as men, everyone gets a custard pie in the face. It's a blast!"

"A custard pie in the face!"

"Well, not you obviously. You're the lead! Any custard pies I guess you'll be doing the throwing, know what I'm saying?"

Silence while she looked out over her pool. Hoffy was peeing on her sofa.

"Hoffy!"

"What?"

"No Harve, I said Hoffy not Harvey."

"Oh, ok. So come on, sweetie? Whaddyasay? Starring role? Christmas in the UK? A glamour route back to the big time? Huh?"

"Ok, I'm in."

And now here she was. Without Harvey - he never flew. Without Hoffy - some issue with animal passports or something which hadn't been arranged in time. Alone, in the UK for the first time. For Christmas. Starring in some kind of play where she'd have to learn lines and shit.

There was a knock on the door.

"Miss Baptiste? Everyone's waiting for you."

Blysse got to her feet and smoothed down her outfit with her palms. Showtime, sweetie. Remember: tits and teeth.

"Welcome to Edinburgh, Mr Krupchenko. Local time is 16:48."

Vasilij adjusted his watch and turned to Jelena in the seat across from him. She was curling her legs under her slim frame, high heels discarded on the carpet, as she put the makeup mirror back in her handbag and grabbed her iPhone. She was young and ambitious - traits Vasilij had been sure to look for during his protracted search for a PA - and easy on the eye. This last factor was very much a consideration when one was paying handsomely to have someone cater to his professional and personal needs. He was, he knew, no spring chicken, but still very much in his prime. He kept himself in shape, only slightly thickening at the neck and waist, and in excellent health. He had been direct with her at the interview, explaining what may be required, and she had understood and struck a fair bargain. She smiled politely at him now as she waited for the call to connect.

"Feliks? Jelena. We are running slightly late so can you make sure that you have the engine running please? Mr Krupchenko would like to be home for 5.30 sharp."

He ran his manicured fingers through the greying hair at his temple and stared out of the window at the dark sky and rain-streaked concrete, the sodium lights illuminating the dusk. Home today was his estate at Yair in the Scottish Borders. He mostly stayed there when jetting into and out of Edinburgh. Usually his stays were not very long - a few days at a time at most - for tax reasons. But he did love playing the genial host there, engaging with the influential and powerful in politics, business and the media and indulging in his imagined country pursuits of a Scottish laird.

Jelena stepped down the staircase at Yair, a vision in scarlet: she had released some of her dark hair from her bun and trained it in loose ringlets either side of her face. She wore a short chiffon dress with a ragged hem, no sleeves. It was short. Very short. Her legs were bare and her feet were wrapped in elegant silver heels with slender straps climbing up her calves. Vasilij was impressed - he had expected smart casual.

"You look delightful" Vasilij said, holding out his hand for her to take.

"Thank you." She saw his flushed cheeks and wondered if it was lust or the number of scotches he'd downed while she had been getting ready. "I have spoken to Tony - he will call any minute now."

"Hmph." He looked at his watch.

"All arrangements for tomorrow's site visit are in place. Feliks will pick you up at 10am and drop you back around 1pm. Your flight leaves at 4pm."

"Must it always be business?" Vasilij sighed.

"Just doing my job, Vasilij. It is what you pay me for, isn't it?"

"Yes. Business before pleasure." He mused. "How are preparations coming along for my Christmas party?"

"Well in hand. Invitations have been sent and I have a meeting with the party planners on the yacht next week - decor, food, music, et cetera."

"Good. And date?"

"The fourth."

"Right. I am due back here in two weeks or so, end of November, correct?"

"Yes" she checked the calendar on her phone. "Currently pencilled in to arrive back in Scotland November 30, staying until December 5."

"Excellent."

As they made their way through to the dining room his phone rang,

"Hello, Tony. Do you have some news for me?"

"Good evening, Mr Krupchenko. Yes, sir, news and good news at that."

"Excellent. Go on."

"You should hear on the news this evening about a fire at the Aquamarine Seafarms hatchery in Lochcarron. The facility is destroyed with the loss of over two million fry and seven million eggs. Aquamarine will not be re-stocking Lochcarron with salmon for a long time!"

"Marvellous. And Georgi?"

"He is due to put the plan into action first thing this morning. I did call him at 8am to confirm completion but he was, um, busy. I will try again later."

"Good. Please call me tomorrow after speaking to him." Vasilij looked up and smiled at Jelena. "Well, enjoy your evening Tony. I fully intend to enjoy mine."

Later in his bedroom, Vasilij flipped the TV to the BBC news channel to wait for Tony's promised bulletin, sat on the bed and took off his shoes. In the mirror he briefly caught sight of Jelena's naked back as she let her dress fall to the bathroom floor and unpinned her hair. Turning back to throw the remote onto the bedside table he saw a full-blown media scrum at an airport, photographers jostling for pictures, cameras held high over their heads snapping hopefully. Their focus was a platinum blonde struggling to make headway through the crowd, tottering on stilettos in a dress which was simultaneously incredibly tight and impressively revealing.

Vasilij watched intently as her minders wrestled her through a side door, catching a glimpse of her in profile as she disappeared. He tried to shake the image of her from his head - something about her was electrifying - and stared at the TV, waiting, all thought of Jelena forgotten.

The shot cut to a room setup for a press conference, a top table draped in red velvet scattered with clusters of microphones, a jug of water and some glasses. To one side a pair of double-doors opened and the blonde catwalked in and up to the table. Vasilij felt an erection spring unbidden to his groin. He fumbled for the volume control and frantically pressed the up button as she started to say something. The journalists and photographers were shouting over each other to attract her attention.

"Bliss! Bliss! This way! Bliss!"

"Bliss! Over here! Can you blow a kiss for your fans in Scotland?"

The TV cut back to the studio where the news anchor was sitting in front of a giant screen now bearing her photo. Vasilij listened with his pulse racing.

"… arrived today at Glasgow airport for the start of her first ever run in panto. Ms Baptiste flew in from New York this morning and held a press conference at the Glasgow Hilton. Large crowds had gathered outside once her arrival had been leaked on social media overnight. Our entertainment correspondent, John Draper, reports."

Vasilij sat enthralled, listening and drinking in every glimpse and sight of her. This vision. This Bliss Baptiste. Who was she? He had to know. Had to meet her. Had to have her. He jumped when he felt a hand stroke his shoulder and spun to see a naked Jelena walk around the bed to stand in front of him, drop to her knees and unzip his trousers. As she took him in her mouth he continued gaping at the screen and when he came thirty seconds later he cried out her name, Bliss.

4

The road out of Peebles wound its way through the valley and the Lexus took a left fork which turned into a single track road with frequent passing places. Sitting uncomfortably at the wheel in suit, tie and cap, Feliks was a bulky ex-wrestler, bristling with muscles and stubble, his neck a mile wide. Any attempt to corral his form into something with a collar was never going to end well for either him or the shirt. Despite the chill winter weather he was sweating heavily, wiping his brow with the cuff of his shirtsleeves which were too long for the jacket.

Several miles further and the road became rutted and split by snow and ice. Feliks slowed the 4x4 and kept it to the middle of the road as they wound their way through the trees and fields. Manor Water burbled to the left and, to the right, there was forestry where some felling had been done recently. In places the trees gave way to dirty stumps and mounds of needles and twigs, stacks of neatly cut logs piled by the roadside.

Inside the car Jelena stopped prodding her phone when she realised she was out of range of a usable signal. She wore a pale blue suit with her dark hair up in a tight bun which accentuated her Slavic heritage: almond eyes, olive skin and cheekbones you could slice a ham with. Slightly agitated that she now had nothing to do she retrieved a folder from her large handbag and shook out a folded A3 blueprint.

"What's the scale on this thing?"

"Hmm?" Vasilij looked up absent-mindedly. "Oh, not sure. The actual dimensions though will be several hundred meters in each direction."

Vasilij was in his fifties but could easily pass for younger. He had a sheen and a gloss that only money could effect and he spent more on a pair of shoes than Feliks earned in a month. Despite it all, Feliks liked him. There had been times when Vasilij had gone postal - Feliks had witnessed the aftermath - but he had never been its focus and never felt that the shimmering madness which undercut his boss's success would ever shine in his particular direction.

Jelena looked out at the bleak landscape for any signs of development.

"And CCS?" She pointed to the legend on the blueprint. "What does this stand for?"

Vasilij, sensing an opportunity to continue her education in her new role as his PA, seized it.

"Closed Containment System."

"Is that like CCTV?"

Vasilij barked a laugh. "No. It is a way of farming fish on land instead of sea."

She gave a tinkling laugh. "But Vasilij, even I know you can't grow fish on land! You know the phrase 'like a fish out of water'?"

"You misunderstand. The fish grow in water but in water tanks. Great vast water tanks in a controlled environment. Indoors."

She unfolded the plans and turned them this way and that, trying to make sense of them.

"So, it's like a great big fish tank in a warehouse or something?"

"Or something." Vasilij smiled at her. "This whole facility is basically one big aquarium for salmon only. But we have salmon at all their different life-cycle stages - eggs, hatchlings, infants, teenagers and adults. They all need different environments to thrive in, different food to eat. So we have a number of different zones and circulate water and feed throughout them, cleaning, oxygenating and heating as we go. As the fish grow, we move them from one zone to another. When the adults are big enough we take them out and sell them. This in turn frees up space for the other fish to move up to their next habitat and when a nursery is freed up we put more eggs into it. It's just one big glorious circle with new fish popping in one end and adults ready to eat popping out the other."

"So they never get to live in the wild?"

"Absolutely not! That's the whole point!"

"But I mean the water, it's not real is it?"

"Of course it is real. We're not in the business of manufacturing water!"

"No but I mean it's not like a river or the sea?"

"Well no, it's not. And I'm quite pleased about it. It's as if the fish permanently live in an air-conditioned building - the climate perfectly controlled to suit their needs - so they never need to go outside."

"But don't salmon like salt water?"

"Well, I think *like* is perhaps not quite the right word. Salmon are a kind of superfish: they are born in freshwater and grow in freshwater. But when they reach puberty - those difficult teenage years - their bodies change and become adapted to salt water. In the wild they migrate to the sea and grow to maturity in salt water.

When they're ready to breed they return to freshwater to lay their eggs and start the cycle all over again.

"But they don't have to." He continued. "They are perfectly able to live in fresh water without ever being exposed to saltwater. Their biology will still adapt to be able to cope with saltwater - and they will perhaps have an instinct to seek it out - but it won't do them any harm if they never come into contact with it. And that is the beauty of closed containment. Do you see?"

Jelena looked at him, unconvinced, and then back at the blueprint.

"I see what looks like lots of circles in a rectangular grid. What I don't see, I guess, is the point."

Vasilij smiled and hitched himself along the backseat, proud of his new pupil taking an interest.

"Look. Every salmon farming site I have involves massive fights, prolonged pressure to get it built, keep the fish healthy, not pollute the environment, keep it open. The environmental agencies complain about ecological impact and waste discharge; local communities about the aesthetic impact on the landscape and local fauna; eco-protest groups about disease and pollution harming seals and wild fish stocks."

"I lose sleep wondering whether the summers will be too warm and cause algae bloom which chokes the fish or increases the incidence of disease; or if the winters will be too cold and stop the fish from growing to full size; or if bad weather will damage the sites, the nets, the cages, prevent us from harvesting the fish, treating the fish, feeding the fish. If the local seal population will decide to feast on our stocks or if the discharge from the cages will wash into neighbouring habitats and have us shut down; I have to make sure we don't have too many fish in a

47

cage and exceed the consent we've been given to farm in that location. I pay a fortune in medicines to treat ill or diseased fish, or a fortune in vaccinations to prevent them from getting sick. A hundred and one issues and problems and costs."

"And every single one of them disappears like the morning mist when you use a closed containment system instead. Every. Single. One."

Jelena looked out of the window hoping to catch a glimpse of this promised nirvana. Instead she gazed at a scabby hillside sculpted into a muddy plateau pegged out with string, some large diameter concrete pipes lying as though discarded next to a couple of bright yellow diggers. As they came to a halt she could see no-one about, no sign of movement.

Feliks got out and came round to open the passenger door, first for Vasilij and then for her. He handed them both a pair of white wellingtons he had taken from the boot and waited patiently while they removed their shoes and tucked their trousers into the tops of the boots. Vasilij sprung out first, clutching the plans, striding confidently across the site. Jelena sat glumly looking at the sea of mud and the grey sky.

Vasilij strode around gabbling excitedly to Feliks, who wasn't listening, and Jelena, who was still sitting sullenly in the car.

"You will come in here." He paced along the site line markers, counting. "The recirculation centre lies here and then over here …" Pace again. "… is the entrance to the hatchery tanks."

He was, he knew, a visionary - taking others with him who didn't share this belief - this certainty - he had that closed containment was the saviour for salmon farming.

The figures and forecasts spoke for themselves, and Vasilij was confident that his plans would be hugely successful. On the other hand, it didn't hurt to have some insurance, some extra leverage, to help increase the chances of success and maximise the financial upside when it came. That, he smiled to himself, was where Tony came in.

At their first meeting, Vasilij had been sitting in his conservatory, watching the Tweed glisten in the summer sunshine, when Jelena had knocked and ushered Tony into the room. He wore a Forty-Niners football jersey, his long hair loose to his broad shoulders, and a deep tan. Vasilij reckoned he was late thirties/early forties and looked every inch the typical US jock - muscly, limbre, confident, at ease, just dumb enough to be dangerous.

"Mr Stafford, pleased to meet you. Do sit down."

Tony sank into one of the two leather Chesterfields situated either side of a large Turkish rug.

"May I offer you a coffee? Or tea perhaps?"

"I'm fine thank you, Sir."

Vasilij smiled lop-sidedly. "Thank you, Jelena. That will be all"

"Scotch perhaps?" Vasilij offered as he poured himself a healthy tumbler from the decanter on the sideboard.

"Not for me. Thank you."

"Are you sure? It is one of Scotland's finest malts."

"Really, I'm good."

Vasilij stopped and frowned. "As you wish. Cheers." He sipped appreciatively for a few seconds in silence before continuing. "Mr. Stafford. Tony, you are probably wondering why I wanted to meet with you?

"Well, you're in the salmon business, I'm against the salmon business, so I figured you might be wanting to try and dissuade me from continuing my program of protests and pay me off or bribe me to stand back and let corporate greed roll."

He smiled and seemed genuinely open and unabashed - this was a simple business transaction and whilst he was against the salmon business that didn't mean he was against business. Vasilij grinned broadly and decided he liked Tony.

"Ha! Straight to the point. You Americans are so direct, so unaffected. I have spent so long dealing with Brits - or Scots, not at all dissimilar in many ways - that it is like a breath from the steppes to hear you talk like this."

"Pleased you like it, Sir. But just because I presume this to be the case doesn't mean I am agreeable to it."

"Well, no. Of course. And you may be surprised that I do not want you to give up your protest role."

Vasilij was pleased to see Tony looked genuinely surprised at this, and continued.

"In fact, the opposite is indeed the case."

"You want me to carry on protesting against the salmon business?"

"Quite so."

"But you want me to stop protesting against your salmon business?"

"Well, naturally, I am hoping we can come to some sort of mutually beneficial arrangement."

"Well, Sir. I'm intrigued, I'll give you that."

"Good." Vasilij smiled and topped up his glass. "To business, then. You, Tony, are a recognised - indeed infamous - thorn in the side of the salmon industry. You rile against the ecological damage salmon farms do to wild salmon stocks and the environment in general. You organise media stunts, issue press releases against Big Salmon, attend seminars and speak at conferences, all the time pressing home your narrative that the salmon industry is bad for the environment. Salmon company executives and owners like myself have to spend an annoying amount of time defending our actions, countering your misinformation, and employing -"

"With all due respect, Mr Krupchenko-"

"Please, call me Vasilij."

"Well, Vasilij, with all due respect, it is not misinformation. I have a wealth of scientific and academic research which clearly shows-"

"Whatever" replied Vasilij, irked for having his flow disrupted. "- and employing unnecessary staff, money and resources to manage the situations which you create. Let me ask you a question, Tony: how do you afford to do what you do?"

"Excuse me?" Tony was discomforted by Vasilij's flash of anger and the question caught him off guard.

"How do you fund your lifestyle? You travel the globe, staying in hotels, paying for PR agents and setting up publicity stunts, sponsoring research - all of this costs money." Vasilij walked around his desk and stood in front of Tony, still seated on the chesterfield. "Where does the money come from?"

"Well, I have some small benefactors - like-minded people prepared to donate small sums to my campaign to keep me operational. I operate a registered charity based out of Sacramento which does fund-raising from time to time and I have a Justgiving page which I advertise through social media where anyone who wants to can donate anything from a dollar to a thousand dollars. It ain't funding a jet-set lifestyle, you understand, and compromises do have to be made, but it's enough to get by."

"Hmm. I admire your resourcefulness and application."

"Thank you."

"If not your methods."

"Ah." It was tough for Tony to hear that anyone didn't admire his pioneering stance and independent approach. Of course, as a millionaire owner of a business Tony was constantly clashing with he wasn't expecting Vasilij to give him a medal. However, he was proud of the fact that his reputation preceded him and he was, he assumed, the biggest big shot in the anti-salmon farming movement. Globally. As he had equivocated to Vasilij, his livelihood was something of a hand-to-mouth existence and he had to spend far more of this time than he would like chasing donations or funding when he would rather be globe-trotting and grandstanding for the world's press at jamborees and high-profile media events. Nevertheless, he was proud of his profile and his accomplishments.

"So I have a proposition for you." Vasilij continued with just a hint of menace, Tony thought. "One which will, I hope, serve us both well in meeting our aims." Vasilij topped his glass up again and continued. "I am offering to be your patron. I will privately fund your operations up to a value of $500,000 a year, allowing you free rein to organise, prioritise and target your activities as you see fit. The money will be advanced to you on a monthly basis and you will keep in regular contact with me personally to ensure I am aware of your activities and the results they yield."

"You're offering to put me on the payroll to the tune of half-a-mill a year?" Tony immediately wondered if he could reconsider Vasilij's offer of scotch.

"No. There will be no direct connection between my business and yourself. You will not be an employee or hired in any formal capacity which can be traced. This would be a personal arrangement between myself and you - or your charity if you prefer - where I make regular, anonymous donations to fund your activities. This is not a salary and it is not money to be spent purely on personal outgoings."

Tony's face fell slightly...

"Although, it is up to you to decide how the money is to be spent and what proportion is required to cover your own expenses."

... and rose again.

"OK, half a million dollars, right?"

"Yes"

"In advance?"

"Each month, pro rata, of course."

"For me to spend as I see fit?"

"Absolutely."

Tony paused to let this sink in.

"What's the catch?"

"There is no catch but there are three conditions which I will require you to comply with."

"O....K..."

"Firstly, you must ramp up your activities. Half a million dollars can fund a lot of activity and is, I assume, a substantial increase on the levels of funding currently at your disposal?"

Tony kept a poker face.

"So, I will expect a significant increase in your profile in the media, your ability to gain headlines, and your effectiveness in disrupting my competitors. If I give you $500,000 I do not expect you to continue your activities as they are."

"You want me to speed up?"

"Speed up and muscle up."

"Muscle up?"

"Yes. I am not funding a bigger leafletting campaign. I want mass-scale damage inflicted on my competitors. I want you to wreck their facilities, their image, their reputation, their profitability, their stocks."

"In the market?"

"In the water. And in the market."

"So, you want me to get heavy?" Tony was getting agitated while Vasilij was simply nodding. "Ramp up into actual eco-terrorism? Industrial sabotage, destroying fish and damaging livelihoods?"

"Is that an issue?"

"Absolutely not." Tony breathed. "No problemo."

"I have a number of resources which I can place at your disposal. If you marshal them effectively you will be able to target several different sites or areas at the same time, allowing you greater and faster impact"

"Resources? You mean, like, men?"

"Yes, like-men." Vasilij smiled at his little joke, unaware whether Tony was picking up on it. "You will liaise with and coordinate these like-men. They have other duties and responsibilities, and I will have first call on their time if I require it, but other than that they will obey you as if your instructions came from my own mouth."

"And if I don't wanna use these guys?"

"You will. It is condition two."

"O-k. And condition three?"

"Condition three is that you avoid doing any damage to my own business. My sites, my fish, my staff, my reputation must all remain untouched by whatever you get up to. In a word, immunity."

"Alrighty!" Tony enthused "So, to recap: you will pay me monthly in advance to the tune of half a million dollars a year and, in exchange, I get to use your goons-" Vasilij winced at the word, "- to damage as many premises, businesses, farmed fish and reputation as I possibly can and as long as your own business is unaffected I am free to plan and coordinate this as I think best?"

"And you keep me in the loop on a regular basis."

"Yeah, and we keep in touch. Say, what - weekly?"

"I will consider it. Meantime here is a cellphone to keep us in contact." Vasilij tossed him an iPhone from his desk drawer. "In the address book is my private number and those of my *resources*." He emphasised. "Do. Not. Lose. It"

"OK. When do I start?"

"Well, let's see. It is late July now, you will need some time to plan, meet my like-men and get the ball rolling. How about the beginning of September?"

"And the first payment?"

"Is already in your account. It will appear as a payment from a pension fund in Jersey."

Tony was impressed. He stood to shake Vasilij's hand.

"Looking forward to working for - er, with you Mr Krupchenko."

"Likewise."

"One question: I get my mission funded, resourced and supported. What's in this for you?"

"Mr Stafford. Tony. Salmon - Scottish salmon - is a premium product. It commands premium prices and has a finite supply. As you know, it takes up to two years from hatching an egg before you have a product you can sell and when you have sold that product in the following six months you have to start all over again. During that two years, all sorts of events can damage your profitability: weather, disease, pollution, accidents, market forces. It is a precarious business and the price of salmon is extremely volatile. One week it is £6 a kilo, the next it is below £3. Imagine, if you will, the run up to the busiest time of the year for salmon buying - Christmas - when salmon prices are at their peak. Imagine if, at this time, there was a massive reduction in the number of salmon brought to market, perhaps because of unforeseen accidents or acts of God. Imagine how the price of salmon would go through the roof. And imagine if, due to circumstances beyond anyone's control, it transpired that only one company had salmon which was healthy, available, sellable. Imagine the killing they would make and the market domination they would have if it took their competitors another two years to get back in the game."

"And that one company would be yours?"

"I imagine."

Vasilij stood by the rail on the lower deck of his motor yacht, *A Crewed Interest*, waiting for the weather to lift. The stillness on the Clyde was disturbed only by the occasional sound of Viktor's shotgun as he indulged in his favourite pastime of shooting seagulls. Like some demented version of clay pigeon shooting, when bored he would get one of the cooks to toss morsels of food into the air off the port bow while he took aim and blasted the birds to bloody smithereens with lead shot.

The yacht was Vasilij's favourite toy. Registered in the Cayman Islands, it was 40 metres long with three decks and a top speed of 24 knots. It had four cabins and a saloon lounge, all kitted out in cool tones and blonde wood, with all amenities and luxuries he had thought to bestow - even a custom built wine store beneath the master suite. Moored here at Largs Yacht Haven he used it as a mobile base which allowed him to visit many of his salmon farms in the Western Isles when he was in Scotland, and as a Mediterranean floating home from home when the Scottish weather got too much for him.

Which wasn't often. For lovers of Scotland the weather was an asset, not a liability, and Vasilij was mostly a lover. He knew many who weren't - Jelena for one, it appeared. She could only see the damp, the grey, the gales, the cold. He saw a beautiful seasonality - a year-long parade through weather patterns and sky changes: winter that could be snowy and cold, icy and wet; spring that blossomed into vivid green, new lambs, mint fresh; summers of enormous skies, scudding clouds, unexpected beauty; autumns of mist, sparkling chill, crystal clear air. No two days the same and yet a cycle that clearly moved, changed and repeated, ticking off each year like a child's calendar.

Today, though, he was still waiting on visibility improving to make any journey worth making. His plans had been to pop across to Arran for a long lunch but as the morning wore on he realised that this wasn't going to happen and, for some reason, his thoughts returned to the blonde he had seen on TV the other night - as they had done on several nights previously.

The day after her press conference he had googled her and found out all about her, including the correct spelling of her name, Blysse. Increasingly, he found his thoughts returning to her at the most unexpected times - usually accompanied by a sudden tightening in his groin. She had also feature rather prominently in his recent dalliances with Jelena and he wondered if she had noticed his air of detachment - or, indeed, whether she cared. He looked at his watch now and wondered where Jelena was. Why hadn't she yet come in and told him of the need to cancel his lunch plans. He stepped inside and buzzed her on the intercom.

Jelena had been furiously hammering on her laptop when Viktor had sneaked in behind her through the sliding glass door onto the deck. He had leant his shotgun up against the wall and silently pounced on her, clawing at her with both hands and pulling her to him, kissing her neck roughly.

"Now? Here?" Jelena she had pretended to resist as Viktor hungrily made it clear what he thought. "Vasilij is upstairs. He could call at any - " He put his hand over her mouth and she writhed as his other hand ran down to her panties.

When the intercom buzzed the pair were thrusting away madly.

Jelena grappled against Viktor's lunging hand but managed to reach it before he could stop her, the pair scuffling as they both groped for the button and tried to match their thrusting at the same time.

"Vasilij?"

"Jelena." Vasilij paused. "Are you ok?"

"Yes. I'm just… helping Viktor… uh… come aboard."

"Really?"

"Yes." She improvised. "Discussing arrangements… uh… for the party." Did he know about her and Viktor, she wondered? Did he suspect?

"Ah, splendid." He bought it, she thought, as Viktor continued pounding away behind her. "On the subject of the party, I was - erm - wondering, could you please extend an invitation to Blysse Baptiste?"

Jelena, struggling as she was to focus, was thrown. "Who?"

"Blysse Baptiste. The American actress over here in panto."

"Oh. Yes, of course."

She released the intercom button and reached around to grab Viktor to better direct his thrusts.

5

This was just dumb, Blysse thought, as she watched the director stride across the bare boards on the stage and proceed to show the chorus line how to swagger in the style of middle age peasants. She knew that panto was an English thing with its own history and traditions and that, as an American, she couldn't be expected to understand the nuances. But this was just plain daft. She was dressed as Robin Hood in a play about two children who die in a forest which was being put on at Christmas time for the entertainment of children where she spent most her time setting up punchlines for Friar Tuck and having to slap her thighs before almost every line - for some reason which no-one had quite managed to satisfactorily explain to her. Her costume consisted of thigh-length leather boots with stiletto heels, bright green hot pants and waistcoat over a crisp white bustier which (ok, she admitted) showed off her assets to the very best effect, topped off with a gaudy green hat with a long white feather sticking out of the top. No men in tights. No Little John. No Maid Marion. No sense.

She sighed and looked out into the auditorium of empty velvet plush seating and elaborately gilded ceiling and chandeliers. The ornate gold carvings framing the circle, upper circle and boxes off to the side had perhaps seen better days and the whole theatre seemed to project this air of faded and dusty grandeur but there was certainly nothing like this back home.

Back at the end of the first day's rehearsal she had called Harvey.

"It's dumb"

"Come on, sweetie. You gotta give it a chance. You gotta enter into the spirit of it."

"Harvey, it's dumb. I mean, just plain dumb. I don't get it."

"Look, Blysse. Give it some time. Let yourself go, sink into it. Immerse yourself, yeah? It'll do wonders for your profile!"

"I don't want it to do wonders - "

"Yeah, sweetie. You do. Really." Pause. "Think about it?"

"Harve, it's dumb."

"Will ya stop saying that for chrissake? Look, it's been one day. You're rehearsing with new people. British people. Different sensibilities, different ways. You're not in the theatre, you're still in some bare room somewhere, right?"

"Yeah. Just sitting around some tables reading lines."

"So, give it some time. See what it's like when you get to dress and rehearse *in situ.*"

"In situ?"

"Yeah, you know. In the theatre! Get the feel of the place. Tread the boards. The roar of the greasepaint, the smell of the crowd. Like proper actors!"

"*Proper* actors?"

"Yeah, you know. Proper act-ors. Dames, Sirs, Lords, Ladies. This is history sweetie! Hopkins, Dench, Mirren, Olivier. They've all done it. They all cut their teeth in places just like where you are now!"

"I guess."

"Just be willing to make fun of your own persona. The Brits will take you to their hearts and you will become a national treasure. I'm tellin' ya."

"I'll give it a week."

"Good girl!"

Roll forward that week and here she was. Still not overtaken by the mood. Still not yet caught up in it. Right now she was just bored, uninspired and wondering what the hell she had let herself in for.

"And one and two and turn and kick and five and six and seven and twirl!" The director was mincing across the stage showing the chorus what he wanted from them.

She sighed again.

This is how they had split the duties: Tony had done the research and calculations, modelling and analysis; Vasilij had sourced the larvae. Tony didn't ask how, how much or from where - all he knew was that he was to meet someone called Henry at the ferry terminal in Portavadie. Henry would be driving a tanker coming off the ferry from Tarbert and the tanker contained millions of sea lice larvae suspended in 20,000 litres of seawater. Tony's job was to take the tanker to the best dispersal point around Loch Fyne and then, at a time Tony deemed most propitious, dump the contents into the loch and wait for all the farmed salmon in Loch Fyne (some 30,000 tonnes scattered across numerous farms throughout its length) to become infected as the sea lice were dispersed throughout the loch system.

Tony sat in his car consulting his maps of the loch, of which he had many: 3D maps showing the topology of the seabed beneath the loch, tidal flow charts showing sea levels, tides and currents, Benthic habitat maps showing biological fauna and sediment types for the loch, and Imray nautical charts showing harbours, shallows, navigable channels, wrecks and so on. He kept them all in a battered leather pilot's case which he'd been given by his father when he graduated from UCSD. This was sitting on the passenger seat as he looked up to see the tanker rolling slowly off the ferry. It pulled up at the quayside and the driver climbed down from the cab. Tony walked over to him.

"Henry?"

"Aye. Tony?" Henry was a grizzled old man, short, with a scruffy beard growth and permanent glower. He was wearing an old red lumberjack shirt tucked into work overalls and a very dirty pair of boots.

"Yep."

"She's all yours. Back here by this time tomorrow to catch the ferry back. Don't know what you want it for and don't want to know. Paperwork is all in the cab above the visor. Only thing I can't help you with is HGV license if you don't have one."

Tony hopped into the driver's seat and made himself at home.

Loch Fyne is the longest of the sea lochs in Scotland at nearly 70 kilometres from its head near Cairndow to its mouth in the Clyde estuary. It is long and narrow with two sills which cross the loch creating its shallowest points: one near the mouth of the loch, the other by a sandy spit at Otter Ferry. Like all sea lochs it is tidal and the water exchange period - the time taken for water in the loch system to be effectively flushed and replaced with new water - would vary with the weather and tides, but was taken to be in the range of 13 - 17 days.

Tony knew all this because he had studied the loch system years ago as part of his Master's degree, looking at the biodiversity of the area: from mussels and anemones, wading birds and gulls, to basking sharks and bottle-nose dolphins. He had also performed sampling and analysis of sea lice in a loch system and was familiar with their life-cycle stages and behaviours. He knew that sea lice went through plankton stages until they became free-swimming. At this point their bodies contained fat reserves enough to last them ten days or so. They needed to find a host and latch onto them within this period if they were to survive. Once latched onto a host they then moulted into their next life-cycle stage where they fed off their host.

No-one really knew how these sea lice found their hosts, but they did and had been doing so effectively for millennia. Tony had taken samples around fish farms and found that sea lice magically gathered at these points almost in anticipation, only to disperse later once fish had been harvested out of the water. Perhaps they were sensitive to low frequency vibrations in the water, vibrations given off by swimming fish. Whatever the mechanism, they were tremendously effective at it and, anyway, who gave a fuck? Tony had a tanker full of millions of baby parasites desperately looking for a home and was about to tip them into a loch full of healthy hosts. Come my little beauties. Go find your salmon. Go directly to your salmon. Do not pass Go. Do not collect $200.

He was glad he was doing this on his own. Georgi and Viktor were clearly strangers to the concept of subtlety and subterfuge - the last thing Tony needed right now was drawing attention to a silver, 40-tonne road tanker while illegally dumping contaminated liquid into a geographically protected marine habitat.

He'd only met Feliks, Georgi and Viktor together one time, back in late summer - Vasilij had thought it best. After bringing Tony on board, briefing him and depositing a hefty down payment into his bank account, he had pretty much left him to get on with it as Tony saw fit. But one of his demands had been that his human resources - Vasilij's term for them - were used as unknowing point-and-shoot instruments. They were to know nothing of the bigger picture, activities of others or ultimate plan. This was to be run strictly on a need-to-know basis and Tony had agreed to do so.

The three looked at him, bored rather than expectant, and somewhat underwhelmed by what they saw.

"Good afternoon, gentlemen. Together we are going to cause an awful lot of carnage and mayhem in the salmon world!"

Georgi leant over to Viktor and mumbled something in a very deep, slightly slurry, voice. Tony couldn't make out what it was but it didn't sound like English. Viktor started moving his hands about and whispering Georgi. Tony wanted to nip this in the bud.

"Problem Viktor? Georgi?"

"Is no problem." Viktor replied. "Georgi has no good English. I translate."

Viktor had dead eyes which gave Tony a fuck-you glare. Tony tried hard to ignore this.

"Ah, I see. O.K!" Tony said this loudly and slowly, giving Georgi the A.OK hand sign for good measure. Georgi looked at him, squinting, as if he had shit on his shoe and let Viktor unnecessarily translate this.

Georgi was about six feet tall and heavily built, with mid-length dark hair, tangled, greasy and untidy. Everything about him was thick: lips, eyebrows, nose, neck, hands. Tony thought he looked the part if nothing else. He was wearing a short black leather coat of no particular fashion or period, it just looked generically dated. It also looked as if he had no shirt or layers on underneath - Tony could see bare chest above the first button. His fingernails were bitten and dirty. He wore baggy, brown army fatigues on his bottom half, many-pocketed, tucked into a pair of scuffed tall, fully-laced army boots.

Tony thought there was a smell of cheap booze, diesel and body odour coming from him and, as if in response, at that point Georgi pulled out a small bottle of vodka from a trouser pocket, unscrewed the cap and took a long swig. In silence, still glowering, he put it back in his pocket and waited for Tony to comment or continue. Tony chose to continue.

"Mr. Krupchenko has asked me to plan a number of operations around Scotland and kindly volunteered your help to assist me in this." Viktor started speaking in a low voice to Georgi as he continued. "I am still sorting out the details but will soon be contacting you each individually to allocate duties to you. It will mean you will have to travel around the country but I will try and make sure all arrangements are in hand for you to -"

"Georgi no drive." Viktor again, smiling this time.

Tony looked at him and sighed. Somewhat younger than Georgi - mid-thirties Tony guessed, Viktor was slimmer but looked muscly enough. Another with a swarthy complexion, he had shoulder-length black hair and a short beard, neatly trimmed. He was wearing a brown lambswool V-neck sweater with nothing underneath, black jeans faded at the knees and a pair of beige Timberland boots. Over it all he wore a full-length black wool coat with deep lapels and one large button halfway down the front, his hands thrust deep into the pockets. Tony thought he looked like an extra from The Matrix who's cooperation it seemed he wouldn't necessarily be able to count on.

"Not even an automatic?"

Viktor and Georgi conferred briefly. "Is OK. Automatic." Grateful for this grudging acceptance from Viktor, Tony continued.

"I will make arrangements and contact you with instructions. I will try and give you plenty of warning -"

"Will need."

"Sorry?"

"Warning. Will need. Plenty." Viktor didn't have a word to spare it seemed, although he was starting to sound a bit like Yoda, thought Tony.

"Yes?"

"I drive ship. Krupchenko ship. He need me."

"Krupchenko ship?" Tony was non-plussed.

"Viktor is skipper on Mr Krupchenko's yacht. If Mr Krupchenko need to use yacht, he will need Viktor. Is what he means: he'll need warning in case he is needed two places at once." This was Feliks. Heavily accented, no doubt he was Russian too, but his English was clear as a bell. Tony brightened at this and looked Feliks up and down. He too was a six-footer, Tony reckoned, but unlike the others he was paler, almost ginger-haired, with a face which was heavily scarred and battered. He was also an absolute bull of a man: huge neck, fists and shoulders, massive thighs, biceps bulging dramatically from under his tight T-shirt. Tony figured him for a weightlifter or gym devotee. Good to know he had at least one who could understand English.

"Ah, OK. I see. Well, no problem really. I'm sure Mr Krupchenko wouldn't have offered your services if he knew you would be unavailable."

"Me too." Feliks again.

"Sorry?"

"I am Mr Krupchenko driver and bodyguard. When he is in this country."

"Oh, OK."

"When he is in this country, I need be with him." Feliks looked over at Viktor as if to say *Hey, I'm needed too, pal* and then back at Tony. "I will need plenty of notice also."

"OK. No problem." Tony looked across all three of them. "Is there anything else I should know about which might affect your, erm, availability?"

Feliks shook his head, Viktor translated for Georgi and received a mumbled reply.

"Georgi say he like sleep late." Viktor smiled his shit-eating grin again.

Fucking hell, thought Tony, Vasilij's given me The Marx Brothers.

Tony kept driving until he reckoned he had about another 30 minutes of daylight left which would do him nicely. He smiled to himself at his cunning plan. After all, it wasn't a simple matter to park a large commercial vehicle by the side of a loch and discharge its contents through a 9" diameter hose without it looking a bit suspicious. You had to get right up next to the loch side for a start - the hose wasn't very long - and there were few places you could do this without either stopping traffic or standing out like a sore thumb. Pulling out a ten metre silver hose and plunging it into the loch in broad daylight was tantamount to pulling over in a lay-by to have sex with your girlfriend on the hood of your car while waving at the passers-by.

So, where could you pull up a tanker up at the loch side safely? And where was near the head of the loch to get maximum impact from the tidal flow? And where could you discharge the tanker's contents without arousing suspicion? Step forward, the Highland Skye processing facility in the Ardkinglas estate. Down right on the shoreline, fed by a winding track down through acres of woodland along which tankers, containers and refrigerated lorries trucked daily. This one factory processed more than half the salmon harvested in Western Scotland each day, starting at 6am and sometimes continuing well into the night. It had no security gates, no barriers, and a large section of hard-standing to the north of the factory where trailers could park, turn or wait. Every hour or so one would arrive or depart, either dropping off fish for gutting and filleting, or collecting boxes of salmon in large refrigerated lorries bound for a central distribution hub on the outskirts of Glasgow. Who would notice one more tanker heading down towards the plant?

Shortly after 6pm he pulled out of a lay-by and drove the last few miles to the estate. The dirt track down to the shoreline was potholed and narrow - enough for him to fit the tanker but he had to drive carefully to avoid coming off the edge of the track. To his right was a culvert and a winding stream which tumbled down into the loch. The track levelled out at the end and a sharp left turn opened out into a wider road on which a few businesses traded: a truck repairer and a local haulier next to each other. At the end of the road was the processing facility itself. All lights were off save for a few emergency ones illuminating the loading area. He drove towards the plant and then bore right onto a large hard scrabble area used for parking. Off to his left were piles of pallets and some large empty plastic tubs used to hold the fish from harvest. He was also pleased to see the another silver tanker parked, without its cab, not too far from the shore. He pulled up as close to the loch side as he dared and applied the air brakes. Startled by the sound he looked around to make sure no-one could see him. On the far side of the loch he saw a flash of headlights from a car heading west on the road to Inverary. He doused his headlights and sat quietly in the dark silence to steady his nerves.

After a short while he climbed down from the cab and walked round to the back of the tanker. It took only a few minutes for him to unhook the discharge hose and lead it across the hard standing and dip it into the water. He opened the release valves and waited until he could hear the plash of water falling into the loch, and the sea lice load with it. He got back into the warmth of the cab and waited, watching the gauge on the dashboard dropping as the tanker load was emptied into Loch Fyne.

It might take an hour all told to empty the contents but, when it was done, he intended to hook everything back up and skidaddle back to the main road before anyone was any the wiser.

6

A man in a leather cowboy hat was striding out over Horse Hope Hill and across to Glenrath Heights, eager to get to wherever home would be tonight. He had a fresh breeze in his face and the fading light of the day splayed shadows from the forests to his left and right. The sky was glowing steadily pinker as the sun was setting and the odd flash would glint off ahead as its rays hit a window from a far-off farmhouse or steading.

As he walked, one flash kept blinking and winking, a sharper steelier light than the others. It stood out as a brighter shard, a pinprick of light nagging him with an irregular pulse. He pulled out a small pair of binoculars and peered over in its direction. It took him several seconds to place it accurately and he waited for it to glimmer again before he could be sure what it was: a theodolite being manoeuvred by a figure in a hardhat. Presumably there was another one nearby but out of view. What was this he wondered?

He diverted across and down the hillside until eventually he was sheltered in the lee of the hill. Looking down on the valley he could see Langhaugh Farm to the left and over to the right what looked like a full-blown construction site with work substantially underway. He scanned the area with his binoculars.

There was an access track, well-defined and gravelled, and a strong, reinforced bridge leading across Manor Water to the only road into and out of the valley. If this track had been purpose built he could see that it had been there a long time and that is was substantial. Permanent. This was not some interim track generated by passing traffic - this was a deliberate road, possibly with drainage, meant to carry heavy plant and large vehicles.

At the road's end was a newly flattened area covering several acres, banked and buttressed into the hillside. There were piles of large concrete pipes - the sort that would be set underground to carry sewage and water - and a large pyramid of black and brown plastic tubing pipes, smaller in diameter and presumably used to house wiring and smaller pipework. Over there a few large cubes of stacked breeze blocks gathered together by plastic binding, a cement mixer, a smaller crane, and two portaloos. Over here were concrete footings and wooden stakes hammered into the mud at regular, precise intervals. To one side a yellow mobile generator and two clusters of portable floodlights stood idle, behind them a portakabin and some rolls of rusting caging used to reinforce concrete.

A small digger was standing idle on the hillside, the ground around it disturbed and ridged with caterpillar tracks. On the digger was written MacPherson Construction and a Peebles phone number. The man made a mental note and scrambled back up the slope, heading home.

November days like this, Tony knew, were few and far between in Scotland, but when they were here, they were glorious. When he had first travelled to Europe, many years ago, he had learnt to reluctantly wrestle with the Celsius scale that the non-American world seemed to prefer over the clearly superior Fahrenheit one. He'd even composed a little rhyme to help him: *30 is hot, 20 is nice, 10 is cool, 0 is ice.* Time later spent in Scotland had caused him to update it to: *30's irrelevant, 20 is damp, 10 is damp, 0 is damp.*

But not today. The sun shone through a crisp autumn sky, the trees blazed in a hundred colours and the majestic granite peaks stood sunlit and shadowed looking down on blue-green waters that splintered and sparkled in the glare. He pushed the car round the twists and bends and floored the accelerator when he wasn't stuck behind lorries or trailers. When he reached Dunoon he pulled into the lane of cars queuing for the ferry, got out and walked over to the ticket office. The ferries ran roughly every half hour so he knew he wouldn't have too long to wait and then he'd be in central Glasgow by lunchtime.

First, though, he was in need of another top-up from the Bank of Kim.

There was an ATM inside the ferry ticket hall and he moved over to it as he heard the tannoy announcement of the inbound ferry encouraging passengers to ready themselves for boarding. He stabbed his fingers at the buttons as he heard the sound of some car horns coming from the queuing traffic and wondered if his vehicle was the cause of the frustration. The silver keys on the machine were sticky and sluggish and the zero key didn't seem to want to play ball. *Come on! Stab, stab, stab.* He felt himself reddening as he imagined the angry drivers stuck behind his car in the queue punching their horns with increasing fervour. With his anxiety now increased, his clammy hands became even less effective on the ATM keyboard. *Stab, stab, stab.* Register my key presses, damn you! *Stab, stab, stab. Enter.*

Tony had unwittingly woken the machine with his injudicious push of the Enter key. As if bursting from a dam, this key unleashed a torrent of zeroes which the machine had been holding back from his key presses thus far. Snapping immediately to life, with some whirrs and clicks, the ATM proceeded to spit out £5,000 in twenties. Tony looked on in horror as the thick sheaf of notes was regurgitated from the newly opened maw and the machine started beeping to incite him to take the cash and be gone. The beeping of the ATM, the bleating of the tannoy and the staccato car horns congealed into a symphony of red mist before his eyes.

He grabbed the stack of banknotes, pocketed them out of sight from any envious eyes, dashed over to the ticket counter to pay for a single to Gourock and then escaped out into the open air, the cold breeze hitting his red sweaty face hard and causing him to catch his breath slightly as he ran to his car. There were no cars in front of him, and a line of some half dozen behind him. Hemmed in by iron railings into a blocked corridor, at least one of the drivers was out of their vehicle, standing around Tony's car scanning the landscape in all directions for the idiot who had abandoned his car.

"Sorry!" Tony shouted, trying to stay calm, not looking anyone in the eyes, head down moving towards his car. "Sorry. Coming now." The other drivers walked back to their own cars mouthing obscenities to themselves semi-audibly. "Fuckin' eejit" being one of the most polite he could make out from the selection. He started his engine and accelerated along to the end of the line where the railings stopped and the gangway to the ferry met the pier.

Driving off the ferry, Tony followed the signs to Glasgow, on autopilot while he tried to marshall his thoughts. He thought about Kim and how she would surely find out about him stealing her money. Normally he would keep withdrawals to limits such as £100 or £200 - small enough he'd always thought to not register on an account which was always many thousands in credit and which was topped up monthly by her allowance. Once he had rashly withdrawn £500 in a single transaction and had sweated and worried for days about being found out. As the time passed and Kim seemed none the wiser he eventually relaxed and, while he didn't often do it again, he felt more secure in his assumption that amounts below £200 would not appear on her radar. And now here he had just nabbed five grand in one go. Surely this would be noticed?

He thought about Viktor, the violent cretin. He needed to find a way to tame this idiot and keep him in check. Appealing to Vasilij wouldn't do any good as Vasilij would just smile calmly as if indulging a small child. Trying to talk to Viktor himself was like explaining particle physics to a deranged wolverine: the animal had been selectively bred over generations to have no interest in anything which didn't involve violently shitting, drinking, eating or fucking.

He thought about Georgi and whether he would survive their next face-to-face encounter after the barrage of Russian abuse he had been on the end of during his last phone call. Tony wasn't aware of what had happened and would no doubt get to be fully brought up to speed via the usual medium of gestures, mime and other varieties of hand-puppetry which the drunkard brought to bear whenever his English failed him - essentially always. Christ, if this pair were the best Vasilij could provide him with how was he expected to orchestrate a coordinated program of destruction and sabotage across Scotland's salmon industry without being detected or getting himself killed in the process?

He was still bemoaning his luck when he realised he had missed the turnoff he wanted to get him to Buchanan Bus Station. Muttering and cursing, he came off at the next junction only to find himself tormented by Glasgow's one-way system. Afraid of U-turns in case the Scottish cops enforced traffic violations with the same relish as their US counterparts, he followed signs he hoped would take him close but never seemed to. After fifteen tortuous minutes of crossing and re-crossing the motorway he gave up and pulled into the first public car park he came across. The street map standing outside the car park showed him he was only about half a mile from the bus station. He cheerfully took off his jacket in recognition of the sunshine, stuffed it into his rucksack containing the IEDs and headed along Renfrew Street.

The glass entrance doors were open as he passed the Pavilion Theatre on the other side of the street and the music coming from the foyer made him look across. Someone called Blysse Baptiste was starring in Babes In The Wood. Her image dominated the hoarding and posters, loose blonde curls coiling down around her shoulders to frame an impressive cleavage. Intrigued, he stopped and crossed the road, letting his pants compass lead the way.

There was a life-sized mannequin standing in the centre of the foyer and somehow projected onto it was a moving image of the blonde, hands on hips, pouting and saying something drowned out by the music. His attention was caught by her mouth. As she talked he stared at it, watching it move and the tip of her tongue playing over it. It reminded him of an old High School girlfriend and he suddenly found himself searching her features for other familiar signs. There was something about the eyes and the chin, and the way she flicked her fringe out of her eyes. Was it Amanda - this Blysse Baptiste - albeit now with blonde hair, newer tits and maybe a nose job?

As the animation looped, he pulled out his phone and googled Blysse Baptiste. Her wikipedia entry said *born Amanda Hardy, California, 1978*. Christ, it was her! Although, that date was wrong - she had been in the same year as him, which would make her 4-5 years older than the entry said. Appeared in a minor sitcom where she played a ditsy busty blonde and then shot to fame with the lead role in the spoof action movie *Doom Raider: Cindy Anna Jones and the Pharaoh's Curse*. This was shortly followed by *Doom Raider II: CAJ and the Midas Touch* and then, sometime later with *Doom Raider III:CAJ and the Jesus Scrolls* ending the series following the law of diminishing returns. Blah blah.

He walked up the steps and into the foyer and watched closely as the mannequin spoke to him. Tony shook his head, smiling in disbelief, as he recalled the time he'd tried to get Amanda to swallow his Love Python in the back of his car - and how he'd have tried even harder if she'd looked then like she did now. Christ, she looked amazing! Maybe he should go look her up - for old times' sake?

Then he remembered the nine remaining bombs in his bag. He stepped back out of the foyer, crossed over onto Killermont Street and then walked across the bus stands into Buchanan Bus Station. He carefully stashed the bag in a left luggage locker off the main concourse and put the key in his pocket.

As he did so he thought about Amanda. Or Blysse if she preferred. Was this a sign? Gaia once again showing him the synchronicity of things: as an unfortunate withdrawal meant he would have to sever relations with one blonde before she severed a part of his anatomy, so the planet presented him with an unexpected appearance of another blonde who could take her place.

Whistling a happy tune, he strolled back out into the sunshine and headed towards the Pavilion Theatre.

Sitting in the darkness of the stalls, all alone, two rows from the back, Tony felt like a bit of a creep. Some sad old man stalking a starlet, gawping from the shadows in a raincoat, hat over his eyes. Ok, so he wasn't wearing either a raincoat or a hat, and he definitely wasn't old, but here he was nevertheless, gawping absolutely. Entranced even. She was simply gorgeous.

He had still had his doubts, despite Google, but now, seeing her on the stage - moving about, her movements unrehearsed and natural - he knew it was her. Blysse was Amanda, Amanda was Blysse.

She was wearing some outlandish costume which seemed to hinder her movements somewhat. Her high-heeled boots made her totter as if on stilts and the feathered hat didn't seem to sit right on her head. Too much hair or too little hat? Either way, that would need some serious anchorage come showtime. And she wore one of those headset mikes - they all did - which disappeared into her curls and was only visible from certain angles as an extra-large mole hovering to the left of her pink lipsticked pout.

He watched as the actors went through their lines, pausing every so often to refer to their stage notes. For some reason she slapped her thigh at the end of every pronouncement. Tony wasn't sure if the director knew what he was doing. Their voices rang out sounding awfully loud and echoey in this empty theatre, the shoes rapped harshly on the boards and the whole effect was of a hollow, over-amped open-mike night where no-one was funny and they were all dying on their arses (as the Brits say). She looked like a million dollars but this production stank, Tony thought.

Tony sat watching for another twenty minutes or so until he felt he had got the gist of the thing and wanted no further part in it. He rose from his seat and went in search of backstage. When a burly janitor blocked his way and told him it was restricted to performers only, Tony slipped him a few of the £20 notes from his plentiful supply and told him he was an old friend. The janitor waved him through.

Blysse was finally getting into this panto concept. It was very weird and she wasn't sure how her friends back in the US would take it, but there was something about it which was definitely growing on her. Sure, the jokes were corny - hell, she didn't even understand some of them:

who was Gok Wan anyway? She poured herself some Evian and adjusted her bust in the tight-fitting corset. She was repainting her nails when there was a knock and a pony-tailed head with a wound dressing taped to it poked itself round the door. Forty-ish maybe, tanned, well-muscled in a red T-shirt, a navy blue USCD Tritons jacket over his shoulder. The newcomer looked at her meaningfully with light blue eyes under heavy pale brown brows and a spark of recognition leapt in her.

"Tony?"

"Hey, Amanda?"

"Oh my God. Tony!"

"Hey again."

"What are you doing here?"

"Come to see you." He sneaked the rest of himself into her dressing room and closed the door behind him. "Mind if I come in? I wanted to see if Blysse was really you."

"Oh. My. God."

"How are you? It's been a long time."

"Yeah, I guess." Of the many thoughts racing through her head right now one, with a mind of its own, rose up unbidden to her lips. "Christ, look at you. You used to be such a jerk!"

"Well, I've gotta Masters degree from Stanford so I guess that would be no longer the case." He smiled, smugly, and instantly it all came flooding back - the fumblings in the back of his car, the practical jokes, the secret diary, the prom, the break-up. The being a jerk. She recovered quickly.

"Sorry, that's was stupid of me. I mean, wow, you look great! Did you really come here just to see me?"

"Well, you sure are something to look at these days" his eyes strayed to the place men's eyes usually strayed to, but came back up to hers. "But no, I ... well, I live in Scotland right now so I was in Glasgow and was just passing the theatre here, saw your poster and thought *"it can't be, can it?"*

"What's with your head?"

"Oh, this?" He reached up to stroke the dressing at his temple. "It's just a scratch."

His eyes were scanning her face closely. Looking for familiar features? Seeing if he could detect the work she'd had done? She looked him up and down. He had matured well, she thought. Very well. He had always been a bit of a beefcake and he hadn't let himself go, she could see that.

"So, what're you doing in Scotland? You work here?"

"Yeah. I'm an ecologist? I'm working on a project campaigning against Big Aqua - the damage industrial fish farming is doing to the environment."

"Wow. Heavy." She paused, wondering what more she could say. "Who's Big Aqua?"

"Not who, what. Big Aqua is the aquaculture industry. Aquaculture is the euphemism they use for fish farming."

Nope, she hadn't really caught any of that. Better keep winging it, she thought. "And fish farming is killing fish?"

"Well, yes. In the same way that cattle farming kills cows - for meat. But it's the harm that farming does to the environment, other species, the ecosystem: that's what I'm campaigning against."

"Cattle farming is killing the ecosystem?" Now she was getting it!

"No. Fish farming is." Ah. No she wasn't.

"Oh." She pursed her lips and pouted, unsure of her next line. Tony smoothly stepped in, transitioning effortlessly into his practised expert mode.

"Yes. Big Aqua consumes 80% of the world's fish oil - that's oil made from killing other fish - to feed these fish farms. Thousands of fish crammed into cages so they don't have enough room to move around. They spread disease and discharge huge amounts of waste into the sea affecting the marine environment and other animals -"

"That's awful! I am a vegan and I deplore the caging of animals." Genuinely - albeit naively – earnest.

"And if that's not enough, fish farmers deliberately shoot marine mammals like seals in order to protect their stocks."

"No! Seals are my absolutest favourite animal!" She pointed to a stuffed seal toy by her makeup mirror as if to prove this point. "Oh my god, they're so cute!"

"Well, that's what is happening today. Not just in Scotland but around the world."

"That's, like, unreal. Someone ought to do something."

"That'll be me, then."

"Well, good for you, Tony. I'm pleased that seals have you fighting on their side."

"Serve and protect, ma'am. Serve and protect." Tony gave a mock salute. "Perhaps you could help me drum up some publicity for the seals of Scotland?"

"Ooh, how gorgeous! But I can't, I'm in a panto Tony! See?" She pirouetted in her outfit and Tony got an eyeful of curves and swerves; a noseful of vanilla and peach perfume and choking hairspray.

"Yeah." Said Tony, thoughtfully. "What's a panto?"

"It's like a funny play they put on at Christmas in the UK."

"Right." He didn't seem impressed, she thought.

"It's Babes In The Woods and I'm Robin Hood." She slapped a thigh obligingly.

"Obviously."

"Yeah. I mean, I didn't get it, at first. Until Harvey - he's my agent - explained. He says it'll re-energise my profile. Help get me back on the road to the A List. He says playing on my image is *post-modern ironic*." These last words enunciated carefully as if from memory.

"Yeah. I guess. Don't you - "

A double-knock interrupted them and a voice came through the door, newly ajar. "Back on in five please, Ms Baptiste!"

"OK." Blysse called to the disappearing voice. "Thank you!"

"Look, I better go." Tony turned to leave. "It was great seeing you Aman-, Blysse. You look amazing."

"Tony, look. Don't be a stranger ok? I'm here for an eight week run and I don't know anyone else here, other than the cast and the director. And they're nice an' all but they're all awfully..." she searched for a suitably derogatory term, her nose beautifully scrunched up. "...British."

"Ok, I'll try. I'm travelling quite a lot right now but I'm sure I'll be back here at some point."

"Well, you know where to find me."

She stood on tiptoe to give him a peck on the cheek, and he walked back through the theatre and out into the open air with a spring in his step, a smile on his face and a Rising Rooster in his pants.

7

The Exhibition Centre was emptying out and many of the stands were being taken down as Tony wandered in. There were only a couple of hours to go before the conference officially ended and, this late on a Sunday, there was no point anyone checking his identity or searching through his bags. Kim saw him out of the corner of her eye as she tore down the large poster behind her and she beamed and waved as he came towards her. She turned to the other woman on the stand and nodded towards Tony.

"Would you mind being a love and finish up here for me, Val?"

Val was somewhat older and stouter than Kim and held a mild maternal view of her as a valued colleague and rom-com-by-proxy conversation piece. She smiled a tolerant "Of course. Off you go.", took the poster from Kim and started rolling it back up into its tube. Kim grabbed her handbag and skipped off across the dirty carpet into the arms of her beloved.

"Tone!" she squealed delightedly. "It's been an absolute age, cowboy. Come here my little Audie Murphy you!"

Kim grabbed his hair and pulled him towards her. Hands and arms wrapped him, writhing up and down his torso as she embraced him and generally tried to suck his face clean off. Manfully, he did his best not to resist and waited for her to finish. When she finally came up for air she was flushed and licking her lips as if she'd just eaten a massive T-Bone.

"Oh boy, sorry. All went a bit Kate Winslet there for a mo. Your fault, really. You look good enough to eat. If I squeezed you any harder you'd turn into a diamond."

"I'll take that as a compliment."

"Oh you should! Of course, you should. I've been stuck in this desert all week being pawed and ogled by sweaty middle-aged business men doing their best to up the halitosis quotient of Edinburgh - as if it needed upping - and here you are as luscious as a ... well, you're like a dry martini to a drowning man. Or something."

Aware she was babbling now and not particularly making any sense she had the decency to stop and look him quizzically in the eye, her head tilted to one side enquiringly.

"You're very quiet for someone being greeted by their guaranteed lay for the night. What's up?"

"Nothing. Really." He looked into her eyes. "You're just overwhelming sometimes, is all."

She dipped into an attempt at a wild-west old-timer accent.

"Well, stop your grinnin' and drop your linen. I'm ready to whelm all over you, pardner. You just say the word."

"The word."

"Much obliged. Now let's make like a tree and get out of here."

"Back To The Future, right?"

"Right. And if you'll kindly convey me to my room -"

"They kept your room? But the conference is finished."

"Listen, Buster! I've been sweating my nuts off here all week, least they could do is give me a complimentary room at the end of the conference."

"Cool."

"Yup. And we can eat and drink on expenses - for one night only!"

"Extra cool."

"After."

"After what?"

"After I give you such a thrill you'll think you've been hit by 1.21 jiggywatts."

"Great Scott!" Tony smacked his forehead dramatically as Kim dragged him to the elevators.

"Come on, Kimchi. We need to get moving."

Tony was shaking her gently, trying to rouse her from her slightly-sozzled slumber.

"Whaa?"

"… moving, Kim. Got to be on our way. It's after eleven, we haven't had breakfast and checkout time is noon. Come on!"

" 'Kay."

He waited ten seconds. She didn't budge. He shook her again, not quite so gently this time.

"Kim?"

" 'Kay."

Grudgingly she tried to open one mascara-stuck eye to the day and held her temple with one hand.

"Attagirl" Tony helped her to her feet and then ushered her through into the bathroom, steering her shoulders towards the shower cubicle. He turned the shower on full, left her standing naked in front of it and went back to packing their cases.

When he'd finished he lay on the bed and listened to the sound of the water slopping and cascading off her body as she washed. For a moment he entertained the idea of slipping into the bathroom and joining in her in the shower and started playing it through in his mind's eye: he was slowly stepping into the bathroom, naked, opening the cubicle door and peering through the steam at her half-seen naked form, hair pinned up in a ragged bun. She was soaping her face and turned towards the draught he was creating, letting in the cold air from outside the shower. She rinsed the last of the soap from her eyes and opened her hands to reveal the face of Amanda/Blysse gazing up at him

He snapped to with a start and went into the bathroom to check on her progress. As near as he could determine, she was sleeping standing up, leaning against the cubicle frame still on the threshold to the shower, the steam swirling all around her and Kim still bone dry. Feeling like a heel, he pushed her in and shut the door to, holding it closed.

At 11.45 Kim was finally ready. Dressed in T-shirt and jeans, tired flat slip-ons, no makeup and her hair still wet she wasn't going to win any prizes for best turned out hotel guest from the night before, but fortunately any such competition would have long since been held, judged and awarded when all the other guests had probably checked out some two hours earlier.

With Kim sitting like a zombie in the passenger seat, they drove out of Edinburgh in silence.

Later, sitting at a table in a Frankie & Benny's, Tony ordered coffee and two cooked breakfasts. Kim was still having difficulty concentrating or making sense.

"Christ, Kim. How much did you have? I thought you were fine but you must have got shit-faced"

"Don't 'member."

"Here, have some coffee. See if you can greet the day."

"Ugh! Sugar! I need sugar!"

"Sorry, hang on. There. Try now."

"Mmm. Better. I need a doughnut. Or a pastry."

"I've ordered a cooked breakfast for you."

"I might just bring it back all over you."

"I thought you liked a Full English?"

"I do but not this early in the morning."

"It's almost 1pm!"

"Your time, maybe. I'm operating on Kim Standard Time and I think I may have forgotten to put my clock back."

A waitress came over with a large round tray containing two plates heaving with bacon, sausages, fried eggs, tomatoes, mushrooms and baked beans. Kim took one look at it as it was placed before her and dry-heaved.

"That's a bit better."

"Told you."

"No actually, you didn't tell me. You ordered a fry-up and expected me to eat it. That was a pastry designed to get my blood sugar up."

"Ok, but I ordered it with a view to it making you feel better after your bingefest."

"Oh really."

"Yes. Look Kim, it was on the menu under Healthy Options."

"Really? What font was that written in - sarcastica?"

"Ok, fine."

"You know, you're quite getting the hang of this Englishness thing aren't you? You've earned a credit for the use of the word 'fine' to mean any number of different things except fine; and you're well on your way to a distinction in the various different ways to express drunkenness in one's partner."

"Yeah, well you must have drunk an awful lot."

"Well some of us can hold our drink."

"I can hold my drink."

"Yeah, right."

"I just choose not to drink often."

"Is that often choose not to drink or choose not to drink often? There's a difference you know. One of them is a simple statement, the other is a snide way of calling me an alcoholic."

"I meant the first one." He smiled thinly.

"Well, fine."

"Fine."

They sat in silence for a while until Kim's phone buzzed noisily. She rooted around in her bag for a while trying to find it.

"It's a text from the bank." She struggled to focus on the small text on the screen. "Says there's been a withdrawal from my account which has taken me overdrawn."

Tony froze and the phone buzzed again.

"Bollocks. Battery's low." She switched it off and stowed it back in her bag. Tony was watching her intently, breath held as she stared vacantly into space briefly before recovering herself.

"Must be some admin error. The usual Dreary Deidre confusing a one with a zero, that kind of thing. I'll give them a call later."

She looked up to find him staring at her, oddly.

"You ok?"

"What? Oh yes. Fine."

Coming round the blind bend, the Subaru kicked up stones as it skidded and snarked its way along the single track road. The wipers thrashed wildly in the downpour, headlights ineffectively buffeting the heaving mass of damp fog. In the passenger seat, Kim wasn't even watching the road.

"Can you slow down a bit, please?" She still felt nauseous and the scenery whizzing past wasn't making her feel any better. She wasn't entirely sure she wasn't imagining it when Tony leant across her and dexterously opened the door one-handed.

"What the hell are you doing?" she yelled, as he flicked her seatbelt open and pushed her out in one smooth but aggressive movement.

As she tumbled and rolled down the muddy bank, slipping with soaking jeans as the grey and green spun in her head, she thought she could hear a belated "Sorry!" faintly sing-songing down the valley. Her bones jangled as she hit humps and divots, sore and bruised as her rough descent continued. By the time she had rolled to a standstill the sound of engine, exhaust and tyres had given way to a blanket of wet, gray silence. The complete absence of sound hung in the damp chill like an enormous sign that said You Are Cold, Wet and Angrier Than You Have Ever Been. You Are Also All Alone, And No-one (Including You) Knows Where The Hell You Are.

Welcome to The Scottish Borders.

"Bollocks!" Kim swore, shouting at the storm. "Bloody BOLLOCKS!"

She'd never felt so cold. She was, she thought, almost frozen to the bone. Her teeth chattered and her fingers and bare arms were a waxy white, not yet blue (this reassured her as her expectations were that if your skin started turning blue then you were truly done for). But cold, oh so cold. Only the absolute purest rage that she felt towards Tony was keeping her alive.

"BASTARD! Fucking BASTARD!" The sheer effort of forcing out the words into the teeth of this bastard weather made her feel physically weak. Her knees buckled and she staggered across some clumps in the heather. Her feet, in her flimsy canvas shoes, were ragged, numb blocks of icy granite. Standing upright with another fierce push of energy she took stock of her situation:

Lost. Cold. Wet. Unsuitably attired. Still not entirely sober, but getting there now. Hungry. Oh God, yes, now she thought of it she was starving. Oh, she could have cried for something – anything - warm, comforting, solid. Why hadn't she had that breakfast when she had the chance? Something which would warm her from the inside out and stop her from dying of exposure out on this miserable shitty hillside. Shit, shit, shit …. SHIT! SHITTY HILLSIDE!!! Swearing mindlessly at her plight as if the very expletives could save her, she had to find shelter, had to get out of this weather. She really was genuinely at risk here, she thought. Come on, girl, get a grip. Think. Do a sitrep. Let's get the brain cells working while you still have breath left in you.

They had been travelling out from Edinburgh, south? West?. They'd been driving, what, an hour? Maybe a bit less? She hadn't been paying attention to the roads he'd taken, just staring listlessly out at the filthy rain and wild countryside, trying to not to decorate the car interior with abstract patterns. This was "border country" as its inhabitants proudly called it (and unjustifiably proud, in her view). So, she could be anywhere really. She wasn't familiar with the Borders and would only have clutched at her sense of direction when a Motorway sign had revealed itself. Which it hadn't. So, somewhere between Edinburgh and an unnumbered motorway, without a real clue as to settlements, towns, villages, names – bloody names – of places that might be en route.

Q: Where the fuck was she?

A: She could be, sadly, anywhere.

Ok, let's forget about the specific location. We can come back to that. What about general directions? Looking around her there was no sun, no stars, no visible indication of which way was North. Didn't moss grow on the north side of trees? Not that there were any fucking trees anywhere around her. Ok, stones then – north side of stones. Or was it the north side where it didn't grow? Bollocks. Look around. Look for moss. Christ, there was fucking moss everywhere. God, she wished she'd paid more attention at the few Girl Guide meetings she'd attended when she was younger. Why hadn't they done orienteering at any of the finishing schools she had attended and never, er, finished?

Shaking, Kim tried to take a careful look around her. She had tumbled about 50 feet from the road, down a slope clumped with heather, long grass and the odd jutting rock. She realised she had been fortunate to not hit any of those on the way down. The road from that point curved around the contours of the valley and twisted out of sight about half a mile further down. Above it the hills blended together to form a ridge which surrounded her. She couldn't gauge the general height but she wouldn't want to have to climb them to reach safety.

Below her was a stream which twisted and wrangled its way into the mist. At its narrowest points it looked jumpable, elsewhere it broadened and looked about wading depth – again, not something she wanted to attempt in this bone-crunching cold wearing these pathetic shoes barely better than ballet slippers.

The general outlook, then: cold and soaked through, rain continuing to fall and mist/fog meant the browns, greens and greys bled seamlessly into the murk with only a few swirling patches where the mist had mysteriously evaporated and the dark, moist colours stood out in relief.

Possible routes out:
1. climb back up to the road and follow it;
2. scale the ridge and see where she was;
3. follow the stream and keep going downhill in the hope of hitting some kind of settlement.

These, she guessed, were her three sensible options and she immediately ruled out the ridge and was inclined to keep to the road in case another vehicle should come by. As she couldn't recall the last place they had passed through to get here (wherever here was), she decided to follow the stream downhill, away from the road, hoping that some place would unveil itself through the fog. With a heavy heart, but a sense of purpose from having thought it through and come up with a plan, she lifted her gaze upwards and started scrambling down towards the tumbling water.

Her watch read 2:28pm. In this fog, she reckoned she had less than an hour's usable light left before she was in even bigger trouble. She took one last look up at the road and the direction that Tony had driven in realising she was saying goodbye both to him and that chapter in her life. Tony - hereafter to be known as TTT (Total Twatface Tony) - had abandoned her violently and without warning and if she got out of this alive she swore she would track him down and make him pay. In the meantime, she put her last ounces of purpose and strength into her shoulders and headed downstream, praying to meet someone, or some thing, which could keep her alive.

The wind whistled through a small gap in the window frame and spat a few raindrops onto the rotting sill. The firewood crackling in the grate warmed the room against the wintry, desolate weather. Inside it was almost cosy; outside the elements hammered at the small building's structure.

The sleeper stirred slightly, scratched himself, tugged his sleeping bag up past his chin and rolled gently away from the draft to face the fire. And smiling, farted.

By the fire a battered tin kettle and a similarly jaded mug stood guard. A few stray sparks floated upwards on the fire's hot air but faded before reaching the flammable material of which his sleeping bag was undoubtedly made. He was lying on a top bunk of three and perched on the bedpost was a battered leather cowboy hat.

The man slept on, blissfully unaware that somewhere out on the moorland behind him a poor girl, clad only in T-shirt and jeans, was slowly suffering from exposure and hypothermia.

Kim was stumbling in the dark and unable to see where she was treading. Rocks and tussocks and small ruts in the track made her sway and scrabble for her balance. A small shattered gatepost on the track held a roughly scratched chalk arrow pointing up and left, a faint muddy trail indicating that people had been this way before. As she squinted she decided she could make out a small light coming from a building and, though she realised she didn't really have any other options right now, she decided to make for this, whatever it was. It was shelter and that would do.

She knocked, got no answer, and tried to lift the latch. Her numb fingers and hand couldn't seem to muster the dexterity to make it move but she grabbed it with both hands and yanked upwards.

She felt the heat of the room before she saw the fire in the grate. It was the only light source in the room but she had never been more grateful to see anything in her entire life. She inhaled the smell of the fire deeply and noticed another, more earthy, note which underpinned it. Her nostrils flared - it smelt as if a large damp dog had eaten the rotting remains of something organic before licking her face and wagging it's tail under her nose. She gagged briefly and peered around for its source.

Two tiers of three wooden bunks lined the walls, a wide rough wooden ladder connecting the tiers. Four of the six bunks lay empty: one was partly filled with a pile of clothes spilling from a binliner and a large rucksack. The other bunk, the top right as you came through the door, contained a single occupant, in a sleeping bag, snoring intermittently, the firelight splashing warm red shadows on his face. He didn't exactly look clean. As if he could feel her eyes on him, he woke lazily and looked straight at her.

"Hi" she stuttered, shivering anew. "S-S-Sorry."

"Huh?"

"Sorry. For s-s-staring, I mean."

"Don't be. I was asleep." He sat up and unzipped his sleeping bag, revealing a hairy muscular torso and a tatty pair of boxers. He kicked his legs out of the bag, swung his feet out over the platform, jumped down unself-consciously and padded off to what she assumed was the toilet. The back of his boxer shorts was caught up somehow and he was showing a large patch of hairy pale, untanned buttock which he scratched at as the earthy odour accompanied him past her. She turned her head away but the toilet door was already shut.

She rushed over to the fire and tried nursing her icy limbs back to life in front of its delicious heat.

"What's your n-name?" she called through the door only to hear the sound of plashing in the toilet bowl.

"What?" he shouted over the noise.

"Your name?" she shouted, artificially louder this time.

He finished, flushed the toilet, snicked the lock back and came out rubbing his hands over his head like a bear waking from hibernation. He exhaled slowly, as if thinking about whether he should tell her.

"Cullen." Quietly, over the sound of him cracking his knuckles. "You?"

"K-K-K-K-K-Kim." Christ, she was cold.

"Can I call you Kim for short?"

She tried to laugh but it came out only as a faint rasp, empty of sound. He looked at her curiously, silently tilting his head looking her steadily in the eye and she suddenly became painfully aware of her current appearance.

"Tea?"

"Oh fuck, yeah. I mean, yes please. God you have literally saved my life."

He threw the contents of a battered tin mug into the sink and re-filled it from a kettle which had been sitting next to the flames, handing it to her. She looked at it in disgust but put it to her lips anyway. The scalding dirty water burnt her mouth and tasted like day-old distilled nappies but its warmth seeped through her putting some colour back into her skin.

She looked over at him as he scratched around in a large rucksack. His nose was broken – twice, perhaps – and his eyelids had long pale lashes the same sandy grey colour as his hair, which was thick and curly on his head. What looked like a few day's worth of stubble covered his chin and throat which was lined and tanned, liberally littered with creases and wrinkles. There wasn't much fat on him but he'd clearly seen plenty of the outdoor life if his face was anything to go by. He caught her looking at him and threw a large shape towards her which turned out to be a sleeping bag. It smelt bad.

"You can use this and bed down over there." He pointed to the bottom bunk of another three-tier arrangement on the wall behind her.

"Just like that? You let me come in and sleep here just like that?"

He ignored her and kept pulling things from the rucksack. A scruffy fleece which he also threw in her direction, and a line of rope which he tied between the fireplace and the end of the bunks.

"I mean, you don't even know who I am?" she protested.

"You're Kim and you like to talk."

"Yes, but…"

"You tired?"

"Yes, but…" Suddenly she realised just how totally exhausted she was.

"Me too. Hang your wet clothes on the line." He climbed up back onto his bunk and started crawling back into his sleeping bag, his back towards her. "They might be dry by morning."

She eyed him warily, afraid to undress, even though he seemed completely uninterested in her presence any longer.

"But don't you want to know what I'm doing here and-"

"Tell me tomorrow."

Reluctantly, she peeled off her outer layers, shrugged the smelly fleece on while she took off her bra, and then stood inside the sleeping bag while she removed her knickers. Shuffling across the floor like a bag lady coming last in the sack race, she hung her soaking clothes on the makeshift line and watched them drip onto the bare floorboards.

Still wearing the sleeping bag like a chrysalis, she heaved herself onto the bed and curled up into a ball to reduce the amount of her body in contact with this foul-smelling dirty bag. She zipped the bag up as far as it would go and when she looked over at him he was softly snoring.

8

A wet Wednesday matinee in Glasgow and Blysse was all out of good humour. She sat in her dressing room applying her makeup, mentally crossing off the shows between now and the 4th of December when she would get her first day off. On the dressing table she had a few limp greetings cards - one from Harvey, a couple from some fans - and a small pile of unopened fan mail. She attacked the pile of envelopes.

The first contained a polaroid of a mans genitals in an aroused state and was written in red ballpoint. She put that straight in the bin as soon as she saw the photo. The second contained a letter smelling of a pleasing aftershave and written in attractive, sloping hand. She started reading it only to recoil in shock as the letter invited her to masturbate with her left hand and call this number with her right. Again, straight into the round tray.

There was a knock at the door, the usual head popped round the side and said "Curtain in 15 minutes, Miss Baptiste" and disappeared again. She opened the next letter and found a lavishly embossed card - an invitation:

Mr Vasilij Krupchenko is delighted to have the privilege of inviting Ms Blysse Baptiste to his Christmas Party on board his luxury yacht on December 4th. Sailing from Largs Marina at 9pm, carriages at 1am. RSVP.

Who the hell was Vasilij Krupchenko and why was he inviting her to a party? She turned the invitation over looking for clues. On the back it showed a photograph of a large sleek white and gold boat - a motorboat, no sails, windows of smoked glass - with a small power launch shooting in front of it to give the picture some depth. The launch was coming out of the photo trailing a small wake, driven by a handsome young man with long dark hair. Sitting in the launch laughing and running one hand through their wind-blown hair were two beautiful young things in bikinis holding glasses of champagne. *Hell, count me in*, she thought. The date was her day off and the young man looked quite yummy. She had no idea where Largs was - one of the cast could enlighten her.

All through the first half she had been daydreaming of what might be, to the extent that she had missed her cue a couple of times and had to be hissed at from the wings. She decided she would call Harvey after the performance and see if he could find out anything about this mystery Russian with the long dark hair. When she got back to her dressing room at the interval there was a newspaper on her dressing table and an article circled in red felt tip. She picked it up and realised it was a review of the panto from the previous night. She inhaled slowly, preparing for the worst, sat down and began to read. She had been right to sit down:

Babes In The Wood, Pavilion Theatre, Glasgow
Reviewer: Tom Nettleston

Blysse Baptiste - One Babe I Woodn't

Babes In The Wood is one of those pantos which doesn't get performed very often but when it does tends to attract a particular type of performer, requiring as it does excellent comic timing and a troop of supporting characters who all have to be shoe-horned into a plot that mixes English myth with European fable. All too often it shines but here in Glasgow the tarnish is all too visible.

The cast, of whom Blysse Baptiste is the most prominent, appear to be enjoying themselves but the same could not be said for the audience. At almost three hours this performance is a survival of the fittest (and Baptiste certainly has the fittest 'lungs' on show) but the setup is creaky, the jokes mostly weak and the songs - apart from the rousing final number - fail to ignite the show.

Those hoping to catch a glimpse of the erstwhile sex symbol would be advised to not sit too near the stage and lower their expectations prior to taking their seat. With dainty pins and a prominent embonpoint, Baptiste strides around in thigh-length boots and a crisp white outfit which shows off her California tan to good effect. However, her voice is thin and she doesn't appear to be fully aware of the camp over-the-top style a good panto requires from its performers. Here and there she is mildly amusing and joins in as a good sport on some of the bawdier gags. But overall, this isn't a comeback for the former American beauty, more of a comedown.

She boiled as she read it again. How could someone write like this? Not just about her but about any actor or any show. Giving a bad review was one thing but phrasing everything so passive-aggressively just made it all the harder to stomach. It was like being fed chocolate from one hand and stabbed with a stiletto by the other. When she heard the "five minutes" for the second half she tried to compose herself but wasn't entirely sure she had succeeded. Anyone sitting in the front rows this evening was going to have an excellent view of slightly smeared mascara and a forced smile.

Changed out of her costume, makeup free, Blysse called Harvey around 10pm UK time. It rang several times before he picked up:

"Hey Sweetie? How's it goin'?"

"Hi Harve. I'm not so bad. Not so good either, though."

"Aw, hey. How are rehearsals?"

"We're through rehearsals. We're previewing now until the weekend when we're fully live."

"OK. But you sound quite down."

"Yeah, just gotta bad review from the local press. It's kinda hit me hard, you know? I was getting into it and well, it is a bit of a schlep - doing the same thing over and over, twice a day. Was looking forward to my day off an' all but now I feel like I'm wasting my time. And -" she started to cry quietly.

"Hey! Sweetie! Come on, *tits and teeth*, remember?"

"Yeah." She sniffled, dabbed her eyes with a tissue. Tried to brighten, then remembering the party invitation genuinely did brighten.

"Hey Harve, can you do me a favour?"

"Sure. Whaddyaneed?"

"I've been invited to a party by some guy I never met and I wondered if you could google him for me. See who he is?"

"Google him? Is this some local hunk who wants to sweep you off your feet or what? He ain't gonna have any kind of profile."

"No the party's on a yacht. His yacht. Surely he must be rich and famous or something?"

"A yacht? In Scotland!"

"'S'what it says. There's a photo of it too. Looks like a real James Bond boat!"

"OK. What's his name?"

She retrieved the invitation and read his name carefully over the phone, spelling Vasilij's surname.

"Ok, hang on… Krupchenko… ok, here we go… Vasilij Krupchenko, Russian business multi-millionaire. Wow, jackpot sweetie! *Multi*! I mean, *multi* is good right? Blah blah blah… construction… salmon… property… bachelor! Woo-oo! Ker-ching.!"

"Harve. I don't know him, He doesn't know me." She chewed her lip thoughtfully. "Is there a photo?"

"Wait up…. Yep. Here we are… Not bad, sweetie. Not bad at all."

"Does he have long hair?"

"Nope. What makes you say that?"

"Oh. No reason." She lowered her expectations and her pulse did the same. "Can you describe him?"

"Well, I'll text you his picture… hang on… there. But he's, what, fifty maybe? Quite handsome, something about him that's definitely Russian-looking but can't put my finger on it. Seems in decent shape. Sharp dresser."

Blysse waited for the photo to come through on her phone. What she saw confirmed that the man in the photo at the helm of the launch wasn't her man - which was a shame. But the man in the photo was really quite handsome and, when you threw in the fact that he was an eligible bachelor worth many millions of dollars, he appeared increasingly more attractive the harder she looked at him. Roll on December 4th, she thought.

Things in this dreary damp dismal country are finally looking up.

Blysse was gathering her stuff into a holdall when Tony stuck his head round the door.

"Hi. Me again."

"Hey Tony. Come in, come in. I wasn't expecting you."

"Oh, sorry. Should I come back? When's better for you?"

"No, it's OK. It's fine. I just wasn't expecting you, is all. Don't worry. How've you been? It's good to see you again."

"I'm good. Good. You?"

"Yeah, not bad. Think I'm getting the hang of this, you know? British humour? Not sure I'm getting the hang of the British critics though - or winning them over for that matter."

"Ah, bad review?" She nodded and showed him the circled clipping in the paper. "Harsh" he grimaced when he'd read it. "Very harsh."

"I thought so."

"Yeah, well look. This is probably some typical Limey snob with his finger up his ass and pissed off at the world because he's been sent to the ass-end of Scotland to live in permanent drizzle when he could be living the high-life somewhere much better. You ain't gonna get anything positive from someone like that, but that doesn't mean you deserve it. You have talent, Blysse. Always had."

"You think so?"

"I know so. Talent will out."

"Well, that's kind of you Tony, but it's all the harder to get people to come when the little publicity we have is so… negative."

He passed the paper back to her and thought for a moment. "Listen Blysse. Do you remember I told you I was in Scotland campaigning against Big Aqua? Damage to the environment and marine wildlife by industrial salmon farming?"

She nodded, not really listening. He ploughed on unaware, caught up with the novelty of a new idea.

"Well, one of the things I've been thinking about is doing some kind of photo op to highlight my campaign. You said seals were your favourite animal and, well, seals are one of the victims of these aquaculture firms behaviour. How about we cooperate on this? I get a world-famous movie star to highlight the plight of seals. You get a guaranteed slot on the news to promote your panto and remind the UK of your, erm, undoubted qualities?"

She looked at him, listening now but having only caught half of what he said. She was reluctant to admit this so kept silent.

"What do you say?" he prompted.

"Well, how would it work?" she asked, hoping he would recap and she'd be back up to speed on what he'd originally said.

"What do you mean?"

"How would I get a slot on the news?"

"Right. Well, I'd setup some demonstration - let's say I arrange for some camera crews to come to a salmon farm. Knock out some placards and a few volunteers: Farming Salmon Kills Seals. SOS - Save Our Seals, that kind of thing. Tell the BBC and the press that Blysse

Baptiste will be there, helping to highlight the plight of these animals -"

"I could get Harvey to use his contacts to tell people about it as well!" she enthused, now she had the gist.

"Yeah! More the merrier." He was impressed with her thinking. "Then all you have to do is shoehorn in some plug for the panto."

"Hmm." He face dropped at this. "How do I do that?"

"Maybe Harvey will have an idea? He's all about raising your profile isn't he? He should be all over this."

"I could wear a T-shirt advertising it?"

"Sure."

"Yeah. Oh-" She was crestfallen again, a perfect pout beneath beautiful sad eyes. "But I don't have any time off until the 4th."

"OK." Tony now thinking on his feet. "Well, I'll choose a site close by. There are loads of salmon farms around Loch Fyne, the Murray peninsular, Loch Striven. They're all within an hours drive of here. We could get you there and back before the matinee. Or even in between the matinee and evening performances. Bit tight, though."

"Nah, I usually stay here after the matinee. Keep in costume for the evening."

"Yeah? So if we did it then, between performances, you'd be in costume when we did the photo op! Thigh-high boots and miles of cleavage would go a long way to getting us on The Six O'Clock News. And News at Ten."

"OK! I'm in"

"Cool! Right, give me your number and let me get things moving." She read out her mobile number and he typed it into his address book. "I'm gonna aim for the day after tomorrow which is - the 30th. Or the day after that if I can't get everything arranged by then. So 1st Dec absolute latest, okay?"

"Sure."

"I'll call when everything is in place."

"Tony, you're the best." she beamed at Tony and he felt a familiar stirring in his groin.

The road to Benbecula - if it could be called a road, thought Georgi - twisted and dipped like a politician on Newsnight. Distended by a covering of ice and snow, he struggled to keep the van on the road, its skinny tyres almost bald. He hadn't thought to check the quality of the vehicle he had stolen, just the capacity. Now he was regretting his choice.

To compensate for the van's steadiness he swigged from a small bottle of chocolate vodka recovered from another off-license he had raided the night before. Total haul: one bottle of chocolate vodka (small); one bottle of Grey Goose vodka (large, consumed); one packet of Anadin Extra (chewed); one packet of Marlboro cigarettes (smoked); one hand towel (blood-soaked); one box man-size tissues (half-empty).

He'd tried to use the towel to strap his leg wound but it hadn't worked and all he had ended up doing was worsening the bleeding. The sixteen painkillers he'd chewed through, in two batches of 8, had stopped the pain for a while but increased the bleeding further by thinning his blood. He was now working his way through the tissues, using them as make-shift bandages which he strapped to his leg with some duct tape he had found in the back of the van.

The end result of this was that his usual unkempt appearance was now looking unachievably dapper. On a scale of 1 to 10, where 10 was David Beckham and 1 was Hagrid, Georgi was currently registering somewhere around the -25 mark. His combat trousers were torn and bloody, his jacket stained and muddy. He was unshaven now for five days and his hair looked like it had been cut by tying a strimmer to a ceiling fan and turning it on. His breath and body odour were off the charts.

On the ferry over from Harris he had tried to avoid arousing suspicion but ultimately failed since there was no-one who didn't notice the dishevelled appearance (and limp) of this stinking stranger, and no disguising his unfamiliarity with the vehicle, driving on the left or, indeed, the English language. The sidelong glances and whispered asides amongst his fellow passengers weren't lost on him but his recent intake of painkillers and vodka, combined with his standard demeanour of *zero fucks given*, meant that his focus was on one thing alone: attempting to recall Viktor's instructions for the Peters Port site. Try as he might, the best he could come up with was *something something nets*. It wasn't much to go on - *nets* - but he brightened considerably with the sureness of one who required only the odd noun or verb here and there to provide ample instruction. It was this absence of detail which allowed him to flesh out his role in proceedings with the flair and artistry that gave him such job satisfaction. That, and the opportunity to filch vodka wherever he found it, were the poles in his personal moral compass.

As he crested the brow of a hill he saw the ever-thinning road ribbon down to a small harbour where a couple of colourful boats bobbed. Out to sea a short distance were the unmistakable circular frames of another salmon farm. It was mid-morning with a lowering grey sky draping everything in winter drab. He looked left and right and peered out to sea but, try as he might, Georgi couldn't see a soul anywhere. No time like the present, he thought, to roll his plan into action.

He steered the small boat out from the harbour into the water. He'd chosen the blue one as he liked the colour, thrown his canvas tool bag into the bottom and tumbled himself in after it. In the bag were some bolt cutters, tin snips, cable cutters and other assorted tools designed to cut, scissor or saw through materials of various weights. He wasn't exactly sure what material salmon nets were made from - mostly because Viktor wasn't sure either so hadn't been able to enlighten him - so he had come prepared for everything. He may have trouble regularly wrestling the puppy Memory to the ground but he was resourceful enough to compensate for this shortcoming.

As the barge and salmon cages grew nearer he took a more considered look at the layout of the whole thing. There were ten circular cages, each perhaps 20m across, arranged in two rows of five. Each cage was edged by a kind of handrail made of drainpipes around three feet above the water level and with a mesh walkway all the way around which held the cages together in this rectangular pattern. Between the cages snaked several tubes and pipes of different colours and thicknesses, all the pipes feeding back to the floating concrete barge which sat at the head of the stack of cages.

He saw flashes of silver breaking the surface of the water and watched intently as the mass of writhing fish - huge things many of them, almost as big as his arm span - fought for the food which was being scattered onto the surface of the cages by a large rotary sprayer. Fascinated he almost collided with the barge as he kept gazing at the salmon in their cages. From their vantage points on the barge cabin, a handful of seagulls looked on.

He tied up, threw his tool bag out on the barge and sprung out of the boat. He was surefooted enough on the barge but once onto the pontoon the swell of the waves took over and he reeled a little as he stepped more gingerly down the walkway towards the first cage. The soundscape was calm and soothing: the quiet slopping of waves on cage sides; the rhythmic whizzing of the feeders as they shot pellets out in the water. Georgi paused briefly in contemplation before taking a swig of his chocolate vodka and stepping over the tubing onto the walkway surrounding the cage on his left.

He knelt on the walkway to get a closer look at the net system. It appeared that the nets were made of thick blue nylon, knotted, perhaps 15-20mm thick. They were attached by hooks to the cage perimeter below the underside of the walkway and Georgi thought he should be able to reach down to them with his long-handled bolt cutters. He put down his tool bag and steadied himself on the walkway as the cage rose and fell in the sea swell. Taking one last look around to check there was no-one who could see him, he started moving around the cage snapping the net away at each anchor point as he went.

Donnie MacIver brought a cup of his coffee back to his desk, sat down and did a round-robin check of his monitors. Four large screens in front of him showed images from cameras across three sites on the island. Each site had a number of cameras capturing images every second or so and sending them out onto the internet so that he could login in from home and check the feeds. The cameras mounted in cages showed him the fish feeding and whether there were any crowding issues; those on the barge heads gave him a birds-eye view of the cages at each site so that he could check for storm damage or loose pipework; the ones at the shore-base were there to act as security monitors in case of unauthorised visitors.

He cycled around the views on each site as he sipped his coffee. From the barge head camera at Peters Port he thought he could see a figure leaning into the cage from the walkway, pausing then moving on, working his way around the cage. The figure had his back to him and the images were grainy and black and white so it was hard to tell quite what the person was doing. Donnie checked the log book to see who was scheduled to be on site at Peters Port that day: no-one until after lunch. He squinted at the image again and checked to see if anything was showing up at the shore-base. Flicking again to the cage-mounted camera he suddenly saw all the fish on screen change direction and disappear out of shot to the right. He waited a few refreshes but they didn't come back into view. Weird.

He put down his coffee, threw on his waterproof and grabbed his car keys. Peters Port was only a ten-minute drive away.

As Georgi reached about halfway round the cage he felt the walkway start to move and sink slightly in the water. Annoyed he looked down and could see hundreds of fish streaming beneath him and away to the far side of the cage. They'd noticed the net sagging from the cage top where he'd severed the nets, leaving a big gap out to open water. Biggest fish first, smaller ones following, the salmon turned as one and herded themselves to freedom. The huge shift in biomass from one side of the cage to the other, and the influence of fish getting themselves caught in the loose netting as they surged for the gap, caused the cage to tilt in the water. Out of sync with the tide, the waves started slapping into the walkway more violently as it pitched a foot or so in the sea. Georgi steadied himself with the handrail, smiling grimly, and carried on - more slowly now - snapping the nets from the rest of the cage. His plan was working.

The seals appeared as if from nowhere and Georgi at first didn't notice the commotion. He had knelt down to steady himself - his limp was more pronounced now from the rocking of the walkway which had angered his wound - when he saw the dark flashes out of the corner of his eye. Some marine animals, like dolphins, use echolocation to help catch their prey - determining the location of their prey by measuring how long it takes an echo to bounce back from it. Many fish species have what is called a lateral line system that helps them detect the movement of prey in dark water. Grey seals have neither, but they do have tremendously sensitive whiskers. Using these they can detect a hydrodynamic trail - the movement of a fish - in even the darkest, murkiest waters from hundreds of meters away. When several thousand salmon simultaneously flood the airwaves with a hydrodynamic tidal wave, to grey seals it is like God is ringing an enormous dinner bell.

The seagulls didn't wait for the dinner bell. As a dozen adult seals started to feed themselves silly at the salmon banquet of their dreams, whole gangs of the sea birds called to each other and swooped down into the frothing water. Salmon, seals and seagulls writhed and roiled, silver scales and red fish blood churning the sea into a foamy broth.

Georgi bent low to protect himself from the dive-bombing seagulls. As the net slipped free from the last anchor point on the cage, the walkway pitched heavily one last time, dipping his legs into the freezing water. Crying out from the sudden shock of the cold, he lost his balance and watched his bolt cutters fall away into the darkness. He was kneeling in the water like some kind of mini-Poseidon when he was hit full in the chest by 400lb of sleek all-male seal with a thrashing salmon in its mouth. He fell backwards and started to sink down through the water.

Unable to swim, Georgi lashed out desperately for whatever he could grasp. He clawed for the walkway and held onto it behind his head. Freezing quickly, he tried kicking hard to pitch his body towards the walkway and safety, like a demented child learning backstroke at the side of a pool. The salmon beneath him started to swarm away, taking their now unanchored net with them out into open water. As he kicked, his trailing foot snagged and became tangled in the departing net.

The grip of an overweight drunk male - freezing cold, soaking wet and afraid of drowning - is no match for several tonnes of well-fed Atlantic salmon in their element (literally), collectively swimming for their freedom. Georgi held his grip for what seemed like an eternity as he was stretched and stretched on this marine torture rack until he could feel his fingers uncurling and, with a final gasp, his body was dragged beneath the waves.

It was a minute or so before an empty bottle of chocolate vodka bobbed to the surface.

PART 2

Use what you have

9

In the background, Martin could hear the tannoy announcing the closure of flight EY602 for Alicante. On the other side of the glass, travellers hurried left and right, zigzagging to avoid colliding with each other. This side of the glass was a nondescript office, all air-conditioned whiteness and silence. Still not quite 6am, Martin counted down the minutes to the theoretical end of his shift. 98. 97. 96. He wanted to go to bed and sleep for a hundred years. Was this too much to ask? As if in answer, the door opened and Chief Inspector Dominic Maxwell, Border Policing Command, entered.

"Martin." he nodded. Martin jumped out of his chair and stood to attention, waiting for the signal that he could be seated again. There wasn't one. "All those about to go off-shift take one step forwards. Not so fast, Jenkins."

"You. Are. Joking."

"Ok, yes. I am. But only a little" He gave Martin an apologetic smile and put his hand on his shoulder. "I want you to go home, get a few hours kip, then get your arse up to the Highlands and find out what the hell is going on."

"Fuck. I'm beat." He gave an enormous sigh and closed his eyes. "Sir." Mid-thirties, tall, athletic, with a narrow face and piercing green eyes. Throw in the close-cropped blonde hair and the charming smile and he could winkle a confession out of you in no time. But right now he did look very tired indeed.

Martin opened his eyes, his shoulders slumped. "What's the story?"

Detective Inspector Martin Jenkins was the senior on-duty officer of Border Policing Command at Edinburgh airport this morning. The Chief Inspector was only here for some drive-by management on his way to a strategic liaison committee with the Assistant Chief Constable and the Head of the Organised Crime and Counter Terrorism unit.

Set up in 2013, the BPC was a specialist crime division of Police Scotland responsible for border security. Able to call upon resources and intelligence across Scotland as well as liaising with other international agencies, in theory its focus was on terrorism, money laundering, drug and human trafficking. In practice, because of its reach, if it involved suspicious activity at, into or out of any Scottish border point, the BPC got involved.

Not much, then, to deal with.

In addition, Martin was a Small Ports Officer with responsibility for all small, non-designated ports, airstrips, harbours and marinas which could act as gateways into or out of the country. This being Scotland, these "ports" were distributed widely and remotely across the whole of the country. Due to some organisational accident originating in the merging of various Scottish forces into the single, unified BPC, Martin had ended up with responsibility for sites on the west coast of Scotland - despite the fact that he was mostly based in the east. So, instead of regularly visiting sites from Berwick to Aberdeen he was lumbered with Ayr to Ullapool. It didn't make any sense but that, to Martin, was par for the course.

The Chief Inspector sat on the edge of the desk and slapped a manila folder down on it.

"I've got a report here of a shooting at a salmon farm on Harris, couple of weeks ago."

"Okay." Martin said, folding his arms, waiting.

"A fire at a salmon hatchery in Lochcarron the same day." *Slap.* Another folder. "Another one of criminal damage at two salmon farms on Lewis last week."

"Right."

"Another one a few days ago of an intruder at a salmon farm on North Uist." *Slap.* "And another one here -" *Slap.* "- of an intruder at another salmon farm on Benbecula yesterday."

"And these." *Slap slap slap slap.* "Reports of thefts, break-ins and other shenanigans the likes of which the Western Isles have never seen before."

"Sounds like a Hebridean crime wave. Maybe the local boys should get right on it."

His boss was in no mood for flippancy this morning. "The local boys did get right on it. They wrote up these reports. And I'm giving these reports to you."

Martin bit back his tiredness. "May I ask why, Sir?"

"Because here-" *Slap.* "Are the recent movements of our old friend Mr Krupchenko who, you will see, has been coming in and out of the country in his private jet like a man possessed. Edinburgh, Kirkwall, Stornoway, Prestwick. And he's due in again in two day's time."

Martin waited, there had to be more. There was.

"There's a pretty good correlation between the dates of these incidents and the dates he's in the country." The Chief Inspector continued. "And one of his major business interests is ... ta-da, salmon!"

Martin wrinkled his nose. ""Yes, well. Freestyle conclusion jumping is what it is."

"Well, my spidey senses are tingling. I want you to check these reports out. The regional boys are going nuts - never seen anything like it."

"Really?"

"Yes, really." Maxwell snapped. "These are all in your bailiwick, ok? And, last time I looked, shit rolled down hill." He sighed heavily. "Martin, just put your A level in Pure & Applied Circle Squaring to good use and see what you can come up with, hmm?"

"Sure. But, I predict -"

"What? You predict what?"

"Nothing."

"Martin, predictions are difficult. Especially about the future." The Chief Inspector looked over at him, archly. "Neils Bohr."

"Yeah, well. When someone tries to tell me just what my future holds, I already know." He rejoined. "Twain."

Maxwell didn't recognise the quote. "Mark?"

"Shania."

When Kim woke to the smell of cooking she was facing the blank wall. She struggled trying to turn in the sleeping bag and found she was all knotted up but once she had wrestled herself over she could see the stranger sitting cross-legged in front of the fire, scraping scrambled egg into his mouth with a fork in one hand, straight from the pan, and a tin mug of tea steaming in front of him.

He had placed her underwear, now dry, next to her bed, atop a baggy pair of paint-splattered jogging bottoms. Her jeans and T-shirt were still gently steaming on the line. She dressed quietly, still inside her sleeping bag.

"Well, Kim." He emphasised her name as if he didn't quite believe she was telling him the truth about it. "Breakfast?"

"Oh God, what are you - some kind of guardian angel watching over me? Christ on a bike, er - "

"Cullen."

"Right, sorry. Look, Cullen, here you are giving me warmth and shelter, a bed for the night and now offering me breakfast. Why aren't you looking at me as if I've just walked into your house and pissed on your kids!"

"No kids" he shrugged, looking around him.

"But I have just walked into your house."

"Well, yes and no." The quiet way he said this somehow sucked all the energy out of the room and made her realise for the first time, that she was actually alone here at the mercy of this stranger and no-one would know where she was should anything happen to her.

"Oh, shitty trousers! Tell me this is your house."

"Yes and no."

"Meaning what? Do you live here?" Panic rising in her throat.

"Sometimes."

"When *sometimes*?"

"Now, for example."

"Cullen - if that's your real name - you sound as if you're being incredibly economical with the *actualite*. Do you own this house?"

"No."

"Do you rent it?"

"No."

"Are you here with the owners permission?"

A pause. "Yes."

"Aargh! Can we stop with the Twenty Questions and can I prevail on your better nature and just let you know that I am out of my mind, at the end of my tether and obviously - if you look at my condition and the way I arrived here last night - in a not inconsiderable spot of bother. Not taken to ordinarily wandering the wilderness unsuitably attired, natch. If you are my guardian angel can you please put me out of my misery and tell me who you are and what you're doing here. And where *here* is. 'Cos - hello! - I am clueless and getting more than a little scared by your Man Of Mystery act."

She extracted herself from the sleeping bag and flopped onto a chair. She ran her fingers through her hair and then put her head in her hands, trying at all costs not to cry and having a certain difficulty with same.

"Relax." He smiled, which somehow made her feel less safe and more afraid. He handed her a plate of eggs and a mug of what had last night passed for tea. "You talk too much."

She gulped at the hot "tea" and almost retched. It was foul.

"Sorry. No sugar"

"S'okay. I'll manage." She swallowed it down, delicately, making sure to keep her gag reflex under control. The eggs were much better and really not bad at all. Cullen watched in silence while she ate. Only when she was scraping the plate did he speak

"OK."

"This place …?" she gestured with her fork.

"… is a bothy."

"Excuse me?"

"A bothy. An unmanned shelter for walkers and backpackers, maintained by volunteers and owned by - well, actually don't know who owns them. Charities, government, council, someone. But they are available for anyone to stay in as long as they leave them in the condition they found them. I don't own it or rent it. But I am entitled to stay here - as are you - and, currently, that is what I am doing."

"They?"

"They who?"

"Yes, you said *they* are available to stay in. This isn't the only one?"

"Oh, no. There are many all over Scotland. Usually in out of the way places, not too far off signed walking trails. I know half a dozen, maybe."

"O-ka-a-y. And you are…?"

"… not a serial killer, escaped prisoner or fugitive from justice. You're safe. If you choose to stay here for a while that's fine. If you choose to leave, I'll help you get to where you want to go."

"And you are here because…?"

"… I choose to be."

He was sitting back on his bunk, leaning against the wall picking the fingernails on his left hand with those on his right. She crossed over to the window and looked out over a valley, green and rolling, no particular landmarks, some forest ahead stretched over to the far right, no roads or other buildings she could see. She could have been anywhere - well, anywhere in the Borders.

"Ok, we'll come back to you later Magnus - "

"Cullen."

"I know, it's a joke. Magnus - I've started so I'll finish? Never mind. Where are we then? Where is *this* bothy?"

"Midway between Peebles and West Linton."

"And where is that?"

"Scotland?"

"Yes, ok, wiseguy. From being zoomed all the way you've zoomed right out. Where is Peebles?"

"Where did you come from last night?"

"Edinburgh. Well we were driving from Edinburgh and - "

"We?"

"Yes. I had a - let's call it an *incident*. We'll come back to that too - once I have some idea where I am."

"Well, Peebles is about 25 miles from Edinburgh - due south. West Linton's about the same but due southwest. We're midway between the two. Sou-souwest?"

"Whoa, it's all gone a bit Captain Jack Sparrow."

"You asked."

"Yes. Yes I did, didn't I? Perhaps I had better get used to asking *differently*." It was all a bit too much like Twenty Questions. You had a question, you asked, he answered. You didn't get the answer you wanted? *Bzzzt*. Sorry, guess again!

"How did *you* get here?"

"Walked."

"From… ?"

"Peebles."

"How far is that?"

"A few hours."

"And how long have you been here?"

"Couple of days." He angled his head and looked at her. "What day is it?"

"Er, Thursday."

"Hmm." Cullen nodded, letting this sink in.

"Cullen. Why are you here?" She realised she was intrigued by this quiet, solitary man who didn't seem to want or need much other than perhaps to be left alone.

"Why are any of us here?" *Bzzzt.*

"No, I mean why are you *here* - in this bothy?"

"I wanted somewhere to think."

"Ok, look. See this?" She held out her hands in front of her, holding an invisible parcel. "This is my patience. Oh, wait, look." She held up her hands, swivelled her head and look around wildly. "Where's it gone? Oh no, I've lost my patience."

Deadpan from Cullen. No smile, not even in the eyes. No recognition of her little tantrum, not incomprehension. Just nothing. Waiting. After a few moments, when Kim didn't speak, he went back to examining his fingernails. Kim gave a deep sigh.

"Cullen. Will you help me? Please?"

"I said I would."

"I need to get h-." She realised as she spoke that she didn't actually know what she wanted to do right now. Going home meant getting back to her own flat in London, but she hadn't been there for a few weeks now what with having been on the road for these bloody conferences and the like. She suddenly wasn't in the mood for being on her own. And all her belongings were still in the back of Tony's car."

"I need to get my stuff back."

"Stuff?"

"Yeah, personal belongings, clothes, credit cards, keys. You know."

"Ah, thought perhaps it might have been a drug reference."

"What? No! Do I...?"

"I don't know. I don't know anything about you other than you arrived here last night like ... like, you weren't intending to."

"Right, Buster. Brew me up another cup of tea and let me tell you a story." She proffered her mug back to him. "Actually, on second thoughts, let me make it. What have you got I can use which won't strip the varnish off my nails?"

Martin had spent over an hour waiting at Kyle Fire Station for the crew to return from a 999 call and, with still no sign of them, he was getting tetchy. The fire station itself was up a road from the harbour into a small industrial estate just across from the railway line. It was modern, functional building, purpose-built as a fire station. Round the back of the building was a small yard which contain a tower and some burnt-out car carcasses used for training. He had quickly tired of the immediate scenery and gone for a walk down to the harbour, watching the gulls on the shoreline and the odd seal lazily surfacing and then disappearing again. Not riveting by any means but better than sitting in his car watching his wipers.

When the crew finally arrived back at the station there was a prolonged commotion as uniforms discarded, showers run, mugs of tea brewed and voices flung taunts, jibes and general banter across the station until it all eventually died down as the on-call crew members drove away and only the handful of permanent staff on duty remained. Martin caught the eye of the Watch Manager, Stewart, and eventually managed to corral him in the duty room, just the two of them. Stewart had been the officer in charge on the night of the hatchery fire.

"Who raised the alarm that night?"

"Davy Jackson. He's the hatchery manager. He'd got an alarm call down the pub. He was on site when we got there, monitoring the systems and trying to minimise the damage."

"Alarm call?"

"Aye, it's a hatchery you know - fish eggs and baby fish being hatched and grown an' that? The different tanks have temperature controls to maximise fish growth and health and all that - Davy could tell you much better than me, like. But they're all these temperature monitors and such and there are alarms which trigger when the temperature rises or falls outwith the desired range. The main office building on the site has these control panels and camera and pumps and flashing lights and so on so you can see what's occurring, like, and shut things down if things start going wrong. The alarms are set to call a phone number under certain circumstances an' all so, like, you don't have to have someone on site all the time - as long as the person on call can get to the site within a reasonable time if their phone goes, you know?"

"And was there much damage? I've asked for a copy of the insurance report from..." Martin consulted his notes. "AquaMarine but I haven't received it yet."

"Aye, there was a fair bit mind. Most of the buildings containing the fish were write-offs by the time we'd put the fire out. They were essentially glorified metal sheds you know, no real structure to them. The actual brick buildings - the offices and that - they were untouched. Could have been worse."

"Could it?"

"Oh aye. There were stockpiles of fish feed in one of the site buildings. Given enough time that could have gone up like a bonfire."

"Fish feed is flammable?"

"Well, it contains fish oil which is technically flammable. But it only ignites at temperatures exceeding 230F and we had the fire well under control before it got to that point, like."

"Right. And did the, er, systems show what caused the fire?"

"No, although Davy did reckon that something was wrong with them. He said that many of them should have gone off but they didn't. Seems to think they'd been fiddled with or something."

"Fiddled with?"

"Or something."

Martin made a note.

"How long did it take you to get to the hatchery?"

"About half an hour."

"That's quite a long time, isn't it?"

"Well, it's 20-odd mile to the hatchery, mind. The roads aren't great. Not much we can do about it, really."

"Any signs of what may have caused it then?"

"Oh aye. There was one clear ignition point in the portakabin next to the outbuildings. There were fragments of a metal bin, desk and chair. Scorch marks and burn patterns across the unit consistent with some kind of small explosion and focussed fire source."

"So, it was started deliberately?"

"Aye, and a pretty amateurish effort it was an' all."

"Why do you say that?"

"Well, you plant an explosive in a building which doesn't have any fish in it, and which will be a dead giveaway to any fire investigator, tamper with the alarms so that the fire can develop unhindered but do it in such a way that the tampering can be easily seen. Then you need the fire to build long enough for it to get to 230F so it can ignite the fish oil in the feed. I mean."

"Aye." Martin nodded. "Does seem an awfully long-winded way of doing it"

"Plus *why* anyway? What's the point of burning down a fish hatchery?"

"Well, Stewart. That is a very good question."

"A man called Tony has my stuff." Kim was curled up by the fire, drinking the tea she made. Cullen's donated fleece and joggies swamped her but kept her cosy at the same time. "Tony is - scratch that, was - my boyfriend. Here on in he is only to be referred to as TTT: Total Twatface Tony."

"Nice."

"We'd been staying in a hotel in Edinburgh, TTT was driving, and I was still a tad "tired and emotional" from too many drinks the night before. On some road somewhere, in the pissing mist and rain and cold and almost dark, we came round this bend and he just opened the car door across me, like this, and pushed me out of the car!"

As she retold the events from last night, it seemed more outrageous the more she said it out loud.

"I mean there was no reason or warning or anything! One minute I'm staring out through the wipers trying to keep my food down and the next I'm tumbling through wet green rocks and mud and he's calling a cheery "Bye-e-e" in his rear view mirror. I fell down a steep bank and didn't know where I was. Started walking, dressed as you found me, and fortunately found this place just as I was trying to get my story straight for St Peter."

Cullen squinted at her, a look she took as disbelief.

"I really thought I was going to *die*." And then the tears came. Her bravado collapsed and the full extent of how close she came to a needless, random end flooded into her. She heaved and sobbed and snorted and shook, uncaring and unthinking, letting it all flow out of her: the shock, the fear, the release. Cullen sat awkwardly in silence until she'd calmed herself. She wiped the snot and tears from her face with the sleeve of the fleece and then realised what she'd just done.

"Oh, sorry."

"So, why did he do it?"

"I don't know." The squint again. "I just told you - I don't know!"

"He must have had a reason."

"Yes. I quite agree with you. But. I. Don't. Know. What. It. Was." Hello, her bravado was back.

"Can you think of a reason he *might* have had?"

"No."

"Had you said something to him?"

"No. As I said, I was fairly silent the entire time. More worried about keeping my stomach contents where they were than focussing on conversation."

"What about earlier. Or the night before?"

134

"No." Hesitation. "Don't recall a lot of it tbh but no, don't think so."

"You don't think so?"

"Well, I don't know do I? And if we had had a row, wouldn't he have made some reference to it at some point? Do you think our relationship consisted of slight disagreements escalating instantly to silent ejection from a speeding motor vehicle?"

They both sat in silence for a while, each with their own thoughts, until Cullen broke in.

"Where will he be now?"

"No idea."

"Really? Where we you going when he pushed you out?"

She realised, for the first time, that she hadn't actually known where they had been heading. "Don't know. Doesn't matter. Tony will be stopping over. Somewhere."

"Why?"

"He lives out of hotels. Doesn't really have a place of his own. He'll stay with me now and again - for a week or so, maybe - then disappear off for a while."

"Where does he go?"

"All over. Depends."

"Hmm." Cullen sat still, his silence representing doubt. Kim finished her tea, put her mug down and took a deep breath.

"OK. TTT is a - an itinerant eco-warrior. He's big in fish - salmon mostly - and is something of a celebrity as far as it goes. A kind of Salmon Swampy but with more money."

"Huh?"

"Never mind. Think Richard Branson without the beard - or the business acumen. Look, he has a talent for publicity. He travels all over the world giving talks, demonstrating, doing publicity stunts against the salmon business. He gets hired by vested interests to promote an anti-farming agenda, heads up protest groups, fronts campaigns in the press and generally acts as the *spokesperson for the environment*". Kim made air quotes with her hands. " - and how salmon farming damages the delicate ecosystems something something."

"And you're not a believer?"

"Well not like him. He's a salmon nut. Lives and breathes it. I mean I imagine that intensive fish farming isn't as good for the fish as if they were left in their natural habitat but it's not like they're pumping fumes into the atmosphere or pouring radioactive waste into the water supply or anything."

"Right. So is he working on some particular campaign right now? Something that would give us a clue to where he might be?"

"Well, he's doing some stuff on and off for a Russian guy. Vasilij someone. Been spending a lot of time in Scotland the past few weeks."

"Well, it's not much to go on."

"Well, sor-ry, Sherlock. Perhaps I should have been taking notes and keeping tabs on him seeing as he's been my boyfriend for the best part of a year and I trusted him and everything and had been thinking we might have had a future together."

She started to tear up again and Cullen looked down at his feet to avoid her gaze. After sniffling a minute or so, she visibly straightened, re-wiping her face on the sleeve of his fleece, unguiltily this time. Cullen stood up and went over to his bunk, rummaging in his belongings.

"I need to go out for a while."

"Where to?"

"Out." He pulled on a waterproof and grabbed a rucksack from by the door.

"Oh no you don't, Buster. You're not leaving me here in the middle of nowhere."

"Look, it's OK. I'm going into Peebles - run a few errands, get some more food. Trust me, I'll be back before you know it. You're not really in the best of shape to be out just yet."

"But how long will you be gone?"

"Don't know. Why don't you get some more sleep. You'll feel better."

"But supposing someone comes? I can't even lock the door!"

"They won't."

"How do you know?"

"No-one ever comes here except me."

"I did."

"Ok, look. Take this." He took out an old-looking brick phone from his waterproof and handed it to her. "You can get a decent signal here so if you need to call for help…"

"Thanks. Very reassuring. Who am I going to call? Ghostbusters?"

"I'll get another phone in Peebles and call you. Check in, make sure you're OK. OK?"

Kim's shoulders sagged as she realised he wasn't going to take no for an answer. He took his battered hat off the bunk post, jamming it unceremoniously on his head. She

137

watched him stalk off across the hillside until he disappeared from view.

10

Cullen wheeled into the courtyard, opened the glass door and took the stairs two at a time up to the library on the second floor. Jennifer looked up from her counter and smiled brightly when she saw him enter.

The cowboy - that was how she thought of him - had his hands in the pockets of his waterproof, his shoulders hunched. The leather hat on his head was beading with moisture and covered in dark patches where the rain had started soaking through. He lifted it off, shook it and then put it back on his head. He was wearing stout leather walking boots, camouflage trousers, a lime green Berghaus waterproof which had seen better days and a tattered fleece underneath, which he revealed as he unzipped his coat.

"Hello again" she said, looking up at him from behind her desk. "I'm afraid we're closing in 15 minutes for lunch."

He leant one hand on the counter and fiddled with a pen chained to a small stand.

"That's OK. A quick in and out. All I'm after."

Was he making fun of her, she wondered?

"Do you need any help at all?"

"In the book department?"

She blushed slightly. "Yes, in the book department."

"Not today. £1 still?"

Jennifer smiled and turned to the log book. As she wrote the entry of his session on the right-hand page she could see on the left a series of previous sessions all bearing his incomprehensible scrawl of a signature. He'd been in every day for the past week almost, often staying several hours at a time.

He turned and strode up the slight ramp into the main reading room and turned sharp right to where the computers were. A small set of desks each hosting a very old desktop PC connected to the internet which library card holders could use for £1 a session.

She had spent all morning so far cataloguing 598.0222 through to 598.138 - books on birds, basically - and had had her fill of ornithology. A shy, plain maiden she may be but she could still dream, and she allowed herself a little daydream now. Never mind marsh warblers. After a morning of Dewey Decimal filing she'd be more than inclined to let him stamp her overdue in the reference section.

He re-appeared suddenly in front of her. "Sorry. The mouse is kaput."

She looked up into his eyes, startled from her reverie, preparing to apologise.

"If you'll wait a few moments I can…"

"No problem. I'll come back after lunch!"

She flipped the log book for him to sign.

"Would you like me to-" she looked up to the sound of the door swinging shut.

A shiny pound coin was gleaming on the counter.

It was after 3pm when he returned and his eyes were shining. She felt herself held by them as he spoke softly. After a few moments of silence she realised he had asked her a question.

"I'm terribly sorry, I didn't catch that?"

"I said: Peeblesshire. Back issues?"

He was talking about the Peeblesshire News, the local weekly newspaper. "Oh, yes. Well, we have some editions on hardcopy - last twelve months or so - but if you go too far back they get transferred over to microfiche."

"Right."

"But, we don't have a microfiche reader any more." She looked to her side to check no-one was overhearing and then whispered. "Council cuts, I'm afraid."

"I see."

"So we transferred them to an external hard drive instead."

"Right. Well, 12 months should be plenty." He smiled and she thought she might be blushing again.

"They're, um, over by the magazine section? At the far end, there's a set of red leather binders on the bottom shelves. All numbered."

"Thanks. And old council records?"

"How old? Parish council?"

"Borders Council. Planning applications, notices, that kind of thing."

"Oh, well the Scottish Borders Council have a public web portal which provides online access to lots of information for planning and the like. I think it covers the last 12 months but you'd have to check. If you search for Borders E-planning on the computer you'll find the links. If you need something older than that, say three years old, I'm afraid I think you probably need to contact the council directly and make an FOI request."

"FOI?"

"Freedom Of Information. It allows members of the public to request information from public bodies about almost anything - provided it's not classified information and the like. I'm afraid, though, that all FOI requests have to be submitted in writing and there is usually something like a 28 day response time. It's not quite the same as the interweb I'm afraid!"

"You seem to be awfully afraid." He looked intently into her eyes. "Don't be."

Cullen was striding back across the hills to the bothy, hiking faster than he would normally while his mind whirled and ideas spun. He'd left the library late and knew it would take at least two hours to get back to the bothy in the dark. He unslung his rucksack and pulled out a headtorch and PAYG phone he'd purchased earlier. First he'd called Kim, as he had promised he would:

"It's me."

"Hello me."

"Sorry, I got carried away and lost track of time."

"I'm fine, thanks for asking."

"I didn't."

"I was being sarcastic. I thought it would be just common decency when calling a woman who you abandoned in a strange house with no means of escape."

"Whom."

"Sorry?"

"Whom you abandoned."

"Fine. Whom you abandoned with no means of escape."

"OK. And are you by the fire?"

"Yeah?" Off-balance, uncertainty in her tone at this sudden swerve in the conversation.

"Do you see that thing to the right, made of wood? It's called a door. Common means of escape round these parts."

"Don't get sassy with me, Buster. Will you be going past an IKEA on your way back here?"

"No." Cullen's turn to be blindsided by the strange topic shift.

"Shame. I was going to suggest you popped in and assembled yourself a sense of perspective."

Cullen sighed, audibly. "I'm on my way. Be a couple of hours. You ok?"

"Two hours!"

"I'll be as quick as I can."

She hung up.

He picked up his walking pace and turned on his headtorch. He was labouring uphill when he called Big Paul, sweating as he walked, cursing every time a foot hit a pothole or uneven ground. The headtorch helped a bit but not much and he didn't want to lose time - not even a few seconds - by stopping to check his watch.

"Beep?"

"Alright Mate, How's it goin'?" Paul wasn't entirely clear who was calling him. The caller's number hadn't registered with any of the contacts in his address book but anyone calling him Beep (short for BP which was short for Big Paul) obviously knew him well, and Paul called everybody *Mate* so this would serve beautifully until the caller, who sounded a bit out of breath as it happened, revealed their identity.

"Today? Beautifully. Ow, fuck! You?"

"Yeah, I'm good mate. Triff?" Did he know anyone with Tourette's?

"Listen Beep, I'm rushing round right now and don't have a lot of time-" his breathing was more laboured, Paul wondered what he was up to. "- but I'm in a bit of a tight spot and wondered if you could help me out? Bastard!"

"Ah, well. I'm a bit short myself at the moment, you know. DVLA on my case, an' that."

Paul was still unclear who he was talking to but this was the generic sort of conversation that seemed to make up most of his time these days. Mates were mates - whoever they were - but he was brassic and in no position to be tapped for a few quid. Giving the topic of money a body swerve, he ploughed on regardless: his relentless sunny optimism telling him that all would be for the best, in this best of all possible worlds.

"Don't suppose you know if there's any work going do ya?"

"Well." resumed the mystery caller. "That is where I was hoping you could help me out."

The clouds parted, as Paul knew they would, and the sun illuminated him like his namesake at the moment of his Damascene conversion.

"No worries, mate." The moniker *mate* now more apt than ever, despite the anonymity. "What do you need?"

"Someone with a strong pair of hands and some - fuck, fuck, fuck - common sense in their noggin."

"I'm there, mate. I'm there. What's the deal?"

"Well, if you're game I can fill you in when I've caught my breath. Can you meet me in Peebles say, tomorrow. 2-ish?"

Paul mentally consulted his diary of engagements and found much of it reading *This page intentionally left blank*. He attempted to sound as if he was considering the suitability of the suggested time.

"Yeah. Tomorrow? Yeah, can we say the back of 2?"

"Fine." The back of 2 meant anytime between 2 and 2.30 - if you were Scottish. "At The Trust? Fuck, ow!"

"Yeah. Yeah. OK. Cheers, mate."

Good choice, thought Paul. Tourette's at The Trust.

By the time he reached the bothy he had formulated a clear plan. Kim was asleep, curled up in a ball by the fire. He tootled about as quietly as he could but the movement must have disturbed her because she woke and looked silently at him for a while - he could feel her eyes on him but he carried on sorting through his stuff waiting for her to let him know she'd woken. The silence lasted a few minutes by Cullen's count but he wasn't in the least put out by it. Eventually she stretched and yawned loudly as if to announce: *Madam is now officially awake and available for pleasant discourse. Commence!*

"Sorry. Trying not to wake you."

"It's OK. I've slept enough already. God, I'm hungry though. Do you have anything to eat?"

"I've got beans, soup, bread." He itemised each item as he pulled it from his pack. "And wine."

She eyed the bottle warily. "Is this some kind of lousy date?"

"No." He checked the label, in all seriousness. "Elderflower I think. Gift from Rosalind at the newsagent." He looked sheepishly at Kim.

"Are you for real?"

He looked at her blankly so she continued.

"I mean, I'm not making you up? Not delusional and at death's door. Am I really lying frozen in a ditch somewhere while my mind conjures up some last minute fantasy as my body shuts down for the last time? Is this Life On Mars?"

"Bowie?"

"No. The TV program."

"Don't have a TV." He indicated around the bothy.

She skimmed through the food he'd brought. "Is this it? Didn't they have anything…" she searched for a diplomatic adjective and then gave up: "- decent?"

"There's trout, sausages, milk and bacon in the cold store. And we've still got some eggs left."

"Cold store? What cold store?"

"Out back." He thumbed over his shoulder. "There's a kind of lean-to, outbuilding - around the side there. I keep food stuffs in there, bundled up in a tarp up on a rafter - so nothing can get at it."

"You are amazing, you know that? I guess I couldn't make you up."

"How so?"

She counted out one finger: "Well. One, you're resourceful enough to have a fully-stocked coldstore. I mean, I bet you even caught the trout yourself, yes?"

He nodded. "I didn't cure the bacon, though. That's from a shop."

She laughed out loud at this and extended a second finger: "Two, you're so *whatever* that you didn't bother to tell me about it while leaving me here alone, ostensibly without food, for the best part of a day."

"You could have looked."

"I could have looked! Yes, now why didn't that occur to me?"

"Because you thought there was no visible means of escape?"

She cocked her head to one side and looked at him carefully, weighing him up. Assessing him. Was he her knight in shining armour or a complete fruitcake? Ray Mears or Screaming Lord Sutch?

"Who are you?"

"Cullen."

"Yes, but who is Cullen?"

"I am."

"You know what I mean. Who are you? Where are you from? Why are you here? How did you get here - in your life? What happened for you to be here now?" She stood up, stretched again and picked up the kettle. "Tea?"

"Please."

"I mean, I don't know anything about you." She filled the kettle from the tap and put it on the stand by the fire. "I told you my flaming life story last night. Your turn."

Kim watched him as he told his story. It didn't take him long but he never met her eyes, just stared off into space running the fingers of one hand over the knuckles of the other as he did so.

"I used to be in the Police force. Many years. Joined straight from school. Never really thought about anything else. Took early retirement - few years ago now. Sold my house, my stuff. Decided to just ... be."

"Be what?"

"Just be." He looked at her now - as if she was slightly retarded, Kim thought. "Exist. Live."

"Like this?"

"Yeah." He shrugged, looking around the room.

He looked uncomfortable, but sincere, talking about himself. His face was lined and weatherbeaten - she couldn't tell quite how old he was but she figured on 50-ish - with pale blue eyes beneath quite heavy brows. His ears were quite large, she noticed, partially hidden though they were by his tousled greying hair which was showing no sign of thinning. And his hands were large, with thick fingers, short nails neatly trimmed. No rings or jewellery, no tattoos. No markers of any kind which could identify him. She wondered if this was part of him: a need for anonymity, to be hidden. Alone.

"Use only what I need. Have only what I can carry." He nodded to the pack lying on his bunk.

"But what about …" she struggled, not wanting to use the word *everything*. She gave up: ".. everything!"

"Who wants everything?"

"Me, I do. Everyone does. Don't you?"

"No."

"Why not?"

"Well." He smiled, looking around again. "Where would I put it?"

"But what about money? Food? Clothes?"

"I have some money. I buy food. Clothes when I need them. It's not often."

"Family?"

"Dead."

"Friends?"

"I have some people I know that I can call on, ask favours, that sort of thing. Friends, I guess."

"Work?"

"I told you: I'm retired."

"Books? Music?"

"Library."

Kim was exasperated. "But what do you *do*? With yourself, I mean."

"Whatever I want." Like explaining to a child.

"Don't you get bored?"

"I have… projects. Keep me busy. When I want to be busy."

"Projects?"

"Yeah. Got one now, in fact. Why I went into Peebles."

"What is it?"

He looked at her again, thinking. "Not sure. Yet."

"Oh you're just… odd."

"Thanks."

"Sorry. I mean, well it is … odd, don't you think? Living like this? No fixed abode? Away from everyone, like some kind of hermit?"

"I'm not a hermit."

"Aren't you?" She held out an invisible microphone. "In what way, would you say, are you unlike a hermit?"

"I…" he pondered.

"The first rule about being a hermit is we don't talk about being a hermit, is that it?"

Cullen frowned. "I know what's going on in the world. I don't hide myself away, I just keep myself to myself." He looked her in the eye. "There is a difference."

"I s'pose." She thought for a moment, dropping the microphone. "You do have a phone."

"Well, you have it."

149

"Yeah but you can have it back."

"It's ok, keep it. I've got this one now." He held up his new purchase, almost proudly. This brick, this throwaway ugly brick that no self-respecting person would be seen dead with.

"Don't you want to swap the SIM?"

"Why?"

"To keep your …" She was going to say *contacts* but stopped herself. "Number?"

"No." He was unconcerned.

"What if someone wanted to get in contact with you?"

"I'd contact them."

"But if someone wanted to contact you and you didn't know it?"

"I wouldn't want them to."

"But what if you needed help?"

"I don't."

"But what it you *did?*"

"I. Don't. Need. Help."

"Well." she said. "That's a matter of opinion."

He made a kind of stew using the sausages, soup and beans which they ate with crusty bread. It was, she admitted, really good and she hadn't realised how hungry she'd been. While he chopped and cooked she kept glancing at him, looking at how he moved. He had a strange smoothness about him - like he could almost glide. He would slip from one position to another, from door to fire, from fire to bunk, and each movement was a kind of seamless process where you weren't aware of him moving until he'd finished and was no longer where he'd been.

She finished scooping the last of the stew from her bowl and wiped it clean with some bread and broke the silence: "So, what's your project then?"

He looked questioningly at her. "The *not sure* project you mentioned earlier?"

"Oh. Right."

He stopped. She waited.

"There's some construction work going on over in Manor Valley. Big development. Some kind of factory being built or something."

"And?"

"It's all being done, well, in secret almost."

"What do you mean, *in secret*?"

"Well, this isn't the big city you know. You don't just go round putting up new housing developments or factories or offices or anything without anyone knowing about it. No-one seems to know much about this site. People might object."

"Why would people object?"

"This is the countryside. Unspoilt views, historic landscapes, families been here centuries. Aye been - it's a saying round here. It has always been - you don't just start digging some bloody big facility without having to go through rigorous planning applications, being subjected to intense scrutiny by local communities, protest groups, etc."

"You sound like Tony."

"You mean TTT?"

"Whatever."

"Well, look. If you build housing then that means more people which means a need for more school places, more traffic, more water use, more sewage and so on. These things need to be planned for and taken into account in the context of the rural communities that exist here."

"Bit negative isn't it? More houses means more people but that also means more customers for local businesses, bigger communities means more social activities, more clubs, more money coming into the area."

"Aye" He looked at her sadly. "But most people who move to the Borders will be employed in cities like Edinburgh, Glasgow or Carlisle. Any money they spend will be mostly spent there - so newcomers tend to consume local resources, damaging the environment or quality of life for people already here - while the benefits they bring aren't felt here. Local sentiment is against it. Usually."

"Whoa. Don't let your mind wander, Buster, it's too small to be outside by itself. Seems awfully short-sighted to me. But anyway, this isn't housing you said. This is some kind of factory?"

"Yes."

"Well, that means jobs doesn't it? What community is going to complain about more jobs available in the area?"

"Depends on the type of jobs. Zero-hour contract, menial jobs? Businesses quite often open in the Borders to take advantage of low pay levels - this is one of the poorest regions in the country."

"Which country? Scotland or the UK?"

"Either. Both. It may look like a beautiful rural idyll but a lot of it is really just subsistence farming. Families just getting by."

"Right. So a new factory brings jobs - that may nor may not benefit the local economy. Jury's out if we don't know what the factory is yet."

"Then there's site traffic - and not just construction traffic. Factories need to be fed and they produce goods which need to be transported. That means big lorries, traffic congestion on small country roads, pollution, potholes. Then there's the water. This factory is going to use a lot of water. Water comes from somewhere and needs to go somewhere. So we have risks of water shortages elsewhere, detrimental changes to the water table or natural aquifers, increased run-off into the Tweed increasing changes of flooding…"

"God, what a Cassandra you are!"

"Then there's the aesthetic impact. Blot on the landscape. Beautiful rolling hills marred by ugly metal boxes. Concrete. Tarmac."

"Hmm." Kim was unconvinced and not impressed by the sudden similarity between Cullen and TTT. Was she destined to always come up against enviro-nutters and eco-mentalists? "What do they need all the water for?"

"Don't know."

"Well, come on! What *do* you know? Seems like you don't know jack, but you've already decided all the bad things are going to happen anyway. Come on, Mr Policeman. Where's the data? Where's the evidence?"

"I'm still gathering it… but you're right, I do need more."

"Well, how are you going to get it?"

"The library?"

"Go, Indiana."

He gave her the confused squint again. A look she was beginning to realise he gave her a lot.

"I mean, not exactly action-packed excitement, is it? The library."

"No." He stayed silent for a while, thoughtful again. "But anyway, if I'm going to help you find your ex-boyfriend I need a plan."

"Ooh, this is more like it. This is all a bit more Mission Impossible. Your mission, should you choose to accept it…" She didn't wait for the look of incomprehension this time, instead ploughed straight on. "So, what's the next step?"

"Well, first I need you to hire a car…"

"Can't you - ?"

"No."

"OK. I'll hire us a car. And then?"

"Then we need to talk to Big Paul."

"Who the hell's Big Paul?"

11

Paul was six foot five, and a good eighteen stone in weight. He was broad, heavily-muscled, tanned and bearded. But his physical stature belied his true nature which was that of a smiling, cheerful, happy-go-lucky chap for whom life's continued blows were just more reasons to bounce back. All the girlfriends he'd ever had who'd stuck around long enough (not a very high percentage it has to be said) had ended up calling him Tigger. His mates, of whom there were many, just called him Big Paul.

Big Paul was currently residing on a friend's floor in a remote house looking out over the Talla reservoir, twenty miles southwest of Peebles. He had recently sold his own property, or his share of it, as his previous long-term partner with whom he had bought a home had returned from a hen weekend in Barcelona having had her head turned by a local romeo and announced quite calmly to Paul that she was leaving and wanted to sell up. If he could be out by Tuesday that would be fine. Shattered by this news, Paul took his two Jack Russells - Penn and Teller - out for a walk to try and get his head together, only to find when he got back that she had packed her bags and gone to her mother's and taken all his good shit with her.

He sat on his living room floor and rolled himself a joint using what remained of his not-so-good shit, opened a bottle of Jack Daniels and proceeded to pour himself into oblivion. He was woken the next morning, still lying on the floor, by Penn and Teller licking his face.

That was Friday.

On Saturday a removal truck pulled up outside his house and the three men proceeded to take every stick of furniture, every piece of crockery and cutlery, all the linen, soft furnishings, ornaments and electrical equipment in the house.

On Sunday he was cooking chicken legs on a gas barbecue in his living room, eating them with tiny prongs used to hold corn-on-the-cob and sitting on a plastic garden chair while watching Teller pull a loose end of carpet to shreds.

On Monday the phone, water and electricity were disconnected.

On Tuesday he was sleeping in the back of his Transit van parked in a layby on the A72.

The van was Paul's umbilical cord. With it he could scrape a living as an excellent (if unreliable) joiner, house his dogs and keep his chin up. Without it he was, he felt, absolutely fucked. The Transit contained all his tools, records and paperwork for his business.

He liked to think that he was a well-organised tradesman but, as everyone else who knew him would say, the opposite was the case. Filing for Paul consisted of making sure that all pieces of paper were "in the van" - somewhere. His calendar was a series of random paper scraps, fag packets and beermats with appointments scrawled on them and left "in the van". That these vital scraps were even located close to each other within the confines of the van was entirely due to the fact that, rustled together into a big pile, they made excellent bedding for Penn and Teller and so, as entirely befitted the man himself, his dogs collectively acted as sort of PA for Paul - they collated his appointments, maintained his paperwork and gave him a reason to keep going.

He had tried to arrange his personal possessions into some semblance of order and keep them separate within the van: all his books (both of them) sat dog-eared and stained at the bottom of a supermarket carrier, beneath his toiletry bag which contained his highly-prized collection of soft drugs in baggies which was in turn beneath a small selection of folded clothes. That was one pile. In the other pile were two pairs of work overalls, roughly folded and pinned in place by an assortment of dog-food tins and a can opener.

Many an expert surgeon or businessman might spend their entire working life never making notes, successfully progressing and building a career and when asked how they managed without ever writing anything down would tap the side of their head, smile and say "It's all up here." In much the same way, in answer to pretty much any question from a customer, potential client or the Inland Revenue, Paul could point to his beloved Transit and say "It's all in there." By that Tuesday, relegated to living out of it, Paul could truly say that everything he knew, loved, possessed and needed was "all in there".

Until a letter from the DVLA told him that he was deficient in the tax disc department to the tune of one.

They set off early in a bright morning sky and a sharp frost on the ground. Despite Cullen's best efforts, Kim was still unsuitably dressed. She had a spare waterproof on top of the fleece she had adopted. Both much too big for her and she felt foolish as well as unfashionable. A quite smart pair of lined over-trousers he had bought in Peebles hung from her frame like a Viking sail waiting for the wind: drawn tightly at the waist using some bungee cord and the length shortened by rolling each leg up inside itself, they still hung loosely and flapped as she walked.

The biggest problem was her footwear. Cullen hadn't thought of this and, having nothing anywhere near her size, she was wearing four pairs of heavy socks and some insoles cut from cardboard inside an old battered pair of walking boots he had stashed in the cold store. The size wasn't now the issue - although they did look enormous - so much as the weight: she felt as if she was wearing deep sea diving boots. Every step was a hardship.

They passed a waymarker which said Peebles 2 miles and Kim asked to stop for a breather. Exhausted she sat on a dry-stone wall and swigged from a water bottle Cullen had given her. He stood, hands on hips, breathing normally as he surveyed back the way they'd come.

"Do you *have* to walk everywhere?"

"I enjoy it."

"Yes. But if something's not within walking distance… I mean, that's why they call it walking distance."

"Everywhere is walking distance if you have the time."

"Huh. Well, if I was suitably attired I *might* see the attraction when the weather's like this. As it is, it feels like my pants are held in place by a belt that's held in place by my pants""

"We can get you some clothes that fit in town."

"But when it's raining and blowing a gale - as it was when I found you - well, that's a different proposition altogether."

"There's no such thing as bad weather, only the wrong clothes."

"Hmm. Yours unconvinced, London."

"They have rain and wind in London don't they?"

"Not often. You get a better class of weather down South."

He mulled this over for a while. She took a few more swigs from the water bottle.

"I like it."

"What, wind and rain?"

"Well, in context."

"Yes, well let's not quote the weather out of context shall we?"

He ignored her. "There's a seasonality to it. Each season melts into the next but they're all distinct. Each with its own weather. It keeps you in touch with things. There's comforting reassurance about it: fresh, dewy spring mornings with blustery showers; gives way to warm, clear skies -"

"With blustery showers."

He ignored her again. "Gives way to misty, autumnal chill, woodsmoke. Then sharp frosts, snow, biting winter mornings and clear night skies. The calendar has a rhythm." He looked over at her, a bit embarrassed, and she softened.

"Yeah, I guess. A bit like when you were a kid and it always snowed at Christmas and summers always lasted forever in the school holidays." She looked into his eyes. "I get it. I do get it. It's just - not up my strasse."

"Well, I like it."

159

The matter settled, Kim stood, stowed her water bottle and motioned for them to carry on down towards Peebles. As they got closer to the town Cullen seemed to grow more pensive. Kim tried hard to keep up a conversation but he was mostly monosyllabic until they reached the river. Crossing by a single track bridge she saw a man fishing downstream, standing in the middle of the river in chest-high waders.

"Do you fish?"

"Sometimes. In season."

"Is it season now?"

"Just. Finishes tomorrow actually."

"Really? When did you fish last?"

"Couple of weeks ago. 'S where I got the trout."

"You fish for trout?"

"And salmon. The Tweed's a good salmon river."

"I thought salmon lived out at sea? That's what Tony was always campaigning against - salmon farming."

"They do. But they come back to their spawning grounds in rivers to breed, then head back out to sea." He looked at her questioningly. "You never heard of salmon swimming upstream? Salmon leaps?"

"Well, now you mention it. I just never connected the two I guess. Tony -"

"TTT."

She sighed. "Well, he was always banging on about the environmental impact of industrial salmon farming. I guess farmed salmon and wild salmon are different things. What's true for one isn't necessarily true for the other."

"I guess."

"I don't recall any fishing gear at the bothy. Where do you keep it?"

"There's a fisherman's hut. A couple actually. When I bunk there, I'll fish. Leave my kit there. The ghillies know me."

"When you bunk there? How often do you move around?"

"Depends. Sometimes days, sometimes weeks."

"Wow. Where else do you stay then?"

"All over. Bothies, huts, camp sometimes, deserted farm buildings. Got a caravan somewhere." He rattled off this vague list as if it was normal.

"Oh." She was thrown by this but couldn't work out why. "How long do you think you'll be at the bothy for then?"

"Not long if we're going to go after TTT. I'll pack up and be gone. May not be back until next year - although it's always nice in the winter because of the fire. Plus it's handy for town." He pointed down to the left as they came round a shallow bend and Peebles opened up before them.

The Trust wasn't actually the name of the pub - it was called The Bridge Inn, and had been called that since about 1900. However, the pub sat next to the main bridge in Peebles across the River Tweed and when the town elders decided to widen the bridge to make it more suitable for road traffic they had assumed the pub would need to to be demolished or modified in some way, so they sold it to the East of Scotland Public House Trust Company. Somehow, despite the widening of the bridge, the pub remained intact and so the locals took to calling it The Trust and, to this day, The Trust it has remained.

"Will you excuse me for a minute?"

161

"Sure."

Kim had been introduced to this giant of a man, Big Paul, after sitting in The Trust for 20 minutes before he showed up. Now she realised she badly needed to pee. She'd been curious as to what he would be like and she was pleasantly surprised - and not a little charmed - to find this jolly, shambling bear of a man with a genuine smile and a hefty handshake. He'd greeted Cullen like a long-lost brother, mumbling something about putting two and two together after their call and realising who it was. She liked him immediately, but nature called.

Kim stood up and went in search of the toilet. Cullen and Paul remained silent, nursing their pints until she was out of earshot, then Paul said:

"Who's the filly?"

"Kim."

"Yeah, you told me her name. But who is she?"

"Dunno. Turned up at my door a few days ago having been chucked by her boyfriend. Literally. We're going after him."

"Why?"

"Feels … right."

"She *looks* like a bit of alright!"

"Huh." Cullen said, as if it had only just occurred to him.

"And? Any reward in it for you?"

"There's been no mention of money."

"I'm not talking about money." He looked at Cullen knowingly. "Payment in kind, eh?"

"She's young enough to be my daughter."

"Well, I would."

"Well I wouldn't." Cullen's face clearly registering bemusement at Paul's opinion of Kim.

"Christ, Cullen. You're a - "

"What?" He interrupted.

"Touchy bugger." Satisfied that the insult was sufficiently trivial, he lapsed back into silence. Paul, not for the first time in their relationship, prepared to do the heavy lifting on the conversation front.

"So. What's this job you need doing?"

"There's some construction going on down Manor Valley. Near Langhaugh, do you know it?"

"Langhaugh, yeah. Construction, no. What they building?"

"Looks like a factory of some kind. Not entirely sure. That's where the favour comes in."

"Oh, aye?"

"I've got to go away for a few days - with Kim."

"Nudge, nudge. Say no more, squire!"

"No. I've told you. She has a boyfriend. I'm going to help her find him."

"Why?"

"He's still got some of her stuff and she wants it back."

"Then what?"

"Then I'll come back."

"No. Then what'll happen to the boyfriend?"

"That, Beep, is none of my concern. What is my concern…" Paul could see Cullen was getting slightly exasperated trying to keep the conversation on track. "Is that you do what you can to find out about the site and the comings and goings thereof."

"Thereof?"

"Thereof. Thereafter, I shall reward you handsomely with a new tax disc."

"And, until then…?" Paul let the question hang in the air.

Cullen took some notes from his wallet and slid them across the table top. "Until then, see if you can get yourself some good shit to tide you over. Keep you motivated."

"Cool." Paul quickly pocketed the money and scanned the bar area to see if anyone had spotted the transaction. "How do I keep tabs? Thereof."

"There*on*." Cullen paused, thinking. "You busy at the moment?"

"No. Hence the tax disc shortfall."

"Ok, well nip up there on the hunt for a job. See if they need a joiner."

"Right. Top."

"Top?"

"Yeah. You know - top. As in, er, nice one."

"Right." Cullen let it go. "You can use Archie Mac as an excuse if you like."

"Archie Mac?"

"Yes. You know. Macpherson Construction. Proprietor: Macpherson, Archibald J?"

"Ah right. And…?"

"I saw his digger on the site. Had a wee chat. Says he's been retained by McAlpine's to dig ditches, lay pipes, and so forth. Been working on it for a couple of months now."

"And what is it?"

"Some big factory he thinks. He's not too sure because he's only seen the utility schematics, pipes, drainage and that."

"What for?"

"He doesn't know."

"Who for?"

"Doesn't know that either. He's subcontracted to McAlpines. They know who the owners are but he doesn't. Need to know basis."

"Right."

"Well, anyway. You can say you know him and he let you know there might be some work going." Cullen sipped his beer and had another thought.

"You still got your dogs?"

"Natch."

"Right, well take 'em for walks up that way too. Have a mooch about. Chat to the workmen, see what the score is." Paul nodded, understanding. "I want to know what they're building. And who *they* is. Are."

"Got you."

"And see if you can - I don't know, slow 'em down."

"Slow 'em down?"

"Yes. They're going full steam ahead up there. Not messing around. You'll have a better idea than me how far along they are, how much they'd done and how much is left to do. Suss it out."

"Roger." Paul drained his glass and looked at Cullen for another, who ignored him. "Is this all legit?"

"I don't think so. There's something fishy going on, I can smell it."

"I gathered that. I mean me, sneaking around. Slowing them down. Is that legit?"

"It's a free country. You're an honest tradesman, out walking his dogs, passing the time of day, looking some work. And if an accident or two should happen which halts construction for a short while? Well, these little things happen all the time, don't they?"

"S'pose so."

Cullen reckoned Paul was not sufficiently convinced, so threw one last log on the fire: "Archie reckons this thing'll be taking loads of water from the Tweed. Might affect the fishing."

"What? Hey, that's not on."

"No." Cullen smiled, satisfied. "I quite agree."

"Been out lately - fishing?"

"No" lied Cullen. "You?"

"Yeah. Went out last Sunday. Took a few tinnies with some mates. Had a great time. Caught a couple of big salmon. Dogs loved 'em."

"Nice."

"Yeah. We should go out on the river sometime. Me and You." Paul prompted.

"Aye" said Cullen, distinctly non-committal.

"So how much do they need? Water, I mean."

"Dunno. I told you - you'll have to ask Archie. Snoop around. Find out for yourself."

"Right." That settled it, Cullen thought. Big Paul was in.

"Same again?"

"Nah. Think I've got to go shopping."

"Shopping! Christ, you under her thumb already?" Paul laughed loudly just as Kim came out from the Ladies and back over to their table.

"What's so funny?" she asked.

"Just laughing at you managing to get Cullen here to go shopping. I don't know how you did it but I bet thereof hangs a tale."

"There*by*." Said Kim, before Cullen could do it himself.

Viktor was watching the helicopter ferrying back and forth across the Kyles of Bute and out towards Arran. Through his binoculars he could see the pilot of the chopper and the cable running down underneath to the cylindrical tank suspended below it. Each tank contained about 5,000 smolt and this was the fifth run of the morning from the hatchery out to the sea site. Viktor was getting cramp from sitting too long, and cold from the wind whipping in off the Firth Of Clyde. He made a note of the time of departure, got up his from his perch in the rocks and clambered back over the breakwater. Tony had explained that they would be transferring 40-50,000 of these juvenile fish out to sea so this process would be going on for some time.

At first light the next morning, Viktor pulled up at the pier at Arran and waited for the ferry to start boarding. Once on the island he drove through the low brown hills beneath a glowering sky, the clouds choking the daylight and stroking the tops of the hills. As the first chopper trip of the day passed overhead, he could just make out the familiar pattern of circular frames in the water ahead.

The helicopter lowered its metal load onto an area of the barge that had been cleared for the purpose. Ivor was one of the Senior Marine Operatives for Arran and today he was loading the smolt from the hatchery into cage #6. He detached the cable from the full tank and hooked it up to the empty one next to him, waving up to the pilot as he did so. Within a few seconds, the helicopter lifted off with its empty cargo and flew back to the hatchery to load up with more smolt.

Ivor got to work pumping the smolt from the tank through the feeder hose into the cage. Through the transparent tubing he could see a torrent of freshwater and wriggling fish being pushed across the walkway and into the cage, pouring out of the open end hanging about 10 inches above the water line.

He looked up at a sound rising above the hum of the pumps. A small boat was approaching the barge and Ivor could make out some details of the figure steering: tall, dark, long black hair being blown around and back from his face. The stranger carried a rifle with a telescopic sight comfortably in his left hand. Ivor pulled his walkie-talkie from the chest pocket in his bibbed over-trousers.

"Dougie?"

Dougal was in the barge cabin, tapping in some of the data into their feed program. He reached for the handset on his desk and opened the channel to speak: "Aye?"

"Can ye phone ashore. NOW. We need help."

"Say again?"

"Call Archie at the shore. Tell him we need help - we're being attacked by pirates!"

"Away and fuck yersel' yer daft bastard!"

"Fer Christ's sake, Dougie. I'm telling ye. There's a guy closing in wi' a gun and he ain't out lookin' for pheasants! Call Archie!"

Dougal pulled his mobile phone from his coat on the back of the chair and dialled the site manager's number.

"Hi, Dougie." Archie had been site manager at Arran for twelve years, salmon farming for twenty. What he didn't know about fishing wasn't worth knowing and Dougal, Ivor and the team all valued his calm, measured manner and his capabilities as manager.

"Archie. Ivor says we need help out here. There's a guy coming for us in a boat wi' a gun. Archie says it's pirates!"

"Pirates is it?" Archie crossed to the window overlooking the site and picked up the binoculars on the windowsill. It was quite foggy out on the water and he had difficulty making out the barge let alone anything smaller like a boat. "Which direction's he coming from, I cannae see anythin'?"

There was a slight pause, presumably while Dougal conferred with Ivor.

"Ivor says from the west." Dougal sounded panicked now, voice rising. "And hurry, he says he's almost on us!"

Archie moved over the desk housing the site PC and the multiple monitors hooked up to the various cameras mounted around the site. He checked the barge-mounted image: Archie waving both hands up at the camera as if trying to signal a plane. No sign of any boat.

"Tell Ivor to stop the pumps, get back into the barge and lock the door." He had known Ivor for ten years - he wasn't the sort for practical jokes. "I'm coming oot."

He unlocked the firearms cabinet and grabbed a rifle and box of bullets. Usually used for seals and other wildlife, it was hardly ever used and probably rusty. He grabbed it anyway.

"Dougie?"

"Aye?"

"Call the police and the coastguard. Tell them a suspected gunman is attempting to board the barge."

"Right."

"And, when Ivor's inside, make sure the door is bolted and everything you've got is put against that door, ok?"

"Gotcha."

"I'll be there in 5 minutes."

Ivor stopped the pump, leaving the tank half-full of smolt, and checked for the position of the boat.

It had gone.

He whirled round looking in all directions but couldn't see anything. Scared of being thought an old fool and terrified he would turn around to find the stranger pointing the rifle at him, Ivor shot for the door to the barge. From here, stairs led down inside the floating platform. It was the only way in - and out. He bolted the thick metal door, meant to withstand all the elements a Scottish storm at sea could throw at it, and almost fell down the stairs into the arms of Dougal, waiting at the bottom with his mobile phone in his hand.

"You ok?"

"Aye. You?"

"Aye."

They were both breathless - one through age, one through youth. Hearts thumping in their chests nevertheless. Ivor took the phone from Dougal and called Archie. There was no signal out on the water between the shore-base and the farm. Ivor got Archie's voicemail and swore.

"He said he'll be here in 5 minutes." Dougal said.

"Aye, and whit's he gonnae do when he gets here? There's a madman up there wi' a powered rifle."

"How do you know he's mad?"

"Aye, right enough. I suppose you could be sane and out in this weather in a small boat training your rifle on an old man pumping salmon into a cage could ye no'?"

"Aye mebbe."

"Ach, mince. You shouldnae be oot on yoor ane."

Ivor sat down at the desk, swigged from Dougal's mug of cold tea and checked the barge camera to see what was going on. He could control the camera from here - something you couldn't do from the shore. He panned round, peering into the fog for the boat. Or Archie's boat. He lurched suddenly back in his chair, spitting the cold tea unconsciously from his mouth in surprise. A dark, angry face filled the camera monitor and then the screen went black. The pirate had wrecked the camera and now Ivor and Dougal were inside the barge, blind.

Archie killed the motor on his boat when he was about a hundred yards away and saw the boat tied up at the barge. He took a firmer grip on his rifle and wondered whether to carry on or wait for the cavalry he had asked Dougal to summon. Sitting thinking for a minute or so he decided discretion was the better part of valour and, still keeping his distance, he rowed his boat quietly around to get a better view of the cages on the other side of the barge. He saw the smolt tank standing by the walkway and then a figure flicker across and behind it, followed by the sound of the pump being started. *The intruder was running the smolt transfer? What the...?*

He grabbed for his binoculars and traced them onto the tank looking for the figure again. Seeing nothing he followed the tube from the tank down along the walkway and saw that it no longer ended at a cage - the stranger had moved the tube and it was now discharging the smolt into open water. *Right, that does it,* he thought. *Sod the cops, I'm not waiting here watching my fish being thrown away like this.* He moved the boat round further to finally get a view of the man, now standing quietly by the tank watching the fish being pumped through the tube and out to sea.

Archie raised his rifle and was about to fire when he heard the sound of the chopper returning across the loch. He watched as the man finished the pumping, disconnected the tubes and sealed up the empty tank. The chopper closed in carrying a new tank full of smolt. The stranger waved the pilot in and watched as the pilot slowly lowered the new tank down onto the barge. He grabbed it when it was close enough, guided it into place and unhooked the cable. Archie took aim and fired.

Viktor had just disconnected the cable hook when he heard a gunshot and a ricochet off the tank right by him. He let go of the hook, grabbed the rifle hanging by a strap from his shoulder and turned towards the source of the shot in one smooth, easy movement, intending to go down into a crouch as he did so. Simultaneously, the chopper pilot heard the gunshot, saw a muzzle flash and instinctively pulled up on the joystick. Two kilos of carbon steel hook swung wildly at the end of the cable as a result and caught Viktor full square on the back of his head as he turned. He collapsed face first into the water like a cooling tower being demolished. When Archie got to the spot a few minutes later all that remained was a rifle and some blood on the tyres lining the edge of the barge.

12

Vasilij's jet landed smoothly and taxied over to the small hangars that the private jets of successful businessmen called home. He was through customs and passport security and into the waiting Lexus in five minutes and within fifteen he was off the Edinburgh by-pass and being driven by Feliks down to Yair. Within the hour he was sitting in his office, at his desk, looking out from the French doors onto his very own sixty acres of Scotland.

Immediately out from the terrace were steps leading down to a large manicured lawn surrounded by yew and ash stands and a large herbaceous border along the eastern edge. In summer this was a blaze of colour and texture, here in early winter it was a tangle of damp matted green and brown partially hidden under clumps of ice and snow. Out beyond the trees the estate grounds rose gently into woodland, extending out to the west and circumvented by a long gravel pathway wide enough for a golf buggy, which wound its way down to the Tweed and the salmon beat. Along the one mile stretch were several fishing stands, a ghillie hut and a fenced off area for parking. This led on to another gravel track which eventually expanded to a fully tarmacced road which led down to the gatehouse by the bridge and the rear entrance to the estate. From here you could see little of the house itself, hidden as it was by the woods, but if you passed along the river and then walked up the hill slightly you would get fine view of its three storey Georgian splendour, extended by a large bay at the front.

He poured himself a brandy, contemplating the view and mulling over progress. Soon, his would be the only company able to provide healthy Scottish salmon to the market. The spot market was soaring in this run-up to Christmas and the forecasts for prices next year were also rising, enough for his customers to have started renegotiating current contracts so that they could lock into prices now rather than continue to get hit.

He was, he knew, cleaning up - making an enormous profit in the short term and driving his competitors into decline in the long term. In his mind's eye he saw his company become the dominant player in the market for many years. Of course, the share price of his company would continue to rise and, as he was the major shareholder, this would only add to his paper wealth and ability to leverage it into more borrowings for his other business ventures.

Maybe he should look at another yacht, or a home in the Caribbean. He could see himself lying on a beach, daiquiri in hand, watching the surf lap at his feet. And there she was, lying next to him on the sand, tanned and glistening. Damn it. Once again, meaning to focus on business, his thoughts were all too easily replaced with those of Blysse Baptiste.

Fucking Viktor, thought Tony. If he had any more brains he'd be a halfwit. A completely incompetent arsehole, he believed the Brits would say.

His last voicemail, again barely coherent, explained an accident and consequently a delay with proceedings. Fuck that, thought Tony. He'd already effectively had a dry-run at this when he'd tampered with the alarms at Lochcarron. If it hadn't been for Viktor thinking he could hurry things along that would've been a nice clean job. So, enough. You want something doing, you have to do it yourself.

He turned right off the main road into Rothesay and kept on until the road narrowed and climbed through rocky outcrops and scree slopes. After about ten minutes there was a sign which read: Aquamarine Seafarms, Rothesay Hatchery in orange and blue on a white background. A white van was parked beside it and two workmen in overalls looked like they were replacing the sign with a new one. He turned off down a gravel track through a stand of trees which opened out into a parking area large enough for a dozen cars or so and a large dark green warehouse with a giant pair of sliding metal doors.

He parked up and reminded himself of the layout again from the schematics he had lying unfolded on the passenger seat beside him. This small site, hidden away on the edge of Loch Fad on the Isle of Bute, was seemingly of no interest or value to anyone. But Tony knew better. Calling this a hatchery was a slight misnomer - it would more accurately be termed a broodstock facility. This was where the salmon eggs were produced. Millions of them every year, churned out by mature adult salmon, specifically selected for their quality, capable of producing eggs destined to grow into prime Scottish salmon. This one site alone produced half of Aquamarine's egg stocks each year and, since they were by far the largest salmon producer in Scotland, that represented a sizeable chunk of all Scottish salmon farmed. These were, quite literally, the geese that laid the golden eggs and Tony was going to destroy every last one of them.

There seemed to be nobody around and Tony was totally unsurprised. All these remote farming sites were supposedly managed round the clock but, whenever he showed up, no-one was there. He ought to send some kind of whistleblower email to the Directors of these companies - they were being taken for a ride by their staff.

He looked at his watch and did some quick calculations. He had to be out of here by ten in order to get down to the jetty and collect the workboat ready for this afternoon's stunt with Blysse. An hour to decorate it and prime the troops ready, then off we went. Back at the car for five-ish in time to catch the last ferry back to the mainland.

He unpicked the padlock chaining the main sliding doors together and then slid one back. Inside the building was humming with bright overhead lights, pumps and jets spitting fresh water out into a huge array of circular tanks stretching out back to the far walls. He wandered down between them, looking into each. The large ones were taller than him and he had to clamber up onto a steel walkway which extended above the rows of tanks and down to the far end where steps led to the second warehouse building which adjoined this one. A few were empty for cleaning and maintenance, enormous pale blue washing bowls - big enough to stand fifty men in easily - scrubbed white in places, each with a central discharge outlet, like a big plughole in the floor of the tank. In the others, huge monster fish swam lazily around, lurching briefly into action if the feed sprays above the tanks switched on and spat food pellets into the water like lawn sprinklers.

Tony stopped and looked at the fish in one tank in particular. God, they were beautiful. Each was a sleek, silver missile of muscle, almost six feet long from nose to tail, weighing maybe twenty pounds or more, their snouts bigger than his hand. He watched mesmerised for a while, kneeling down and trying to dip his hand in the water to touch them but it was too far below the walkway for him to reach.

He reached the end of the walkway and descended the steps and walked through to the second warehouse. Here again tanks stretched out before him but over to the left was a door with some internal windows running down a corridor along the length of the building. He could see into an office or two, a cheap wooden meeting table and chairs with filing cabinets in one, a desk and a PC in the other. He strode over to the corridor and walked along to the far end where it turned 90 degrees and led to a door marked AUTHORISED PERSONNEL ONLY.

He fiddled with the lock on this door for some time but eventually got it open. Inside was a jack-hammering generator and walls full of dials and junction boxes, pipes and cabling leading in a maze of trunking up through the false ceiling and away to the various containment, management and feeding systems that ran the place. Out along the far wall was another door with a small glass reinforced glass window set within it. He went through this door and was immediately in a completely different environment: cool and quiet where the outer room was hot and heavy with noise.

In here were the servers and controllers for the systems. A large rack housed three servers connected into a patch panel and a single screen and keyboard sat on top of the rack. He turned the screen on and it flickered into life showing a dozen windows, each drawing a graph or histogram depicting water temperature, flow rate, feeding levels and so on - each tank in the hatchery monitored and controlled from this main console. He flicked through the menus looking for a Settings or Calibration screen and found it under Options/Other. He tabbed through each screen and reset the alarm thresholds to zero on each tank and, when he'd finished, applied his changes and switched the screen off.

Back in the outer room he held his breath as he ran down the main array of junction boxes and flicked each control to OFF. One by one, the pumps whirred to a standstill and the whine of the various fans stopped. He left the generator running and re-locked the door behind him. His final act, walking to the far end of the facility was to open the master discharge valve to its fullest extent and then, one by one, he opened the valves on each tank as far as they would go. As he left through the main sliding door and re-clasped the padlock all he could hear was the tumbling sound of thousands of gallons of water draining out of the plant down the discharge pipes and into the loch below.

As Tony drove back towards the main road he passed the sign for the hatchery he'd seen on the way in. The workmen had finished replacing the sign and he glanced anxiously out of his rear view mirror, checking to see whether they had noticed him or, more importantly, his vehicle. He had belatedly realised that his new green Subaru was fairly conspicuous and it wouldn't need anyone to make a note of his number plate to place him

179

at the scene of a crime if anyone noticed the car. Fortunately, it looked like the workmen were too busy to worry about some lone car, so he turned the radio up loud and started to sing along as he drove away in the wintry sunshine, heading for Port Bannatyne.

Vasilij trod gingerly through the mud. Dusted with snow, there were pools where ice had formed and ridges where caterpillar tracks had left their mark all over the site. He was used to the cold - it never really got cold in Scotland if you were Russian - and he was dressed for the winter with heavy coat, hat, gloves and scarf. But when that wind keened and channelled down the valley below Langhaugh Hill it went right through him.

Jelena had told him he didn't need to keep checking the site himself - she was keeping tabs on things and quite capable of updating him accurately. Vasilij, though, felt a deep personal attachment to this development: it was his baby, his idea, his plan. He remembered his excitement at the board meeting last year when he had presented the plans for the site, run through the business case and focussed on the role of closed containment within his business strategy.

He needed to keep involved and feel part of it, even if his involvement was technically unnecessary. He walked the site, blueprints in hand, reckoning progress and looking with interest at the pipes and metalwork that protruded from the reinforced concrete so far laid. Inspecting the metal carcasses which were partially erected across the site, the studwork which partially in place inside, and even some empty tanks lying protected under thick polythene sheets waiting to be connected and cemented in place. Things were clearly taking shape now and within six weeks this place would be operational. Soon. Very soon.

A man whom he took to be the duty foreman exited the portakabin on the far side of the site and walked towards him. Over to his right he could make out a couple of hard-hatted workmen moving iron trellises and wooden pallets into piles. One of the workmen was chatting to a third man, no headgear, large burly figure with a full head of dark hair and a goatee. As the site foreman approached, Vasilij noticed a couple of small dogs running loose near a collection of abandoned gas cylinders. He didn't much care for dogs. Any dogs. When he saw these two small terriers sniffing about, his hackles rose.

"Feliks, please remove the dogs."

Feliks had been leaning against the driver's door of the limo smoking a cigarette. He stubbed it out on the ground with his heel and strode off up the shallow incline towards the animals.

Penn was sniffing around the long metal tubes, Teller was elsewhere. Penn had picked up a trail, an extremely strong chemical taste almost which hurt the back of his throat. He sniffed eagerly left and right, following the scent as it strengthened, the stub of his tail wagging furiously. He barely noticed the large man until he was right on top of him. He raised his head to the man who bent down to get closer to him and Penn could smell the smoke and stale sweat gusting from him in great clouds and waves. The man reached down and Penn jumped left out of his grasp, sensing evil intentions. The man turned

181

and tried to grab him again but Penn barked harshly at the man, his hackles rising. He dug his claws into the freezing mud and bared his teeth. There was a standoff for a few seconds - the man crouching, arms raised with hands out; Penn snarling and pumping himself as large as he could, legs tensed, ready.

Teller heard Penn barking and looked round. He saw a man pulling a shard of metal from his jacket and hold it menacingly as he advanced on Penn. Teller ran to Penn's aid. He launched himself at the man's back when he got within a metre of so. The man must have heard him because he turned just as Teller was in mid-flight and managed to bat him away with a whirling arm. The man was powerful and strong and the swipe knocked Teller back several metres. He hit the ground awkwardly, rolled and got to his feet but was a little disoriented for a second or so. He could no longer see the man with the metal shard. Instead he saw another figure wearing a large furry hat, scowling, standing some way off. As he looked this man waved him away and shouted something gutterally. Teller padded carefully towards him, smelling warm spices and human sweat. He bared his teeth and the man narrowed his eyes. Teller continued his advance and the man started to back away, apprehensively. Teller took this as a good sign of weakness and suddenly sprang forward; the man swung his right foot and hit Teller smack in the belly, sending him to the ground with a crack of broken bones.

Penn, meanwhile, was continuing to bark at the man holding the metal shard - the pair of them circling each other like wary prizefighters, waiting for an opening to launch the first strike. Behind the man he could see Teller whimpering on the ground, another man standing over him. From behind this man there suddenly appeared the looming dark shape of their owner. He didn't look happy.

Paul had been chatting to Archie when the commotion started. He didn't turn to look - his dogs barked all the bloody time, over nothing mostly. No reason to be interested right now when he was trying to tap Archie for some work. When he heard Penn snarl though, that was different. You could tell something was wrong by the pitch of it. Teller never went in much for barking or snarling, just got on with stuff. He tended to be a bit mental and throw himself into things without thinking. Penn was a lot more bark than bite normally, but when threatened would fight like a polecat. This snarl was the sound of Penn being threatened and Big Paul looked round.

Although it was Penn doing the barking the action seemed to involve Teller who, as Paul turned to look, was caught by a huge swing of the foot by a rich-looking man wearing a big fur hat. Teller went down like a bag of spanners and lay in the snow, whimpering. Paul strode over, furious at the stranger who now had his back to him. When he got within a hearing distance he shouted across the the man:

"Here! What the fuck you doing to my dog?"

The man turned to face him and didn't seem to be registering fear, or guilt, or any emotion come to that. Paul didn't need the sight of his injured dog to help him decide what to do next. He got close to the man and let fly with a massive right hay-maker which caught him on the left side of his face, registering surprise as it did so.

There was a loud pop and the man fell to the ground as if chopped off at the knees. By the time he hit the mud, the side of his face was already a bloated, swollen purple and blood was pulsing from his eye socket.

Turning back towards Penn, the sound of snarling had become more muted and Paul could see why: Penn had his jaw clamped onto the man's arm. The man had dropped the knife and was shaking his arm vigorously trying to dislodge the dog. Penn was hanging on for dear life, saliva bunching from his jaws, foaming white on the man's dark sleeve. Paul bounded up and could see that this man, unlike his colleague unconscious on the ground, was built like a fighter - his neck and shoulder muscles flexing as he struggled with the dog. Penn wouldn't be able to keep hold much longer so Paul took an executive decision:

"Penn! Heel! Now!"

Penn obediently unclenched his jaw, dropped to the ground and flashed through the man's legs before he could venture a kick. The man turned to follow the dog and came to face to face with Paul. When he spoke his voice was deep and slow with a heavy foreign accent:

"Take your dog and go."

"Fuck you, mate. You attack my dog, I'm goin' nowhere until you've paid for it."

The man eyed him up, rubbing his bitten arm. They were of similar height and stature, although the stranger clearly had the advantage of muscle and tone. If they were going to fight it would be a close call unless one of them had an edge. He slyly scanned the ground for the knife he had dropped and played for time.

"You want money? How much?"

"No money, mate." Paul drew closer. "I want to see you trying to pick your teeth up with a broken arm."

Feliks woke up to find himself on a chair in an office. There was rope around his chest and around each ankle, tying them to the chair legs. The Dogman was drinking a mug of tea looking out of the window at the rain. Feliks assumed they were still on site, in the portakabin perhaps. The dog who had bitten him was curled up in front of a one-bar electric fire, dozing.

The Dogman looked around, saw he was conscious and put down his mug of tea. He walked over to Feliks, took another chair and sat in it directly opposite him, face-to-face only a few feet apart. He had an olive complexion, short black hair and goatee, dark brown eyes and a large nose which looked like it had been broken several times. His hands were large and rough, with thick heavy fingers and nails ringed with dirt and oil. The knuckles on one hand were bruised and skinned, there was blood on his other hand.

Feliks's mouth, nose, cheek and ribs all hurt. He ran his tongue around his mouth trying to assess his injury while the Dogman spoke:

"Who are you?"

Feliks remained silent.

"Who are you and why did you attack my dogs?"

Still no reply.

"My dog needs a vet. Your boss, I'm guessing, needs an ambulance. You have maybe ten minutes until I call the police. If you don't start answering my questions you may not see them arrive." He took Feliks' knife from a pocket and held it up between them. "Who are you?"

"Fuck off."

The Dogman pushed the point of the knife into his cheek below his left eye, pushing painfully just underneath his eyeball. "What is your name?" He pushed harder.

"Feliks."

"Good. Progress. So, Feliks. Who is your boss and what are you both doing here?"

"My boss owns this facility."

"Really?" The Dogman was surprised and considered this information for a while before speaking again. "What's his name?"

"Krupchenko."

"So Mr Krupchenko owns this place? What's your role?"

"Bodyguard."

The Dogman burst out laughing. "Oops. Tilt! Why does he need a bodyguard? A *bad* bodyguard?"

"Rich men need bodyguards."

"Rich? How rich?"

Feliks shrugged. "Rich."

"What is this place he owns then?"

Another shrug. "Don't know."

The Dogman made a strange sound, like a buzzer. "Oops, wrong answer. Guess again."

"I don't know."

"Do you want to phone a friend?"

Feliks looked at him in stony silence. The Dogman changed tack.

"Why did you attack my dogs?"

"Mr Krupchenko doesn't like dogs."

The Dogman leant in to Feliks, knife point now piercing skin. "I don't like your Mr Krupchenko. And I don't like you." He looked over at his dog. "And my dog doesn't like you and he doesn't like your Mr Krupchenko."

At that moment, the mobile phone in Feliks trouser pocket trilled out a ringtone - Beethoven's Ode To Joy. The dog's ears pricked up and the animal shot up and launched himself straight at Feliks' trouser pocket. Feliks struggled to swivel his hips away from the dog but succeeded only in opening his crotch area to the dog's attack. The animal's teeth closed round the bulge in his trousers and he let out an agonising howl. The dog shook his body, teeth clamped onto Feliks' groin. He could see blood staining his trousers around the dogs mouth and he let out an anguished cry. The ringtone stopped.

"Help me!"

A siren sounded in the distance and the Dogman looked furtively out of the window. He gave a short whistle and the dog unclamped his jaws and sat obediently on the floor, still between Feliks' legs. His mouth was ringed with saliva and blood.

"And he doesn't like bloody Beethoven either."

The man and his dog disappeared out through the portakabin door into the rain as his phone rang again and Feliks passed out.

187

13

The lady at Harrisons' car hire desk was very polite when she explained that Kim's card had been declined. Happened all the time, she said. Nothing to be embarrassed about, she said.

Fuck that, thought Kim. She handed over another card and ten minutes later was driving a 64 plate Focus up from the parking lot onto the Edinburgh Road. She had agreed to meet Cullen at Sainsbury's just down the road and, when she pulled into the car park, he spotted her immediately and jumped in.

"Wait here." She instructed.

"Huh? I've only just got in."

"Wait here. I'll only be a minute."

Kim left the engine running while she got out and went over to the cash machine at the store entrance. She inserted her card and followed the on-screen instructions to view her current balance. When she got back into the car she was pale and visibly shaken.

"What's up?"

"I've got no money." She said these words for the very first time in her life, listening to how alien they sounded even as she said them. "The bastard's almost cleaned me out."

Cullen looked at her in silence, unsure what to say.

"The fucking bastard's taken thousands!" She slammed both hands on the steering wheel, accidentally triggering the horn. An old couple coming out of the supermarket both started at the sound. "Shit. Shit. Shit. SHIT!"

"TTT I assume."

"He's thrown me out of a moving car, taken all my stuff and stolen all my money. Fuck." Her face crumpled and she started to cry. Cullen sat awkwardly silent until she regained herself.

"We've got to fucking get him now." Kim insisted, sniffing back her tears.

"That was the plan."

"Yes, but I mean *really* get him."

"You mean kill him? That's illegal, you know?"

"Wow. Did you used to be a policeman or something?"

"Violence is never the answer"

"Unless the question is *What is never the answer?* in which case violence is indeed the answer." She looked at him with steel in her eyes. "I want to mess him up. Do him harm. You gotta problem with that, Buster?"

He thought for a few seconds before replying. "Not really, no."

The Sainsburys car park was only half full, and she stood under a tree to shelter from the rain while she waited for her bank to take her off hold. She toed the kerb with her left foot, noting how scruffy her shoes were. How had it come to this? Reduced to wearing ill-fitting, charity shop tat, using a 19th century brick phone while chasing down her lowlife boyfriend across half of Scotland in the company of a taciturn hermit with all the social skills of a half-digested -

"Yes, hello?"

189

"The last recorded transaction on your account was a cash withdrawal of £5000 from an ATM at Dunoon Ferry terminal, four days ago."

"Where?"

"Dunoon."

"Oh, well, when you say it twice it becomes a lot clearer."

"Ms Schofield. Whilst I appreciate that having your bank card stolen is upsetting I would like to remind you that you were duty bound to inform us as soon as practicable after the theft. Four days is a considerable time after the incident and if, as it seems, there has been a single transaction of £5000 during that time, I am afraid the burden of proof will lie with yourself to show that it was indeed someone other than yourself who-"

"Are you accusing me of lying?"

"No, Ms Schofield, I am merely-"

"Of stealing my own money!"

"Of course not. I am only-"

"I've never even been to Dunoon!"

Cullen's was walking out from Sainsbury's across towards her. She signalled to him urgently.

"We've got to go to Dunoon." She hissed to him out of the corner of her mouth, then spoke back into the handset. "Yes, of course I want you to cancel the card! Do you think I'm-".

Cullen grabbed her arm and shook his head at her. She covered the phone and hissed again. "What?"

"Don't cancel the card." Cullen hissed back. "If he uses it again, well know where he is."

"But he's in Dunoon!"

"What, when?"

"Ah." Good point, she thought, four days ago. She got back onto the phone. "Erm, sorry about that. Er, look, could I keep the card active please? For a little while."

"Are you saying the card has not actually been stolen?"

"No, it's been stolen alright it's just that-"

"Ms Schofield, I'm sorry. If a card is stolen it is our security policy to stop that card immediately and inform the police so that-"

"No, wait." She looked angrily at Cullen, furious and starting to tear up as she assessed her options. "No, sorry. My mistake. My, er, partner has just informed me he has the card."

"Your partner?"

"Yes."

"Your partner has the card?"

"Yes."

"And it was your partner who withdrew £5000 four days ago?"

A pause, then quietly "Yes."

"With your permission?"

"Yes." Kim wiped her nose on her sleeve. "Bloody yes, alright!"

"Just one moment." There was a silence on the line and the distant sound of typing. "Is there anything else I can do to help you, Ms Schofield?"

"No. Thank you." She hung up and looked disconsolately at Cullen. "Now what?"

"Now, we go to Dunoon."

"Yes, but he won't still be there will he? And she said he used the card at the ferry terminal, so he was obviously going somewhere."

"Glasgow."

"Why?"

"The Dunoon ferry goes to Glasgow. Well, essentially."

"Well, it doesn't matter does it. That was four days ago. He could be bloody anywhere now."

There was no traffic on the Glasgow road, ahead or behind, and they hadn't passed any vehicle for some time now. All around the hills loomed at her, dark and dank, through the swirling rain and clammy fog. The tarmac was slick with great pools forming across both sides of the road where the rain and runoff was too heavy for the drainage to deal with. Up ahead, though, there was a break in the clouds. Bright blue sky flooded through and the edges of the frame showed fluffy white clouds being beaten across the sky like egg whites in a silver bowl.

She decided to break the silence which had been sitting there for a while: "This weather, huh?"

Cullen couldn't have looked less interested. "It's Scotland alright."

"I get it. If you can see the hills it's going to rain, if you can't see them it's raining, right?"

"Yes." He looked across and almost smiled. She leapt on the chance.

"Do we have a plan for when we… you know… catch up with TTT?"

He shrugged again. "We'll just ask him for your stuff back."

"Oh, right. Silly me." She slapped her forehead. "And what do we do if he declines this kind offer?"

"Why would he?"

192

"He's a cunt." She was grim-faced, focussing on the road, scheming and dreaming of the physical torture she would conduct on him when she caught up with his sorry arse.

"Yes, I think we've established that. Why did he steal your money?"

"Because he's a cunt."

Cullen sighed and looked out of the window, searching for another gambit. Conversations weren't his long suit. "What does he need the money for?"

Kim thought for a while wondering how to respond and whether she could shoehorn the C-word into her answer. By the time she had an answer for him she had calmed down.

"I don't know, really. Perhaps he needs it to fund his salmon shenanigans? Although God knows why when he has a Russian sugar daddy bankrolling him."

"A Russian sugar daddy?"

"Yeah. Vasilij someone. I think I mentioned him to you. He's Tony current patron."

"Patron?"

"Yeah." She sighed and explained. "Look, Tony does his eco-stuff, ok? Travels all over the place, giving talks, generating publicity, garnering support, blah blah blah. But he doesn't get paid. He's not employed by anyone to do this - it's his own thing, all off his own bat. So he needs people to give him money. Expenses, travel, accommodation and so on."

She indicated to turn left.

"So people just give him money?"

"Well, yeah."

"What sort of people do that - just give him money because he needs it?"

"Well, me for a start."

"Yes." Cullen pondered. "Why?"

"Because … it seemed like a good idea, ok? We were in love, I thought. I have - correction had - money, he needed it. He believed in what he was doing, so I supported him."

"Does he believe in what he's doing?"

"Oh yeah. He's nuts about it. One track mind, all the time. Salmon, seals, whales. Never shuts up about it."

"So there would be, what, like-minded people prepared to give him money to speak on their behalf? Promote causes they also believed in?"

"Yes. Exactly."

"Huh."

"Yeah. I believe the American phrase for it is *go figure*."

Cullen sat thinking for a while, then said: "You know that blinky thing means turning?"

"What? Oh, sorry." She switched the indicator off. "Miles away."

"How did he get your money?"

"I gave him a card." Kim said sheepishly

"Nice."

"I trusted him, ok? It was for emergencies. Contingencies. Top-ups when he ran short."

"Didn't you ever check your statements?"

"Not really. I've got kind of a Shrodinger's balance thing going, you know?" She looked at him, looking at her. "Christ. Don't you judge me! This is what normal people do when they're in a relationship. They trust each other. Share? You are familiar with the verb?"

"Aye."

"And like I said, this Vasilij guy - he was sponsoring him to do some particular project, I dunno, defending the business practices of his company or something. He shouldn't have needed money from me at all."

"Who is this Vasilij?"

"Don't know." Cullen looked at her and she shrugged. "Never met him."

"What his company called."

"Don't know."

Cullen sighed. "Ok, what do you know?"

She thought for a while. "Tony came home one day, all pumped up. Said he'd been 'hired' by a Russian business man called Vasilij who wanted him to work on a project for him. Would pay him cash up front, lots of it. Put loads of resources his way and wouldn't stop him doing all his other stuff, just wanted his own project to take priority. Said it would involve a fair bit of travelling up and down Scotland for a while - few months. This was back in June. July maybe?

Cullen didn't say anything so she continued.

"I didn't pay much attention really. Not interested in what he actually does although I was bothered about the fact he'd be travelling. Meant we wouldn't see each other so often. Tony started splashing the cash almost straight away. Bought me some nice things. Got himself a new car. I never saw this Vasilij guy - heard Tony speaking to him on the phone a few times and mention his name. That's about it."

"Not much to go on."

"Sor-ry." She glared across at him, her hands white on the wheel. "Look. All I want now is to get my stuff back, get my money back and forget I ever met the fucking creep."

"Ah."

"What do you mean, ah?"

"Well, the money." Cullen sucked his teeth. She'd never seen anyone actually do this before. "I assume he will have spent it."

"Well, he'll have to bloody well unspend it, pronto!"

"I don't think that is practically possible."

"I'm not talking literally, idiot."

"I am not an idiot." He said calmly.

"I'm not being literal there either! Christ, Cullen, you have met people before haven't you? You do understand people use figures of speech. Idiom?"

"Yes."

"He has his own source of funds you know? He's being paid by the Russian guy remember. It's not as if he needs my money."

"Why does he take it then?"

"I told you, I don't fucking know! Point is, we can get him to repay me from his Russian money." She looked at him for some sign of agreement or acknowledgement. Nothing. She picked up a bottle of Diet Coke from the cup-holder and sipped thoughtfully. "Do you have a gun?"

"No."

"A knife?"

"No."

"Er, any weapons at all?"

"No."

"So - what, we give him a Paddington Hard Stare and hope that does the trick?"

"I can be … persuasive."

"OK. And if he sees us and just runs. What then? *'Hey, you there. Stop! Or I'll…. say Stop again!'*"

"Let me worry about that." He tried to look reassuringly at her. "I can be surprisingly creative."

She almost choked on her Diet Coke at his facial expression. "Surprisingly creative?"

"Yeah. And if that doesn't work, we have the police."

Kim whistled. "The police? Nice thinking batman! We're off to ice some dude and you want to give local law enforcement the heads up. What the fuck's wrong with you?"

"Ice some dude?"

"Yeah." She laughed, despite herself. "Ice some dude. Top some loser. Do some wetwork." He sat quietly, staring straight ahead. "Somehow the film noir vernacular seems appropriate." She trailed off, lost for words for once.

"We're not off to ice some dude." He looked across at her now, making a point. "That would be murder."

"Yeah. I mean, no. Yeah, you're right. I'm getting carried away. Sorry."

"We are attempting to recover your property."

"Yeah."

"Property which was stolen from you and which is rightfully yours."

"Yeah. And if recovery of said property requires the use of deadly force…"

"That would be regrettable."

"Yeah. It would." She smiled at him, hoping he would reciprocate. He didn't.

They stopped at a petrol station and Kim went to use the ATM while Cullen filled up. As he replaced the petrol cap she appeared from nowhere.

"Right. Let's go!"

"Hang on. What's changed your tune?" She seemed suddenly as bright as a button, all fired up and raring to go. "Where're we going anyway?"

"Port Bannatyne." She waved a small slip from the ATM in his face. "That's a real place, right?"

Cullen tried, ineffectively, to hide his disdain. "Yes it is. It's on Bute. Quite nice too, actually."

"Well come on! TTT tried to use my card there less than twenty minutes ago. The game's afoot, Watson!"

"I think, perhaps, you should be Watson." She looked at him and swore there was a trace of a smile, just *there*, in his eyes.

"Whatever."

Kim stood at the rails on the small CalMac ferry, looking across to the Isle Of Bute. The surface of the loch was whipped into small mare's tails of foam by the salt gusts and the shadows of the clouds as they raced overhead cast different hues of green, blue and grey on the water. She breathed deeply in the ozone and, chilled though she was by the stiff breeze, she felt the tang and zest of a fresh new start.

Cullen broke the silence, surprising her. "Tell me more about him."

"TTT? You really want to know?"

"Know your enemy."

"Ok. So what do you want to know?"

"Well. How did you two meet?"

"We met on New Year's Eve. Last year. Or this year, depending on how you count it. At a party."

"Go on."

"It was a New Year's Eve dinner dance at Gleneagles. Do you know it?"

"Heard of it. Never been. Pretty swanky." He made the word swanky sound negative.

Kim remembered the night and the raucous atmosphere and the feeling of wanting to throw up from having drunk far too much. In what she'd thought of as an empty room he had just appeared and sat down on the plush and gilt chair next to her. He'd put his hand on her bare shoulder to see if she was conscious. She bolted upright, brushed her hair from her eyes in an over-exaggerated manner designed to give the appearance of sobriety but which illustrated the opposite as clearly as could be.

"Someone's sitting there I'm afraid!" She blurted this out as a loud high-pitched squawk, no grace or finesse. She realised she was rocking a look of smudged mascara and a general air of dishevelment but was unable to do anything about it in her current state.

"I'm sorry. I was just checking - "

"He's gone to the back. Bar shurely. Er, back shortly." Her eyes met his but were having trouble focussing.

Tony had looked around the dining room.

"Are you sure? It looks like everyone's left."

"Rum and coke, thanks."

"Um, really? Do you not think you've perhaps had enough?"

"Fuck off!" She spat this with some vehemence.

"Excuse me?"

"I said 'Fuck off'! I know you Americans have trouble with the language but I would have expected the land of Tarantino to be familiar with the vernacular"

"Excuse me?"

"You. Are. Excused." With a wave of her hand she dropped her head back on the table and started snoring.

Sometime later he had rustled up a pitcher of black coffee from a member of the kitchen staff who had wanted a fiver for his pains and was watching her trying to keep her second cup down.

"Feeling better?"

"Somewhat."

"Is it what the doctor ordered?"

"I'm sorry?"

"It's what you Brits say isn't it?"

"Yes, I suppose it is." She tried on a smile. "I mean, it is what we say but it's not what the doctor ordered. Not unless he ordered a large helping of embarrassment, a side order of shame and a humiliation garnish."

She looked at him, full on, red-faced.

"Thank you for helping me out. I must look a fright."

"Well, actually you do. But, at the same time - divine."

"Divine!" She snorted. "You Americans are so full of shit. I can't believe I'm actually blushing."

"It suits you."

"Oh do give over, for heaven's sake. One compliment is lovely. Keep them coming and it all goes a bit Pretty Woman. If you're looking for a rebound shag to ring in the New Year, look away now."

"Rebound shag?"

"Yes. Look it's a … never mind. I'm sorry. Thank you. For your help." She looked around the empty room. "This place could do with a few more white knights."

"So you're here on your own, then?"

"Looks like it now doesn't it? Bastard's fucked off with someone. I should've known better." She snuffled back some tears and looked at her watch. "Isn't there someone you're supposed to be with, it's almost midnight?"

"No. I'm on my own. Usually."

"Hmph. Well, maybe we can be lonely together then. For the bells, at least. It's not the way one would wish to start a new year but it's better than ringing in the year all alone."

They listened to the shouting countdown from ten leaking through from the open door.

"I'm Kim."

"Tony."

As the bells, gongs and party poppers and hooters all sounded, people cheered and yelled 'Happy New Year'. Kim clinked her coffee cup against Tony's empty wineglass.

"Cheers. Happy New Year."

From the ferry, they drove down the north-east side of the island and soon the narrow loch began to widen as it joined Loch Striven. Her knowledge of Scottish geography wasn't good but Cullen had pulled out an AA atlas from the glove compartment and showed her the locale. She understood that, from here, the two lochs themselves merged into Holy Loch further southward and widened still further into the Firth of Clyde, down the eastern side of Arran and then on into the Irish Sea.

Cullen continued to scan the far side of the loch on their left as she drove and as they were coming into the small village of Ardmaleish he pointed out the windscreen to her left.

"Well, would you look at that, Watson."

Kim glanced over in the direction of his hand and at first couldn't make out quite what she was looking at. Sailing away from them, across towards the far side of the widening loch was a bright orange boat decked out with shining white banners and some kind of inflatable bobbing around on top. The reflection from the water made it difficult to read the writing on the banners and it was only as the road led slightly right and the boat was heading further left that the angle allowed her to see the words "SEALS" and "KILL". Standing at the prow of the boat, thrusting a placard skyward and posing like some figurehead of old was a pony-tailed man wearing a dark padded jacket over a white T-shirt. She knew immediately it was him.

"Fuck! Fuck! Fuckety Fuck! It's Tony!"

"I figured as much."

"Shit. We've missed him. Bugger!"

"Aye, but not by much."

"Where's he going?"

Cullen looked down at the map. "Well there's not much over there according to this, apart from some kind of Oil Depot. But…" and he looked back out again at the boat. "There's a load of salmon cages out there." he pointed. "You don't think -?"

"Fuck, yeah! I DO think." She clutched the steering wheel tightly, then let go and banged it jubilantly with both hands. "Ha! We've got him!"

"Well, not quite. Not yet. See, he's over there and we're over here. On dry land."

"Yes, but Holmes…" And here it was Kim's turn to give him a patronising look. "Unless he's taken to living on the bloody boat he'll have to come back to shore. Back to his car." She was thinking on her feet again. "Which will mean he has parked it somewhere in Port Bannatyne." She gave Cullen a victorious leer, eyes wide. "Find the car and we find the man."

As they were coming into the port, there was a boat yard on their right with dozens of yachts and small boats covered or up on blocks. Immediately on the left was a large area of hard standing where a few cars were parked.

"That's his car." Kim pointed at the shiny green Subaru estate facing the water. She pulled into the space next to it, switched off the engine and hurled herself out of the car. "The bastard's still got my stuff here, look!" As Cullen stepped out of the passenger side, she had her face pressed to the rear windows, covered by her hands, scanning the contents of the bootspace. She tugged at the door handles. "It's locked."

Cullen looked out across the water to the boat, barely visible now in the sparkling distance.

"Could be some time before he's back."

"So we wait, then." She leant against the car and folded her arms. "It's a lovely day. I have no pressing commitments."

Cullen looked around, brow furrowed. "Then what?"

"Then, Holmes, we take the sucker down!"

"Right here? In plain view?"

"Why not?"

"In broad daylight, we just drag him up against the car, beat him up, grab your stuff and leave." He gave the look again. "Well, it's a plan I suppose."

"Ok, well…" Kim looked around. "We drag him to that toilet block over the road, there, and beat him up inside." As she spoke, she heard herself and realised how ridiculous she sounded. She finished weakly, no longer even believing herself. "Then we tie him up, leave him in a cubicle and drive away in his car."

"And leave our car here."

"Er…"

"So they can trace us."

"Well…"

"And then come and arrest us for assault, theft, …."

"Look-"

"Maybe kidnapping. Unlawful restraint."

"Ok, I get it."

"False imprisonment. Who knows?"

"I said, I get it. Ok?"

They both stared silently out to sea each standing on opposite sides of the car. There was nothing but the sounds of the gulls, the wind whipping at a flagpole and the odd passing car. Eventually Kim broke the silence.

"Right. So what do you think we should do?"

Cullen looked at her over the roof of the car and raised one eyebrow. "I have a plan."

14

When Blysse had told him about her idea for a PR stunt, Bernard the panto director had spoken to the theatre manager, and the pair had agreed to cover the cost of a pink stretch limo to take her to and from the location. The minute the curtain call for the matinee had ended, Bernard had whisked Blysse from the wings and ushered her down the steps, along the bustling artists alley thronged with dancers and the children of the chorus, and out into the limo waiting with its engine running at the stage door.

In the back of the limo, Blysse rustled through a clutch bag for her phone and dug out a couple of folded sheets of A4. Bernard started to bite his nails.

"Do we know where we're going?"

"Yes." Blysse squealed excitedly. "I have the zip code here - Tony texted me. And here -" she waved the sheets of paper. "- are my lines!"

"Do you want me to rehearse them with you?"

"No, I'm fine." She gave the postcode to the driver who punched it into his satnav and gave her the thumbs up in his rear view mirror when he had directions he could follow. "Relax." She said, nestling back in the upholstery. "Do you have anything to eat?"

Jock & Ewan McGregor were tying the duty boat up onshore when the first camera van arrived. It churned up gravel as it sped down the track to the farm site, the tight bends catching the driver unaware. After the first couple, he slowed down and took it more gradually, taking in the fantastic view as he did so. Ahead of him lay the calm waters of Loch Striven, laying like smooth black marble out towards the blue hills in the distance. The salmon cages were packed in a group of six only a short distance from the shore, the loch dropping steeply away beneath them to a depth of several hundred feet as soon as you were fifty yards from the edge.

The driver got out and gazed around, beckoning the camera man and producer to do the same.

"Whit the fuck they lookin' at?" Jock scowled at Ewan as the pair looked on.

"Ne'er mind whit they're lookin' at. Whit they fuck they dae'in here?" Ewan had been site manager here for 27 years and didn't take too kindly to the company of anything which wasn't his own staff or his own fish.

"Says SKY News on the side there."

"I kin see wha' it says, yer numpty. Whit I canna see is whit they're here fae." He shouted up as he walked closer to the vehicle. "Hey, you! Whit's your game, eh?"

"And a good afternoon to you too, sir." The producer was a young man, late twenties and no more, with a smooth southern accent and wearing a pair of very clean boots, freshly ironed chinos and a checked shirt. "Would you be the person in charge here?"

"Aye, that'd be me." He took an instant dislike to this smooth Englishman and ignored the handshake offered. "This is private property you know. You canna just come doon here and start filmin' wi'out permission an' that."

"I quite understand." The producer seemed unfazed and removed a large leather pouch from the laptop bag he had slung from his shoulder. "I believe I have the permission paperwork right here." He rummaged around and retrieved an unsealed white envelope which he handed to Ewan. Inside were three crisp £50 notes. He smiled at Ewan "I trust all is in order?"

"Er, aye…" He muttered something to Jock and the pair of them slouched off to the main site building which looked like an abandoned car park toilet block.

Within fifteen minutes another three camera vans had arrived and the white envelopes were flying into the toilet block thick and fast. When the pink limo arrived, Ewan was drinking from a mug of scalding tea. He almost threw it down himself when the pneumatic blonde in thigh-high boots stepped out. "Fuck me. It's a porno shoot!"

The MV Clarissa May was a 15m workboat, with a battered black hull and a pilot cabin freshly painted sunburst orange. Tony had hired it for the day from a fisherman at Port Bannatyne on the other side of the loch, where it was normally berthed, and spent the past forty five minutes tying up his banners and hoardings to the white metal railings that ran down the port and starboard sides. As a finishing touch he had arranged for a 12 foot inflatable seal to be secured to the top of the cabin with cable ties. As the boat came into view around the western promontory to the shore-base, the handful of volunteers he had dragooned into helping him started waving their placards and sounding their airhorns. The camera crews on shore threw down their mugs and flasks and got their cameras rolling.

Ewan looked out to sea from his vantage point in the shore-base. Chugging through the breezy afternoon light was a bright orange workboat decked out with protesters with placards. He couldn't quite make out the words from here but along the port side of the boat was a long white banner which bore the legend SCOTTISH SALMON KILLS SEALS in dark blue capitals. To ram the point home a pair of red hands dripping blood were clasped together at each end of the text. As the boat drew closer he saw a placard which read S.O.S - SAVE OUR SEALS and another saying DOUBLE-O-SALMON : LICENSED TO KILL?

The blonde in the boots started to saunter gingerly down the shoreline towards the small jetty, the cameras following and surrounding her as the boat drew up alongside. She was talking breezily, shooting comments left and right, flashing a piece of paper in her hand for the cameras to see and waving brightly at the protesters on board. He could see now that they were all wearing the same T-shirts - big baggy white ones with huge red letters front and rear which said BLYSSE BAPTISTE - XMAS PANTO - GLASGOW. A man on the boat threw a T-shirt down to the blonde and there was a sudden silence as the cameramen clustering round or zooming in started jostling for position and microphones were pushed into her face. She said some words that Ewan couldn't hear from this distance and then she was lifted up onto the boat. As the boat slowly pulled away from the jetty the blonde tore her crisp white blouse apart, buttons flying, revealing a white lace bra full to bursting with its cargo, threw her blouse to the cameramen and pulled the new T-shirt over her head.

Up by the camera vans, pandemonium was unleashed as the producers and fixers all made a beeline for Ewan's vantage point. Within seconds he had a crowd of young

208

men standing in his office gesticulating at him and all shouting wildly for a boat. Within minutes young Jock was piloting their own skiff out to the cages, trailing in the wake of the Clarissa May, carrying four teams of cameramen, boom operators and news reporters, while Ewan took another swig from a fresh mug of tea and counted the £50 notes out into two neat piles.

The room on the first floor of the Murrayfield Spire Hospital was stifling when Jelena walked in. The room was clad in whites and beiges, very clean but fairly spartan given the money she assumed it must be costing. However, any niceties or luxuries would have been lost on Vasilij since he was hooked up to drips and oxygen and had been pretty much unconscious ever since being punched in the face.

He was tucked in, all hospital corners, with his arms over the covers and a natty pair of turquoise silk pyjamas that she had prevailed upon the nurses to dress him in. To his left was a tray on wheels containing a small pitcher of water, an empty glass and his phone. There was a pair of cashmere-lined slippers on the floor below it. To his right was a chair on which was sitting a paperback, spine up, open midway through. In the far corner by the curtain-covered windows was a TV showing a rolling news channel, sound off. The main room light was off and the only illumination was from a small bedside lamp, adding to the cosy glow of the place.

Jelena stepped quietly across to the chair and sat down, putting the book on her lap. She didn't feel like reading at the moment. She looked at Vasilij and his patched up face: his left eyelid, brow and entire surrounding area were a purple so deep as to be black. He had a row of stitches running down his cheekbone covered in goo and gauze, and the rest of that side of his face was a mess of ugly black and yellow bruises, scratches and healing scabs. His lip had been split and he had a large cut on the right side of his forehead, presumably from where he had fallen after the punch.

She walked around the bed to get herself a glass of water. Something about the movement or the clink of the glass must have woken him because when she looked at him again he was looking straight at her with his right eye, although not seeming to see her.

"Vasilij?"

He tried to speak but couldn't move his mouth. He gently and slowly licked his lips and tried opening his mouth while keeping his teeth clenched together. He managed to issue a croaking groan. "What. Happened?"

"You were attacked. A man hit you in the face. You're in hospital."

He looked around the room with his good eye, taking it in.

"You're okay."

"Don't. Feel. Fucking. OK."

"Do you want some water? Here, have some." She put the glass to his mouth and watched him delicately sipping. It seemed to provide enough lubrication and coolness to visibly rouse him.

"Who. Did. This?"

"Some guy at the site? Feliks saw him - said he was a big guy." Vasilij didn't say anything to this so she continued. "Says he had two dogs. Vicious things. Chewed one of his balls off."

"Feliks?"

210

Jelena nodded. Vasilij winced at the thought.

"Where. He. Is?"

"Yair." He looked at her, puzzled. She shrugged. "Got an ambulance that took you both to A&E. He got stitched up, took some painkillers and declared himself fit." She shrugged again. "I drove him back to the house. I think he's self-medicating on vodka and horse tranquilisers." She smiled, trying to raise one from him. It didn't work.

"Get. Him."

"Feliks? On the phone?"

Vasilij nodded. "Here."

"Here?"

He nodded again. "Now."

"It'll take a bit of time, Vasilij. We're in Edinburgh, West I think. It'll take him about an hour to get here."

"Fine. Not. Going. Anywhere." He slumped back in his bed and Jelena hurried out of the room to make the call.

Almost as soon as his head hit the pillow his phone buzzed. Someone had set it to silent and it hummed and jittered around the bedside tray like a jumping beetle on acid. Vasilij tried to reach out for it but couldn't because of the drip in his arm. He tried to call for Jelena but found his mouth was dry and he needed another drink. The phone stopped buzzing, was silent for a long minute, and then buzzed a single buzz. The caller had left a voicemail message.

Jelena walked back in to find him glaring at the phone. She picked it up, saw it had one new message, put it on speaker phone and pressed play. It was Tony.

"*Hi, Mr Krupchenko. Er, Vasilij.*" He sounded hesitant but chirpy. "*It's Tony. Just calling in to give you an update on how things are going. So far so good is the short answer. But I'll give you the long answer when we talk. I'll try again later today. Bye.*"

"Would you like some soup?"

Vasilij looked at her as if she were demented. "Soup?"

"Yes. It'll give you some nourishment, get your mouth and jaw working. Maybe make talking easier?"

"Hmmm." He didn't look convinced but she recognised that it wasn't refusal either. She made as if to leave to find a nurse.

"TV." He nodded at the screen in the corner.

"You want me to turn it off?"

He shook is head. "Sound."

"Turn the sound up?" She took the remote control from the TV shelf and put it by his right hand. "I'll just go and see if I can rustle up someone who can get you some soup. Feliks is on his way."

He watched her fuzzy form as she sauntered out of the room and then tried to make the buttons on the remote control swim into focus. Eventually he found the volume control and managed to make the TV audible before sinking back into the pillow and blankly gazing at the screen. The images flashed and flickered and hurt his eyes so he closed them for a while.

When he opened them again he thought he must be dreaming. The first thing he saw was her face through a car window but then the camera moved back to reveal a pink limo with tinted windows showing the reflection of other camera crews and reporters. Everybody pulled back as the rear door opened and Blysse stepped out wearing her panto costume: a blinding white off-the-shoulder blouse, nipped in tightly at the waist, exposing mountains of cleavage and the lacy intersection of two white bra cups; Lincoln green hot pants with top-front button provocatively undone; black thigh-length leather boots with roll-top legs and three-inch heels; set off with a jaunty emerald cap, primed with a long white goose feather being brushed by the breeze. The camera had her in long shot with other camera crews jostling beside her and she lifted her right leg slightly off the ground, slapped her thigh theatrically and called out clearly in the chill clear air: "The seals need saving and me and my merry men are here to save them!"

Blysse sashayed - there was no other word for it - down a gravel path and as the camera followed her it revealed a slipway down to a scruffy wooden jetty beside which a couple of small motor boats bobbed gently. In the distance was an expanse of slate grey water framed by dark hills and a cavernous sky of shifting clouds, silver and white. Approaching was a larger orange boat covered with banners protesting against seal deaths and a clutch of protesters waving placards and shouting something which was lost on the breeze. What looked like a large inflatable walrus was bobbing on top of the wheelhouse. Airhorns punctured the general hubbub every few seconds.

At the bow of the boat as it approached was a tanned, muscular man wearing a long white T-shirt advertising Blysse's panto. In his left hand he was hoisting a large placard with a photo of a baby seal with a exaggerated bullet wound to its head, blood everywhere and in his right hand he had a megaphone through which he was repeating the phrase "Save Our Seals". He had his long brown hair tied back in a ponytail and two fingers of red and blue warpaint on each cheek. He white teeth flashed as he grinned and his eyes twinkled wildly for the cameras as they zoomed in.

Tony.

Vasilij's jaw - despite the pain - dropped. The news anchors voice underlay the pictures but Vasilij didn't catch a word as he lay entranced by this circus unfolding. Blysse was being lifted onto the orange boat to huge cheers and "Blysse! This way!" calls from the cameramen. As the boat pulled away she waved and blew kisses and behind it Vasilij could make out the unmistakable shapes of salmon cages in the water.

The video cut to a close-up of Blysse and Tony standing on a platform alongside a salmon cage, their T-shirt legends now hidden by bright orange life jackets which some well-meaning H&S person had presumably thrust upon them. Blysse's cheeks and hair glistened with sea spray and vitality - she was clearly enjoying herself. Beside her Tony was looking all serious and listening to the interviewers question.

"Blysse. What is your interest in seals? Why are you here today?"

"Well, Doug. Seals are my absolutest favourite animal in the whole world and when my old friend Tony -" *Old friend! What?* "- told me about the plight of Scotch seals and how the salmon industry was shooting them and killing them I just thought I should do whatever I could to make this more widely known to the general public. You know, I'm only here for a few weeks - in Panto at the Pavilion Theatre, Glasgow - and I couldn't pass up the chance to see some seals in their natural habitat and experience as much as I could of the marvellous lochs and mountains of Scotland."

She smiled coquettishly at the camera which started to pan back to Tony. Before it reached him, the VT ended and Vasilij was back with the news anchor in the studio. "And finally, -"

Vasilij lay stunned for a few seconds before he waved his hand to Jelena who had just re-entered the room. "Off. Off!"

His breathing was laboured and he felt a little faint.

"Water?" Jelena poured him a glass from the pitcher and held it up to him but he waved it away angrily. Her phone trilled once and she checked it.

"Feliks is here."

Vasilij's phone buzzed again as Feliks walked in. He was favouring his left foot and looked shame-faced. Vasilij motioned for him to sit down while he took the call on speaker-phone. Feliks sat down - gingerly.

"Yes?"

"Mr Krupchenko?" A very shaky voice. Scottish.

"Yes?"

"Er, Sir. This is Davy MacIntyre - Head Of Farming Operations?"

"Yes?"

"Erm, I've been asked by the Chief Exec to give you a heads up on an event that has occurred at one of your facilities on the west coast. The new broodstock site in Bute?"

"Yes." Vasilij had a tightening feeling in his chest as he sensed the caller hesitating. This was a site he'd only just acquired from one of his competitors. The ink on the contract was barely dry and they hadn't even finished changing the signage at the site.

"Well, er, you see, Sir. It seems there's been some sort of accident... malfunction... somethin' of that sort."

"Yes?"

"Aye. Well, you see this, er, malfunction - in the computer systems, you see. And well, they monitor the various environmental sensors for the tanks all year round and trigger alarms if anything threatens to fall too low or rise too high and ... er, well Sir, it looks like there was malfunction in the heating systems as well and ..."

Silence from Vasilij, the caller pushed on.

"... and the temperature rose past normal levels wi'out the alarms goin' off..."

Again, silence.

"... and the automatic backup systems reacted by triggering the drainage procedures when they shouldn't have, see..."

Still no reply.

"....and the master evacuation valve had accidentally been left open so there was no over-ride ..."

Vasilij felt faint and the room began to spin.

"Sir?... Are ye still there, Sir?"

A gulp of air, a long slow exhale and then: "Yes"

There was long gap before the caller came back on the line.

"Well ... er, the thing is, Sir. The tanks were fully discharged."

"How many?"

Long pause. "All of 'em, Sir."

"My. God."

"Aye, sir. All the fish an' all the eggs. Gone."

Feliks watched as Vasilij was taking the call. He sure didn't look too well with his face all battered and swollen like that. Still, the call didn't seem to require him to talk all that much, although towards the end he did go very pale and seem to have difficulty breathing. When he finally put the phone down, Feliks started to get to his feet to see if he could help and then faltered mid-stand as he felt the pain shoot up from his groin.

"You ok, Mr Krupchenko, Sir?"

Vasilij was silent, staring into the middle distance, motionless.

"You don't look too good, Sir."

His swollen face was growing darker and darker and Feliks thought he was starting to shake visibly.

"Would you like some more water?"

"WHAT?"

"Water, Sir?"

"Fuck … water!" He hurled his phone across the room. It thudded into the wall, took a big chunk out of the plasterwork and then fell to the polished tile floor with a dull crack. Feliks didn't dare move his head to look at it and just made a mental note: *No water.*

"Jelena?"

"Just outside, Sir."

"Bring … her … in."

"Yes, Sir."

When Feliks brought her back in she took one look at Vasilij and said to Feliks "Watch him. I'm going to get a nurse."

They let him sleep for a while after the nurse had given him a sedative and adjusted his drip. They sat,

217

silently, in the corridor outside his room. Jelena constantly checking her phone, Feliks occasionally adjusting his posture as his discomfort waxed and waned. Eventually they heard a muted roar from his room and tentatively opened the door.

Vasilij was now sitting up as best he could, he had his head down looking at the bedclothes, moving it from side to side agitatedly, like a caged bear. His colour had returned to a more normal shade and he was breathing more easily.

"Are you ok?" Jelena offered, clearly worried.

"NO! I'm not fucking OK! Do I LOOK OK to YOU?" She shook her head slowly.

"The nurse said you need to stay calm."

"I am calm. I am FUCKING calm, ok!"

"OK." She replied, face down, looking up at him through her fringe. Waiting.

"I am going to KILL them!"

"Who?"

"The. Whole. Fucking. Lot of them."

Feliks and Jelena stood, willing the other to ask Vasilij who *them* was. In the end it was unnecessary. Vasilij's power of speech had clearly returned and he was on a roll.

"The bastard who broke my face. That bastard Tony who … who I trusted to… do his FUCKING job! He has betrayed me."

Feliks seconded the first sentiment. That was the same bastard who's dog had snacked on his bollocks. Retribution was due.

"You!" Feliks looked up to see Vasilij pointing angrily at him.

"Sir?"

"Feliks. You are going to mind my CCS facility."

"Sir?" Feliks was unfamiliar with the abbreviation.

"The building site we keep visiting."

"Oh, yes, sir."

"You are going to go there and stay there and do everything you can to speed up completion of the site. Do you understand?"

"Sir."

"I want you to sit on Mackie, the construction manager, and any of the site managers and other foremen he has there and press and press them every day. I want that site up and running by the end of December. Do you hear me?"

"Yes, sir."

"Vasilij?" This was Jelena, wearing a confused frown. "Are you sure?"

"Of course I'm fucking sure! Don't you see? I am now minus a broodstock facility. My share price will plummet when this news gets out - and it will! I need some good news - great news - to balance it out as soon as I can." He was shaking with rage and muttering to himself. "The AGM is at the end of December. Maybe, just maybe, if I can show the CCS facility on line I can keep this under control."

"Also-" this to Feliks as Vasilij's mind whirled. "Defend it with your fucking life - if you value it."

"Sir?"

"Clearly Tony has decided to fuck me over. When I see him again I will find out why. In the meantime-"

"But, Vasilij, it is only a TV interview. It doesn't mean anything." Jelena again.

"Are you fucking stupid?" Jelena blanched in the teeth of his rage but he didn't notice. "Do you think a broodstock facility would just malfunction like that? Or perhaps you think that there is some other psycho out there going around damaging salmon premises? Hmm?"

"Well, I…"

"No. Obviously Tony is to blame and also, obviously, if he can damage one of my sites, he can damage another. So, Feliks?"

"Sir."

"While you are defending it with your life, you are going to find that fucker who hit me and you are going to bring him to me." *I'll bring what's left of him, after I've finished with him* thought Feliks. "Do you understand?"

"Yes, Sir." Feliks nodded obediently, hands behind his back.

"And you!" Vasilij pointed at Jelena and looked across at his damaged phone lying on the phone.

"Vasilij?"

"Get hold of Viktor. I want him to find that fucker Tony and bring him to me. I want to tear that fucker's tongue out and watch him smile then."

"Yes, Vasilij."

"And -"

"Yes?"

"Stop his money."

"Viktors?"

"NO! Tony's. The fucker is off my payroll."

"Yes, Vasilij."

"And Jelena?"

"Yes?"

"Get me discharged. I want to go home."

As the MV Clarissa May pulled into Port Bannatyne it was getting dark and Tony only had just finished cutting the cable ties that had secured the banners on the port and starboard sides of the boat. Roughly folded into a pile he dropped them on top of the placards stashed upside down in a large plastic tub and pushed them down so that everything was tightly wedged in. He pulled off his loose-fitting T-shirt and stuffed that into a black binliner along with those he had wrangled back off his volunteers and by the time they tied up he was ready to go.

"I'd like to thank you all very much for your assistance today." he shouted to the volunteers assembled in a huddle. "Please tell all your friends to watch the news bulletins tonight. I reckon we'll be on all channels at 6, 9 and 10. Good Job!" He started a round of applause which everyone joined in with, the odd hoop and holler thrown in for good measure.

They all disembarked in good spirits and shook hands with each other as they made their way over to the minibus which had brought them here. Tony gave the bus driver a wad of notes to be distributed equally amongst the volunteers once they were all on board, shook hands with him and waved them all away as the bus pulled off the hard standing and headed left towards Rothesay and the ferry back to the mainland. Within ten minutes of landing he was all alone at the door to his car with the binliner, tub and his own thoughts. *Good Job*, indeed, he thought. All the underhand work for Vasilij didn't give him the same satisfaction as this did - the adrenalin, the buzz, the thrill of making a public point and putting on a show for the media. He was looking forwards to watching the rolling news channels himself when he got back to the hotel.

He had to manoeuvre a few of the boxes and cases in his boot to make space for the tub and considered for a moment leaving it behind but decided he couldn't bear to. As he shoehorned the bin liner into the available space the bag split and a waft of Blysse's perfume from her discarded T-shirt came floating up to his nostrils. He smiled. She'd given the cameras an eyeful when she first put it on and, again, when she came to take it off so that she was dressed back in her full panto gear. There been an almighty scrum - and, Tony suspected, a private auction - amongst the crews to decide who got to give her a lift back on their boat to her pink limo waiting to whisk her back to Glasgow in time for the evening performance. He sighed and sniffed the fragrance again, feeling his Magnificent Mamba stir. He would definitely have to give her a call later and see if she was free to meet up, just the two of them.

He put the car in gear and pulled out onto the main road hoping to catch the same ferry as the minibus. He caught the queue of cars just as it was starting to load and didn't notice Kim in her hire car, pull out from a parking space across the main square from the terminal and join the queue a few cars behind him.

The reception at the Airport Hilton was busy and when Tony finally got to his room he took a shower, sat on the bed with a big white hotel towel wrapped around him and scrutinised the room service menu.

What he wasn't expecting was the knock at the door.

"Who is it?"

"It's the Duty Manager, Sir. You left your passport at reception."

The second Tony opened the latch, the door was thrust violently towards him and he was flung off his feet and some distance back into the room. He looked up to see the door closed and a man and a woman standing over him. The man was rangy and limbre, somewhere in his late forties Tony guessed, with uncombed curly hair and several days growth. He was wearing a green Berghaus waterproof and a don't-fuck-with-me expression. The woman was Kim.

"Get up." She said.

"What the- ?"

"Up." The man repeated for clarification.

Tony struggled to his feet, trying to think at light speed. By the time he was standing he had a plan.

"Kimchi! Hey, it's great to see you."

"Fuck off, cretin."

"Kim!" he pleaded.

"Don't you fucking *Kim-chi* me, you retard." She pushed him and he fell back, and she continued to push him using each thrust at his chest as punctuation, like a mother smacking a small child. "You. Lowlife. Twatfaced. Motherfucking. Turd."

He was up against the window now with nowhere left to go, the man standing right behind her. Kim now screaming spittle into his face, continued to thump him in the chest with the heel of her hands while he held his hands high in surrender and bounced off the windowsill like a boxer on the ropes.

"How fucking dare you? How dare you? You fucking scum-sucking -"

He tuned out and was suddenly watching the scene in slo-mo, the muscles in her face wobbling errily, her eyes flashing wildly and her hair flailing slowly as in anti-gravity. The muscle behind her remained expressionless while her rant dropped to a low drone, a baritone reverberating ever slower on a turntable running down. She slapped him across the face really hard and suddenly everything sped up again and he was back in the scene. He clutched his hand to the side of his face and howled with pain from his headwound the slap had reawoken. He bent down and away from her but she was intent on coming after him again, pleased now that she was actually causing him some pain. She was raising her hand to strike him again when the muscle stopped her arm with the back of his palm.

"Enough, Watson."

Watson? That wasn't her surname was it? Tony was confused.

She glanced bitterly at the man and then, deflatedly, lowered her arm and stood back giving Tony some space. "Your call, Holmes" and she sat down dejectedly on the bed.

The man stepped forward now and filled Tony's field of vision.

"I want your car keys and your wallet." He took a scrap of paper from his pocket and looked at it. "And I want you to repay this woman the £13,850 you took from her."

His cases were standing just inside the door and Holmes came back into the room one final time and rested Tony's overcoat and wellingtons neatly on top.

"Everything else is in the car." Holmes said to Kim who was still sitting calmly on the bed. Tony was sitting in the desk chair facing her not knowing how to start a conversation and unsure what was going to happen next.

"We're done here, Tony." Kim said, finally looked up into his face again.

"I-"

"Don't talk anymore." She interrupted. "You've said enough. I don't want to know why you did it. I don't care anymore. I'm done." There was a finality to her tone he couldn't mistake. She nodded to the man, Holmes, and then looked back at him.

"We just need to tie you up now and we'll be on our way."

"What?"

"We won't hurt you. God knows why." She flashed Holmes an angry look. "It's just a precaution."

"But, but, -"

"We'll leave you lying on the bed and someone will find you in the morning, safe and sound."

"But-"

"And if what you said about the Russian's money is true - and I have no reason to disbelieve you at this point - I will expect to see a deposit of the money you took from me, in my account by tomorrow lunchtime. I assume you'll have been found by then. Otherwise - " She looked across at Holmes who met her gaze and then turned meaningfully to Tony. "Otherwise, you will be found and you will be hurt."

"Badly." Added Holmes and together, they tied him up on the bed and left, closing the door with a soft click behind them.

15

Viktor picked the phone up on the fourth ring, having found it down the back of the sofa when it started to vibrate.

"Hello?"

"Viktor?"

"Yes. Jelena?"

"Yes. Where are you?"

"On the yacht."

"Oh. Ok, good. I have instructions from Vasilij."

Viktor sighed and puffed out his cheeks. He had not long recovered from his prolonged dip in the icy waters off Arran and his head still buzzed and rang like Brunhilde on horseback. Despite the past few days of self-medication on Vasilij's best cognac he still felt cold and would unaccountably shiver every now and again when his body decided.

"Viktor. He wants you to find Tony and bring him back." She sounded all husky and wanton over the phone, breathless and needy. Was it the cognac, he wondered?

"Jelena. I want you."

"He wants you to 'tear his tongue out and watch him smile then.' Unquote."

"Did you hear me?"

"Yes. I heard you."

"Well? I need you. I am in great pain."

"Why?" There was genuine concern in her tone. "What has happened?"

Viktor spoke quickly in Russian. He told her how he had been side-swiped by the helicopters carry hook and dumped into the Irish Sea to sink or swim, clung to a far cage side until the man with the gun had gone back to shore and climbed back onto the barge. He had stayed buried in its cabin until the next morning when he had regained the feeling in his hands and his teeth had stopped chattering only to have to brave the ice cold currents again in order to swim back to the shore and collapse crying in his car where he'd left it. All the while the only thing keeping him alive was the thought of her. The warmth of her projecting itself across the country into his bones and marrow, giving him a hunger that wouldn't leave and a will to keep himself alive only so he could feel her skin again. The breath of her hair, the sting of her touch, the warmth of her thighs.

"Enough!" Jelena slapped him down. "Enough, Viktor. Now is not the time for such talk. Now is the time for you to do what Vasilij asks."

Viktor stung by her rebuke, took another swig from the cognac decanter. "And if I refuse?"

Her tone changed in an instant from menace to breathy seduction. "You will not refuse because you know you want me. And because what Vasilij wants Vasilij gets... and what I want, I get. And you know I want you. So bring Tony to Vasilij and you and I can get what we both want."

Viktor shivered involuntarily, this time with pleasure.

"You persuade me."

"I knew I would." She purred.

Viktor felt himself growing hard to her voice. He reached for the cognac again. "Where do I find Tony?"

227

"Well now, here I have more good news for you." She paused for a beat or two, teasing him. "Vasilij installed a tracking app on Tony's phone before he gave it to him. If you install the same app on your phone, you can see where Tony is. I will send you a link."

Viktor was stunned. *You could do that?* "Why is tracker on phone?"

"Vasilij likes to be… in control."

"Hmm." Viktor considered this for a second, pondering whether there was any connotation here he should be personally concerned about, and decided he didn't give a shit. "Maybe I mess with Tony first, huh? What do you think?"

"Vasilij doesn't care what you do as long as you bring him here."

She hung up and Viktor found himself surging once again with desire for her. He took another swig of cognac, and dialed Tony's number.

Tony hadn't wanted to hang around at the hotel after the whole fuss they'd made. First the maid who found him had shrieked the place down in some dialect he couldn't understand - sounded like a cross between Polish and a Highland cow but what did he know? - and then the duty manager had called the police, despite Tony's protestations, and then the police had asked him questions and suggested he get himself to a hospital since his headwound was now bleeding again. Eventually they let him go, taking his phone number if they needed to contact him again, and he hadn't been able to get out of there quickly enough. Fuck the hospital, he thought, he needed to hide away, heal and think.

Checking out, walking through the lobby, he had felt as if all eyes were on him and all tongues wagging - *"He was tied up in his room you know...", "Some kind of sex thing gone wrong by all accounts...", "...took his stuff and left him to die, they say...".* He'd bundled himself straight into a cab and shot down the motorway a few miles to the city centre where he could be anonymous again.

Sitting in another hotel room, he listened to Viktor's voicemail. The stilted nonsensical patois that constituted Viktor's vocabulary did not really work over the phone. He sounded merely like an angry wasp in a tin can struggling to get out and hoping that excessive use of the word fuck would act like some magic key. He'd listened doggedly to the guttural grammar and discerned that (a) he - Tony - had fucked up big time and (b) that he - Viktor - was going to find him - Tony - and make sure that all functioning parts of his reproductive system would be something something something. He got the general idea.

He dabbed his wound with a damp towel and took some more painkillers. They didn't seem to be working.

What was the problem, he wondered? A little PR stunt - no more than a minor side project, already yesterday's news (literally, as Tony had been unable to find any clips of it on any news channels on the hotel TV). Why would Vasilij be so annoyed? Actually, not just annoyed: angry enough to send Viktor after him to do some damage. Exactly how much trouble was he now in and how worried should he actually be?

He sat on the bed and stared at the minibar.

Some time later, things did seem brighter because he'd had an idea. He'd been looking for one. An astonishingly good one was required and he distinctly remembered having found one. Just before he'd had a little drink and started talking to himself. Now, where was it?

- Have you seen it?

- *No.*

- Did I write it down somewhere?

- *No. No need. Mind like a steel…. thing.*

- No wait! Yes, that was it. I'm going to call Vasilij. Tell him to back off. Explain that it was all a silly misunderstanding. No harm meant, cetera.

- *Yeah.*

- And if he doesn't I'll call the cops. Tell 'em everything. Expose his little racket.

- *Yeah. Go for it.*

- Right.

- *Go on then. Pick up the phone. Make the call.*

- Er-, perhaps a another little drink first? Dutch thing?

- *Good idea.*

A female servant opened one of the double oak doors into the hallway at Yair House and Martin showed her his ID. The servant moved off into a side room and Martin heard a brief conversation and the sound of a handset being dropped back onto its cradle. He was ushered into a waiting room decorated in traditional Scottish baronial style: dark green walls, wooden shutters at the windows, tartan chairs and leather chesterfields, a large fire flaming in an even larger sandstone hearth - the chimney breast embossed with heraldic shields and a stags head. He scanned the side tables, shelves and mantelpiece for photos or personal effects - there were none. The bric-a-brac was anonymous and told him nothing about its owner other than the extent of his wallet.

A side door away to the left opened and a man stepped through it: smartly dressed in an expensive suit and tie, thick greying hair swept back from a proud forehead. He would have been handsome, Martin reckoned, if it hadn't been for the bruising, swelling and stitches to the left side of his face. Vasilij gave a half-smile - a look Martin assumed would have been a full smile were it not for his disfigurement, which he took to be temporary but *who knew?*

"Detective Inspector Jenkins." He said, shaking hands "Welcome. Please excuse my current -" he made a circular gesture around his face. "circumstances. The perils of being too hands-on with my salmon business, I'm afraid."

"Not serious, I hope Mr Krupchenko?"

"It looks bad, I know. But -" he shrugged, still smiling. "But in a few months time it will look like a duelling scar. A badge of honour. A dinner party anecdote. No more. Please, call me Vasilij."

"Did you get it duelling, Vasilij?" Martin raised an eyebrow and waited interestedly for his reply. Vasilij seemed annoyed with himself when he did so.

"No. A -" he chose his words carefully, Martin noticed. "A poor turn of phrase, perhaps. Nothing more." He held out an arm. "Please, come through to my office. It is more comfortable. Coffee or tea?"

"Tea please. Milk and sugar."

Vasilij led them through into a more intimate space, with fewer lairdly artifacts. A working room.

He poured a cup of tea from a pot, using a tea strainer, into a china cup resting on a dainty saucer, both bearing a paisley-type pattern somehow suspended in the porcelain. Martin took it and wandered slowly around the room.

Behind his desk was an extremely large corkboard holding a number of maps, coastal charts and graphs. Martin walked over to the map of Scotland, dotted with different coloured panel pins. "Are these your salmon sites?"

"Yes." He enjoyed showing off his empire, it was evident. "Blue are freshwater sites - hatcheries where we grow the fish from eggs. You can see we have a few of them scattered around. Red are the marine sites - where the salmon are taken when they have developed the ability to live in salt water. This is where the fish stay until we harvest them - we have lots of these all around the coast as you can see. The green sites are our processing facilities - where we process the fish and pack into finished products for sale."

"Brown?" he pointed to a pin up in the Orkney islands.

"HQ." He explained, humouring me now Martin thought.

"Right." He scanned the map and pointed to a pin in the heart of the Borders, not far from where they were right now in fact. "And what about this black one down here? It's not very near the sea."

"Um, research facility." He bristled and moved away from the map. "Still … under construction actually." He poured himself something into a brandy glass and used it to wash down a couple of tablets he had produced from his pocket. He caught Martin looking at him.

"For my duelling scar."

Martin gave a tight smile and then nodded towards the multiple monitors sitting on his desk.

"Nice to see someone who still clings to traditional methods whilst embracing new technology." He sipped his tea. "I'm not the only dinosaur left in Scotland then."

He was smiling but his eyes didn't seem know it. "I don't consider myself a dinosaur, Inspector. A control freak perhaps, but not a dinosaur."

"Your control-freakery seems to be have paid off for you, though. You have a lovely house."

"Thank you. I'm afraid, though, that I might have chosen the wrong line of business. A salmon farmer is never in control." He gave a rueful look. "If I were a sheep farmer or a pig farmer I could count my animals, vaccinate them against disease, take them indoors and keep them warm when the weather is foul. I could easily check on their growth and know when its best to take them to market. And they're contained on a farm - they can't be easily contaminated by other animals in the area unless they come into contact with them."

"My salmon, on the other hand, are in the water. And at sea, you are not in control." He started counting out on his fingers. "I can't see them and there are too many to count. I can put a device in the water which counts and measures them, but only if they swim through it - and I can't make them do that. If I take them out of the water to measure and count them I risk stressing them and stress can damage their muscle tone and affect the quality of the edible end product."

"I have no control over the marine environment: if the water is too cold the fish may not grow fast enough. If the water is too warm it can encourage growth of parasites or algae which can affect the fishes health. I can't do anything about the temperature and if my fish die because of any of these reasons I won't find out until I take them out of the water to harvest them - by which time it's too late."

"If I want to treat them, most times the only way to vaccinate them is to be take them out of the water one at a time and I can't prevent them being infected if some germ, bacteria or disease finds its way into the water system from somewhere many miles away. Or if a competitor's salmon farm across the loch from me decides to dump chemicals into the water to treat its fish and the chemicals disperse over to my farm due to prevailing winds or currents."

"If the weather is bad my staff can't travel out to the cages and check on the fish. Storms - and there are a lot of storms in Scotland, as you know - cause damage to cages and equipment and prevent the wellboats from collecting the fish for harvest. When everything goes to plan I have lots of healthy salmon and a bumper profit. When it doesn't I have a load of dead or sick fish that no-one will buy. As the Scots say, it is a mug's game."

Martin looked thoughtfully at him but, before he could think of any response, Vasilij continued.

"Inspector, salmon farming is like an act of faith. I exert what control I can to try and wrestle stability and success from the business. But, regrettably, it does not always work out that way."

This sounded a lot like a well-worn speech he had given many times before, Martin thought. But, nonetheless, one which he seemed wholeheartedly to believe in.

"Can technology not help improve your control?" he suggested.

"Perhaps. Perhaps not. Technology cannot always be... trusted. It is not always... secure. If I can see a fish, I know it's there. If I can put my finger on a chart I can know the place exists. If I see pixel on a screen..." he let the sentence go, pulling a doubtful face. "Can I get you another?" he nodded towards Martin's tea cup.

"No. Thanks all the same."

"Well, then. What brings you here, Inspector? To what do I owe the honour?"

"Mr. - Vasilij. You sound like someone in a TV cop show. I, uh, hope I don't look too much like Columbo."

"Not at all." He smiled and sat down again. "How can I help you?"

"I understand that there have been a number of incidents at salmon farming properties all over Scotland in the past few months."

"Yes, yes. I was aware of that. We may be competitors in the same industry but the salmon business is very... incestuous, for want of a better word. Everyone knows what everyone else is doing."

"Your business - " Martin consulted his notes. "Caledonian Seafood. Have any of your sites been affected?"

Vasilij felt his skin prickle. "Not so far." He lied, slowly. "We appear to be have been very fortunate in that regard." He chose his words carefully, even as they felt like bile in his throat. "Naturally, we are constantly vigilant and - in light of these events - we have increased our surveillance and security at our sites to try and make sure it stays that way." He scrutinised Martin more carefully, wondering if his lie would be detected. "I'm sure we're not the only company lucky enough to be unaffected though."

"Well, as a matter of fact - you are."

"Really?" It seemed a genuine response to the news, if not exactly showing genuine concern for his competitors. As if to confirm this, he smiled slowly to himself and then quickly dismissed it, pursing his lips in thought. "Do you suppose we are particularly at risk then? You've come to warn me, perhaps, that our turn is due?"

"Yes. But also to ask about your thoughts on the matter. I have spoken to some of your competitors - and intend to speak to them all eventually - and asked them the same question. Do you detect a pattern and are you aware of anyone who would want to damage the industry?"

"You are assuming these are all coordinated in some way?"

"Yes." Martin admitted. "It is an assumption - at this stage. But I think it is a fair assumption, given the pattern of events."

"Well, I am unfamiliar with the detail I must say, so am unaware of any pattern per se. As for likely culprits… well, the salmon industry has always had a fight on its hands - wherever it has set up shop. And Scotland is no different. No worse, no better, no different. There are environmentalists, ecologists, nimbies, animal rights people, countryside alliance people, nutters, old folk, marine biologists, fishermen, anglers… if you want to look for possible culprits, Inspector, you'd better get them to form a queue. It would be an awfully long one."

"I see."

"I don't expect I'm telling you anything you haven't heard already from other salmon businesses?"

"No. That is true." He sighed, put his notebook away, and stood to leave. "It is becoming something of a familiar litany. Annoyingly."

"I don't suppose these events could be unconnected?" he raised an eyebrow.

"You say this because…?"

"Well, when you've been in this business as long as I have, nothing catches you by surprise. There is an infinite line of mishaps which can occur at any time, all seemingly designed to eat into your profit or destroy your margin. Weather, disease, transportation failures, water temperatures, contamination, equipment failure, human error… it's another long list I'm afraid."

"Your point being?"

"My point being that it might be simply that they were individual accidents. Unrelated. Unfortunate, but unrelated."

"Everything happens for a reason, Vasilij."

"Perhaps." He mulled this over. "But sometimes the reason is someone made a mistake. Someone had an accident. Someone fucked up."

"Thank you for your time, Mr Krupchenko." Martin waited to be shown to the door.

"You're very welcome." They walked together back out through the drawing room and into the tiled hallway. Their footsteps echoed in this cavernous space. "Should you need to contact me again, please just let my assistant know. Jelena." He gave Martin his business card. "She will make sure my diary is cleared if that is at all possible."

"Thank you, Vasilij." Martin proffered his own card. "And if you should think of anything which might shed some light on these mysterious events - please: I'm never off duty."

"Never?" he grinned as they shook hands, Martin feeling his smoothness starting to curdle.

"Almost never."

"Shame."

Martin turned and walked carefully down the steps from the front door, feeling Vasilij's eyes on his back all the way to the car.

They drove back in convoy: Cullen in Tony's car and Kim following in the Focus. Kim's plan was to return the hire car and then take Tony's back to London with her where she would leave it in a long-term car park somewhere. The fucker could swing for it as far as she was concerned.

But it was late when they passed the Welcome To Peebles sign on the Edinburgh Road and Harrison's was closed for the night. She pulled up behind him on the other side of the road and Cullen got out to speak to her.

"What now?"

"Well, I guess we come back again in the morning."

"OK. Well, let's leave the cars here and go back to the bothy."

Kim's heart sank as she realised that she'd have to walk several miles across the hills in the dark back to the little hut and then back again in the morning to get here. She felt very, very tired all of a sudden.

"Really? Hiking's not really my thing, remember? How about we stay at a hotel in town for the night? My treat."

"Well...." He looked doubtful she could tell.

"Come on!" She gave him a mock-punch on the arm. "My way of saying Thanks? You've helped me when you didn't need to - we both know it. I couldn't have got this far without you. And it's dark, and it's cold - a little luxury as reward for services rendered?"

"I thought you had no money left?"

"Au contraire. Cash, yes. But plastic? It's fantastic."

He still looked doubtful but relented.

"OK." He thought for a moment. "You've got the Park Hotel or the Tontine. Or the Hydro, of course, if you don't mind being a little out of town."

"Which do you recommend?"

"Never stayed in any of them." He shrugged. "Tontine's the most central."

"Tontine it is" She declared. "Lead on MacDuff."

The next morning they had a late breakfast and she checked her account balance from the ATM across the street to find £13,850 had been newly deposited. *Well I'll be*, she thought. When they both drove their cars into the Harrison's Ford dealership and parked in the customer bays, Cullen got out and came over with the keys.

"Here you go. Good Luck."

"What? Where are you going?"

"Home."

"But -" She blurted as he raised an eyebrow. "I thought ..."

"What? What did you think?"

"I... well... I..." Her shoulders fell. "I don't know what I thought."

"Job done. One bad guy found, justice done. All monies returned." He smiled. "Another case closed by Holmes and Watson."

"I guess." She looked up at him, feeling suddenly small and empty. "I'm going to miss you."

"Really? What *odd* old me?"

She smiled gently. "Yeah, but you're a good *odd.*"

"Thanks. I think."

"What are you going to do? With yourself, I mean." She felt stumbling and awkward.

He looked up at the clear sky and took a big gulp of morning air. "I've got paths to walk and views to see. Be nice to get back to normal."

"Normal?" she snorted, then regretted it. She reached up, put one hand on his cheek to turn him towards her and kissed him on the mouth. "Thank you." He tasted sour and salty and she left her hand linger on his cheek a while longer before he pulled away.

"Plus, I still have some fish to fry."

"Fish?" she queried. "Oh, you mean your other *projects?*"

He smiled again, put a hand up to signal goodbye and turned to go.

"Wait!" she called to his back and he turned round. "Can I give you something? To say thank you?"

"You just did." And he was off, his open waterproof flapping as he strode down the pavement until it ended in a grassy verge and then continued on, around a long bend in the road off she knew not where. Kim watched him until he was out of sight and then she reluctantly turned down the slope to the service desk to return her car.

There was no-one at the desk when Kim walked in so she rang the bell and waited until a middle-aged woman, all birdlike and hesitant, appeared from the office.

"Can I help you?"

"Yes, please. I'm returning my hire car?"

"Ah, yes. Do you have your form?"

Kim handed the paperwork across and waited as the woman typed in her registration number, one finger at a time, with the air of someone attempting to defuse her first bomb. She clicked the mouse and waited. Then waited some more, smiling nervously at Kim. "It's cold out isn't it?"

"Yes." Said Kim, willing the woman to speed up.

"I'm sorry." She said after another pause. "I think there's a problem with our system. Would you mind? I'll just go and get someone who's a bit more familiar with it." And she shuffled off back into the office, hidden by a screen of vertical blinds.

After another minute or so, a more efficient-looking young man came out of the office and spoke to her.

"Can I take the keys please? I need to check the mileage on the vehicle. If you'll just take a seat, I'll sort this for you in a jiffy." She handed him the keys and walked over to the seating area where a breakfast news program was on TV. "There's coffee if you want it." The man shouted as he disappeared outside to the car, the automatic door making a wheesh sound as it slid open and then closed again.

She made herself a hot chocolate from the vending machine and sat watching the TV. After a few minutes she heard the sliding door wheesh again and looked up and a policeman came towards her, followed by the young man.

"Good morning, Miss. Are you the person who hired the Ford Focus being returned?"

"Erm, yes. What is this?" She looked at the PC and then the man, then back to the PC. Neither was giving anything away.

"I need to ask you to come with me please."

"What?"

"Miss, will you come with me please." The PC more insistent now. "To the station."

"What? I haven't done anything wrong. Is something wrong with the car?" She looked at the young man for clarification but he stood behind the PC now, looking at the ground.

"Miss? Will you come with me please?"

"What? No! I will not." Kim felt a rising panic in her throat and a flush to her face. "Not until you tell me what this is all about."

"I'm afraid if you don't come with me willingly, I will have to arrest you."

"Fine. Arrest me, then."

She was regretting this hastiness on her part even as she was being bundled into the back of the police car. She spent the short journey to the police station hopefully looking out of the window to see if she could catch sight of Cullen.

She didn't.

16

Martin hadn't actually read the paperwork yet and walking into the interview room, notes in hand, laid eyes on Kim and seconds later realised he was (a) obviously staring (b) working out how to get his mouth in gear and start the interview. In the end he needn't have bothered because she did the honours.

"My face is up here!"

Uh-oh, he thought. That's torn it. She was very pretty indeed. "Sorry. I was staring - "

"Oh yeah. You betcha!"

"Yes. As I said, I'm sorry."

"Do they send all the young men in to ogle the prisoners first thing then? Is this a new SOP?" She tilted her head to one side and glared at him like an angry bird, challenging him to respond. He cleared his throat and endeavoured to get the conversation back onto a more professional keel.

"Detective Inspector Jenkins. Border Policing Command." She seemed non-plussed - or unimpressed. Either way she remained silent and let him continue. "I'd like to ask you some questions if I may?" he pulled up a chair and sat down without waiting for her permission.

"What's this all about?" She shot forward and thrust her face closer to his across the table. "Why have I been arrested?"

"I believe because, well, you invited it." He flipped through the notes to confirm this and found himself gratefully slipping back into his calmer self. " *'Arrest me then.'* Were your words, I believe."

"Glad to see the police are so obliging when it comes to indulging the wishes of the general public" she snorted, sarcastically. "This some new policy is it? Policing for the 21st century: doing what the bloody public want?"

"Miss, er - " he checked the notes again. "Schofield. Perhaps we could dispense with the sarcasm and faux indignation? I mean, just for the time being? While I ask you some questions?"

She bristled. "It's Ms."

"Sorry, Ms Schofield." He corrected himself. "Would you like a glass of water?"

"No." She was still glaring at him. "Thank you."

"OK. Now, can you confirm that you were the person who hired this car." He showed her a photo of the Focus. "A Ford Focus, registration SN64 ANP. From Harrison's Car Hire on Monday of this week?"

"Can I ask you a question?"

"Ms. Schofield. Perhaps if I can ask my questions first - get those out of the way, if you like - then you could ask me your questions? How would that be?"

"How about if I ask all mine then you ask all yours?" she countered.

Martin sighed. This is going to be a long day, he thought. "What about if I ask one, then you ask one, then I ask one, then you ask one?"

"Oh, it's all gone a bit Silence Of The Lambs!" she smiled and then stopped, thinking better of it.

"If you must, yes." Martin replied. "Quid Pro Quo, Clarisse. Htth-htth-htth-htth-htth."

She burst out laughing at his Hannibal Lecter impression and Martin couldn't help but grin sheepishly and roll his eyes at her. She laughed a bit more. The ice, he realised delightedly, was broken.

"OK. Did you hire this car?"

"Yes."

"Why?"

"Because I... needed a car?" she did the internationally recognised facial expression for *Duh!* "Why the interest in the car? Is it stolen?"

"No. Funny you should say that, though. Because it was last seen leaving the underground car park of the Glasgow Airport Hilton two nights ago in the company of a green Subaru Impreza, registration YX14 HGS, which *was* stolen."

Suddenly she was all quiet. He continued. "The Impreza that belonged - sorry, belongs - to a Mr Anthony Stafford who was found tied up in his room in the very same hotel the following morning."

"Ah."

Martin almost did a double-take. He hadn't expected this. He'd assumed this was some administrative cock-up with an innocent explanation. One which would result in this beautiful woman walking free from here and into his open arms.

"Ah?"

"Yes." She sighed heavily. "I can explain. Kind of."

"I'm all ears." He folded his arms and waited.

Dogman, Dogman, fucking Dogman. I'm coming for you, you bastard. It was all Feliks could think about every time he bathed his groin - which was at least twice daily now. He pulled the discoloured lint away and looked at the mess between his thighs. The stitches showed black, like a trail of ants across his scrotum, amidst the purple-blue swelling and plum-scarlet red of the dried blood. At the hospital they had shaved his pubic hair in order to bathe and stitch the wound and at this particular time of day, when he had been driving all morning, sweating and cursing with every bump in the tarmac and every tight bend of the road, his crotch was sweaty and raw. If he could have brought himself to draw a face on it the overall effect would have been of a human punchbag that had gone twelve rounds with Mike Tyson.

He bathed and redressed his wound and threw the stained towel on the bathroom floor. He had had e-fucking-nough, officially, and someone else - one of Vasilij's flunkies on the boat, or Jelena, or Vasilij himself, anyone - he didn't care who cleaned it up but it wasn't going to be him. Who gives a shit, he thought. Focus. Focus on the Dogman. Sure, Vasilij wants him so that he can have his pound of flesh. Well, that's OK. That's fair. And he was Feliks' employer so he would do the job he was paid for. But if he happened to deliver the Dogman to Vasilij looking like a pile of broken bones held together by wet rags, Vasilij wouldn't care as long as the Dogman was breathing and Vasilij could be the one to deprive him of his last breath.

Feliks came up from below onto the main deck of the yacht and looked up at the sky. Snow was coming and the keen wind whipping in off the Clyde made it feel even bleaker. There was white sprinkled on the hills in the distance and Jelena, standing at the stern rail, was looking out at them.

"It's not Russia, is it?" she sighed, as she felt him approach.

"No. Godforsaken place, this country." Feliks stared out, unseeing, thinking of the Dogman. "I don't like it."

She watched him stare out across the hills for a moment. "How is your, erm, leg?"

"Aching." He glared down at her. "Aching for revenge. And it shall have it." He lifted his lapels and collar against the breeze and thrust his hands deep into his pockets. "I'm off."

"To the CCS?"

"Yes. Call me if *he* needs me."

She watched him down the gangplank, carrying his left leg slightly, gingerly until he was on dry land.

"Tell me again about this Cullen character. Who is he?"

Kim bit her lip and looked honestly at the dishy detective sitting across from her. "See, I know this sounds - well, odd. But I don't really know who he is."

"Is Cullen his first name or surname?"

"Don't know." She raised her hands, palm upwards in front of her.

"So how did you meet him?"

"I told you. Tony pushed me out of his car - his precious Subaru - in the middle of bloody nowhere. I staggered around in the dark until I saw a light. Walked towards it and found his house - with him in it."

"And he offered to help you find Tony?"

"Yep."

"Just like that?"

"Yep."

"A complete stranger?"

"Like I said: he's a bit… unusual. Lives on his own. Keeps himself to himself. Wears a leather cowboy hat." She brushed some loose hair back behind her ear with her hand and tried to throw the detective a meaningful look. He didn't catch it.

"I'll say." He was writing now, in his notebook. "So, where is he now. This Cullen."

"He went home."

"Where's home?"

"Well…" she grimaced.

"You've been there, remember? The light in the dark? You walked towards it?" It dawned on her, that it was entirely possible this policeman didn't believe what she was telling him.

"I know. But it's not his… only home."

"Oh, so he's a millionaire is he? Many homes? A millionaire philanthropist perhaps? Helps damsels in distress? Is he a playboy as well? You sure we're not talking about Tony Stark?"

"Ok, cut the sarcasm, Buster." She was angry but she didn't know what else to say. "He's kind of - an itinerant. Of No Fixed Abode, you might say. Spends a few nights here, a few nights there."

"A tramp?"

"No! Not at all." She felt strangely hurt that someone who didn't know him could dismiss him with such a derogatory thumbnail sketch. "He's … a good man. A kind man. Who helped me out. When I needed help." She missed him already. "And I wish he was here now."

"So do I, Ms Schofield." Agreed the detective, closing his notebook with a finality that worried her. "Because he's the only person who can corroborate your story and

248

if he was here now we'd hopefully be able to get to the truth."

"I've told you the truth."

"So you say."

"I have!"

"And I thought we were getting on so well." The dishy detective looked genuinely regretful.

So did I, thought Kim. *So did I.*

Tony woke and his head still hurt like a bastard. He took some more painkillers and washed it down with a Gordon's.

- What was I going to do?

- *Call someone?*

- That's it! Yes. Call someone. Who?

- *Someone you really, really need to speak to. Important. Vital.*

- Yes. Someone I've been meaning to call and haven't summoned up the courage to do it.

- *Exactly.*

- Who?

- *No idea.*

- Blysse!

- *Blysse?*

- Yes. Beautiful Blysse. I need to speak to her. Tell her how I feel. What a great team we were the other day. See if we she wants to say hello to Tommy the Tunnel Terrier.

- *You the man.*

- Oh yeah. Where's the phone?

- *Where you left it. In the ice bucket.*

- Shit.

- *You want another drink?*

\- Not in the mood.

- Not in the mood for a drink?

\- No, not in the mood for stupid questions.

"Who's Mr Holmes?" Martin asked.

"Sherlock Holmes?" Kim frowned.

"No. *Your* Mr Holmes. Mr Stafford said that the person who tied him up was a tall guy called Holmes."

"That was Cullen."

"Is that his name: Cullen Holmes?"

"No!" It was her turn to roll her eyes. "Actually I say *no*, but perhaps it is. I don't know what his full name is but I think it unlikely that it is Holmes."

"I see."

"No, I don't think you do see. It was a joke, ok? I called him Holmes and he called me Watson."

"Partners in crime." He seemed pleased with himself.

"No, not partners in crime." She leaned across into his face. "Although he did used to be a policeman."

"Who, Cullen?"

"That's what he said."

"When?"

"When I first met him."

"No, when did he used to be a policeman?"

"Oh, I don't know. Said he'd retired. A while ago I'd guess. Look, have you been listening to a word I've said?" She started counting fingers. "One: Tony threw me from a car and robbed me of fourteen grand. Two: I was lucky enough to find Cullen and he said he'd help me track Tony down. Three: We found out where Tony was. Four:-"

"Whoa! Hold up, there. How did you find out where Tony was?"

"Cullen suggested I not report the card stolen so that Tony could use it again and I checked the ATM transactions on my account and found out where the last one was."

Dishy D raised the other eyebrow and Kim found him fetching, once more. He looked at her, arms folded, for a while, saying nothing. She folded her own arms and looked back. He was handsome, smart, clean and smooth. Short blonde hair and honest, intelligent eyes with shimmering shards of ice scattered in the green. A few lines - worry lines, she guessed - creased around the eyes and forehead and he had a lovely, lilty burr of a voice: she couldn't place it but she was much taken by it. A thought occurred to her.

"What am I being charged with?"

"Charge? Nothing. Yet." He squinted while he thought. Cute. "Theft of a motor vehicle."

"I didn't take it. I was driving the Focus."

He ignored her. "Tying him up: could be kidnapping, unlawful restraint, false imprisonment - "

"God." She interrupted. "You sound just like him."

"Him? Cullen, you mean?"

"Yes."

"Hmm. Where's the car now?"

"Which car? Tony's?"

"Yes."

"Parked at The Tontine." She shrugged and then gave him a meaningful look. "Unless it's been… *stolen?*"

Dishy D stood up, and left her alone in the interview room.

Archie Mac was trying to dig out the frozen clods of earth from the caterpillar tracks on his digger when the big bald guy in the black 4x4 pulled up. *Uh oh,* he thought. The events of the previous week were still the talk of the area and Archie had had a ringside seat at the time and was now drinking out every night on the story, embellished and burnished into an anecdote he would bring out at future social fixtures. But he'd seen the real, ugly viciousness of the violence up close and had no desire to be ringside now without the protection of a firearm.

Or Big Paul. Or his dogs.

He watched the big man climb out of the car and anxiously scanned the distance between his digger and his van, wondering if he could make a run for it without being caught. He was a brick outhouse of a man, neck a mile wide, fists like loaves, but he was stepping delicately across the gouged snow and mud like Bambi at an ice rink.

Archie considered his position and decided to sit tight but he shook nervously as the man mountain approached. "Hullo." He ventured.

The man mountain came to a stop a few feet away and reared himself up to his full height, looking around as he did so. "I am looking for the Dogman."

"Sorry?"

"I am looking for the Dogman." Archie frowned authentically and the man understood and decided to clarify. "Man with dogs. The Dogman."

"Ah, man with dogs." Archie nodded in what he hoped showed understanding without recognition. "Sorry, I don't know him."

252

"You know him?"

"No, I said I don't know him."

"You know him." The man mountain was insistent and Archie's apprehension grew. "You talk to him. I see you talk to him."

Archie racked his brains as to where he had been when he'd last spoken to Big Paul and the effort must have told on his face as the man mountain came to his aid: "You talk with him before the fight. Over there." And he pointed to where the pair of them had been standing that day.

"Ah. Yes. I mean, No. I mean Yes, I was talking to him but I don't know him." Archie was aware he was jabbering a bit with the relief. "He was just asking about a job, y'ken?"

"A job?"

"Aye. A job. Here, on the site?" Archie indicated around him.

"What job he want?"

"Well, he's a joiner see?"

"Joiner?" The foreign accent was having some trouble with the word.

"Yeah. Joiner." Archie considered what would be the internationally recognised sign for joinery, couldn't think of one and so ended up miming sawing a piece of wood, adding a noise that sounded a bit like a donkey for good measure, before falling back on the British default of repetition in the face of incomprehension. "Joiner? You know, carpenter?"

The stranger showed no sign of understanding but seemed to dismiss this as unnecessary detail and took another tack. "Where I find carpenter?"

"Yellow pages?"

The man mountain's patience was thin. He snatched at Archie's throat and pulled him upwards until Archie was standing on tiptoe with his nose inches from the bulky forehead and bloodshot eyes of this angry monster. His sour breath enveloped him and Archie turned his head to one side to try and avoid it. The man mountain shook him by the throat until they faced each other again.

"Where I find Dogman carpenter?"

"I don't know!"

"You tell me where he is." The giant squeezed harder and Archie started to feel faint. "You tell me now."

"He... he... walks his dogs near here."

"Where?"

"Near... by." Archie was passing out. "Diff'rent... spots."

"When?"

"Nhnh."

"When?" The man mountain shook Archie as fiercely and violently as he could but it was no good, the little man had gone all limp and Feliks flung him to the ground in disgust. He turned and stalked carefully back to his car while Archie lay still, his pulse slow and faint, with his face smashed into the icy ground.

"You're in luck." Martin explained as he walked into the interview room. "Your boyfriend has decided not to press charges."

"Ex-boyfriend."

"Whatever. You're free to go."

"Finally." Kim looked relieved even as she tried to hide it with her sarcasm. "I was starting to get a little tired of this place. You know, the service is terrible!"

He ignored her. "Sign here, please." He thrust a form in front of her and indicated with his finger. "And here."

She looked at the form and then up at him. "Is this to get the return of my things?"

"Yes." He took the signed form from her. "And don't think of leaving the immediate area just yet."

"What? But I want to go home - back to England, at any rate." She complained.

"Well you have just agreed to abide by these terms as part of your release." She looked at him in horror but he simply smiled at her. "The large print giveth, and the small print taketh away."

"Fine." She snapped. "I'm sure The Tontine will be pleased to have my business for another… what, few days?"

"That should do." he nodded and then goaded her. "I hope The Tontine doesn't mind a suspected criminal under their roof."

"I am NOT a criminal." She put her hands on her hips. "I am thirty-four years old and I have never been in trouble with the police in my entire life."

"Until now." She threw him a disgusted glance and he goaded her again. Something about her meant he couldn't resist. "If a man builds a thousand bridges and fucks just one goat, they won't call him a bridge builder they'll call him a goatfucker."

"Charming." She replied, but she seemed to take his point.

Martin attempted to lighten the mood and at least part on good terms. "Come on, take a few days here in the

Borders. It's a nice part of the world, and it's a nice time of year. People getting ready for Christmas, the promise of snow in the air. Market stalls on the High Street selling mulled wine and mince pies. Relax and enjoy it, before going back to whatever constitutes your usual nine-to-five mundanity."

"Yeah." She seemed reluctant to be brought around. "I'm not really in a socialising, celebrating mood. Need I remind you that I have just, somewhat unexpectedly, found myself ejected - physically, literally and financially - from a relationship I thought had legs." She started to tear up. "I thought maybe this could be it, you know? Now I'm just embarrassed, dejected and not thinking pleasant thoughts." She looked up at him, eyes wet. "I just want to go home and hide myself away. I feel as if everyone looks at me and knows."

He bent down and put an arm around her shoulders. "Come on, be a tourist for a couple of days. Relax. Have fun. I'm sure you've had fun before? So do it again. It's easy. Like riding a bike."

"Yeah, except the bike is on fire. And I'm on fire. And everything else is on fire."

He stood up again, crossed his arms and smiled good-naturedly. "Come on. Why don't you let me buy you lunch or something, hmm?"

She dried her eyes and tried on a lop-sided smile. It suited her and attracted him. "OK." She sighed. "But I'm telling you right now that I'm not going to be good company."

"Why don't you let me be the judge of that?"

Blysse answered on the ninth ring.

"Tony, is that you?"

"Yep." He poured himself a whisky. The glass and bottle audibly clinked.

"Do you know what time it is?"

"Nope."

"It's either very very late or very very early."

"Sorry. Had to dry my phone out before I could charge it."

"What?"

"Ne' mind."

"It's three in the morning!"

"Well, why'd ya ask me if you already knew? Ha!"

"Are you ok?"

"Nope."

"Tony?"

"Yep."

"Can you please stop saying either *Yep* or *Nope*?"

"Er. Yep."

"Tony!"

"Ow, fuck! Did you need to scream at me like that?"

"Apparently I did, yes. What do you want?"

"I love you."

"Tony, have you been drinking?" *Stupid broad, of course he'd been drinking. He was shit-faced, what did that matter?*

"I love you, Blysse. Amanda. I mean Blysse. I've always loved you. I never stopped loving you." Tony had a type of eloquence which only worked when he got the right amount of drunk. To be specific, that amount was: *fucking*. "How about we meet up and play Cindy Anna Jones: Womb Raider?"

"Tony. Go back to bed. It's late and you're drunk."

"It's not late if you're a night owl. I thought you showbiz types were night owls?"

"Ordinarily, I guess. But I have a late night tomorrow so I don't want to be up all night tonight."

"Hmph. Whatcha doin' tomorrow?"

"If you must know I've been invited to a party."

"Whoo! Can I come?"

"It's invitation only. For celebrities."

"Ooooh." A descending cadence.

"On a yacht."

"Ooooh." A rising cadence. *Wait a minute.* "Who do you know who has a yacht?"

"A Russian millionaire, actually. A *multi*-millionaire."

Fear and adrenalin are the two things which can immediately sober up the human body given the right conditions. Tony instantly felt a cold jolt of adrenalin course through his chest and was suddenly completely alert. He shivered and tried to moisten his mouth which was incredibly dry all of a sudden.

"That wouldn't be Vasilij Krupchenko, would it?" he was panicking now, fingers crossed.

"Yes. How did you know? Do you know him?"

"Erm, kind of. Yes." All of a sudden, Tony wanted to end the call.

"Wow! Could you introduce me? Will you be there?"

"Erm, maybe. Yeah."

"Cool! Ok, look I don't mean to be rude Tony, but it is awfully late. How about we both get some shuteye and I'll see you tomorrow at the party?"

"Erm, yeah. OK."

"'Night then."

"Yeah. 'Night."

Oh shit.

17

Viktor was sitting in his car on the outskirts of Glasgow wondering why the tracker app had stopped working. It had been working yesterday - for a while - and he'd seen Tony whereabouts flashing in Glasgow city centre. He'd driven across from Largs towards the capital and then, en route, for some unknown reason the app had said "No signal found."

He had the window slightly open to allow the thick smoke from his Turkish cigarettes to escape from the cabin and the heater on full blast to compensate for the chill leaking in as a consequence. The result was a heaving fug inside the car, heavy with the stench of stale sweat, tobacco and several day old breath. Viktor knew a bath was in order but consoled himself with the vision of taking it in the company of Jelena once he returned Tony to his boss.

He was lost in a daydream, picturing Jelena naked in a vast circular bath full of milky water while he wondered whether to call her and tell her that he couldn't complete his mission because of this technical difficulty. Then he imagined Vasilij's response.

He flicked his cigarette out of the window and tried the app one final time, almost crying out in relief when the map on screen changed to show a light green circle heading almost directly towards him. Never at ease with technology he looked askance at the screen and waited as the circle moved slowly southward and past him. It carried on travelling down a main road so Viktor put his car in gear and followed the signal.

Tony had woken with an almighty hangover and swore to not drink ever again. He showered and dressed, had breakfast in the half-empty dining room and then checked out. At some point last night he had received a text from the police informing him that his car was at Peebles Police Station whenever he wanted to come and pick it up. Tony had no idea where Peebles was so asked the concierge who told him a cabbie would charge him about £80 to get there and it would take around an hour.

He did a quick mental calculation: he needed to pick up his car, get back here, get ready for Vasilij's party and get over there before it started and somehow inveigle himself aboard. Maybe all he had to do was find Viktor or Vasilij and explain this little misunderstanding. They'd let him on no problem, he felt sure.

The ride down to Peebles was uneventful and when he arrived at the Police Station he had only to fill out a form and show them his passport as photo id. They gave him the keys and led him out to a row of parking bays over against the court building with which the police station shared the same grounds. He checked the boot, glove compartment and all the cubbies to see what Kim had left him with. He had a travelling suitcase with a few changes of clothes, a set of waterproofs, his scuba gear and wetsuit, two pilot cases filled with his maps, charts, assorted papers and notes and a small metal cashbox containing a few hundred pounds in cash, a spare credit card and his locker key. He had to hand it to Kim, she hadn't taken anything she didn't need or wasn't owed.

He put the contents of the cashbox in his wallet and drove out of the car park looking for signs for Glasgow. He had three quarters of a tank of fuel and it was not quite 11 o'clock. Plenty of time. He found a classic rock station on the radio, cranked it up, and accelerated the Impreza out onto the A72. Despite the snow on the ground the road had been recently cleared and he reckoned he would make good time. He didn't notice the silver BMW following some distance behind him.

Tony saw the straight stretch ahead and the road markings which indicated a speed camera. In his rear view mirror he could see a large silver BMW speeding blithely up behind him, apparently intent on overtaking while he had the chance and unaware of the camera. It shot towards him and started to pass but when it was level with him, the two cars straddling the full width of the road, it slowed and kept pace with him. For a few seconds Tony thought this was some kind of parallax illusion but was rudely disturbed from this view when the BMW swerved in towards him and scraped along the side of his car.

Tony wrestled with the steering wheel as the car bucked and swerved, skidding on snow off the roadside, its back end swinging wildly. He threw the wheel left and then right as the white scenery blurred past in his peripheral vision and realised had heard the expression "steering into the skid" many times, thought he knew what it meant, and understood now that he really didn't. He risked a glance to his right to look at the BMW driver and found he was looking straight at the angry black eyes of Viktor.

"Viktor!" He screamed through his window, the surprise and shock now rapidly transmuting into rage.

Viktor responded by swinging the wheel again and the BMW bashed once more into the side of his car, pushing him left and onto the kerb, The wheels scraped against the stone and then swung up off the kerb as the nose of the car rose up and Tony felt his car sway and start to tilt. The steering wheel was doing nothing now and he watched in slow motion as the car left the road, now travelling at what felt like a 45 degree angle to the horizontal, smashed through a wooden fence and down a short bank, and crunched to a stop in a snow-covered field.

Tony's face had smashed against the pillar when his car ploughed through the fence, and was battered again by two airbags when the car thudded to a halt. His seat juddered forwards as the dashboard shot backwards to meet him. His left knee smashed against the steering column, his right knee impaled itself on something sharp - he couldn't see what it was but he imagined, in a weird moment of detachment and piercing clarity, that it must be his keys hanging from the ignition.

The world stopped spinning and the slow-mo suddenly sped up to become normality again. From somewhere he felt the cold breath of the outdoors as his door was opened and white daylight flooded in, only to be followed by a large swollen fist. All the cold and white suddenly became warm and black.

Viktor carried Tony's limp body over to his car and dropped it casually on the ground. Tony's face was bleeding from his nose and there was a deep cut on his head somewhere in his hairline. He had lost a shoe and he had a set of bloody keys sticking out from just below his right kneecap. Viktor opened the boot, looked quickly around to see if any cars had appeared at either end of this long straight stretch. Seeing none, he picked up Tony's body, dumped it unceremoniously in the boot and shut the lid. Surveying the scene quickly, he could see that the broken fence and abandoned Subaru were hidden from the road by the steep bank and all there was to see were some skid marks in the snow.

Satisfied, Viktor climbed in and drove off at speed. By the time a few more cars and lorries had passed this way there would be nothing to mark this spot as special at all.

"What's in this?"

"Ham." Martin looked across at her, a single eyebrow raised. "And pickle. Homemade."

Kim nearly burst out laughing and, thinking better of it at the last minute, reduce it to a laugh-cum-snort which she hoped came across as delightful. "You make your own pickle?"

"Of course." He seemed crestfallen. "I mean, if you don't like it…"

"No. No, it's really nice. I do like it. Honestly." She smiled apologetically. "I just… dunno. Didn't think the Old Bill made their own pickle."

"I make a lot of things." He took a deep breath, as if about to blow his own trumpet. "Pickle. Jam. Pies. Bacon. Sausages. Pate. Even tried to make my own haggis once."

"Really?"

"Aye. Didn't work out." He smiled ruefully. "But my other stuff? I think it's pretty good. I know my pork pies are good. I've given them to friends and they've all commented favourably."

"They've all commented favourably?" She mimicked. "Not exactly the Richard & Judy Book Club is it? I mean: *I read this book and I look on it favourably?*"

He didn't take offence, to her relief, but continued to chew on his own sandwich and look out at the landscape. She realised she might have to wind her neck back in if she wasn't going to push him away. This man, Dishy D, as she still thought of him, was a genuinely nice, caring man. Intelligent, thoughtful, considerate and bloody good-looking, let's not deny it. She wondered, not for the first time, what he was like in bed. Then realised he was talking again and she hadn't been paying attention.

"… nice isn't it? I mean, I come up here quite a lot, so perhaps I'm biased."

"Yes." She was being honest. "It is very pretty."

"Pretty?"

"Well, you said nice."

"I said *really* nice."

"Once again, you with your ringing endorsements. Hello, is that the Michelin Guide To The Borders? Yes, could you please alter my entry to read *really* nice? Thanks. Bye!" She mimed putting the phone down and realised she was winding him up it again.

"I think it's just… right, you know?" He looked at her and since her face was now clearly expressing doubt he ploughed on. "I mean, the Highlands are all very well and that, but there's just too much grandeur, you know? Towering granite and endless lochs. It's alright if you like that sort of thing but this is more… understated. Gentler, less in-your-face. And, I think, all the nicer for it."

"More green-and-pleasant-land, you mean?"

He shot her a look of disdain. "No, that's England, I think you'll find."

"Oh. Sorry."

She finished her sandwich and stood up, brushing the crumbs from her lap. They were sitting on a small rocky outcrop near the top of a hill, bounded on two sides by forest, giving a quite impressive view out over several sets of hills all sweeping away into the distance. The rocks had protected them from the wind and when she stood she felt the chill gusts brush her face and quickly sat down again.

"Have you always lived here?"

"Mostly. I grew up on Orkney - my parents are still there - but since going to University and then joining the police I've lived here or hereabouts." He rummaged in his pack, brought out an apple and offered it to her. "'Course since I spend most of my time all over the bloody place I'm not here that often. But I always get a nice warm feeling of coming home when I drive round a bend and get the first glimpse of hills and woodland stretching out before me." He looked like a little boy, recalling his childhood. "Doesn't matter what the weather is, it always looks like home."

"That's nice." She bit into the apple which was cold and sweet. "And country pursuits? Does an interest in them go with the territory?"

"Hunting shooting fishing, you mean?"

"Well, yeah."

"Hunting and shooting - no. Not a big fan of firearms. Fishing? Well, there's a fine line between fishing and standing on the river bank looking like an idiot."

"I don't really get the country. My folks are from down South and I've always lived there or in or around London. I guess I was a country child - all rolling fields and Black Beauty - but I never missed it when I moved to London. The city was just too exciting, too whizz-bang-blink-and-you've-missed-it." She offered the half-eaten apple back to him and he took it. "There's something about feeling that you're at the centre of everything - where it's at. There's nowhere like London, I think." She nodded at him and smiled. "Town mouse and country mouse."

"I'll drink to that." He took a swig from a water bottle.

"Cheers." And she followed suit. "Still, having the right company helps."

"Why Miss Schofield." He fluttered an imaginary fan in front of his face. "I feel perhaps you are flattering me with your intentions."

"Ms." She stuck her tongue out at him. "And I am having a nice time - despite the cold - and, where I come from, its considered normal and polite to share your feelings when you're enjoying yourself."

"Well, where I come from it's considered either emotionally incontinent or crawly-bum-licky." He made a thoughtful moue and then raised his imaginary fan again. "But 'twould be uncharitable of me were I not to return the compliment and concur that I too am enjoying your company on this occasion."

"Only on this occasion?"

"I fear -" he started to continue his Austen impression and then thought better of it. "That's not what I meant. Poor choice of words, sorry."

She picked up his Austen fan and fluttered it animatedly. "Why Mr Darcy, I do declare! An honest emotion expressed so boldly."

They were both standing now and he jokingly half-punched her arm.

"Come on." She said. "These hills won't climb themselves you know."

"I though you said you didn't get the country?"

Vasilij adjusted his bow tie in the mirror and looked at his battered face. The swelling had subsided a little but the major improvements in his appearance had been effected by Jelena with a truckload of foundation and blusher. She had patiently stroked and daubed his cheek, forehead and eye socket and half an hour later when she had given him a mirror he was immensely impressed and flattered at the job she'd done.

"You are a marvel, Jelena." He looked, he thought, like an actor just coming off stage - perhaps having been in Phantom Of The Opera. There was clearly disfigurement under the pancake but you would struggle to work out what it was and, in the dim evening light, it could pass largely unnoticed unless anyone spent time with him. He had plans only to spend time with one particular person tonight and he hoped she wouldn't notice the makeup - or wouldn't mind if she did notice.

He threw down a couple of painkillers and made his way from his dressing room up onto the main deck area at the rear of his yacht. An expensive arrangement of delicate lighting wreathed around the large marquee area with overhead heaters carefully masked by swathes of silk and chiffon in bold colours that swooped and bowed gracefully across and along the roofline. The main lounge which gave out onto the rear deck had been cleared of furniture and arranged into a socialising space with a long set of tables down the entire left side, already being filled with platters of food that the caterers had been working on since yesterday. His sound system had been co-opted by a string quartet who were currently tuning up and rehearsing while miked up. Later they would be replaced by a pre-recorded and mixed set of disco music for anyone wishing to dance once the evening was well underway. As far as Vasilij was concerned he would have retired downstairs by then with Blysse and the party goers could dance themselves silly if they wanted to.

Nervous and wanting to keep his mind occupied, he checked the guest list - again - and conferred with Viktor regarding the weather forecast and tide timings. Feeling like a teenager on a first date, he looked out over the marina with its bobbing masts and lamplit walkways and waited for Blysse to arrive.

18

Tony woke to find himself sitting fastened to a hard chair. His hands were secured tightly behind his back and his ankles were similarly tied to the chair legs. His head hurt, his ribs hurt and his right knee *really* hurt. His tongue could sense the metallic taste of blood in his mouth but it didn't feel as if he had lost any teeth.

Yet.

He could tell by the gentle movement of the floor beneath his feet that he was on a boat and judging by the opulence of the decor he figured he was on board Vasilij's yacht. He made a half-hearted attempt to test the ropes holding him but twisting and jerking didn't produce any movement or slack that he could detect so he abandoned the idea and looked around the room for inspiration.

The door opened and Viktor walked in, grinning when he saw that Tony was awake. Tony thought he could hear violin music wafting through the door.

"Hello my friend. Remember me? Your red russki retard, hmm?"

Viktor was in an expensive suit, silk shirt in the palest blue and even a handkerchief in his breast pocket. His hair was slick and shiny, tied in a neat pony tail and Tony couldn't be sure but it looked like he'd had a manicure. He'd recently shaved and the only mark detracting from the entire ensemble was a large sticking plaster covering a wound of some kind on his right temple. Even to Tony's eyes, he could see that Viktor looked the business with his athletic build and olive good looks. He looked like *Crocket and Tubbs*.

"Wow, Viktor." Tony commented through gritted teeth. "Very, uh, metrosexual."

Viktor smiled but his eyes glowed crazy. "You like?"

Tony almost expected him to give a twirl as he strode into the room. But he didn't.

"It's a good look, Viktor. Suits you."

"Jelena. She like."

"Jelena?" They're eyes met and a brief conversation went unsaid. "I see."

Tony tried to draw his head back as Viktor leant forward and thrust his face close into him. Viktor grabbed his cheeks between his thumb and forefinger on one hairy hand and twisted Tony's head round so they were looking into each other's eyes.

"You feel pain?" Viktor squinted, searching Tony's left eye then right in quick succession. "Hmm? You are hurting?"

Tony tried to nod with his face still held in Viktor's grip.

"You are lucky." Viktor continued. "Very lucky man." He pulled back from Tony and let go of his face. Tony continued watching him silently, listening to him gloating. "My orders: bring Tony to me, says Vasilij. I want hurt you. Kill you. But Vasilij, he must have his way."

There was a bang at the door and a moment later a man and a woman bundled noisily into the study, the woman's blouse half undone, the pair of them giggling and carrying drinks. At first they didn't see Viktor but when they saw Tony tied to the chair they started and then saw Viktor glaring at them menacingly.

"Sorry." The man held a hand up, nervously. "Wrong room."

The couple retreated: the woman still giggling, the man trying to shush her as they left hurriedly.

Viktor turned back to Tony. "Is party. On boat, tonight." He said, by way of an explanation. "When party is over, Vasilij will come." He leered. "Maybe then *you* be over."

"But why?"

"He very unhappy man." Viktor shook his head, sadly, looking at Tony with big cow eyes. "You know why."

"No."

"No?"

Viktor squinted and from nowhere he suddenly had a knife in his hand, winking and glittering in the rooms low lighting. He played it down the side of Tony's face, tracing the contours of his cheek and chin, descending to his neck. Viktor pushed it in a millimetre at his adams apple and Tony felt a ragged burning in his throat and tried desperately not to swallow.

"You make big mistake." Viktor sneered, teeth glinting. "You pay big price."

"I... didn't... do anything."

"You kill many fish." Viktor's breath sour on his face.

"I... was... supposed... to." Tony felt his Adam's apple exploding in his throat. "We... all... were."

"Not Vasilij fish." Viktor wagged a finger in his face.

"I didn't... kill.. Vasilij's... fish."

"You did. And Vasilij want you to pay."

"Wait... wait..." Tony was flailing, trying to think. "How ... I... kill his fish?"

271

Viktor paused and his eyes looked away to the right, thinking. Eventually, as if realising it for the first time, Viktor said: "I don't know."

"You're… mad. You're… all… mad!" This didn't make any sense. Viktor tilted his head and looked into Tony's eyes, searching for something. Eventually he pulled the knife away and hid it inside his jacket.

"Wait! If you don't know what I did, how did you find me?"

"I track your phone." He smiled a winner's smile. "Jelena, she show me."

Viktor moved to towards the door. "Goodbye, Tony." And he left, closing the door quietly behind him.

By the time Blysse stepped onto the yacht Vasilij had already drunk a considerable amount of champagne. Notwithstanding this, however, when she appeared shimmering through the wall of people like an Aphrodite in aquamarine he had to stop himself from standing there with his mouth wide open. She had pinned her hair up at the back and wore it in tumbling ringlets at the front and sides, exposing a lithe tanned neck and emphasising her sculpted cheekbones and delicate chin. Her open, white greek sandals had elegant heels and long tendrils which wound up her leg to mid-calf where they were tied in a bow. Her dress, such as it was, ruffled in the slight wind coming off the sea. Layers of chiffon and mist rippled and bloomed like a tropical lagoon. She came towards him, led by Jelena, and he felt his insides turn to air and scatter in the cold night.

"Blysse Baptiste, may I introduce you to our host, Vasilij Krupchenko."

Vasilij was caught momentarily frozen. When she put out her hand towards him he pounced upon it and lifted it, unexpectedly, to his lips.

"Miss Baptiste. You cannot know how much I have been looking forward to meeting you."

"Gee!" she responded with genuine enthusiasm. "I am delighted to be here. This is just too much!" She leaned in to speak into his ear and he caught a delicious waft of scent and hair. He was without doubt captivated. "I'm used to scuzzy Hollywood types and this…" she gestured, looking all around her. "This is just so sophisticated. So… European!" she squealed and squeezed his hand. Vasilij almost came.

"Please. May I call you Blysse?" She nodded. "And you must call me Vasilij."

"Vasilij, you have a most beautiful boat."

She thought he seemed very nervous and wondered if it was because of the makeup he'd daubed on his face, presumably to cover some birthmark or duelling scar - *oh, those dashing Russians!*

"Perhaps I could show you round?"

"That would be great, thank you." She looked around again. "Now, where could I get some champagne?"

"So, what do you actually do?"

"Hmm?"

"For your job?"

Kim tossed her hair back and laughed. "I'm in Marketing. I don't actually *do* anything, silly!"

"But what is Marketing? I mean, you must do something."

She put down her cutlery and looked at him earnestly. "Well, I organise events: conferences, seminars, and so forth. I manage advertising and PR campaigns, keep our website up-to-date and work with our web design company to keep it fresh and on the first page of search results, where poss. Plus general dogsbody work that no-one else will do: company newsletter, corporate charity events, fun-runs, Christmas party, works nights out, blah blah blah."

"So…" he seemed forced back in his chair by the stream of words hitting him. "You *do* do stuff then. Lots of it, by the sound of it."

"Yes." She picked up her knife and fork and started eating again. "So, not just a pretty face, then."

"I'm sorry. I didn't mean… the way I asked. Sorry." He was genuinely apologetic, dropping his eyes to his plate as he sliced his steak.

"It's OK." She relaxed. "I can come on a bit strong, I know. It doesn't take much to yank my chain. I'm sorry, ok?"

She'd been enjoying the meal - this, well, date almost, and somehow she'd allowed his naive questions to get under her skin. They ate for a while in an awkward silence. When his dessert arrived, she immediately regretted not ordering one herself.

"Can I try some of your tart?"

"Why didn't you order one yourself?"

"I don't want a whole one."

"Well, I do."

Worried now that she was ruining the mood, she changed tack.

"Do you enjoy being a policeman?"

"I'm a Detective."

"Now who's being prickly?"

"Sorry, I'm not being prickly. There is a difference you know?"

"I know. I've seen Morse and The Bill."

"No. You don't know." Now it was his turn to put down his knife and fork. "I'm also a Small Ports Officer."

"That sounds like a euphemism."

"I wish it was. What it is, instead, is a pain in the arse - excuse my French."

She pulled the wine bottle from the cooler and hovered it over his glass. "More tea vicar?"

"Thanks." He took a sip and then looked at her gently, his irritation fading. "You know, I like you. You're funny."

"Oh, way to go kid. Nothing like complimenting a woman on her sense of humour to get into her good books."

"Would you rather I said I like you because you're not funny?"

"No." She thought for a moment. "I'd rather you said you liked me because I was the most beautiful woman you'd ever seen. Or because I make you feel complete. You know, some bollocks like that."

"Really?"

"Yes, bozo. Women want to feel special, want to feel beautiful. What they don't want is to be told they've got nice tits. Or a nice ass. Or a nice sense of humour."

"I didn't say you had nice tits."

"You don't think I've got nice tits?" She pushed them out straining the buttons on her blouse.

275

He looked down at her chest deliberately, long enough for her to feel uncomfortable with her own joke, before speaking.

"I think you have very nice tits." He spoke calmly and smoothly. "But that's not why I like you. Well - it doesn't do any harm. I like you because you're edgy and vibrant and funny and … it makes me open up to you." He looked right into her eyes.

"Fucking hell." she said softly, and felt herself redden. "Well, that went from 0 to 60 pretty damn fast."

After twenty minutes of sweating and swearing, his arms bleeding where the ropes chafed and his ankles crying out for relief, Tony had managed to free one hand and rocked himself in the chair around to the other side of the large oak desk. Another exhausting twenty minutes and he had extended a desk drawer out as far as it would go but couldn't crane his neck round enough to see its contents. He rocked himself one more time and tried to twist but all that happened was that the chair knocked against the drawer at a funny angle and dangled tantalisingly from the desk. The strange combination of movement sent him off-balance and he screamed a silent N-o-o-o! as the chair toppled to the floor and his body let out an involuntary *oof* as his chest hit the carpet.

The force and vibration of his landing was the additional assistance required to cause the drawer to finally dislodge and as it too fell, it tumbled spilling its contents on top of Tony. A knife landed blade down in his left buttock. Before he could bite his tongue from the pain, the butt of an automatic pistol smacked him on the forehead and started his headwound bleeding again.

He managed to reach the handle of the knife with his free right hand and so, with adrenalin flooding his system keeping the worst of the pain at bay, he removed the knife and roughly sawed away at his bonds until he was able to pull his left hand away, his wrist weeping and raw from the ropes.

He lay still on the floor for a long time, feeling the sensation returning to his fingers and arms, letting his breathing return to something like normal while still constrained by the ropes around his chest. When he felt sufficiently calm, he cut through the ropes remaining and lay foetally on the floor for another ten minutes sucking air into his chest and letting the blood flow back into his feet and ankles. When he was finally able to stand and survey the scene he could see a bloody outline on the carpet which looked like a Rorschach of an ultrasound scan taken at twelve weeks.

He did a quick check on his condition - he was bleeding in several places: his old head wound, his new buttock wound and his knee looked like someone had attacked it with a knife and fork. However, he had been, only a few hours earlier, in a position that any sane person would have officially categorised as *fucked*. Through resourcefulness and an appetite for pain he hadn't realised he possessed he had now managed to de-fuck the situation. What he must make sure of now, was that he didn't un-defuck it. He wasn't out of the woods yet - or off the boat, same thing - but he had a knife and he had a gun. But he was in a locked room, somewhere out to sea, and at some point in the next few hours Vasilij was going to come in here and shoot him dead. What he needed now, was a plan.

When Jelena's phone rang she was leaning forward at the rail looking out to sea while Viktor thrust into her. The chain of her purse clanked against the rail and she almost fumbled it into the water as he rocked her back and forth.

"Viktor!" she pushed back suddenly but this seemed only to elicit heightened groaning so she left it at that and manhandled her phone to her ear with one hand as best she could.

"Hello?"

"Jelena." It was Vasilij. "Would you be able to mingle with the guests in my absence, maybe re-engage the musicians for a while? I would like to go below with Blysse."

She wondered whether "go below" was a euphemism and decided it didn't matter much either way, the end result would be the same. She grunted as Viktor's thrusting became shorter and more violent, her own breath now getting more ragged.

"Are you alright?" Vasilij asked. "It sounds like you're in the gym! Doing weights - at this time?"

"No. No. No." She moved the handset away from her mouth briefly to try and gather herself. "Viktor's just… uh… helping me in the stern."

"OK. Well, can you please mingle for me when you've finished? I may be … a while."

"Yes. Certainly, Vasilij." She bit her lip. "I'll be coming very shortly."

While he was thinking up a plan, Tony fascinated himself by watching the little vignettes which the two large desktop monitors were displaying of the various goings on around the ship. The desk was dominated by these screens, each displaying four separate monochrome CCTV images. On one screen he could see a large ballroom with a lot of people all milling about, in twos and threes, engaged in small talk and chatter, all dressed in tuxedos or ball gowns, with one or two exceptions. To the left of that was a view of a luxurious bedroom and then another room with two sofas, both rooms empty and quiet. In the fourth was another bedroom with what looked suspiciously like the couple who had gatecrashed his and Viktor's little soiree earlier. Now they were in various states of undress,

The second screen showed a view of the rear of the yacht, a seating area and deck shaded by a large canvas awning. Alongside that, the bridge, showing two T-shirted crew members having an arm wrestling contest while a third was watching a porn film on a portable TV. And out on another smaller deck area, a man in a suit was fondling the exposed breasts of a dark-haired woman and pumping her from behind while she was nonchalantly looking out to sea as if nothing unremarkable were happening at all. He couldn't be entirely sure but it looked like the man was Viktor.

He sat and watched, entranced, forgetting about his circumstances as the tiny figures moved in and out of shot on the different cameras. Into the room, now, at the bottom left - one which had been empty the entire time - came a distinguished looking figure wearing a white tuxedo and holding a large brandy glass. There was something about the way he held it that Tony recognised but he couldn't place it and the man's face didn't look familiar. The man walked further into the room, closer to the camera and was followed by a beautiful blonde in a short Tinkerbell-style dress - Blysse. The man turned to face her and the camera at the same time and Tony recognised Vasilij. Although something had happened to his face - it seemed frozen, swollen, plastic. Riveted and appalled at the same time, he watched as they moved about the room, talking. Eventually the man sat down on one of the sofas and signalled to the woman to sit next to him.

Vasilij stroked her face and moved to kiss her and Tony sat and watched as Blysse responded and the anger built inside him. As the pair grew more amorous Tony realised he was gripping the knife in his hand tightly and unconsciously carving lines and shapes into the polished surface of the desk with it. By the time she had her head in his lap while he struggled with her bra strap, Tony could bear it no longer. With a silent fury he dropped the knife, grabbed hold of the pistol, pointed it at one wall full of books and pulled the trigger. There was a click and a small flame sprang up out of the end.

He was holding a fucking cigar lighter.

"What the fuck is this?" demanded Vasilij.

The door to his study was hanging open and the door jamb had been clumsily splintered and hacked at with something sharp. Inside there was disarray: an overturned chair, an emptied desk drawer, books littered the floor and some discarded rope lay beside his cigar lighter. In the centre of the desk, standing proud - as it were - was a huge, human turd. Sticking prominently out of this, leaning slightly, was a white iPhone.

"What the fuck is THIS?" Vasilij's repetition remained rhetorical but Viktor flinched nonetheless, knowing this wasn't going to end well for him whether he answered or not.

"Where is Tony?"

Viktor stayed silent while Vasilij thumped both fists on the desk and then leant on it, arms far apart, glaring up at him beneath his heavy brow.

"Where. Is. Tony?" Viktor looked on dumbly. "You said he was here."

"Looks like he escape." Viktor shrugged.

"Escaped?" Vasilij sneered. "Come here."

Viktor hesitated and then slowly paced towards Vasilij watching him carefully. Vasilij stood waiting. Viktor edged closer and closer until they were standing across the desk from each other.

"Give me your knife."

Viktor slowly reached into his jacket and brought out a large hunting knife with a worn-smooth bone handle. He handed it to Vasilij, holding the blade as he did so. Vasilij took it with his right hand and swung it high over his head, grabbing Viktor's hand with his left and smearing it into the turd on the centre of the desk, as his right arm fell and skewered Viktor's hand to the desk in one smooth movement. A muscle in Viktor's cheek twitched but his dead black eyes stared straight ahead and he stayed silent.

Vasilij pulled the knife out, smeared it over Viktor's hand and handed it back to him. "Bring me Tony."

Viktor looked at his bleeding, shit-stained hand and flexed his fingers to test his range of movement. His hand hurt like hell and he tried not to wince in front of Vasilij. He nodded to the discarded phone.

"How can I find him if he has left this?"

"I don't fucking CARE! Bring me Tony, or it will be your face in the shit with my knife through it."

Viktor lowered his eyes, turned and walked out of the room pausing only to mutter under his breath "*My* knife."

PART 3

Do what you can

19

"Good morning."

"Hnh?" Kim felt something warm on her shoulder and opened her eyes a tiny amount. The warm thing smelt good and she closed her eyes again, enjoying her sleep.

"Wakey wakey, eggs & bakey." The voice again, low but insistent, and the warm thing rocking her now, gently urging her to open her eyes. She smelt bacon suddenly, and fresh coffee and the warm smell of *him* and she opened her eyes slowly. "Breakfast?"

"Awww." She stretched delightedly and saw his face, all white teeth and stubble and tousled blonde hair, about six inches from her own. "You're a keeper."

"Well, yes. On a scale of one to ten, to some people I'm only a two, but to others I'm a solid three." He planted a bed tray down over her legs. "Eggs, bacon, orange juice, croissants and coffee. In bed." He climbed in next to her. "Don't move."

"Why, what have you got in mind?" she giggled coyly.

"No, I mean: don't move, you'll spill the breakfast."

"Oh" she tried not to sound too disappointed and raised herself delicately up to a sitting position while he tinkered with clinking cups and a cafetiere. "Sugar?"

"I'm sweet enough."

"Milk?"

"Please."

"Help yourself to er, whatever you like really. Knock yourself out." He grabbed a plate and started piling bacon onto it. "I'm starving."

She looked around for a clock but couldn't see one. "What time is it?"

"Why, have you got to be somewhere?"

"No. I don't." She realised and then snuggled down into the bed in recognition of the fact. "And if I did, I think I'd rather miss it and stay here a while - if that's OK."

"Fine with me. Although, when did you suddenly start asking me for permission?"

"What do you mean?" she buttered a bit of croissant and put it in her mouth. "Mmmm. I can do demure."

"Hmm, perhaps. But I think you're better when you have a bit of spunk in you."

She coughed out her mouthful and caught it in a napkin, looking him archly in the eye. "Well, we know who to thank for that this morning, don't we?"

"That's not quite what I meant" he said, although he started laughing too.

They ate quietly for a while and then his voice dropped a register, all serious now.

"Are you ok? This morning, I mean?"

"Yes?" she raised an eyebrow quizzically.

"Are *we* ok, I mean?"

"Oh, Mr. Dishy D." She said, snuggling into his chest. "I think we're very *very* ok this morning. What about you?"

"Mister Dishy Dee?"

"Yes. That's your pet name, didn't you know?" She moved the tray over and lay it down on the floor beside the bed.

"Uh, what if I don't like it?"

She traced a finger through the curls of his chest hair. "Tough toenails, Buster. My choice, not yours."

"Right. Spunky. Forgot for a moment there."

"Listen Mr. Dishy D. You want spunky? I'll show you spunky. Come here!" And she threw herself head first under the duvet.

"Mmm, yeah Mand - I mean, Blysse."

Tony was nuzzling her neck and swimming in her perfumed hair. He was working on her bra strap without success and the swelling in his pants was becoming unbearable.

"Tony, you're not listening!"

"I am. Try me. Ok? Tell me and I'll repeat it back to you, ok? Word for frickin' word. Ad verbosum… infinitum"

"What?"

"Never mind. Just tell me, ok?"

"OK. My plan is you and me run away and live happily ever after, living a life of riches and leisure."

"Sounds like an excellent plan, Blyssy-boo."

"And Step 1 is I get married to Vasilij."

He pulled back in alarm and sat staring at her as she wrestled her bra back to a comfortable state.

"Whoa! What about you and me? You just said -"

"That's Step 4."

"You mean Step 2?"

"No, Step 4. Step 2 is we kill Vasilij."

"WHAT?"

"Shhhh."

"What?"

"We kill Vasilij. I get married, live with him a short while, then we do him in. I inherit his money - that's Step 3 - and then you and I can be together with all his money. Step 4!"

"Hmmm. How long is a short while?"

"Huh?"

"You live with him for a short while? How long is a short while?"

"I don't know. Not long. Just long enough not to arouse suspicion."

"But what about you and me?"

"Well, we can still see each other, baby."

"Yes, but you'll be … doing it. With him. You'll be entertaining his Bishop With The Bright Red Hat while my Blind Cave Salamander …"

"But I won't be enjoying it." She interrupted.

"That. Is not. The point."

"Look, he's only going to be attracted to me because of the way I look. And these looks won't last for ever, Tony. I gotta start where I am, use what I have, do what I can. Arthur Ashe said that!"

"Arthur who?"

"Ashe."

"The tennis player?"

"Yes."

"Why the fuck you quoting a tennis player at me? Is that supposed to persuade me? You sure you don't wanna quote from Arthur Ashe the brilliant philosopher instead? Or Arthur Ashe the Nobel-winning rocket scientist?"

"Tony! It's a fucking plan, isn't it? You gotta better one?"

Silence and then a sulky: "No."

288

"Right then. Let's go with the plan!"

"But you'll be … fiddling with his Fat Finger."

"This is your problem? This? Not the fact that we've somehow got to kill a guy and not get caught?"

"I assumed you had worked that out as well."

"Hell no. I don't know how we're gonna do it."

"What! … Well, why are you calling it a fucking plan, then? It's a bit light on, you know, detail."

"Well, I thought I'd be able to leave that detail to you."

"Wow. Thanks a lot. You're banging his brains out and I'm left trying to work out how not to get life for Murder One."

"I won't be banging his brains out." She paused. "Unless you think that's a good way to knock him off?"

"No!"

"Right. Well, you work on that - Step 2. I'll work on Step 1."

"But, you and him…" Whiny now, not attractive.

"Tony. Baby, listen. Don't dwell on it. It doesn't mean anything." She rummaged for an analogy. "Think of me as a pre-owned Ferrari, huh? You know you're not the first but, really, do you care?

She mussed his hair and held him close, issuing whispered assurances and rocking him gently on the sofa. He nuzzled her again and she took his right hand and led it between her legs.

Alone in his hotel room, he woke with a thud as he fell off the bed. He had ejaculated in his pants during the dream.

Again.

Wrestling with an enormous spreadsheet, dispersed over the entirety of his two large desktop screens, Vasilij couldn't quite decide whether he should be laughing or crying.

On the upside, he had managed to corner the Christmas market in Scottish salmon due to the success of his sabotage campaign at competitors sites. The situation was changing all the time, and the salmon price had never been this volatile, but undoubtedly he was making huge money hand over fist and would continue to do so in the next week or two until the market demand was sated and he would be able to take stock.

He picked up the Business Section and re-read the article:

Scottish Salmon prices leap past 50 NOK/Kg

Spot and forward prices for Scottish Salmon spiked today as the markets reacted to adverse news of supply in the lead up to Christmas and Q1 & 2 supplies for next year. Only last Easter, salmon was trading at 30 NOK/kg but the traditional rise in Q3 & 4 has seen it shoot past the 40 mark and keep going.

According to Fish Pool, the start of next year will see prices averaging higher still and volume customers with contracts up for renegotiation early next year are going to find the going extremely tough.

However, it is the conventional Scottish "premium" which has also come in for some significant movement. Traditionally, Scottish salmon is priced around 3-5 NOK higher than the Norwegian spot price but as of now this premium has leapt to more than 8 NOK and is threatening to hit 10. Analysts say that this is primarily due to the news coming in from the main Scottish salmon farmers of large

---

> *reductions in volumes due to disease and other - unspecified - operational farming losses. There are also rumours in the run up to the end of Q4, when all the major companies will declare their result, of smaller than average fish sizes which will also put upwards pressure on the per kilo price for larger fish sizes. If this is the case it will mean further price pressures for the newly resurgent US market where customers traditionally prefer large fish.*
> **STOP PRESS:** *See related story, p11.*

He may have to wait until all the companies figures were in next year before he could gauge the true financial extent of his competitors losses but here was a pretty good indication of the scale. So far, so good.

On the downside, his farm managers were reporting some impact of the infections intended for his competitors. He had expected as much - you couldn't completely protect your own sites from lice or other disaster spread through the water, after all.

His major concern was for the impact on his loss of broodstock which, while it wouldn't hit his harvest volumes for the next year, would have a dramatic impact on his company's valuation (and hence his own personal shareholding) if the news became public knowledge. His difficulty: how to acquire the eggs he would now need for the next two generations of adult salmon without it becoming plain that someone was buying up surplus egg production (if, indeed, there was any) and that someone was him.

Better start preparing for the AGM statement, he thought. He unconsciously stroked his eye socket in what was now becoming a nervous habit. This slight touch made him wince so he took a couple of painkillers before turning to page 11 to find out what the breaking story was. As he read it, his face fell.

Caledonian Seafoods: whistleblower claims brood stock disaster for west coast firm

A confidential source at Caledonian Seafoods, a leading Scottish salmon farming company, claimed yesterday that there has been a massive loss of salmon at the company's dedicated broodstock hatchery on the west coast of Scotland.

Only recently purchased from one its main competitors, the facility was capable of hatching ten million salmon eggs annually and over the course of two years, this would normally be converted into 50-60,000 tonnes of high quality salmon to be turned into much-sought after Scottish smoked salmon, mainly for export.

If the allegations are true it could mean an almost complete wipeout for salmon production in the company for the next two years, since eggs from other sources will be difficult to source at this stage in the lifecycle and may not conform to the company's stringent technical and biological standards.

With their annual report due in early January, all attention will now turn to the AGM scheduled for December 31st to determine the scale of the impact this will have on future revenues. Shares in Caledonian Seafoods closed 8% lower on the news yesterday. A spokesman for Caledonian Seafoods was unavailable for comment.

"She's a fine looking woman." Martin said, down the phone.

"Yes, so I believe." Chief Inspector Maxwell waited for him to get to the point. He knew there would be one. Martin just liked to work his way up to it, scattering sarcastic remarks as he went - like chaff to disorient the anti-aircraft fire of your attention.

"Great big... tracts of land."

"I'm sure. Look, Martin." Maxwell swept on, impatiently. "This theatre manager keeps ringing me up, complaining about unwanted fan attention after this PR stunt she pulled. He's a friend of the Assistant Chief Constable. There's no pleasing some people. I wonder if he'd call me up if she wasn't pulling in the audiences."

"Yes, and while I am honoured to be asked to keep, ahem, abreast of her movements. I can't help feeling that it is both unnecessary and a waste of what I would like to think is a valuable BPC resource. Namely: moi."

"I quite agree."

This rocked Martin back on his heels a little. "You do?"

"Yes." Maxwell sighed. "Look. Delegate. Get some PC to stand at the stage door after each performance. Keep order. It's not some kind of stakeout."

"Hmm."

"Listen, if she's so stacked, surely you'll be fighting volunteers off for this duty with a shitty stick won't you?"

Maxwell hung up just as one of the PC's walked into the room.

"Inspector?"

"Yeah." Martin sighed and pushed his head back, stretching his neck against the back of his chair. He'd had his feet up on the desk and now he had pins and needles. He swung his legs down from the desk and rotated his feet to get some feeling back in them as he looked at the PC.

"That Subaru Impreza? With the number plate? You asked me to keep an eye out for it?"

"Do all your sentences have to be questions?" Martin grumbled.

"What do you mean?"

"Never mind." He picked himself up and walked over to the coffee machine. "What about it?"

"It was picked up a speed camera on the A72 this afternoon."

"Ooh. Our Tony's a naughty boy isn't he?" He looked at the PC. "Wilkins?"

"Yes, sarge."

"Wilkins, it is not illegal to break the speed limit. Well, actually, ok, it is." Damn he needed a coffee. "What I mean is, he'll get a letter. And a fine. And points on his license." He poured some coffee into a dirty mug and tasted it, pulling a face. "Fucking hell, who made this?" The PC waited obediently for Martin to resume. "Look, let me tell you a story: once upon a time I didn't give a shit. The end."

He looked at the PC who seemed crestfallen, realised he was being a bastard due to coffee withdrawal, sighed and attempted to make amends. "What I mean is, if he was caught speeding then it's not really a matter for us is it? It's not an *arrestable* offence."

"He wasn't caught speeding."

"I thought you just said he'd been picked up by a speed camera?"

"Yes, but he wasn't speeding."

Martin looked at the PC askance. "So why did his car have its picture taken by a speed camera?"

"Because it was run off the road by a car that *was* speeding."

"What?"

Along Glenrath Heights was Big Paul's favourite part of the loop. He didn't do it often - at somewhere around 16 miles all told, he couldn't afford the time to - but once in a while he would stride out from Peebles along the Old Drove Road and up Birkscairn Hill, and keep going across Dun Rig, and Glenrath Heights, before looping round to Stob Law and Hundleshope Heights and back down to Peebles.

His dogs loved it too. It wasn't something you would do in the winter unless you knew your way. The hills here had a habit of getting tangled up in fog and snow - bad weather blowing in as if from nowhere while down below it could be a beautiful winter's day - so tracks would disappear and you'd be left wandering, lost and exposed, hoping the weather cleared or some other lunatic would come wandering by.

And today, wouldn't you know it, was just such a day when the fog and snow left the hilltops hidden. But Big Paul knew his way so he didn't need the assistance of the fellow lunatic walking slowly up from Horse Hope Hill. Walking slowly. With a limp.

Penn & Teller were some way off, sniffing after some animal or other, scuttering across towards one of the many piles of stones that littered the hilltops. Big Paul was about to call them back before they went too far when something about the approaching lunatic rang an alarm bell in his head. The bulk of the man, and the limp, and the menacing intent all said: Feliks, the bodyguard.

Except today, he didn't look like a bodyguard - he looked like two.

Big Paul was immediately alert but, this time, it wouldn't do any good. He was tall and heavy and had plenty of heft, strength and stamina. What he didn't have was agility, sheer gripping power and an upper torso like a elephant seal.

Feliks did. Many years ago, Feliks had been a professional wrestler, winning titles and starring in TV commercials along with the likes of Hulk Hogan and The Rock. His sheer bulk combined with his astonishing muscle mass meant he was a formidable opponent and he had been spotted by talent scouts for what was then the WWF who would regularly tour the eastern European and Asian circuses and strongman circuits, looking for *the next big thing*. For a while, Feliks had been the next big thing - Boris "The Spider" Beshanovski had been his WWF name - a huge Russian (Boris being the universally recognised name in America for Russian men) with a trademark move: the Spider, where Feliks would arch over his opponent and pin him to the floor, wrapping his arms and legs around his opponents torso and crushing the life out of him.

On a lonely white hilltop, 700m above sea level and hidden by cloud and snow flurries, his dogs too distant to hail, it was an uneven match, swiftly resolved.

Feliks came towards him and dispensed with the pleasantries, immediately using his technique to good effect. He grabbed Paul by his collar and twisted him right and down as if he was driftwood, using the momentum of his bodyweight to hoist Paul over before he could grab anything to hold on to. Paul threw a punch in the direction of Feliks's face but it glanced off his shoulder as he was spun around and met with a knee in the gut as he crumpled to the ground.

He tried to lift himself up but Feliks was on him like a shot, his full weight and strength pressing down in a Spider move.

"Not so clever now, eh Dogman?" Feliks breath heavy in his ear.

"Get... off... me... you... fucker." Big Paul was already struggling for breath, Feliks' weight pressing down on his ribcage making it hard to talk.

"You give me great pain last time. Now, is your turn." He punched Big Paul in the kidneys with one hand, a blow like a concrete hammer. "You keep away from me. You keep away from the site." Feliks was pressing his elbow into the back of Paul's neck, pushing his face into the snow and threatening to snap his neck with the force of it. "You understand? Keep away from me. Keep away from site. Grown up work. No children allowed."

There was one final thrust from somewhere up above him and Paul felt himself sliding down, down, down. The wet blackness, somehow cold and warm at the same time, opening up and swallowing him whole.

The wind whipped up Martin's coat as he stepped from the car onto the hillside. The site was busy with workmen everywhere. A chainlink fence was being erected around the site, beginning and ending at the portakabin which seemed to serve as some kind of entrance/reception. Martin walked over, leaning into the wind, knocked brusquely and entered without waiting, climbing two steps up into the warmth as he did so. The office was hot and heavy with cigarette smoke and the smell of BO.

"Can I help you?" A balding, middle-aged man stood from behind a desk cluttered with dirty mugs holding down plans and blueprints. On the walls were schematics, a year planner containing various coloured symbols and a calendar from a Builders Merchants showing a topless brunette in a hard hat and an open hi-viz tabard leaning provocatively on a cement mixer.

"Detective Inspector Jenkins, Border Policing Command." Martin showed his badge but the man looked unimpressed. "You in charge here?"

"I am the construction manager, yes. George Mackie."

"Mr Mackie, we've had reports of a number of unconfirmed incidents at this site and -"

"What sort of incidents?"

"Unconfirmed incidents." Martin continued, not taking kindly to being interrupted. "Which I am duty bound to investigate."

The site manager shrugged. "No idea. Don't know nothing about any *incidents*." He emphasised the word as if he suspected it of having been smuggled into his baggage at the airport.

"There's been a large man asking around? Big fella, bodybuilder type. Heavy foreign accent?"

"Mister, -"

"Inspector. Please." He smiled coldly.

"Half the bloody workforce here are Poles an' that. Barely speak the language, mind, and all built like brick shithouses y'ken."

Martin looked around at the portakabin office then stooped to look out of the window onto the snow-splattered building site. "Mind if I take a look around?" he said, grabbing a hard hat from a hook on the wall.

"No. Help yourself." Mackie turned back to his desk and immediately forgot about him.

Martin stalked out into the cold and walked over to a large building frame with a roof and three walls of corrugated metal being bolted to it. The sound of electric screwdrivers, drills and nail guns volleyed around the hillside and once he was inside the building the sound was worse, gunshots echoing off the metal walls. Against the far wall were two men in yellow surveying a large chart they held between them. He walked over to them, glad at least to be out of the wind, and flashed his ID at them.

"I understand there've been a few disturbances on the site lately?"

"Like what?" asked the greyer of the two. He had a small, wizened face with snaggly yellow teeth. His partner was the more rotund of the pair and wore glasses with thin silver frames, a tuft of brown curly hair poking out from under his hard hat.

"You mean the thing with the dogs?" his partner added, earning a dig in the ribs from the grey one.

"Dogs?"

"Aye, weren't nothin'" said the grey one. "Bloke was out walking his dogs, touting round looking for work apparently and some visitor riled one of the animals, got bit for 'is pains."

"Visitor?" Martin prodded. "You get many of them up here then?"

"Mebbe." The grey one pondered. "More'n you'd expect I reckon. There 'us the one who got bit -"

"And the big guy, askin' round." Added his mate, all keen to chip in.

"Aye, and the bugger wi' the cowboy hat."

"Cowboy hat?"

"Aye. Tall guy, wore a leather cowboy hat. - looked like someone out of High Plains Drifter" the other added, and they both laughed.

Martin was suddenly all ears. "What can you tell me about him?"

When Paul came to, the snow was falling again. It hurt to breathe - he felt blood in his mouth and possibly a cracked rib or two - and he could see his fingers were starting to turn blue with cold. He nursed himself to his feet, standing bent over and straightening himself gently as he assessed the damage. Getting his bearings, he turned to head for home and suddenly heard a low keening moan, long and painful, growing into a rushing, echoing roar. It was coming from him.

Lying beside him were the torn bloody remains of Penn, his tongue still lolling from his severed head. Teller was a few yards further away, entrails strewn over the ground in a bloody smear, a knife buried to the hilt in his neck. Paul knelt to the ground and wept like a child, his huge frame racked by sobs as he gulped air and howled in grief over the remains of his beloved pets.

20

For Kim, normal service had been resumed. She was back in London and Martin was up in wherever the hell part of Scotland it was this nano-second, and all she had was a nightly call when they were both curled up in bed. When he had a signal. If he had a signal. She wasn't happy with this as a working arrangement *at all*.

Val had told her she was worrying over nothing. It was all perfectly normal something something something. She had found a lovely man. True, she had. And said lovely man was showing true affection and keeping in touch when he could. True, he was. *But it wasn't enough!* Val sympathised - up to a point.

"Kim, it's called real life."

"Is it buggery-chuff, real life."

"Yes, Kim, it is."

"Well not for me, Buster!"

"Look." Val persisted. "There are two types of people in the world, ok? Left-brained people and right-brained people, right? Left-brained people are logical, analytical, evidence-seeking; right-brained people are imaginative, focussed on feelings, non-rational -"

"Typical left-brained comment." Kim snorted.

"Look, the point I'm trying to make is that you're not being rational about this. If you were a bloke you'd call it *thinking with your dick!*"

"But I like his dick!"

"Christ, where's Groucho Marx when you need him!" Val looked to the ceiling.

"Er, sorry. Whoosh!" Kim sliced one hand over the top of her head.

"Hmm, OK. Probably before your time. Groucho Marx used to host a quiz show and one time he had this woman contestant on who had eleven children or something. When he asked her why she had eleven children she said 'because I love my husband'. Quick as a flash he said: *Well I love my cigar, but I take it out my mouth once in a while.*"

Kim scowled at her and mimed picking up a phone. "Hello, is that the Samaritans? Do you have a vacancy for a sympathy and support councillor? You do? Excellent. One moment please."

The phone rang again now and she looked at the clock. 10:55pm. It was Martin.

"Hey, Dishy D."

"Hey you. How're things?"

"Lonely."

"Same here."

"Lonely, wet and cold."

"Ditto."

She snuggled down into her quilt and tried to hold the phone closer. "Where are you tonight, Mr Intrepid Traveller?"

"Today I've been back near Peebles. Tomorrow, Largs."

"Peebles! Our old stomping ground."

"Indeed. And of your old friend with the cowboy hat."

"Cullen?"

"The very same. Seems I may get to meet him yet."

"How is he? What's he up to?"

"Well, that I don't know. But there is a plot thickening here that I just can't get my brain round."

"Ooh, let me help! We can be … Mulder & Scully."

"I may be unable to work out what's going on, but I'm pretty sure there's no aliens involved."

"Ok, then. Well, Cagney & Lacey."

"They were both women."

"Oh, right. Well, never mind that. Come on, share with the group!"

"Well, OK. Not sure where to start, really, though."

"Just start at the very beginning." Kim sang. "It's a very good place to start."

"Right, ok, Julie Andrews." Martin took a deep breath. "So, we have… *one*: a number of separate incidents, all destructive, at a number of salmon farming businesses around the country that have been taking place over the last month or so. *Two*: some of these incidents have occurred at some kind of secret salmon site being built outside Peebles - "

"Ooh, secret site."

"- one of them involving Cullen."

"Really?"

"Unless there's another weirdo walking around wearing a cowboy hat."

"He's not a weirdo."

"Says you."

"So what's his involvement?"

"Don't know." He brushed this interruption aside. "*Three:* known anti-salmon farm protester, Tony Stafford, is run off the road and then disappears after having a week previously been robbed and tied up by a mysterious woman and said man in cowboy hat."

"Run off the road!"

"And disappeared."

"Hanging's too good for him."

Martin ignored her. "*Four:* the car that ran him off the road was a silver BMW registered to Caledonian Seafoods. A salmon farming company that owns the secret site near Peebles."

"Oooh!"

"*Five:* the Port Authority at Largs report that this Beemer is frequently logged at the marina there."

"OK."

"Where, *six,* there is currently a luxury yacht moored - also registered to Caledonia Seafoods."

"Nice. The have's and the have-yachts. So…" she took a deep breath.

"I haven't finished yet. *Seven:* Caledonian Seafoods is owned by a rich Russian guy, Vasilij Krupchenko."

"What?" Kim squealed down the phone. "Well, clearly -"

"Steady with the *clearly's* there, Kim." Martin interrupted. "I'm not sensing many *clearly's* here."

"Ok, look. Tony was obviously hired by this Vasilij guy and is going round sabotaging salmon sites."

"So…" Martin's head was starting to hurt. "Tony's working for Caledonian Seafoods? Going round sabotaging their competitors sites? So… why is Caledonian Seafoods after him?"

"Maybe they're not after him. Maybe they're helping him?"

"By running him off the road?"

"Well, maybe he's been piddling in their pot noodle!"

"Translation please?"

"Well, maybe he tried something on at this secret site - which they own - and now the Russian is mad at him and wants to rub him out!"

"But the site's not even finished yet. There's nothing to sabotage." Martin butted in but Kim was in full flow and didn't hear him.

"And Cullen found out and, knowing what a heel Tony is…"

"I think you've been watching too many Sopranos box sets."

They lay at opposite ends of the phone line in silence for a minute or so, each trying to get their brains to settle.

"What does it all mean, then?" Kim wondered.

"I told you, I don't know. I can't get my brain round it."

"And if there is a connection here, tying all this together - exactly what crime has been committed in all this?"

As usual, Kim had cut to the very heart of the matter. Martin sighed.

"I have absolutely no fucking idea."

Blysse was lying dishevelled and warm in Vasilij's bed on the *A Crewed Interest*. The morning light filtered in through the curtains and bled a bright line about six inches wide across the pillow, brushing her cheek. Vasilij was gone and she had the room to herself. The clock said 9:20am so she had hours before she needed to make her way back to the theatre but, right now, the prospect of skipping the matinee and staying here with Vasilij seemed infinitely preferable.

For the past few weeks they'd been playing this game of chauffeuring her down to Yair after each matinee, spending the late afternoons in lazy delight, and then whisking her back in time for the evening performance. It was a tight deadline and slick timing was needed - not to mention, aggressive driving from Feliks - in order to accomplish any meaningful length of time together. Jelena's desk drawer was stuffed full of speeding tickets accrued as a consequence. Vasilij had toyed with the idea of getting a room in a Glasgow hotel to make things easier but found the idea rather sordid. As a compromise he would quite often accompany Feliks in the car to collect her. Despite the opportunity to indulge themselves in the back of the car, it always felt rushed and well, not cheap - Vasilij didn't do cheap - but somehow unsatisfactory.

This, on the other hand, was much more like it. Here on the yacht she felt she had the time to luxuriate and relax. Live the multi-millionaire lifestyle rather than just visit it.

Last night had been a very good night, she realised. And the night before. And the night before that. Vasilij may be older than her but he was gentle, vigorous, and considerate. His body was still taut and muscled and he smelled of tar and masculinity, soap and musk. One moment he was all over her, like a boy in a candy store, pressing and kneading, stroking and kissing. The next he relaxed, took his time, made her feel … feminine, desired, wanted, cherished, appreciated. Loved. Whole.

Was this what romantic fiction meant? What she'd been missing without realising she missed it? She'd heard the phrase, read the books, watched the chic-flicks and romcoms - women always looking to be *whole*. She'd always thought of that as oneness with the universe, at ease with yourself and your nature. She wasn't religious but her therapists over the years had encouraged her to explore the spiritual. Search the different routes to enlightenment, seek the goal, become complete.

Had she overlooked - all this time - the real way to completeness? A oneness with a man who desired you above all things, worshipped you body and soul. And fucked you until your ears bled.

She stretched and rose to look out of the window. The yacht was moored again and rocked gently in the marina and across the Clyde she could see the sloping hills of the lowlands gradually rising, in tiers, until the blue mountains of the Highlands could be seen in the distance. The sky was its usual grey splotch but there was something majestic, permanent and peaceful about the place. She wouldn't have to spend her life here - yachts moved, you know - but returning here for a month of so, at certain times of the year? Yes, she could see that. Summering in the Caribbean or cruising the Adriatic and then returning for Hogmanay, seal-watching, going to Up Hellya.

She'd surfed and read up during the downtime in her dressing room these past few weeks, feeling an obligation to get to know her public and the country they called home. And it had grown on her. She'd always be an LA child - perma-tanned and happiest near the surf - but places like this with their rugged, rough-hewn beauty and their sense of being eternally part of nature, part of something bigger than you could ever be? They could draw you in, hold you close, keep you coming back.

"Penny for them?" Vasilij had appeared from nowhere and she started at his voice.

"Just enjoying the view."

"Me too." He walked over and put his arms around her. She sighed appreciatively.

"Do you ever get tired of the climate here?"

"Often." He laughed. "But, as they say here, if you don't like the weather - wait a minute."

"It's all so very …"

"Different from California?"

"Yes." It was her turn to laugh. "Different from Russia too, I guess?"

"Well, yes. Scotland is very… wet. Russia is not. Cold, yes. Wet, not so much."

"California isn't cold or wet. It's always warm and sunny."

"Yes. I have been. Many times."

"To California?"

"Yes. LA. San Francisco. Las Vegas."

"Vegas isn't in California. Is it?"

"Ah, just over the border I think - but I have only been when staying in California so…"

"Maybe we saw each other!" She was immediately excited by the prospect but Vasilij didn't seem so keen to reminisce.

"Maybe."

She turned in his arms, their noses almost touching. "You always seem to clam up when the conversation turns to your past. Or your work. Why?"

He looked sheepish. "There is not much to tell, really. Mostly boring." He forced a smile at her. "Who wants to hear about the mundanities of making money when they could be spending money?"

"Me. Sometimes." She gave him a peck on the cheek. "I really don't know much about you, you know?"

"Look. There is not much to tell, really. I was an independent businessman in Russia during *glasnost* and *perestroika*." Blysse half-recognised the terms but didn't know what they meant. She was too glad to have him opening up to her that she didn't want to interrupt his flow. "There was a lot of money to be made buying and selling western items. Many were luxuries to Russians then. Jeans, CD players, that sort of thing. I had contacts in Europe. Bought them at the market rate and then sold them at good profit. I built my business over a few years."

"You made millions selling CD players?"

"Not to start with. Later, when Yeltsin came along he privatised many state industries - almost all industry was state-owned back then. They distributed vouchers - basically shares in these companies - to everyone. Many people didn't want them, or were prepared to sell them cheaply and I had enough money and... influence, to be able to buy them - lots of them. So, I became a major shareholder and when the stock market stabilised and the economy prospered I was able to sell my shares and plough those profits into other businesses."

"Like salmon?"

"Yes. You see, it's all very boring and very uncomplicated. Buy low, sell high."

"And why salmon?"

He shrugged. "I don't know, really. Maybe it's another example of old luxury items from the West? Maybe it's just because I liked smoked salmon. There is good money to be made there."

"Is that how you met Tony?"

Vasilij's mood immediately darkened. "I thought we had agreed not to talk of him again. After our first ...conversation?"

Blysse was relieved he hadn't said *argument* or *row*, and kicking herself for having stupidly blundered into this again. It had been an extremely difficult *conversation* with Vasilij after the TV and other press coverage of the seal demonstration which she and Tony had engineered. It was, she had felt, only the continued discomfort from his facial injury which had kept his temper in check on that occasion. Well, that and the blowjob.

"I'm sorry." She put her head on his chest and listened for his pulse. "I did explain that it was all an enormous coincidence. But I did date him at High School - briefly - and he did just turn up out of the blue in my dressing room one day."

"I understand." His voice was calm but his heart was thumping. "The man's ubiquitous. You have to try very, very hard to avoid him. But I find that it's well worth the effort."

"I'm sorry, V." She only employed this diminutive of his name when she felt it necessary. "Remember - I didn't know you then."

"I know."

"On the bright side, the theatre audiences shot up after I was on TV. Bernard is very pleased. Although I now have to have a policeman at the stage door because of the increased fan attention." She slipped her hand through his shirt and stroked his chest hair. "*Male* fan attention."

Vasilij's heart kept thumping but, she hoped, for a different reason.

At the rear of the facility was a small pebble-dashed extension with a flat roof and a single thin strip window of frosted glass. The external door, when open, almost touched up against the perimeter chain link fence and both times Cullen had climbed over it, the door had been unlocked and he'd been able to see inside. It was basically a glorified toilet block.

Along one wall were two toilet cubicles and a urinal. The opposite wall was one long line of coathooks with a bench beneath them. White wellies stood under the bench, white overalls hung from the hooks. On the third wall, opposite the window, was a white-tiled shower area with a single privacy curtain and a short run of worktop holding a stainless steel sink and, underneath, a washing machine.

Cullen stood behind the open door holding a large black bucket. Billy over at the farm had watched him earlier collecting slop, waste, manure and other crud from the farmyard into the bucket and swill it round with some rainwater from the water butt. Cullen had not been particular and Billy had not been inquisitive - all he cared about was that he got his bucket back. He chewed the inside of his cheek absentmindedly as he watched Cullen scooping.

"How lang'll ye be then?" he'd asked.

"I'm only going over the way, Billy." Cullen nodded over to his left. "I'll be back before you can say five fit Fife firemen fight four fir fires in Forfar forests."

Billy had snorted and watched him stalk off down the drive back to the road, his open coat starting to flap as the wind picked up again.

Cullen readied himself, now, as he heard footsteps coming round the corner across the gravel towards the door. He balanced his weight evenly over both feet and held the bucket in front of him with an easy grace. As the man called Fletcher wheeled round the corner, Cullen flung the contents of the bucket straight at him, point blank.

"Whthefcheurgh!" he spluttered and put his hands to his face, blinded. Cullen brought the empty bucket down on Fletcher's head, passed it into his left hand and then punched him in the midriff with a deft swing of his right. Fletcher doubled over and toppled to the ground, winded and mystified by this sudden and silent attack.

By the time Fletcher had struggled to his feet and smeared his eyes clear with the back of his hands, there was no-one there. He staggered into the block and dropped his filthy overall onto the floor. He'd been about to clock off shift for the day but now he had to get this foul-smelling shit out of his hair, eyes and nose. He peeled off his own clothes, which seemed to have survived the disgusting onslaught intact, and hung them up on a peg before stepping into the shower enclosure.

He had a shower in the hottest water he could stand, convinced that he could still smell shit even if he couldn't see it anywhere. Unaware that, on the other side of the shower curtain, his attacker was rummaging through his clothes on the peg, looking for a mobile phone.

"Okay. It's… not getting any less complicated."

"And good evening to you, Martin." Kim retorted. "What sort of way is that to start a romantic phone call with your beautiful lover stuck hundreds of miles away in her lonely bed?"

"Sorry, look. I'm all excited-"

"Ooh, do you want me to talk dirty to you? While my warm fingers roam tantalisingly over my lithe and voluptuous body?"

"Not now, Kim. Really. I think I'm getting somewhere."

"Hmph. Not with me, you're not."

Another evening, another long distance phone call. Kim looked forward to them daily, even as each one reminded her of what she was missing. They were a poor substitute for having Martin in her bed.

"Hang on, that's a good idea. Why didn't I think of that before?" She could have kicked herself.

"What?"

"We could Skype each other? Then I could see you, you could see me."

"Erm."

"I could be your private webcam performer, Martin."

"Yes, er, hang on. That is a good idea. Only I don't know how to do any of that. Not a big technofan, if I'm honest."

"Really! Come on, Dishy D. It's peasy. Look, grab your laptop and I'll talk you through it."

Fifteen fumbling minutes later, the two of them were finally connected. Lying in bed with her laptop on her chest, she could see his nervous face inches away from hers. She could hear paper rustling at his end.

"Are you sitting comfortably?" he asked.

"I am. Doesn't look like you are." She smiled at his discomfort with this new arrangement.

Martin ignored her. "Then I'll begin. Can you see that?"

"What?"

"This. The photo."

"No, I can see you and you alone, my sweet."

"Erm, OK. Hang on." His face disappeared and there was copious off-screen clicking until another face filled the screen, Martin's own relegated to a smaller thumbnail in the top left hand corner.

"How about now?"

"Yep. Some middle-aged bloke." Kim scrutinised his features. "Quite imposing."

"This is Vasilij Krupchenko. Multi-millionaire owner of a number of businesses, most prominently Caledonian Seafoods. Paper worth around £100 million but varies - the value of shares can go down as well as up."

"Vasilij! The man who hired Tony."

"Yes. Interestingly his net worth has soared in the past few weeks due to a massive spike in Salmon prices."

"Ah! A motive. I wondered when you were going to bother with one of those. I know they're quite insistent on them in TV cop shows."

Martin ignored her and a second face appeared alongside the first. "Tony Stafford. Noted eco-protestor and marine animal welfare campaigner."

"Ugh. Take it away, take it away!"

Tony's photo disappeared and was replaced by an angry looking man with a ponytail.

"Viktor Chorney. Ukrainian national, registered maritime pilot and all-round nautical bod. Criminal record as long as your arm and tattoos from several Russian prisons to prove it. Works for Krupchenko on his yacht - if you please - sailing the seven seas, and

314

identified by two salmon farmers on Arran as 'strange man carrying a firearm'. Apparently tried to argue with a helicopter and was last seen being dumped into Arran Bay with a bleeding head wound. Whereabouts unknown, presumed drowned -"

"Cool. Chalk up one more bad guy!" Kim interrupted.

"Georgi Sidorenko." Another photo, this time of a swarthy unshaven thug with heavy brows. "Russian national and known associate of Chorney. Formerly on payroll of Caledonia Seafoods. Wanted by Stornoway police for a number of minor offences. Current whereabouts unknown. Suspect #1 in the Outer Hebrides Crime Wave Stakes."

Another photo. "Feliks Beshanovski. One time professional wrestler now employed as chauffeur and general dogsbody working for Krupchenko. Identified by A&E staff at Borders General Hospital as the man attacked by a dog, believed to have taken place at the new Caledonian Seafoods facility in The Borders -"

"Is that the place where - ?"

Martin ignored him and ploughed on. "Said dog, a Jack Russell terrier, owned by this man." Another photo came up on the board showing a heavyset, slavic-looking man with a dark goatee and black threatening eyes. "Paul McInnes, aka Big Paul. Joiner and carpenter based in Peebles, currently of no fixed abode. Known associate of ..." Another photo, this time the image was of a middle-aged man with stubble and a full head of hair, and ears that stuck out a little too far. "Mungo James Cullen. Former police officer for the Hong Kong constabulary and then later Lothian and Borders Police -"

"Huh?"

"Retired on mental health grounds 2008, currently of no fixed abode, believed to be living in the Tweeddale area, whereupon he came to the rescue of a Ms. Kim Schofield."

"Mental health grounds?"

"According to his record."

"Hmm." His photo showed him looking several years younger but it was definitely Cullen. "Mungo, did you say? What kind of name is that? No wonder he wanted me to call him Cullen."

"Mungo? Perfectly respectable Scottish name." Martin sniffed. "Patron saint of Glasgow, you know."

"Whatever. So, this is our cast of characters is it?"

"Yep. Well, actually not quite. May I present the piece de resistance to this wonderful array of motley fools. Ladies and gentlemen, I bring you none other than… Blysse Baptiste." A photo of the movie star appeared next to the others. Kim's jaw dropped.

"You are kidding me?"

"Nope."

"Cindy Anna Jones?"

"Yep." Martin enjoyed the brief silence while Kim was speechless. "According to a doughty PC who has been placed nightly at her stagedoor, she has been engaged in daily dalliances with Mr Vasilij Krupchenko since early December and - get this - is an erstwhile High School sweetheart of one Tony Stafford."

Kim smiled ruefully, despite herself, and slowly shook her head. "The immovable mountain of silicon that is Blysse meets the Mohamed of money that is Krupchenko and … stars collide. Tale as old as time, song as old as rhyme."

Martin joined in, tunelessly. "Beauty and the Beast."

"So I was kicked out of a moving car, jilted for a movie star?"

"You're a poet and you don't know it."

Kim puffed out her cheeks and tried to collect her thoughts. "OK. Can we go back to the motive thing again?"

"In what way?"

"Well, perhaps I should rephrase: What the fuck is going on?"

"Ha! Ok, here's my version. Our man Krupchenko here wants to corner the market in Scottish salmon, scupper his competitors and generally make a killing. Only, being Russian, is genetically incapable of identifying an above-board, honest way to do this so is resorting to skulduggery, criminal deception and out-and-out sabotage. However, not wishing to get his hands dirty he hires Tony to orchestrate a series of unfortunate events which will hamper or disable his competitors clearing the way for him to clean up. Somewhere along the way Tony gets greedy, or careless or bored or whatever. He makes two mistakes: firstly he jettisons you, forgetting you will stop at nothing to wreak your revenge."

"Hey! He stole my fucking money. And my stuff! And threw me from a car. That's assault!"

"Secondly, he screws up somehow and brings down Krupchenko's wrath on him. Tony teamed up with his old flame Blysse to go on a PR march against Big Salmon, On TV, no less. Maybe that was the mistake that Krupchenko took against, Tony risking drawing attention to his crazy scheme. Whatever - he instructs his henchman to take Tony out of the game. Tony goes to ground."

"Where is he now?"

"No idea."

"And Cullen, I guess he's irrelevant in all this, right?"

"Hmm. Appears out of the mist to come to your aid, helps you track Tony down, and gets one of his mates to set his attack dogs on one of the bad guys. Doesn't sound irrelevant to me."

"Um." Kim grimaced slightly. "Might have been self-defence."

"Yeah." Said Martin, playing along. "Could have been a complete coincidence."

"Hey, wait a minute. I never asked him to go sniffing around some secret -" Kim brought herself up sharply. "Hang on. This site, where did you say it was?"

"Just outside Peebles. Area's called... Manor Valley."

"Shit."

"Would you care to elaborate?"

"Ahm, well this secret site had kind of come to his attention independently, so to speak. He mentioned it as one of his projects."

"Uh-huh. And what was his exact interest in this project?"

"Well, uh." said Kim, reluctantly. "He was against it."

21

Tony had been enjoying his time on Orkney and was having difficulty keeping the smile from his face. In the past week he had been out across Scapa Flow getting the full tourist history lessons about its naval role during the first and second world wars. Okay, it wasn't Pearl Harbour but it was hell of a lot easier to get to. He'd been seal watching out past South Ronaldsay and now here he was en route to Gairsay via Puldrite Bay where there was another seal colony and - according to some of the locals in the hotel bar last night - recent sightings of killer whales too.

The air was bright and bitterly cold and the sea was choppy and flecked with white. He wrangled the boat out from Kirkwall keeping a respectable distance from the shore and keeping an eye out for the buoys which littered this expansive harbour. Once he was out past the promontory he cut the engine and let the boat drift in the slight swell. He wanted to see what he could using his binoculars, whilst mulling over his three-point plan.

Point One: the processing factory. This was an ugly two-storey building of metal, bare breezeblock and unpainted concrete, wind- and weather-beaten. In the parking area to the left as he looked were a couple of refrigerated lorries and several stacks of wooden pallets. It was Sunday and there seemed no-one around. This was Caledonian Seafoods main processing plant, on Crowness Road. It took fish from the whole of the northern coastlines of Scotland - Orkney itself had five sites and there were many more sites as you went around the coast anti-clockwise from there: Caithness, Sutherland, Ross-shire & the Outer Hebrides. Fifty thousand tonnes of salmon processed each year. Not the company's entire stocks but the lion's share. And if, heaven forbid, something should happen to it - perhaps taking it out of action for a while - why, then, the company's revenues would collapse almost entirely overnight.

Possibly they could ship their fish to other factories - competitors perhaps - but only if they had spare capacity (which would be unlikely at this time of year with everyone working flat out to feed the Christmas market). But, just in case, he wheeled his binoculars round to Kirkwall harbour for his Point Two: the wellboats.

These multi-million pound pieces of seafaring sophistication were expensive to own and operate, and very often temperamental. Costing upwards of £100,000 a week, the salmon companies leased them and their crews: twelve men who spent three months on and three months off, all year round. It was a lucrative line of work, but hard, and the wellboat owners knew better than to stint on luxuries for those rare times when the crew were at rest. Christmas was one of those times. Processing factories would shut down for two, possibly three days over the holiday and there would be no harvests, no pickups or put-downs, no need to sail. For three whole days, the crew could dock in a harbour and get out of their heads without worry.

They weren't here yet but, come Christmas Eve, they would be nestling in the natural shelter of Kirkwall harbour - the three wellboats that between them served the salmon industry in the North Atlantic, North Sea and Outer Hebrides fisheries.

And there, behind the row of low-slung buildings that lined the harbour front, was Tony's Point Three: the tallest building on the island (which, okay, might not be saying much) was a modern four-storey arrangement of smoked glass and wood, incongruous on the skyline amongst the fishing vessels, Victorian brickwork and damp concrete hard scrabble of the local architecture. This imposing structure was the main employer on the island, home as it was to the headquarters of Caledonian Seafoods Ltd. The jewel in Vasilij's crown.

How unfortunate would it be if some harm should come to this building as well? In fact, imagine some hypothetical disaster which could, in a single evening, wipe out the man's HQ, his main processing facility and all available wellboats which could help the company out in an emergency. If such a thing could happen, his company would be in severe financial difficulty - a difficulty from which their recovery would be, at best prolonged, at worst impossible. Wouldn't it be absolutely awful if something like that was to happen? Oh, and then when Blysse came to him, standing before him, letting her clothes fall to the floor and kneeling down to slobber on his Sherbet Serpent, would that be sufficient retribution for Vasilij trying to have him killed? No, but it was a fine start.

Tony lowered his binoculars and started up the engine. He smiled as he headed back to Kirkwall, taking a sweep right past the main harbour wall until he reached the jetty where he would moor up for the night. Tonight he would wine and dine in luxury. Tomorrow he had a Christmas card to post. But first he wanted to double-check the incendiary devices he had rescued from his locker at Buchanan Bus Station.

Cullen rose and left the bothy as he found it, packed his rucksack and headed off towards Horse Hope Hill some eight miles away. When he got there he found Big Paul sitting on a groundsheet beneath a battered old tarp, binoculars to his face and a flask of Irish coffee at his side.

With the demise of his pets the life and animus had left him. He seemed to have visibly shrunk and the laughter creases which had brought humour to his eyes now seemed worry lines, etched by pain into his tanned face. This new mission was the only thing giving him purpose right now - he'd abandoned scouting for work until the New Year, hoping he could start afresh then - and his eyes glinted with anger and hatred. More than anything, when he raised the binoculars to his face, he wanted to see the fleshy outline of the man mountain who had taken his dogs. The man on whom he would wreak his cold, hard revenge.

"Morning." Cullen said as he sat down next to Paul.

"Ah, decided to join me have you? Finally."

"Been busy." Cullen mumbled. "Had to see a man about a dog."

"Say what?"

"I said, I've been busy. Putting two and two together."

"Oh, right. And coming up with?"

"This…" Cullen indicated grandly down towards the large featureless metal building below them. "Is Caledonian Seafoods' Closed Containment Site."

"Oh, I knew that." Said Paul, eyes still trained on the activity below.

"What?"

"Caledonian Seafoods Limited. Archie told me. He found out by looking through the records at the hut on site - when the foreman weren't watching."

"Oh."

"Needn't have bothered, mind." Paul put down his binoculars and pointed down towards the access road. "See, I found an old parish noticeboard down near the main road, hidden by some overgrown bushes? Faded old notice an' that but still wossname, legible. It's only a bloody planning notice ain't it? Supposed to alert the general public and they stick it out o' sight down some backwater somewhere." He read from a scrap of paper from his pocket. "Caledonian Seafoods proposed development of a Closed Containment Site. Site access agreed by P.F. McHenry."

"Oh." Cullen was deflated.

"Cheer up! I don't know what a Closed Contact Centre is."

"Closed Containment Site."

"Yeah. That 'n' all."

"Well, I do." Cullen brightened. "And I know who P.F. McHenry is."

"D'uh! So do I. He owns Langhaugh farm."

"Yes. And?" asked Cullen.

"And... that is here? Where this building is?"

"No, actually. Because P.F. McHenry has sold them this land." Cullen pulled out some paperwork of his own. "For a massive price to boot."

"Yeah, but still. Planning permission?"

"Well now, you see, our Mr McHenry has been rather economical with the *actualite*."

"Come again?"

"Sorry. Picked it up from a friend. Look. Poor farmer applies for planning permission. Way back. New outbuildings for extra livestock, chickens maybe - all very run of the mill. Planning permission gets waved through. Construction starts, all still in the guise of additional farm buildings. Only once the building is underway, he submits a change notice. Same zoning, new use. No horses startled. No major ruckus. Buries the info about impact: traffic, drainage, water, et cetera. Place has already been approved. Just tweaking the definition of what's being built." Cullen folded his papers up and jammed them back in his pocket. "And if, by any miracle, anyone does notice or complain the poor farmer just applies for retrospective permission. Job done."

Paul nodded slowly. "So, the farmer gets permission for some bog standard expansion, sells land to Caledonian Seafoods-"

"Ah, not so fast. Ownership passes to Caledonian Seafoods on commissioning of the site only."

"So?"

"So the land is still technically registered to the farmer, the building work is being done under his auspices, but when it is all ready to be switched on, the land and site passes to Caledonian Seafoods who say *'Nothing to do with us guv, we just bought the place.'* And the farmer pockets a pretty penny for his troubles."

"Surely they can't do that?"

"Looks like they have."

"Right." Said Paul, scratching his head. "So when does it get switched on?"

"December 31st."

"New Year's Eve? Funny date to pick isn't it?"

"Yeah, that's what I thought. I wondered if maybe it might be something to do with tax - you know build it one tax year and operate it at a profit in another or something."

"Hmm, tax." Paul responded gloomily.

"Not a strong point?"

"Not really. There's always a lot of month left at the end of the money, if you know what I'm saying."

"But it isn't to do with tax at all - I don't think."

"Really?"

"Yeah. Guess what else happens on December 31st."

"Hogmanay!"

"Yes." Cullen looked at him as if at a small child. "And the Caledonia Seafoods AGM."

"Ah." Paul attempted to nod sagely. "Which means...?"

"Well, I guess it could be coincidence. Could be a tax year thing. But it could be a good way to make a big splash at your AGM - announcing the opening of your shiny new facility."

"Hmm." Paul resumed scanning with his binoculars. "So, these tankers are going to keep coming and going 'til the 31st then, are they?"

"No. I reckon today will be the last of them. Tomorrow they'll tidy up and knock off early for Christmas and not be back until Tuesday next week. So Archie says. That leaves us, what ... four or five days to clear the place out. Should be enough."

"Clear the place out? Of what?" Paul looked across at Cullen. "What's in the tankers?"

"Fish."

"Fish?"

"Yes. What did you think? Salmon. And water."

"We're going to steal their fish?"

"Technically, no. We will just, ah, relocate them."

"Right. And they'll be good enough to leave this place unattended for us, will they? With all this fish inside? Must be worth a fortune."

"Automated alarms mostly. Systems monitor water temperature, oxygen levels, feed remaining. All that. If anything falls outside defined thresholds the alarms trigger and call a cellphone number. Someone's on call, they respond." Cullen was starting to sound quite the expert. "Otherwise, some nightwatchmen might do a drive by every once in a while to check the fences and gate haven't been disturbed. 'Bout it, really."

Paul smiled. "So how do we disable the alarms."

"We don't." Cullen took his own flask from his rucksack. "Tea?"

Martin was picking pastry crumbs from his lap and nursing a styrofoam coffee cup. The radiator on the far wall made spelunking noises but didn't seem to be giving out any heat. Through the window above it, Martin could see the snow flurries blowing left and right across the tarmac at Prestwick airport.

"Let me see if I've got this right" Chief Inspector Maxwell started in. "You're saying that Krupchenko the mad Russian is now after Tony's blood. For reasons unknown. And you think Tony isn't going to stand for it. Wants his own back. Maybe he feels shortchanged on the money front. Maybe he's just pissed off that Krupchenko is boffing his old childhood sweetheart."

"Anyone who's prepared to throw their girlfriend from a moving vehicle and rob her of fourteen grand, whilst continuing a campaign of criminal violence against numerous salmon sites around the country, isn't going to just roll over and play dead when his Russian sugar daddy cuts the money supply and puts a contract out on his head."

Maxwell scrunched his face up. "I'm not buying this."

"Well, buy this then. Suppose there is a Caledonia Seafood AGM on New Years Eve."

"Is there, Martin?"

"Yes. And further suppose that Tony decides to make a big splash of some kind to disrupt, discredit or destroy Vasilij's business or his reputation on the event of the AGM."

"Okay."

"Caledonian Seafoods HQ is in Kirkwall, did you know?"

"No." Maxwell wasn't fond of Martin's games. "Your point, Martin? I do hope you have one."

"Well - on a hunch - I thought I'd give a couple of hotels in Kirkwall a call…"

"Right. And?"

"And staying at the Kirkwall Hotel, checked in a few nights ago, is a Mr Tony Stafford." Martin was triumphant. The moment didn't last long.

"Well, in that case, I suppose… you'd better get yourself to Orkney."

"What?"

"Get yourself to Orkney." Maxwell was brusqueness and decisiveness in a snap. "You've got family there haven't you?"

"Yeah."

"Right, so what could be nicer than a Christmas with Mum & Dad?"

"Well, actually I was hoping to spend Christmas with my girlfriend in London."

"Well, change of plan. Get down to London. Invite her to Orkney for Christmas." Maxwell smiled sarcastically at him. "So romantic."

Martin inhaled deeply. "You want me to take Kim to spend Christmas and New Year with my parents on Orkney-"

"Yes."

"While trying to stop Tony from committing some unspecified crime, or crimes, on the Caledonian Seafoods HQ -"

"Yep."

"And, at the same time, make sure Tony doesn't get whacked by any passing Russian bad guys?"

"Exactly. Merry Christmas."

Martin shook his head in disbelief. "Ho ho ho."

"AGM?" Vasilij asked Jelena as he traced his way down his notes with a finger.

"Yes. So, I have…" she riffled through a stack of papers she had pulled from a large briefcase. "Last year's papers, annual report, minutes, Chairman's Q&A, agenda, presentations from Finance, Sales & Production. And…" she searched for something else and then, unable to find it, stopped: "That's all. What I don't have is your introduction for the report."

"OK. Well, I can do the report intro this evening, so that it can go off to the printers tomorrow."

She pouted. "We are cutting it tight for circulation to shareholders. With Christmas post and everything."

Vasilij shrugged. "Can't be helped. I have decisions to make about what to say and how it is to be said. Information is still…." He chose his words carefully, even for Jelena. "Coming through."

"As you wish." Jelena made a scribbled note and left him alone with his thoughts.

With the recent bad news and fall in his share price he wanted to impress the analysts with a demonstration of his company's strengths. He wondered if he could get a live video feed from the CCS site into the AGM presentation. Video that showed advanced preparation for an industry-leading future, investment in new technology, and financial projections illustrating stratospheric growth to back it all up. If he could arrange for some poor financial info from his competitors between now and then it would be the icing on the cake.

When Kim got home that Friday evening and Martin was standing waiting at her front door with flowers and a suitcase she wept and hugged him so hard she thought she would injure him. She fussed and flapped over him, kissed him and talked and talked and talked and kissed him some more. And all the time she was doing so he was looking on slightly bemused while a part of her brain (*the left-part, Val?*) was sitting back in its chair saying *Well this is new, isn't it? You've never done this before. You've never felt like this before have you? You know what this means, right?*

By the time they'd eaten she had calmed down and was content to sit at the table across from him and hold his hand while it was his turn to talk. She wasn't really listening to him, she'd tuned out in some kind of delirious trance and only gradually became aware that he had stopped talking.

"Kim? Kim?"

"Hmm?" she was startled from her reverie.

"Well, what do you say?"

"About what?"

"About coming up to Orkney?"

"Oh my god, I'd love to!" she beamed. "When?"

"For Christmas." He frowned. "Have you been listening to a word I've said?"

"Yes. Yes. Of course." She tried to mollify him. "I just... zoned out for a moment there. With happiness."

He didn't seem convinced. "That's happiness is it? That weirded out vacant look? Doesn't suit you."

She slapped his wrist - literally. "Tart! Look, I'm sorry to get all serious on yo' ass, bro, but I have really really missed you." She grabbed his hand again and held it to her face. "Christ, you can't know how much I have missed you. Did you miss me? Never mind. Look you can tell me about Orkney or Christmas later. What's more important, right now, is that you ... Get. Your. Kit. Off."

Half an hour later she turned to him in bed. "So, tell me all about Orkney then?"

"I thought it would be nice to spend Christmas up at my parents. On Orkney."

"You want me to meet your parents?"

"Yes, but don't get all heavy on me. I wanted to see my Mum and Dad over Christmas and I wanted to see you and I thought: why not try and kill two birds with one stone? Plus Orkney - have you ever been?" She shook her head so her carried on. "It can be really pretty, really special at Christmas."

"Well, you can count me in." She kissed him ceremonially on the lips. "When?"

"Well, I need to get flights sorted first. I just wanted to check that you could do it before I booked anything."

"Right, well now you've checked, we're good to go." She paused briefly. "And tomorrow you can come shopping with me and help me choose some new outfits!"

"Er… really?"

"Yes. Really." Kim could see he wasn't brimming with the enthusiasm she had anticipated. "You will still be here tomorrow, won't you?"

"Yes. I don't have to fly back until Sunday night."

"Right, well that's settled then."

"Right." He agreed reluctantly. That was denial ticked off the list, now to try bargaining. "You do know that Orkney isn't really any different to anywhere else in Scotland, climate-wise?"

"So?"

"You know, it's not where Orcs come from or anything? You don't need special clothing."

"Oh yes, my precious, hmm. Christmas-in-Orkney-wear we needs, yes." She dropped the Gollum impression for a moment and clasped his face in both hands, planting a kiss on his forehead. He still didn't look keen. "Come on, it's all in vogue and totes essench!"

"I'm not really a shopping person." He said weakly.

"Hmmm. People who don't like shopping?" she pulled the sheet up and looked down at him. "Nasty little hobbitses."

"No, squeeze trigger. Not pull."

Viktor was trying to show Vasilij how to use his shotgun but Vasilij was proving remarkably useless with a firearm and an atrocious shot. Perhaps it was the amount of brandy he'd drunk. The rocking of the boat and the fact that each seagull looked suspiciously like two. Who could say?

The shotgun went off and bucked against Vasilij's shoulder, sending him flying back against the stairs to the bridge. The seagulls squawked harmlessly away

Jelena had been right - with Blysse's arrival on the scene, Vasilij was now entirely hands-off with Jelena and Viktor somehow felt less need to violently couple at every given opportunity as a result. The upside to this was that Jelena was now seeking *him* out which gave their sex a new sparkle and fizz.

Jelena appeared from behind the smoked glass doors carrying letters on a tray. She glanced nervously at Viktor as she walked towards Vasilij.

"Vasilij. You have some more Christmas cards."

Vasilij showed no signs of caring and was leaning against the steps rubbing his sore shoulder with one hand and gulping more brandy from a tumbler in the other.

"Put them in the car."

"I think, perhaps, you should look at this one." She took an opened envelope from the top of the pile and handed it to him. Vasilij looked at her drunkenly, placed his tumbler unsteadily on her tray and clumsily tried to remove the card from the envelope. "Be careful when you -".

A shower of glitter tumbled out and covered his trousers and shoes.

"Fuck!" He attempted to shake the glitter away but succeeded only in distributing it more liberally across the deck. "Fuck's this from?" He ripped it open - more glitter - and glared at the writing in the card:

Merry Christmas Fuckface -
Hope your AGM goes with a BANG!
Tony

Vasilij reeled around at Jelena, red in the face. "What the fuck's this? What. The. Fuck. Is. This?"

"It's a Christmas card." Jelena said redundantly. "From Tony."

Vasilij couldn't seem to take it in and kept staring at her.

"It's postmarked Kirkwall" she added helpfully, glancing at Viktor again.

"Kirkwall!" Vasilij raged. "Fuck! Viktor." He wheeled around to look at Viktor. "He's going to destroy my Head Office. On Orkney."

Viktor looked over at Jelena and back at Vasilij, waiting for some instruction.

"Vasilij?" Jelena prompted.

His eyes focussed briefly. "To coincide with the AGM."

"Vasilij?" Jelena again. Vasilij seemed to snap into a calm sobriety for a moment.

"Viktor. Get to Orkney. Now. You have to stop him. Bring him back to me, if you can manage. If you can't…"

Viktor waited expectantly.

"Make sure he suffers as much as humanly possible." Vasilij spat and threw the card overboard.

22

The Jenkins' family home sat on Scorradale Hill, commanding expansive views over Scapa Flow to the south and the Hoy hills beyond. It was a drab, single storey smallholding with an acre of land they had given over to vegetable patches, a few pigs and a chicken run. As he drove up the hill towards it Martin smiled nervously at Kim as she looked left and right for a sight of the place she would call home for the next few days. He hoped she would like it. He loved it more than anything.

He pulled into the drive and parked beside his father's battered old VW. "Here we are."

"Wow. What a view!" Kim got out of the car and walked over to the side fence. The bay of Scapa Flow was wide and foam-flecked beneath an expansive blue sky decorated with fluffy white clouds. Snow on the far hills reflected the low sunlight and made her squint.

Martin smiled happily. "Good isn't it? Come on, let's meet the folks." He led her across to the front porch, rang the bell and then opened the front door without waiting for an answer.

"Martin!" Kim scolded.

"It's OK." He reassured her. "No-one locks their doors, they know we're coming, and the bell doesn't work anyway." He grinned foolishly at her and then shouted down the hall. "Mum! Dad! We're here!"

Viktor sat in his car waiting for the Kirkwall ferry to start loading, feeling like death. He'd been drinking beer to stay awake - his last two bottles rattled loosely on the passenger seat - and wasn't sure it had worked. His thinking was based on some muddled logic involving the fact he'd read somewhere that the human body was 80% water and, according to the label, the beer was only 5% alcohol by volume - which meant that it was 95% water. So that meant that drinking beer should actually sober him up.

He was dog tired and totally pissed off with his lot. When Vasilij had demanded that Viktor "Get to fucking Orkney. Now" that, of course, had meant right now. Which meant driving right across the fucking country in order to catch the next ferry from Aberdeen to Orkney - wherever the fuck that was. And, of course, the first ferry had been fully booked so he had unsuccessfully tried to sleep in his car overnight waiting for the next one. Which was 5pm the next day. One fucking ferry a day. What a joke.

And his left hand still hurt like fuck. After Vasilij had stabbed it with his shitty knife, he had poured cognac all over it to prevent it getting infected, but he wasn't sure if that had worked either.

And Jelena had been surprisingly curt when she waved goodbye from the yacht - he didn't know why. And now he was away from her, over Christmas, just as their sex life was revving up nicely.

And now he had a fucking six hour crossing to look forward to.

His eyelids were dropping and he was surfing in and out of sleep when he felt his car rock suddenly. He looked in his rear view mirror to see the driver behind put an apologetic hand up sheepishly at him. The bastard had bumped his car coming up behind him and his last two bottles of beer had rolled down into the footwell and smashed amongst the empties. Viktor clambered out of his car, the freezing wind instantly snapping him awake, marched back to the car behind him and, without even waiting for the driver to wind down his window, smashed through the glass with his fist and, in one swift movement, punched the drivers head down hard onto his steering wheel. The car's airbags deployed and its alarm started wailing plangently in the night air.

Viktor stormed back to his car and caught a glance from the man in the next car who immediately looked away as if had been slapped. This fucking country, thought Viktor.

"More tea, dear?" Mrs Jenkins hovered with the teapot.

"No thanks, Martha." Said Kim, through a mouthful of scone. "These are lovely by the way."

"Thank you, dear. Martin?"

"Not for me, Mum." He watched as his mother scurried around, all pinny and petticoats. Fussing and adjusting, fetching plates of what looked disconcertingly like freshly made scones, cakes and other treats. Small and white-haired, with stubby cheeks and twinkling eyes, she had a lilting celtic accent inherited from her Western Isle upbringing which sometimes jarred with the Orkney locals - even after she'd been resident here for most of her life. She never made this fuss when he visited normally. Was this because he had brought a *lady friend*? His mother had taunted him gently when he'd phoned inviting himself up for Christmas, delighted as he knew she'd be, but she was all business-like just the same when she explained about the rules underneath her roof as regards members of the opposite, erm, gender. Kim had almost staggered in disbelief when he'd told her the sleeping arrangements he'd agreed.

"Separate beds?"

"No, separate *rooms.*"

"But you're a grown man!"

"Glad you've noticed."

"You're in your thirties!"

"That's right."

"But…" words failed her.

"It's just the way they are. They way it is up there. I'm not surprised, I expected it." Martin had, genuinely, not been surprised in the slightest at his mother's stipulations.

"Do we have to go to church on Sunday as well?"

"Come on. It's not that bad. You're thinking of The Hebrides. Nothing moves there on a Sunday."

"Well, if we're going to be in separate rooms, there'll be nothing moving at all, never mind bloomin' Sunday."

This, as far as Martin was concerned, was Kim's acquiescence. Now, here she sat, sweet as pie, smiling and minding her p's and q's as his Mum pushed baked goods on her like they were going out of fashion.

"Ever been to Orkney before?" his Father asked. Now this was a first - his father starting a conversation. Martin began to realise that this was the first time he'd ever introduced any of his girlfriends to his parents, the first time they'd ever had any proof that he actually had a girlfriend. Stooped and damaged from a working life as a fisherman in the unforgiving North Sea, his father now spent his days sitting in his wheelchair, painting the view from his conservatory window and keeping a record of the puffins and seabirds which visited in a neat black logbook he kept on the sideboard with his binoculars. Taciturn and considered, he wouldn't talk to you unless there was good reason, or answer you unless he was sure.

"No. No, I haven't." Kim replied. "But Martin's told me a lot about it and I'd love a tour."

"I'll leave that to you, son." His father nodded to him, happy to have thus concluded his verbal duties for the day.

"Well, it'll be dark soon so-" Martin excused.

"But it's only three o'clock!" Kim interjected.

"Aye." Said his mother, as if that explained everything.

"Oh. Right." Kim's shoulders dropped slightly and Martin couldn't help feel a pang of desire.

"Look, let's unpack and change. Then I can take you into town and we can have a wee mooch before the shops shut. Maybe have a drink overlooking the harbour?"

"Mooch?"

"Aye. Mooch." He declined to enlighten her in front of company. "Maybe we'll see the Northern Lights."

Kim brightened at this and snaffled the last of her scone, ready to get underway.

"I have a confession." Martin offered as they sat in the pub that was gradually filling up with drinkers as they finished work for the week.

"Is it to do with mooching?" she pulled a gormless face at him.

"Don't mock me please, Kim. I feel bad enough about it as it is."

"Mooching?"

"No, not mooching. Will you stop going on about bloody mooching."

"But I don't know what it means." She pleaded with him, as if he alone had access to some awful secret.

"It means a bit of a wander, shufty at stuff. Just meander where the mood takes you in pleasant surroundings, is all."

"Oh." She seemed disappointed, as if expecting something more exotic. She considered the word, the sound it made. "Mooching. Well, it's a nice word. I think I'll use it."

"Excellent. Now, can I get back to my confession?"

"OK. Do I need to prepare myself? Get hot water and towels or anything?"

Martin ignored her flippancy and dived in. "Tony's here."

She looked around the pub, interestedly. "Tony who?"

"Tony."

"Oh." She didn't explode as he'd been expecting, but her face fell and she just sat looking at him and thinking. He let the silence linger and then, unable to bear it any longer, broke it.

"Is that all?"

"What did you want me to say?"

"I don't know. I just… needed to tell you."

"Why? Is that why we're here? In Orkney?"

"No… Yes… No."

"Make your mind up."

"Look, Kim, I wanted to be with you. Spend Christmas with you. It just so happened that my boss knew Tony was coming here and wanted someone to keep an eye on him."

"Really?"

"Yes. He thinks ... well, we think... he's going to try and... do something." Martin looked glum. "So he hit me with the old carrot and stick switcharoo: first they hit you with a stick, then they hit you with a carrot."

"So you brought me. As the carrot."

"Yes... No... Well, yes, obviously I brought you. But I wanted to be with you."

Kim leaned in close, staring into his eyes. His soul. "Would you have asked me to come here, with you, at Christmas, if Tony *hadn't* been here?"

"Yes." Martin's reply was instant, from the gut, and he knew for certain then it was the truth.

Kim leant back in her seat and regarded him coolly. "Well, that's alright then." She said quietly.

She looked sad and Martin didn't know what to do or say. They sat together in silence for a while, sipping their drinks and looking over each others' shoulders into space. Once again, Martin felt the need to break the quiet.

"Are you ok?" he asked gently.

"Yes." She replied, still subdued.

"Are *we* ok?"

"You tell me."

"Oh, please don't be like that."

"Be like what?"

"All cryptic and moodiness."

"Well, pardon me Buster!" she flushed and waggled her head sarcastically.

"That's more like it." He smiled at her, trying to break the mood. It didn't work.

"Don't patronise me. I'm not some performing seal, putting on a show so you can pat me on the head and say *good girl*."

"That's not what I meant at all."

"Well, what did you mean?"

"I mean I like you. I like you a lot." He put a hand on hers and she looked down at it. "Enough to want to spend Christmas with you. Enough to bring you here to meet my parents, see my childhood home. Enough to be upset that I may be fucking this up because of a coincidence that is out of my control that I am being honest with you about." His eyes were now tearing up. "That's what I mean."

Kim put her other hand on top of his and looked up, her eyes now moist as well. "Val was right. You are a keeper."

23

Christmas Eve

The snow was falling in heavy fat flakes, dusting the woodland and the lawn at Yair with white. Blysse was sliding a present underneath the lavishly decorated Christmas tree, Vasilij was standing at the French doors looking out into the softly illuminated dark. She had watched him take tablets for his eye pain and his left hand still held the empty brandy glass. The fingers of his right were jiggling strangely behind his back.

"Blysse?" He spoke to the window pane, his breath visible on the glass.

"Hm-mm?" She came up behind him and stood sharing in the silence.

"May I ask you something?"

"Hm-mm."

He put his glass down on a side table and turned towards her. When he dropped to one knee she felt her eyes moisten and her breath catch in her throat. She saw something sparkling, a huge white flash nestling in a dark plush box in his hand and despite her best efforts, when she looked into his eyes to give her answer, Blysse Baptiste began to cry.

The last men locked up the main sliding doors to the plant. One climbed into a Mitsubishi Shogun wearing Caledonian Seafood livery and made a phone call. The other walked over to the gate and waited for the truck to leave the compound before he padlocked it shut. Paul watched through his binoculars as the second man got into the passenger seat and the pair drove off down the freshly laid cinder track.

"We're good." He shouted to Cullen, who was taking a piss off the edge of a small crag away to their right. He shuffled up from his seating position and started to pack away his gear and the tarp. Cullen walked over zipping his flies and lent a hand. Within fifteen minutes they had climbed down from their protected spot on the hillside and were marching up the track towards the main gate.

Paul took out a set of bolt cutters and sliced through the padlock chain. Cullen swung the gate open and walked over to the main entrance above which winked a blue light - the main site alarm. He punched in some numbers on the keypad at the door: the light went out and there was an audible click. He pulled on the metal door and it slid easily open just enough for the pair of them to creep through and pull it close again.

"OK." Said Cullen. "Now the tricky part."

The building was full of enormous circular tanks connected by a maze of pipes and tubes in an assortment of sizes and colours. Most of the tanks were a pale translucent blue and in many you could make out the ghosts of fish as they swam around within. Each tank was taller than either of the men and some were more than 10 metres across. Walking between them Cullen felt as if he was moving through a scale model of an aquatic oil refinery. He found his way across the main floor and up a metal slatted staircase to some offices suspended beneath the corrugated roofing. There was an eerie light emanating from each of the tanks, Cullen thought, perhaps to simulate daylight. He flicked on the strip lights in the offices and went over to a row of filing cabinets behind a desk.

"What are we looking for?" Paul asked.

"Blueprints. Plans. Drawings. We need something which shows us the layout of all these tanks and pipes."

"OK." Paul started rifling through the top drawer of a cabinet, Cullen started at the other end of the row. "Then what?"

"Then we flush the system."

"What?"

"Look. This whole place is one big recirculating system. All the tanks and pipes are interconnected. Water, fish and waste will get channelled down different tubes and pipes to move them from one place to another. Water will get purified and fed back in and any top-up water will get fed in from the reservoir outside. 95% of the water will stay in here for ever, pretty much. All we need to do is find a way to flush all these tanks and pipes down into the river."

He moved on to the second cabinet, working swiftly as he talked. "It's quite interesting actually. As the fish grow they'll get moved from tank to tank, graded as they are moved so you keep similar size fish together. Different size fish eat different types, sizes and amounts of feed - that's the stuff being sprayed out over the tanks by those rotating lawn sprinkler things. Uneaten feed and fish crap gets sucked down into the base of each tank and channelled out along some of the tubes and out into the exhaust pipe, so to speak, which discharges all the shit into the river."

"How do you know all this?" Paul was impressed by any display of knowledge beyond his ken.

"There's something these days called *the internet?*"

"Oh yeah. I heard about that." Paul moved on to the next cabinet. "I thought that was for porn."

They continued in silence for a while until Paul pulled out a sheaf of A3 papers. "This do?"

Cullen cleared the desk with a single swipe and laid the sheets out on the wooden surface. "Yeah. Let's see. This bit... here... is that array of tanks over there... here's the filtration unit... hmmm. Ok, this may take a while."

Paul pulled out the desk chair and sat back in it, tilting the seat with the lever underneath so he could rock back and put his feet up on the desk. He pulled out a small tin and started making a roll-up.

"You want one?" he offered it to Cullen when he'd finished.

"What's in it?"

"That shit you got me."

"Ah. Nope." Cullen went back to the drawings. "Thanks all the same."

"Suit yourself." Paul lit the rollie and inhaled deeply, looking up to the ceiling and exhaling loud and long. "Mmm. That's better." He smoked in silence for a while, mellowing all the time. Eventually a thought occurred to him. "Cullen?"

"Un-huh?" Cullen said, absent-mindedly. He was still struggling with schematics, making scribbled notes on a pad.

"You gonna help me nail him?"

"Who?"

"The big guy. Guy who did my dogs."

"Hmm. Violence is against my nature." He looked across at Paul, slightly hurt.

"Really?"

"Well, mostly." Cullen sighed. "Tell you what: I'll find him, you do him."

"Deal."

"OK." He shouted with relief. "Here we go!"

"Really?"

"Oh yeah. In about twenty minutes 3,000 tonnes of precious biomass is going to start emptying into the Tweed."

Half an hour later they left the building and reset the alarm. Cullen re-threaded the severed chain through each arm of the main gate and loosely joined it with a spare link he took from his pocket. Unless someone walked up and physically yanked the chain they'd never know it wasn't properly locked. As they walked down the cinder track to the trail leading back up the hill, Cullen's phone went off in his pocket.

"You gonna answer that?"

Cullen pulled it out of his pocket and looked at the Caller Id. "No need. The tanks are draining nicely."

"What do you mean?" He looked over Cullen's phone at the screen. "Hey! Is that the alarms going off? How did you get the guy's phone?"

"I didn't. Just switched the SIMs."

"How did you do that?" Paul was lost in admiration.

"Need to know, Beep. Need to know."

The weather outside the small window was atrocious. Hail and sleet battered at the glass, thrown by a vicious wind hurling itself across the bay into the sanctuary of the harbour. Sitting cosily on a high-backed trestle bench looking out, a healthy fire burning in the open hearth next to them, were Viktor and Georgi. They sat in a comfortable, familiar silence each turning a glass of apple schnapps in their hands, a half-empty bottle of the clear liquid standing between them.

Georgi didn't look too bad for a dead man, thought Viktor, but he certainly smelt like one. He had listened as Georgi, in animated Russian, told him how he'd almost drowned while on Harris, found his way back to the mainland and managed to hook back up with Jelena at the boatyard. He'd figured that Jelena would have handed him a wad of cash and pushed him out of the door with instructions to get himself to Orkney and meet up with Viktor - as much a tactic to rid herself of Georgi's unwelcome olfactory assault as one to increase the chances of success for Viktor by uniting him with his old sparring partner.

Pondering his position now, the pair quietly drinking and thinking, he wondered at the appeal of this shambling cesspit and how best to put this act-first, think-second asset to use. He needed a bath. And a shave. And some new clothes. It didn't look, or smell, as if he had changed any item of clothing since he'd managed to swim ashore. But it was late Christmas Eve so nothing would now be open for a few days and, even then, options on Orkney were severely limited. He figured the best bet would be to get round the back of the marine chandlers off the harbour front and steal some work gear.

He spoke softly to Georgi and rose to leave. Georgi picked up the bottle of schnapps and followed him loyally out of the door into the teeth of the storm. The drinkers in the bar let out a collective, audible sigh of relief as the door closed behind them and the opportunity to breathe normally through their noses was handed to them as an early Christmas present.

In the end, getting into the processing facility on Crowness Road had been the easy part. For whatever reason, the last car out of the staff car park left just after noon and by 3.30pm the place was dark and deserted. He had plenty of time. Tony smiled a crazy smile to himself and padded softly through the empty reception area and across through the security doors. The building was arranged over two floors: the first floor was offices, meeting rooms, kitchen and a staff canteen; the ground floor was the processing facilities, the heart of the operation.

At the far right of the building were two large shuttered roller doors which, when raised, would reveal a giant loading bay. Here the tankers carrying recently killed fish would be attended by forklifts, scooping up the large plastic bins full of dead salmon and ferrying them into the factory. Hydraulic lifts raised these tubs and tipped their contents out onto a conveyor belt which carried the fish down to huge metal maws, glistening stainless steel mouths of the gutting machines. From here the fish would be graded, de-headed, trimmed, sliced, deboned before being packed for onward dispatch.

Tony surveyed this massive surgical array of mechanised slicers, trimmers, rollers and strippers spanning the size of a football field. The cold, clinical efficiency of the place made him weep at the thought of the sheer tonnage of biomass destined for slaughter each and every day so that facilities like this could be fed and justified. He hardened his resolve and stepped through a set of strip curtains and the changing room through to the stairs up to the offices above. The corridor ran down the middle of the building and offices gave off to both sides, each with windows out onto the factory floor below. The fluorescent lights and unnatural quiet - even the ice machines and generator were silent - gave the place a feel like a film set: the innards of an alien spaceship perhaps, or an intense form of purgatory dressed in white light and steel.

Working carefully, he placed the homemade incendiary devices in waste baskets in each of the four corner offices and then two in the middle of the corridor for good measure, and set the timers all for midnight. He placed the baskets amidst piles of files or other papers and adjacent to items of wooden furniture or fabrics to try and maximise the speed with which the fire would take hold.

He checked his watch and saw that it was nearly 5 o'clock - this was taking longer than he thought. The knee wound he had mysteriously collected in his last encounter with Viktor had healed over but not returned him to full mobility. He was having to hobble and limp, wincing as he went down the corridor, back down the stairs and out of the main building turning off the fluorescent lights as he went. He drove gingerly back down Crowness Rd and right around the harbour onto the High Street where he turned a quick left and then right to bring him round to the rear of the office building which dominated the skyline.

"Will you stop that?" Martin wriggled in the driver's seat uncomfortably as Kim wrestled with his zip.

"That's not what you usually say."

"Kim! We're on a stakeout."

"Stakeout." She guffawed. "What's that? They've poisoned the waterhole? Quick, let's saddle up a possie and get after those varmints."

"Someone might see!"

"It's pitch black."

"Someone might still see."

"Well, good luck to them and Merry Christmas." She released his belt buckle and put her head in his lap. She was quiet for a while.

"Shit!"

"Nhhnhh?"

"It's him! Tony. He's going in!"

"Nnhnnn."

"Ah, Christ! Kim. Not now. Ah, no please."

She came up for air. "Do you want me to finish or not?"

Martin was torn but looking up could no longer see Tony. "No. Maybe later. Quick, we've got to get after him." He jammed his dick back in his pants and did his trousers back up. Kim checked her hair and face in the vanity mirror of the sunvisor and then sprung out of the car.

"So, which one of us is Sundance and which one of us is Butch?"

Martin looked at her in exasperation. "Do you want to be Butch?"

"Ahm, no. Silly question." She looked up and down the empty street. "So, now what?"

"We go in. Catch him in the act. Arrest him. Lock him up. Have a Merry Christmas."

"OK. Sounds like a plan."

He led her across the street and into the side door that Tony had disappeared into. Christ, did no-one on this island lock their door? They were in a bare corridor, the only illumination coming from dim emergency lighting in the ceiling and a bright shaft of light showing under a door someway down on the right. They almost tiptoed down the corridor towards the door and Martin motioned to Kim to stand to the side. Taking a deep breath, he mentally counted to three and then put the whole weight of his shoulder into the door.

It didn't budge.

"Whoops. How's that plan looking?"

"Hmm. Mike Tyson said: *Everyone has a plan until they are punched in the face.*"

"Well, shoot the lock out with your gun."

"What gun?"

"You don't have a gun?"

"I'm a Detective in the police force, not fucking John Wayne."

"You mean, Butch Cassidy?"

"Whatever. Do you have any helpful suggestions?"

"Right, said Fred. Time to knock the walls down."

"What? You're not making any sense."

"Sorry, I'm so excited. I'm all adrenaline. I could drown a toddler in my panties right now."

"Now, there's an image." He thought for a moment. "Look, he wouldn't bother locking the door behind him so I'm thinking this isn't the way he came in. There must be another door somewhere. Let's try round the corner."

They moved down to the end of the corridor and Martin poked his head round to see what was round the corner. Answer: more corridor but with a door at the end from which light was dimly escaping. An open door.

"Come on."

Martin led the way down the corridor to the open door and looked through to a long, open plan office with no sign of Tony. Lit only by the odd desktop lamp which had been left on and the street lighting reflecting through the windows, they walked through slowly, looking for signs of disturbance he might have left but saw nothing.

"What do you think he's looking for?" she whispered as the neared the end of the office.

"Dunno. A safe? Some incriminating files?"

"Maybe he wants to get access to a particular computer?"

"Yeah, well this conjecture is useful. Let's keep doing this. Oh no, wait … that would be pointless! Let's find the bastard instead."

They continued on, through a series of open-plan areas, each as identical and uninteresting as the next. When they reached the fire exit marking the end of the floor they took the stairs up to the next level and repeated the same procedure. By the time half an hour had passed, they had covered what felt like the entire building, each floor empty with no sign of Tony.

"Looks like Elvis has left the building." Kim urged, no longer bothering to whisper. "Let's go."

Martin walked to the window, looked out over the harbour and sighed. "He wanted to be here for a reason. What is it? Why break in, wander around and then leave?" He turned back to Kim. "Where the fuck's he gone?"

"Don't know." She shrugged. "He's a slippery bugger, though. Bear in mind he's been doing this clandestine act for a while now. Probably getting good at it."

"Nah." Martin mused. "Rank amateur. Hatchery fire had signs of deliberate damage. Found evidence of foul play at his other targets. Raffles he ain't."

A hard look came across Kim's face. "No, more like Mola Ram, trying to rip out Indy's heart in The Temple Of Doom. Tony - prepare to meet Kali!"

"You're not over him?"

"Oh, I am *so* over him. Fucker can rot in hell."

"You're in denial."

"No, I'm not!"

Martin smiled. "It's just you said *rip your heart out.* Seems maybe you loved him and didn't realise it?"

"Look, Buster. Don't try and psycho-analyse me." She put her hands on her hips.

"Kim, you can be hard as nails. You really can. Come across all sass and self-confidence." He put his hands on her shoulders. "But underneath ... well, it's ok to be human you know? It's not a sign of weakness. You must have had good times with Tony, must have been happy - at least now and then. To have stayed with him -?"

"Until he threw me out of a fucking moving car!" She was angry now and shook his hands away. "Lied to me about stealing my money. Not to mention stealing my fucking money!"

He saw that she was upsetting herself and reached for her once again. "Kim-"

"Let's go." She turned to leave. "Let's find the bastard and really hurt him. Hurt him like he hurt me, only worse."

"You don't mean that." Martin appealed, still trying to calm her down. "Let it go."

"I do mean it and I won't let it go." She looked him straight in the eye. "If I had a gun with two bullets and I was in a room with Hitler, Stalin and Tony, I'd shoot Tony. Twice."

Tony looked up at the three wellboats. These queens of the seas were always given girls names and tonight the piercing lights of the Sonja Explorer, Helga Norvic and Katja Poseidon shone across the harbour, beacons in the empty dark. Right now, with only a hour or two before midnight, he fully expected the crew lounges to be full of drinking, sleeping or puking crew members. Those with families would be phoning home, those without would be drowning their sorrows by watching movies in the onboard cinema or playing pool in the games room. No-one would be on duty, no-one would be sober and no-one would notice him as he boarded each in turn.

Viktor and Georgi, though, were watching, sheltering in a doorway overlooking the harbour, finishing off the last of the schnapps. The storm had subsided now and the wind was merely buffeting desolate snowflakes about beneath the street lights. Now fully equipped thanks to the generosity of the chandlery, both he and Georgi were able to withstand the cold wind blowing across the empty dockside, the boats bobbing in a slight swell, their masts pinging in the night air. They watched as Tony tottered up the gangplank onto the Poseidon, climbed a ladder up behind the bridge and disappeared inside. Ten minutes later he emerged from the same door, slipped down the ladder and off the boat and limped round to the Norvic moored beside it.

When Tony stepped inside this time Viktor smacked Georgi on the arm and pointed. Together they threw their empty bottles to the ground and jogged unsteadily down to the water's edge and started up the gangway to board the Explorer, slipping on the greasy surface. This was the smallest of the three vessels and no lights showed anywhere on board, the crew having abandoned her and decided to join their colleagues on the Poseidon. Viktor and Georgi crept through the first door they found and felt the relief of relative warmth, quiet and absence of wind immediately. Viktor scanned right down a dark corridor and then turned to see Georgi padding away to his left.

"Where are you going?" He spat furiously through his teeth.

"Drink." Shrugged Georgi and plodded off into the darkness.

Martin and Kim came down the fire escape stairs and back out onto the street where they'd gone in. The street was still empty and it was now getting close to 11 o'clock. The pubs would soon be closing and people would be milling around on their way home for Christmas. They climbed back into the car and pulled slowly away, turned left at the end of the road and did one final sweep of the main harbour road to see if they could see any sign of Tony. Kim stared disconsolately out of the window, seemingly done paying attention for the night.

"There he is!" She pointed, sounding surprised herself. "That's him."

She was pointing out down into the harbour itself where a number of vessels, big and small, had moored up. The wooden walkway linking them was lit by a string of street lights and as the lone figure passed under each, the profile and pony tail were clearly distinguishable.

"What's he doing now?" Martin asked.

"No idea."

They watched as he approached a large ship with cabin lights blazing and a blue hull. He disappeared from view behind the boat but didn't appear on the other side of it. Martin turned the car around and headed back to the car park at the entrance to the harbour. They pulled up and sat watching. Here they had a clear view of the large ships - three of them - moored up in a line. After a few minutes they saw Tony march down the entry way from the biggest ship and walk over to the second one and up onto that.

"Right, let's go." Martin moved to open the car door.

"Where? Onto the ship he's just got off or the ship he's just got on?"

Good question, he thought, puffing out his cheeks. "How about-" he paused mid-sentence as he saw two large dark figures appear beneath one of the dockside lights and stride purposefully down towards the ships. The lead figure was tall and lean, the second burlier and more shambolic in his gait. "Hold on."

The pair walked to the end of the walkway and climbed up onto the last and smaller of the three boats, disappearing inside.

"Oh fuck." He said.

"Wait, is this the Orkney Christmas Hide-and-Seek Championships or something?"

"No. Unless I my eyes deceive me, those two ne'er-do-well's are Viktor and Georgi - the Russian bad guys charged with meting out Grevious Bodily Harm to your friendly neighbourhood ex."

"Ok, and …?"

"Ok, let's see." Martin started thinking. "There's three of them and two of us."

"And three boats." Kim added.

"Yes. And three boats." Martin's mind raced. "We need backup."

"Right!" chirped Kim, relieved. "Go on then, call for backup."

"Who from?"

"From whom." Kim corrected.

"From whom?"

"The Orkney police, of course!"

Martin laughed in her face. "Are you out of your mind? The Orkney police force probably consists of two men, one who is nearing pensionable age and one who can't read and is currently on another island a long ferry ride away."

"OK. What about the crew from the boats?"

"Brilliant idea!"

"You're welcome."

"Ok, I'll take the lead boat - this one with all the lights on. You take the second one."

"Whoa, I know it's Christmas but Ho-ho-hold the fuck up, Buster! I'm not going on a boat full of blokes. On my own. In the dark."

"Right. Sorry. Yes, stupid idea. Ok, stay here or come with me."

Kim thought for a nano-second. "I'll come with you."

Turning right at the end of the corridor, Viktor shook his head and wondered where Georgi was. Then the lights came on and the corridor suddenly exploded into brightness as Georgi casually flipped light switches as he went.

"What you do?" Viktor whispered.

"Looking."

"But, why turn lights on?"

"To see." Said Georgi, obviously. He tried a door handle next to him, which opened and he stepped through. Inside was some kind of lounge with two large corner leather sofas, a pool table, large flat screen TV and a small kitchen area with a breakfast bar. Georgi moved over to the kitchen and started opening cabinets. Shortly he turned back to Viktor clutching a dark bottle and beaming a big grin.

"What is it?" Viktor hissed.

"Balsam." Georgi eyes lit up as he pulled off the top and took a large swig. He wiped his mouth with the back of his hand and handed the bottle towards Viktor. There was a sudden echoing clang and the pair of them froze. The sound of footsteps in the corridor meant Tony was on board. Viktor smiled and drew a pistol from inside his jacket. He motioned with his head for Georgi to stand behind the door while he moved over to a sofa where he'd be facing the door when it opened. They waited for a minute without a sound other than Georgi gently guzzling from the large bottle, each raising eyebrows at the other as they listened. Eventually, Viktor walked purposefully over to the door and flung it open with his right, the pistol ready in his left.

The corridor was empty.

Signalling Georgi to stay there, Viktor stepped slowly down the corridor leading into the ship. Tony looked like he had been following Georgi's example and putting lights on as he went so Viktor just followed the lights until they stopped and then looked at the door options available to him. He heard the sound of feet again somewhere below him, echoing metallically through the belly of the boat, and saw one of the doors to his right was slightly ajar. He stepped through and onto a white-painted metal flight of steps leading down. A glimpse of Tony's green waterproof coat flashed below and to his right and Viktor fired a knee-jerk shot in that direction. The bullet ricocheted off a wall and the sound was incredibly loud.

He heard a door slam shut and footsteps fading away. Bounding down the steps he saw an exit door away at the far end but when he reached it found it locked. Cursing he bounded back up the steps and ran down the corridor he'd entered from. He shouted for Georgi as he passed the lounge door but carried on running until he was outside on the boat. He could just make out Tony's outline as he slid down a harbour ladder into a small motorboat tied up at the dock. The bastard was getting away.

"Police!"

Martin burst into the lounge room of the Poseidon holding one hand up in front of him and his credentials in the other. They had hollered and halloo'ed loudly since they had first boarded the boat but no-one had heard them and they had followed the muted sounds of music and voices until they came to this room on the boat which seemed like it might be the only one occupied. When they opened the door they realised why.

Perhaps thirty men were crowded into this space meant for half as many. The air was thick with tobacco and the sweet smell of dope. A large number of the men were passed out, either through drink or the dope, and a good handful more were sitting stoned on bar stools away to Martin's left watching a porn movie on a large screen TV, oblivious to their entrance. The blue baize of the pool table was littered with empty bottles and cans and an ipod speaker which was blaring out something by Eminem.

Martin's first thought was: *these blokes are going to be no use as backup*.

Seeing the porn movie, Kim clung close to Martin and kept her eyes focussed on a happy bearded man in an open-neck short-sleeved shirt and fine set of perfect white teeth. His eyes sparkled as he stood and came over towards them, hand extended.

"Merry Christmas!" he had a European accent - Dutch perhaps, Danish maybe. When Martin didn't extend his own hand the man frowned slightly and looked around at his fellow drinkers. He reached over to the pool table and turned the volume down on Eminem. "I am Captain Olafssen." He extended his hand again. "And you are...?"

"Detective Inspector Jenkins, Border Policing Command." They shook hands. "And this is my, er, colleague, DC Schofield." Kim nervously extended her own hand to be shaken and the Captain lifted it to his mouth and kissed it.

"Charmed." He said, and Kim blushed. "What are you doing on board my ship?"

"We, er, need your help."

"Really." His eyes narrowed. "You, at least -" he said, nodding at Kim. "Are not a police officer." Kim blushed again. "You-" he pointed at Martin. "You, I don't know. I am not familiar with British police identification." He scratched his beard thoughtfully. "Who are you really, and what do you want?"

Martin recovered some of his official demeanour and straightened himself. "I am DI Jenkins even if, as you say, this lady is not a colleague of mine. But she is assisting me in my enquiries… which have led me to this boat-"

"Ship." Interjected Olafssen. "It is a ship. My ship. And, as is standard maritime practice, on board my ship I have sole command and *you* have no jurisdiction."

"Captain." Martin attempted to reason with this most eloquent man. "I do not dispute your statement. And I have no intention or interest in whatever substances you and your crew have been using to, ah, enjoy the festivities. It is Christmas after all." He smiled at the Captain who kept eye contact noncommittally. "But we do need your help. Right now."

"Captain!" A heavyset man bundled himself into the room looking somewhat the worse for drink and still doing up his fly, leaning on the door jamb and breathing heavily. He saw Martin and Kim and froze.

361

"What is it?" Olafssen demanded impatiently. When the man seemed reluctant to talk in their company the Captain signalled the pair of them. "It's OK. What is it?"

"Ahm, …" the man continued, weakly. "I think there is a bomb on board."

Martin felt goosebumps shoot across his skin and took control. Immediately, he realised what Tony's plan must be. "You-" he pointed at the Captain. "Get everyone off this ship. Now! And make sure no-one is on the other boats either." he pointed at the heavyset man. "You, show me where this bomb is. Kim, come with me."

The man led them down metal stairs into a white-painted hold with large standing tanks and wall-mounted boxes and tubes running everywhere. All the doors out of the area had large locking wheels on them. They stepped across some raised bulkheads and over to a large wall-mounted control panel. At the foot of the wall, where the metal tube ran into the wall and disappeared were three sticks of dynamite wrapped with duct tape and a black lcd timer counting down. As they watched it flicked from 42:00 to 41:59. Martin looked at his watch and looked at Kim. "Get off this boat and get back to the car. I left my phone in the cubby under the dash. Dial 999 and get whoever you can to evacuate this area and the area around Krupchenko's offices."

Kim looked suddenly very scared and vulnerable, all her brassy veneer gone. "But Martin, can I stay with you?"

"Kim. I'm serious. Get off this boat and dial 999." He held her shoulders again. "Then look in my contacts and dial Maxwell's number-"

"Who's Maxwell?"

"My boss. Tell him what's going on and that I'm asking to mobilise whoever he can to evacuate the High Street and harbour areas. An unknown number of explosive devices are set to go off at midnight."

"What are you going to do?"

"I'm going to see if I can find Tony."

The storm had abated slightly and Tony was able to steady himself on the launch and start the engine without having to fight with the elements. The gunshot had been his first shock of the night, catching him completely by surprise. He hadn't expected any of the crew to be on board at all, let alone armed - and he had shot off the wellboat as fast as he could, before he had time to set a bomb on board. Never mind, it would have to do - the factory, HQ and the other two wellboats were all now fully primed and ready to go off on cue at midnight. In the dark he hit the boat headlights and searchlights and then pointed them out towards the harbour entrance. As he approached the mouth and saw the swell on the sea ahead he flashed a last look back at the ships moored at the quayside. His second shock of the night was seeing the lights on the Explorer all lit up and the prow of the boat pulling out slowly from its berthing.

The wellboat was coming after him.

Viktor surveyed the equipment on the bridge. Some of it was familiar, much of it completely incomprehensible and, he hoped, all to do with the wells and tanks on board rather than navigation or stabilisation. Georgi had helped untie the ship from its moorings and then gone in search of more booze on board. Viktor didn't have time to think of what else he could usefully be doing - his focus was on getting Tony and he was making his plan up as he went along. But he had a size advantage since the wellboat, small though it was, was about three times the size of Tony's launch and probably many more times powerful than that. Also Viktor was a qualified and experienced navigator and skipper - Tony wasn't. The way Viktor saw it, Tony had only two possible advantages: he had full use of both hands, and he might actually know where he was going.

Viktor followed the launch out past the safety of the harbour wall and immediately felt the moderate swell take effect on the boats hull. He steadied the starboard engine and trimmed the boat to keep it into the wind as best he could. The lights from Tony's boat were hard to make out in the darkness but Viktor could see the white trail of his wake in his own lights so followed it. Within minutes he was out of range of land and all lights other than his own.

Martin raced down the walkway from the Poseidon just as the Explorer pulled away from its moorings. He looked in disbelief as the wellboat slowly accelerated after a much smaller motorboat fast disappearing out of the harbour mouth.

"Shit!" he shouted to the sky. Who the fuck was driving the boat? Was that Tony? Then, who the fuck was piloting this huge wellboat? "Jesus. Suffering. Fuck!"

He stood hopelessly at the water's edge as the two boats slowly pulled away into the night. After a while he was aware of some footsteps and turned to see Kim panting towards him, her skirts billowing in the breeze, holding his phone in her hand.

"I made the calls." She was completely out of breath. "Maxwell wants a word."

"Huh?"

"Your boss." Kim panted. "Wants a word." She handed him the phone.

"Hello?"

"Martin? I've scrambled Bomb Disposal from Aberdeen and an army unit from Lossiemouth. They're all being ferried over in Sea Kings. Be with you in twenty minutes. The local fire brigade, army reserve and paramedics are also being briefed as I speak. Are you sure we only have until midnight?"

"I don't know. I've only seen one bomb on one ship and that was set for midnight. I don't know how many others there are, where they are or when they're set for. Maybe there are none, maybe there are loads!"

"Is there anything else I can do?"

Martin watched as the Explorer's lights winked out of view. "Yeah, can you call the Coastguard?"

Tony headed for Puldrite Bay. There was a salmon farm in the bay itself, about half a mile from shore, and between the harbour and the bay was a small rocky islet with a short jetty. If he got close enough into the bay the shallows would prevent the wellboat from following him in, its draft needing a lot deeper water than his own launch. This was the edge Tony needed as he heard the wellboat's superior engines gaining on him without needing to look around.

Viktor fiddled with one of the monitor screens on the bridge in front of him and realised it was displaying a sonar image of the area around the boat. Like a radar image in green, he could see 360-degrees out to a distance of several miles. He could make out the moving dot of Tony's boat and, some way ahead of it, the now-familiar circular shapes arranged in a grid formation which were the tell-tale sign of a salmon farm. He decided to change course and cut straight to the farm and try and cut Tony off. The waves were growing and the wind was picking up, hitting the boat and cascaded the sea water over the prow, brine and ozone plashing the windows on the bridge. Viktor increased the engine speed slightly and kept his eyes on the monitor as the salmon cages started to quickly draw closer.

Tony could feel the wake of the wellboat affecting his own course now and realised that it was no longer right behind him but was trying to attack him from the side and that he wasn't going to make it to the bay shallows in time. He needed a plan B and all he had was the farm barge and cages so he turned into the wellboat's course slightly and herded his motor as high as he dared. His small launch was now rocking alarmingly in the growing swell and he could only see the farm ahead briefly when he crested one wave before dipping into the trough of the next.

Georgi was starting to feel decidedly unwell. The 75cl of Black Balsam on top of a litre of apple schnapps might have had something to do with it but Georgi put it down to the motion of the sea and the nervousness he always felt in rough weather. One of nature's landlubbers, he viewed this moderate swell as a hurricane-level storm and believed with each wave crashing onto the deck that his end had come and he would meet, for real this time, the watery grave he had so miraculously evaded. He struggled out of the nearest door and onto the deck, almost up-ending himself as the wind threw the heavy door back at him. Staggering to the side of the boat he leant over and immediately threw up. His head was spinning with the combination of alcohol and swaying motion, his vision blurred by the spray and vomit-induced tears. Never one to trust his own senses too much, his natural sangfroid was nonetheless shaken to its core when he saw an enormous black fin scythe past his peripheral vision and, turning to gape, was convinced he saw a gleam of creamy whiteness and a razor sharp smile the size a dining table before another tonne of spray broke over him and all was dark.

Tony made it to the floating concrete barge and tied up to see the wellboat slowing and arcing around towards him less than 50 metres away. That was when he saw Viktor on the bridge.

"You fucking retard!" He shouted across the storm.

In response Viktor simply stepped out of the wheelhouse, raised his left arm and fired a pistol at him. Tony ducked out behind the raised stairway and felt the splinters from the door frame scatter over his back with the impact from the bullet. He scrabbled around the back of the barge keeping the wellboat on the far side of the doorway and peeked out as Viktor fired again. Seemingly forgetting about piloting the boat for the time being, Tony watched as it veered gently away to the left and brushed one of the cages on its starboard side. Viktor sensed his mistake and charged back into the wheelhouse to correct the boat's course but it was too late. The boat slammed into the two cages nearest the barge, breaking their perimeters, and careered slowly but inevitably towards the barge itself. The sides of the cages crumpled away in slow motion and started to topple as the mass of writhing fish within them sensed freedom and moved as one towards the gaping route to open water. Within seconds there was visible a silver river of fish, pulsing out in a flood either side of the wellboat as it drifted into a collision with the barge. Tony stood entranced as, out of nowhere, he saw flashing grey missiles of seals appear amidst the boiling torrent of salmon, swooping and curling over and under the water like some aquatic *cirque du soleil*. The wellboat crunched finally into the barge, tipping it down at the front by a couple of meters, the boat almost rising up onto the barge at its prow. Tony fell back on impact and then felt himself slide inexorably down into the icy water.

From being in slow-mo, all of a sudden time seemed to speed up and everything then happened very quickly. Tony felt the shock of the cold as he hit the water and turned as he fell, looking for something, anything to latch hold of.

Viktor seemed to have thrust the wellboat engines into reverse and the water around the stern of the boat was now churning up with spume and pink foam, interspersed with shining chunks of freshly chopped salmon shooting into the air. The sea was alive with roiling silver, red fish blood and flashing sealskins.

The boat struggled but started slowly turning and Tony paddled furiously back away from it as the barge righted itself and spooled its own wake into the churning sea. He grabbed hold of a cage rim and tried to pull himself out of the water.

The wellboat managed to turn through 90-degrees but then found itself pulling against some unseen force. Viktor could hear the engines straining and kept the power on full but the boat was barely moving and the sound of straining and screeching metal was starting to be heard over the roar of the wind. He kept the power on and the boat slowly started to keel to port as whatever force was holding it continued to resist its pull. He looked out from the bridge window to see if he could make out what the ship was caught on and thought he saw a dark lurching figure on the side of the wellboat suddenly tip overboard and drop silently into the foaming red and white. Before the figure could come back up for air, he watched in awe as a glistening black shape curved majestically from the pink-grey sea, it's massive frame rose and rose and then fell and fell, a huge dorsal fin surfacing and then diving. It rolled away to the left, white and black, and he knew straightaway it was a killer whale.

Tony was splashing in the bloody foam and froth as he saw the whale and immediately dolly-zoomed to his first meeting between shark and seal, in the balmy waters off California. He froze for a moment, a mannequin reflecting on the circle of life and the savage beauty of nature in the raw. He couldn't tell whether the whale had taken a man or a seal but his main concern now was making sure it didn't take him. As the boat continued to lurch in the water Tony managed to climb soaking onto the cage walkway and as the waves pounded into the side, he caught a severed rope and started to bind himself to the platform to keep himself afloat. He watched the propellers churning through the ragged mesh of cage netting and cables as the boat's engines desperately raged trying to cut themselves free. He felt the walkway jerk beneath his feet and, looking down, saw the water level rising to his knees.

Viktor locked the wheel in place and tore out of the bridge to look astern. The wellboat was now gathering steam and pulling away from the farm, taking with it two cages which it had torn from their moorings. They bobbled and dipped in the swell and were now empty of fish, nets half torn away and one of the platforms sliced in half by his propellers.

The farm site was a scene of watery carnage, pieces of dead fish littered the sea, pools of red dispersing and combining with blotches of grey spume and engine oil. Appearing and disappearing like conjoined hoops of a gigantic sea serpent were flashing darts of grey seals, feeding on the remains and the live salmon still departing the site.

On the far side of one of the cages was the drenched and beaten figure of Tony, shivering with cold and tied to a stanchion on the walkway. He was helpless as the boat towed the cage he was standing on out into open water.

Viktor pulled his prize hip flask from his coat and took a warming swig of apple schnapps, feeling the wind hitting his face and the salt breeze spinning the hair away from his face. As the small clock on the bridge gently chimed midnight, the mainland behind him exploded in a staccato display of light, flames and thunder. Viktor flashed a huge wide-eyed grin: *A merry Christmas to all, and to all a Good Night!*

24

Boxing Day

"OH NO HE ISN'T!"

Down in the front row Blysse could make out the twinkling eyes and happy smiles of kids with their parents, yelling out "OH YES HE IS!" with gleeful abandon. Roared hoarse by the end of the show she had watched from behind the curtains as parents led their happy and exhausted offspring out of the auditorium and realised that she was actually enjoying herself, happy in her work, giving families enjoyment and spreading festive cheer. The weather may be completely shit in this god-awful city but, by god, the people threw themselves into Christmas like nowhere else she'd ever been. Harvey had been right and she'd been wrong. So be it. That's why she had an agent - someone who could make informed decisions on her behalf and leave her to excel at her core competencies of pouting, bosom-thrusting and hair-tossing.

Blysse realised she'd be sorry to leave the show behind, but she had to come to some arrangement with them now - she was getting married. Vasilij had suggested a wedding on board his yacht, and a romantic honeymoon sailing round Orkney and the top of Scotland looking for seals and whales. When he'd mentioned this she had squealed with astonishment and delight. After the show she showered and changed and went in search of Bernard.

"Blysse, sweetie. You were marvellous. Marvellous. So much zip!" The director kissed her on both cheeks and held her hands together. He had been chatting to the sound man in his booth in the upper circle, comparing notes after the performance, and turned to greet her.

She glanced over at the sound man who was suddenly busy with his dials and sliders.

"Could we talk somewhere private?"

"Of course." He put on a slightly puzzled look but led her down the stairs into the upper circle lobby bar and across to the rear stairs that took them down to his office between floors. In reality it was little more than a large broom cupboard, with no windows, space only for a lonely chair, desk and filing cabinet, and with the single added feature of a phone line installed He had done his best to make it homely by hanging framed posters of past panto's on the walls and he glanced at them now as he plonked himself on the edge of his desk and motioned for her to sit in the chair. "Ah, The Hoff in 2010. Now *that* was a show!"

"Had he done many panto's before?"

"No" Bernard coughed a laugh. "Didn't have a clue what panto was - not like your own good self." Blysse kept her face straight and let Bernard continue. "I had to coach and coach and coach. Gosh, he was hard work. But what a trooper! Once he'd got it he was a diamond. What a star! And so-o-o camp." Bernard twinkled at the memory and Blysse let him wallow in it for a moment before trying to kick the conversation her way.

"Did he see out the whole season?"

"Of course!" He couldn't have looked more shocked at the thought. "My dear, he'd got it in his blood. He couldn't keep away. If we'd ran until Easter he'd still have turned in 110%"

"Right."

"So, what was it you wanted to talk to me about?"

Come on, she thought. Deep breath. You don't owe him anything. "Well, you see. Bernard, unlike The Hoff, I'm afraid I won't be able to finish the run. Sorry."

"Sweetie. What do you mean?"

"I won't be able to stay until the season ends." She looked at his mystified face, not wanting to have to spell it out any more. This was harder than she'd hoped. "I'm getting married? On New Year's Day."

"Wow, darling. Congratulations!"

"Yes, but my future husband doesn't want me working after that. He wants - we want - a honeymoon."

"Ah. I see. Well-" She could see the wheels turning as he searched for a solution. "I'm sure Cindy can stand-in for you for a night or two. I'm sure we'll manage."

"No, my husband doesn't want me working when we're married. Period."

"But the season runs until the middle of January!"

"I know."

"Blysse, sweetie. Your contract states you're committed for the run." His tone was starting to rise sharply and she could see him consciously struggling to stay calm. "You can't just walk out midway through. Married or not."

"My husband-to-be is … a very rich man. He's prepared to pay for the inconvenience."

"Darling, the money won't help. We need you and your star quality. We're sold out! People have paid to see you and if you're not there we'll lose reputation. Trust. And so will you." He looked sternly at her, like a parent scolding a toddler. "Your public will look at you in a completely different light. The press will have a field day. Your name will be mud." He looked over his glasses at her. "Blysse, honey. Do you really want to let your fans down?"

"He'll pay you £200,000." She watched him blanch. "If my last performance is December 28th."

"28th! But that's only two more days. You said you're not getting married until New Year."

"Yes, but there is preparation to do. Plus travelling time."

"But. But." Bernard spluttered, reality sinking in. "That will leave us …" he did a quick calculation. "… 30 shows short! That works out at less than £7000 a show."

"OK." Vasilij had prepared her for this eventuality. "£250,000."

Bernard gulped visibly but then his eyes narrowed. "£300,000 or I'll sue you for breach of contract and you'll never work in the theatre again."

"Done." And they shook hands.

"You useless fuck!" Vasilij was stamping around the drawing room at Yair, kicking furniture and thumping walls.

"He is dead." Viktor tried to remain unworried in the teeth of Vasilij's wrath but wasn't finding it easy.

"Is he?"

"I think."

"You. Fucking. Think." He spat into Viktor's face. "I am ruined." He put his face right into Viktor's - so close they were almost touching. Viktor could smell the sweat and anger but remained motionless. "Give me your knife."

Viktor obeyed and stood silent as Vasilij brandished the knife in his face.

"Remember what I said I would do if you failed me?" Viktor nodded imperceptibly. "I am a man of my word. I keep my promises. Give me your hand."

Viktor held out his left hand which, although still bandaged, had nearly healed.

"Your other hand." Vasilij hissed. He held Viktor's right hand on the desk and plunged the knife down hard into the back of it. Viktor trembled as he stayed upright, the knife embedded in his hand.

"There are only two reasons you are still alive."

Viktor wondered what they were but waited in silence.

"One: you will get my yacht to Orkney. I want to be in Orkney for New Year's Day and spend the next few days after that sailing around the islands. Lodge berthing plans, plot a course, do what you have to do. But you will take us there."

"But I just come from there." Viktor said, confused.

"And you will take us back there. On my yacht" Vasilij snarled and twisted the knife into Viktor's hand. "I am getting married."

Viktor looked doubtful as to how this could possibly serve as an explanation. Vasilij obliged.

"In Orkney. On board the yacht. On New Year's Day."

Viktor nodded imperceptibly.

"Two: you will marry me."

Viktor's eyes widened in shock.

"To Blysse. You will enact the ceremony."

"No understand."

"You will marry me and Blysse. On board."

"Cannot." Viktor replied, reluctantly.

"You can. And you will."

"No, cannot." Viktor realised he was risking his life at this moment just by disagreeing. He switched to Russian to explain that standard maritime law did not grant ship's captains the legal capacity to perform marriages on board.

Vasilij sneered in his face. "I don't care. Just do it. Leave the legalities to me."

"OK." Viktor shrugged.

"And if you can manage to do these two things without fucking them up." He tweaked the knife again. "Perhaps, I will let you live."

Vasilij swept out of the room leaving Viktor standing, his hand still pinned to the desk.

25

New Year's Eve

Cullen got out of the taxi and walked up the few steps into the lobby of The Scotsman Hotel, ignoring the doorman's outstretched hand and his look of disdain as they passed. The sign in the lobby for the Caledonian Seafood AGM was standing on an easel at the foot of the main staircase and he ascended the plushly carpeted steps and turned right on the mezzanine level towards the reserved reception room. He was early and the room was still largely empty with some staff at the front and on the stage putting out carafes of water, pencils and pads, and erecting posters and hoardings with the corporate logos on.

He sat at the far right of the very back row, nearest the exit but with a good view of the stage and the large screen acting as a backdrop, currently showing a rolling corporate video with no sound. A copy of the agenda, voting slips and annual report were on each chair and Cullen perused these, waiting while the hall slowly filled with people.

The big projection screen had been split into three sections: the lion's share of the screen was a head and shoulders shot of Vasilij Krupchenko, sitting in a book-lined study. He seemed to have something wrong with the left side of his face which looked slightly discoloured compared to the rest of it and appeared to move a beat or two behind the right side of his face. Cullen wondered if he'd had a stroke or something. Down the right hand side of the screen were four smaller camera shots, each showing a head and shoulders of different young men in white shirts and expensive haircuts. These had been introduced to the room as "The Analysts" and each was wearing a discrete earpiece and microphone which wrapped around the side of their face. Finally, along the bottom was a ticker display, scrolling right-to-left, showing live market share prices, quoted in NOK, with Caledonia Seafoods (CSL) price displayed in bold.

Cullen watched the faces, not listening, while Krupchenko droned on, reading from the prepared statement which was included in the annual report. He watched as Krupchenko finished his speech and threw the floor open to questions from The Analysts and kept an eye on the share price scrolling across the bottom of the screen, watching as it ticked up and down with each question and answer. It had started the meeting at 8.5 NOK and, after some heavy sweating and shaky gesticulating from Krupchenko, had fallen to 6.0 before making a bit of a rally on the back of some bravado hand-waving, palms open and earnest furrowed brows which took it back to 7-ish. A few bar charts and other diagrams he couldn't interpret had the price wavering again and struggling to keep above 7 before it took a final knock to its resting place when the session ended at 5.5. There was a short break where tea, coffee and biscuits were available along a set of tables on the far wall before settling down again for agenda item #4.

The main drawback to not being at the AGM in person was that Vasilij couldn't see what was going on in the room. He could see the thumbnails of his inquisitors - the analysts - on his monitor but he couldn't see the presentations. Plus, he didn't like the constant scrutiny of his webcam while sitting still for ninety minutes without trying to sweat, drink or need to pee.

He also couldn't see the rabble in the hall. He could hear them if the ushers handed them a microphone for specific questions but that was about it. These idiots who only owned a handful of shares and who wanted to exercise their rights to take the company to task once a year for whatever their personal agenda was. Fuckers didn't seem to realise that it was *his* company.

He'd done his best to mitigate the disastrous news haemorrhaging from all areas of his business over the last few weeks - the lost broodstock, the lost wellboats, the damage to Head Office - and tried to offset this against the equally unfortunate issues his competitors were facing through increased sea lice infestation rates and lower growth projections as a result. The whole industry was being hit and the only silver lining had been the astonishing rise of the spot price of Scottish salmon in the run up to Christmas. It alone had rescued his annual figures and the share price now rested on plans for the future.

Viktor had failed to bring Tony back to him - said he had disappeared. That simply wasn't good enough. He had been humiliated and shamed, his plans destroyed. There was a price to be paid now. And it would be paid, he would make sure of that.

He had done his best to control his black mood and his hopes had improved gradually as the meeting progressed without any sign of dissent or disruption. When he heard the exceptional CCS presentation announced his heart rate jumped briefly. Here was the moment he had waited for: to win them back over and take the market sentiment in the right direction once more.

Viktor came inside her with a powerful final thrust and flopped forwards, pinning her to the mattress. Jelena grumbled and grizzled trying to shift his weight until he reluctantly rolled to her left. While he lay gaping vacantly at the ceiling, she thought she could hear a low buzzing sound coming from the table next to the bed. She leant over and opened the drawer to find her phone skittering around in the drawer, vibrating its heart out.

"Viktor!"

"Uh?"

"Did you hide my phone in here?"

"One time" His speech was slurred and slow. "Always he interrupts."

"Viktor!"

She picked it up and answered it.

"Yes?"

"Jelena! Where have you been! I've been trying to call for ages. You have to stop this. You have to tell Vasilij now!"

"What? Feliks, is that you?"

"Yes. Jelena. Please! Tell Vasilij to stop it now."

"Stop what?" She sat up in bed, the urgency in Feliks' voice hitting home. "What are you talking about?"

"The AGM!" Feliks was shouting at her now. "He has to stop it. The CCS site is destroyed."

"What?"

"It has been drained! There are no fish. There is no water All the tanks are empty and -"

"What?"

"It's ruined!"

"What?"

"Please! Please stop saying 'what?'! I need you to tell Vasilij to stop the live transmission."

"The live - ?"

"He wants to cutover from the AGM presentation to live camcorder footage of the site during the AGM! If we do that it'll be a disaster - the place is a war zone."

"I don't understand." Jelena was desperately trying to kick her mind into gear.

"Didn't you know?"

"What? No!"

"Someone has drained this place and Vasilij is expecting - as a surprise - to cutover from the pre-planned presentation to my camera footage in... less than FIVE minutes!"

"Fuck."

She dropped the phone, grabbed the sheet off the bed tried to wrap it around her and rushed out of her cabin. Vasilij's study was two doors down the corridor and she burst in without knocking.

Cullen watched as Krupchenko's image shrunk down to a small picture-in-picture thumbnail at the bottom left and then a voice-over started. A simple black-on-white appeared: Closed Containment - Strategic Vision Becomes Reality which dissolved into a montage of photos showing a bright new factory interior, close-ups

382

of various tanks and fish, a series of large white numbers superimposed on the images fading left and right. A general appreciative murmur from the room indicated that this presentation was being taken well by all concerned: as it came to a close, the stock ticker showed a much improved price of 7.8.

There was a huge round of applause and the beaming smile of Krupchenko enlarged back to fill the main portion of the screen again. The smile rapidly left his face for a moment, replaced by a look indicative of him having superglued his jaws together. A black scowl passed across his face before the smile reappeared, albeit somewhat less genuine than before. "Ladies and gentlemen, let me now take you - LIVE - to our new Closed Containment site." There was a ripple of appreciation and surprised exclamations as Krupchenko's image disappeared once more and was replaced with somewhat shaky handycam footage.

Vasilij looked up, startled at the door opening, to see Jelena wearing nothing but a sheet. She was slicing her hand across her throat in the sign that usually meant "cut". What Vasilij wanted to say was "Get out! I am on camera with the analysts. I will deal with you later." But instead he just glared at her, doing his best to keep calm, while still facing the Skype webcam. He clenched and unclenched the muscles in his jaw to try and keep his anger down. Jelena stood and glared back at him, eyes bulging out of her head. He ignored her.

Vasilij recomposed his smile and looked straight into the webcam again. "Ladies and gentlemen …"

There was no voice-over on this presentation, but the juxtaposition between the previous slick company video and this one was made all the starker by the difference in what was being shown. No longer were thriving silver torpedoes of salmon, writhing and snarking in large blue tanks. Now these tanks were pale and listless and empty, a few water trickles at the bottom of a muddy silo the only movement. Where once there had been thousands of tiny creatures, surging in waves beneath sprinklers of feed, now there was only a handful of miniature carcasses scattered across the sides and bottom of alga-covered sumps. Then the vivacious hum and murmur of pumps and circulation units, now only the staccato whine of feed units still sporadically spraying out pellets wastefully into rotting piles.

Some in the audience had risen to their feet and were shouting at the table on stage, insisting there be an explanation for this: Who was in charge? What was this? Is this a joke, a hoax? Where is Krupchenko, what does he have to say? The analysts were bellowing like bulls for an explanation: their European accents thickening as their voices rose and they sometimes lapsed from their second language of English into their native tongue. The video picture went wonky and then black.

As the share price ticker rolled inexorably from right to left and the numbers sank lower and lower, getting closer to zero, Cullen quietly rose and walked from the room.

Vasilij cut the microphone while Jelena frantically explained, and then listened blind and frozen as the meeting broke up into shouts and the sound of chairs being overturned. He heard the analysts firing questions at him, all shouting over each other in the general hubbub. And looked at Jelena, slack-jawed and helpless, as the share price plummeted on his screen past 6, then 5, 4 and 3 before coming to rest at 2.5 when the Skype call went dead.

The small pub was packed to the gills and thick with body heat and the smell of spilt drink. Kim and Martin had trouble edging their way out from the bar with their drinks and through the throng out to the doorway and the cold night air. The freshness on their faces snapped them into something approaching sobriety and Kim huddled into Martin's coat, holding her drink away from her as she did so.

"That's better." She sighed and snuggled in closer. "So choking in there, I thought I was going to faint."

"The warmth of an Orkney Hogmanay." Martin smiled and kissed the top of her head. He inhaled deeply and exhaled in a loud, slow breath. "Can you smell that, though?"

"What?" She breathed deliberately, trying to taste the air, detect something significant. "I just smell cold."

"That." He sniffed sharply. "The smell of a new year. A fresh start."

"You're a soppy bugger sometimes, you know that?"

"Maybe. But look at those stars, that sky. Just look at it. Doesn't it make you feel as if anything is possible? A billion billion worlds out there, places we'll never see, spaces we'll never cross. And us, here, small and insignificant, caught up in our little squabbles, our petty politics, our trivial issues."

"I guess." She looked up at the blackness sprinkled with brilliance and glitter. A sky she wouldn't ever see back home, a view she'd never really noticed. It wasn't hard to see the grandeur he was seeing, but wasn't sure she could muster the necessary awe.

"The enormity of it - this infinite arrangement of matter. Stuff. Life."

"I didn't have you down as deep or spiritual." She was teasing, he could tell.

"I'm not, I don't think. But when you look at this and realise that, in a heartbeat, we'll be gone. Dust. And all this-" he swept the sky with his right hand. "This immense splendour will just carry on regardless. Uncaring and unknowing. We had the chance to do something in that blink of an eye, that tiny fleck of life that's ours - all the time we have, all the time we'll ever have - and if we don't seize that opportunity we are truly wasting it." He looked down into her eyes. "This will never come again. The universe doesn't care if we're happy or sad; if we spend our lives in drudgery and shame or delight and endeavour. It's all the same to it. But it's all we have and I don't want to waste a precious second of it anymore."

"Christ. That was - poetic."

"Thanks." He said, sarcastically.

"No. I mean it. It was so affecting, so… beautiful."

He rested his chin on her hair and breathed deeply. "Should be. I was up all last night rehearsing it."

"What?" She laughed, still sniffling. "Martin Jenkins! Well…"

"Well what?"

386

"Well …" For perhaps the first time, she was lost for words. "Fuck me."

From inside the pub came the sound of the chanted countdown to midnight. "10… 9… 8…"

He smiled a happy smile. "Maybe later."

26

New Year's Day

The yacht cut through the swollen sea with merely a hint of spray. The day was clear and bright, the North Sea calm and quiet. The sun glanced off the water and threw dappled reflections onto the polished steel and smoked glass on the boat.

Viktor had plotted a lazy loop around the main Orkney islands passing through Scapa Flow and up round to Westray before turning back to the mainland via Ronaldsay. A loud colony of grey seals basked on the rocks in the watery sunshine, individuals easily identifiable even at this distance. Off to the horizon, the occasional lazy black hump of an orca briefly broke the surface.

Blysse had been on deck watching for a while, lost in the tranquil beauty and chill, cold air. Wrapped only in a towelling robe she had quickly grown cold and retired behind the sliding doors, reluctant to leave the view alone in case it disappeared for good.

Now below in her cabin, she looked at herself in the mirror as Jelena adjusted the short train of her dress. This past week, her mind had been in turmoil about her upcoming wedding, and now it was here. If it hadn't been for the distraction of her last few panto performances she felt she would have worried herself into a frenzy.

Daily, even on Christmas Day itself, Vasilij had grown more short-tempered and distracted. He didn't share his business dealings with her so she had no idea what was behind the changes in his mood. She could only assume she had upset him or he was as nervous about the wedding as she was. Although it was a cliche for wedding day nerves, she really wondered now if she was doing the right thing.

"Jelena, what do you think Vasilij will be like as a husband?"

Jelena looked at her reflection and weighed up the best response. "You are nervous on your wedding day?" She smiled. "It is natural, of course."

"Yes. Yes, I am" she admitted. "But what will he be like, do you think? You must know him very well."

"Yes, I know him well. He is very kind man. Very loyal." She thought for a moment. "He will protect you and care for you."

"But he can... have a temper?" Blysse searched out Jelena's eyes but she kept them down, focussed on the dress. "These last few days he has been very angry. Have I done something to upset him?"

"No. No." Jelena kept her eyes down. "It is not you. Vasilij has had some bad news from his business. He has been upset. Your wedding will help him forget this, I think."

Blysse wasn't as reassured by this as she felt she should be.

Have you ever... disagreed with him? Had an argument?"

"Yes."

Blysse felt the curtness of Jelena's reply spoke more loudly than her words. "And what happened?"

"He was right. I was wrong." She shrugged, matter-of-factly.

"Has he ever threatened you? Hit you?"

"No." She looked up at Blysse now, kindly. "You are worried? Afraid?" Blysse bit her lip and didn't answer. "Do not be. Vasilij is very strong man, very rich man. He can be angry and violent. But not to you. Not to woman he loves."

"Really?" Blysse brightened and she looked afresh at herself in the mirror, twirling her long white dress and watching it play in the light.

"Really." Replied Jelena, thinking she should have finished her sentence with *Ah, but once he no longer loves you...*

Caught between the attraction of Jelena and the fear of Vasilij, Viktor was stuck. All he could think to do was await his fate stoically and hope that a married Vasilij would be more merciful and commute his stay of execution into something less final. Something which allowed him to keep Jelena.

He had had to bone up on conducting a wedding ceremony: the words, the procedure, the rigmarole. Here he stood, waiting alone on the rear deck as the ship bobbed gently past the island of Eginsay. Uncomfortable in his newly pressed uniform and captain's hat, his only prop a small Gideon bible which he clutched in his newly bandaged hands. His first of the two tasks assigned him having been done, the second minutes away.

He repeated to himself under his breath: "Do not fuck up. Do not fuck up."

Jelena, as usual, had done all the work. It was she who had arranged for caterers, florists, beauticians and dress designers to be flown in by helicopter to this godforsaken northern outpost and get everything ready for today. Vasilij had, for once, expressed no interest in budget and left the details to her. She had unilaterally decided, without bothering to obtain any evidence, that Orkney would have nothing suitable in the way of quality for any of the services she required and consequently, London's finest had all been drafted in to measure, quote, advise and create. Now the day was finally here she had, she belatedly realised, undertaken it as if it were her own and, in her official role for the day as bridesmaid and witness, she was officially becoming quite teary and emotional about the whole thing. She tried to put from her mind the stubborn concern that Vasilij's interest in his new toy would rapidly wane and the ramifications for Blysse that would ensue.

Vasilij straightened his tie in the mirror and smoothed his swept-back hair with his hands. Hands that were shaking uncontrollably.

He had done his best to hide his rage and despair from Blysse after the AGM yesterday but wasn't altogether sure he had managed it. He was still too much in shock to take it all in and comprehend the extent of this latest damage that had been done to him. He had not contemplated postponing the wedding - not for an instant. The bastards would have truly won, then. For now, he had to assess his losses, short and long term, and consider his options. As long as he had fish in the water there was still money to be made and value in his business but there was no getting away from the fact that his net worth on paper had fallen hugely and his personal reputation massively impacted.

First he would make sure Tony Stafford was dead. Then he would track down and deal with these other trouble-makers who had defiled his new facility - whoever they were. And then, perhaps, he would address the issue of his own staff: Viktor, Georgi and Feliks. They too had all failed him and all would have to pay the price.

His forehead burnt - the headache he'd had for the past eighteen hours refusing to be cowed by the painkillers he'd been taking. He washed another few down again with a stiff brandy and tried to calm himself.

Dressed in his newest, sharpest grey suit, almost silver, he admired his trim figure: thickening at the waist and neck certainly, but no more than middle-age would necessitate, certainly not overweight or flabby. His face almost healed and now devoid of makeup, apart from the merest hint of eyeliner that Jelena had insisted he apply to make his irises pop and draw attention away from the slightly discoloured skin around his left eye.

He checked his watch, took some long slow breaths, and patted his pocket down to make sure he had the rings still. He checked himself one final time in the mirror, made only a minor, unnecessary, adjustment to his shirt cuffs, and swept out of his cabin and onto the deck. He nodded to Viktor, who stood patiently at the rail, went to his position and awaited the arrival of his new bride.

Blysse stepped lightly up the steps onto the deck as some gentle choral music lilted from the loudspeakers on board and the rest of the crew crowded around on the deck above, straining out of sight of Vasilij to catch sight of this famous blonde. She looked nervously up at the peering heads above and then down at her feet, anxious not to step on her own dress. Jelena, behind her, held the short train: the dress was white silk and lace with long sleeves which tapered to her narrow wrists, and with deep pleats into her waist, emphasising her hips and breasts. The neck was scooped gently to show only a hint of cleavage and she wondered, briefly, if this was the most demure outfit she had ever worn and whether Vasilij, who had yet to see it, would be dazzled or disappointed. She was wearing her hair up again, as on the night of the party, with delicate ringlets curling either side of her cheeks and her slender neck garlanded by a thin gold chain Vasilij had presented her as a Christmas gift.

She shuffled forward to stand next to him and saw that he was beaming at her, his handsome profile and sparkling eyes making her catch her breath as the sea breeze gently brushed her hair. Viktor coughed quietly and drew their attention to him so that he could begin the service. Jelena stood slightly off to one side and waited. The music faded and Viktor began to speak.

It was her train, in the end, that saved her, Blysse believed. When the ship had keeled unexpectedly to one side and Viktor and Vasilij had suddenly vanished overboard, her train had caught on Jelena's heels as she felt herself also tipping backwards on the deck. The rocking motion caused her to arch her back and then twist as she fell and her hand reached out and grabbed at anything she could find. The anything happened to be Jelena, who had herself reached for, and held, the handle of the door leading from the side of the deck to the reception room laid out with food and drink.

The pair clung to each other as the boat righted itself and a huge wave of freezing seawater washed down across them, cascading down the stairs behind them to the deck below. The sudden shock of the cold made Blysse gasp and lose her grip but by this time Jelena had caught her with her other hand as she herself was being held by one of the deckhands. All too swiftly, some of the crew had seemed to realise what was happening and their survival training had immediately kicked in.

She had seen the look of surprise on Viktor's face as he fell backwards from her view. He had been scouring his bible intently, reciting words with a fierce concentration, his left hand gripping the spine of the book so that she could see the whites of his knuckles. In slow motion she saw his head rise, his eyes widen and then his shoulders fall away as he plunged over the rail and into the water, suddenly churning with white.

She hadn't seem Vasilij at all. One moment he was at her side, the next he had gone and she had to conclude that he had ended up in the water as well. As she sat wetly stunned on the carpet, her dress ruined and one shoe missing she couldn't piece together what was happening. Her ears had lost all ability to discern sound and all she could hear was a vague humming and blurry noises coming at her from all directions. She saw Jelena's face up close, her lips moving, but was unable to make out any words.

Blysse shook her head, wondering if she had water in her ears, but nothing would make the background wash she was hearing crystallise into coherent sounds. Around her all was movement and action while she sat transfixed, observing disconnected motion through a sound fog and a slo-mo filter. She felt Jelena put something cold to her lips and she automatically turned and sucked on it. The burning alcohol shot through her and the whole world burst back to full volume, the sound and noise congealing suddenly into shouted English and Russian.

"Where…?" Blysse couldn't tell if she was shouting or not, a cacophony around her.

"He's gone!" Jelena shouted. "We can't find him!"

"What…?" How long had gone by - seconds, minutes?

"He went overboard. Viktor too, but he's managed to climb back. We're going to circle around, try and find him."

Viktor was standing at the rail, now, soaked through with a blanket over his shoulders, scanning the sea for signs of Vasilij. Jelena leant over her, shivering in her own thin dress, until a crew member passed a blanket around her shoulders too and handed one to Blysse, still sitting in shock on the floor. She struggled to her feet and toppled gently over to the rail herself.

"We've got to get back to port." Viktor announced. "We are taking on water. Starting to list." He was hanging over the rail now looking down at whatever damage was visible. Another member of the crew came up from below and spoke closely in his ear. "Ladies, up to the bridge if you can. If we need the launch I'll let you know."

"What about Vasilij?" Blysse heard herself screaming. "We need to find him."

"Is too late. He is gone." The finality of the words shone in Viktor's eyes. "Priority is this ship. People on board. You." He turned and disappeared down the steps out of sight.

Blysse stood stunned at the rail as the boat turned slowly, floating wreckage bobbing past on the water. Jelena put her arm around her shoulder and tried to lead up through the reception room and up to the bridge but Blysse couldn't seem to move her legs.

"What happened?"

"We were hit." Jelena explained. "A collision."

"With what?"

"I don't know."

Jelena led her slowly through the reception room to the stairs. All down the starboard side, the whole length of the room one long smoked glass window, Blysse could see more wreckage and floating junk. As she watched, a large curved piece of metal curled into view: tubular, black, pieces of netting hanging from it. Then another, and another. As she watched the sections span slowly in the water and she could see that they were in fact all one, an almost complete circle of black tubing surrounded by a fringe of mesh and a ragged sheets of netting drifting around and across it.

At one spot on the circle there was a protrusion, some solid lump that she couldn't identify, holding its place like a black stone on an engagement ring. The circle continued to slowly turn as it rolled past the window, the protuberance cycling closer to the ship.

"What is it?" Blysse squinted, intrigued, as this mysterious object drew nearer and turned to face her.

"I can't tell." Said Jelena, also staring. They both stood entranced as the frame turned inexorably towards them in the slopping waves and they both screamed at exactly the same time as the object on the frame bumped up against the side of the ship. Tied to the mesh walkway around the salmon cage was the body of a man who, despite his face being exposed to seawater and feeding seagulls for several days, was still recognisably Tony Stafford.

27

On the banks of the Tweed between Walkerburn and Caddonfoot is a large wooden fisherman's hut. With windows and a wood stove and basic furniture, it is a safe haven used by fisherman and ghillie's throughout the season and, out of season, by Cullen as another place to lay his head. New Year's Day was clear and bright, the low sun as it climbed sending glints up from the frost-covered banks, glimmering reflections in the eddies on the river. Just before noon, Big Paul knocked and entered to find Cullen making coffee in a percolator sitting on the stove top.

"Happy New Year." Paul cried and thrust out his hand to shake with Cullen.

"Happy New Year." Cullen shook his hand, not bothering to get up. "Lovely day."

"Isn't it, just. Any coffee left? Smells good."

They sat and shared from Cullen's battered tin cup, looking out through the open doorway at the beautiful winter view. Paul sat dressed all in green: rubber galoshes that rose to a chest bib and braces, floppy hat with assorted flies hooked to the brim, woollen army jumper with patched elbows and epaulettes. He'd dragged into the hut with him a large catching net, folding stool, coolbox, rod and travel scale. Cullen sat amidst the clutter without comment. He had acquired a tattered pair of waders, which he wore under his fleece, that a previous occupant had left in the hut; his cowboy hat sat in its usual place. The only sound was birdsong and the odd distant rumble of a car from the road some distance off behind them.

When they'd finished, Paul rolled a joint while Cullen cleared away.

"What do you think, then?" Paul offered, licking his rizla.

Cullen stared out of the window at the burgeoning Tweed. "I think we'll be lucky."

Paul stood, stretched and gathered up his gear. Cullen collected a rod propped up in the corner of the room and together they marched out in the crisp glare of the morning and walked along the bank until they stopped at a gentle bend where the river bellied out before meandering off into the distance and out of sight beyond the far wooded slopes. They left their gear on the bank and both waded into the icy water as it tumbled and flowed past them.

Within an hour they were back sitting on the bank, seven large adult salmon glistening on the grass beside them. Paul took out a small hip flask, offered it to Cullen and, when he declined, opened it and took a swig. He surveyed the fat river bend and the catch beside them with a satisfied air.

"Blimey, like shooting fish in a barrel." He looked over their catch. "Must be 30-odd lbs of salmon here. What do you reckon?"

"Aye." Cullen replied and looked contemplatively upstream as the sunlight continued to dapple the water. "Reckon that's all of 'em flushed, judging by this. River's thick with 'em, all shapes and sizes. Look." He pointed further up the river where you could see fish leaping out of the water, perhaps one every ten seconds or so.

They watched in silence for a while, Paul continuing to take sips from his flask, Cullen content to smell the clean air and feel the chill on his face from the slight breeze. Eventually Paul stood again.

"Well, I was going to spend the whole day but… well, seems like there's no point. I ain't goin' to be able to eat my half as it is, and…" a cloud passed over his features, "… no-one else to feed it to."

Cullen looked at his friend and tilted his head to one side. "You can take my half - I don't want it." When Paul looked at him as if he was retarded he reiterated his point. "No, go on. Sell it down The Trust or something. And can you give one to Rosalind? I owe her one."

"You sure?"

"Positive." Cullen looked up at Paul, squinting into the light. "Never really liked salmon."

Postscript

The assets of **Caledonian Seafood Limited** were acquired by Aquamarine Seafarms when the share price remained below 3 NOK. The site of the damaged Head Office in Kirkwall was sold to property developers who demolished it to build luxury apartments and a residential care home. The closed containment facility in Manor Valley was bulldozed and sold back to the landowners at a nominal £1 valuation. The processing facility on Crowness Road is still in operation.

The market Spot price for salmon persists in fluctuating unpredictably. The CEO's of all the major salmon producers continue to congratulate themselves on their prowess, and reward themselves disproportionately, when the price is high and curse the vagaries of the market when the price is low.

The body of **Vasilij Ivan Krupchenko** was found washed up on a beach on Stronsay. The coroner verdict was accidental death from a heart attack brought on extreme hypothermia and an adverse reaction to painkilling medication taken against doctor's advice. His estate of $40 million included the proceeds from the sale of his shares in Caledonian Seafoods Limited. It was divided between his PA, Jelena Stiachkov, and his three sisters living in Estonia where his body is now buried.

Viktor Alexei Chorney was arrested in Kirkwall for piracy, specifically for unauthorised piloting of a wellboat. He pleaded guilty, on legal advice obtained by Jelena, and was given a suspended sentence in view of his guilty plea, the fact that he returned the vessel undamaged and for his efforts in helping to save the lives of those aboard the *A Crewed Interest*.

Jelena Maria Stiachkov was bequeathed $5 million in Vasilij Krupchenko's will. She married Viktor Alexei Chorney in Monaco where they now live and run a superyacht leasing business.

Feliks Beshanovski was admitted to Borders General Hospital with head injuries consistent with those caused by a nailgun. He was unable to identify the perpetrator and, after initial treatment, was committed to the Whim Hall Nursing Home in Lamancha where he receives round-the-clock care. At lunchtime every day he entertains the 30 other residents, all with chronic mental health issues, by barking like a dog. No nailgun was ever found.

Georgi Vladimir Sidorenko was never seen again, missing presumed drowned, after falling from a wellboat in Orkney.

The coroner pronounced that **Anthony Jermaine Stafford** had died from exposure after floating in the North Sea while tied to a un-moored salmon cage and ruled it as death by misadventure. His remains were flown back to California where they were cremated and his ashes scattered in the Pacific Ocean. His father bestowed a $1 million trust fund to UCLA in Pasadena to have an eco-maritime scholarship founded in his name.

Blysse Baptiste (aka Amanda Hardy) returned to the United States where she sold her engagement ring for $1.2 million. She used the money to rent a theatre off Broadway where she produces and stars in a highly successful year-round programme of panto for tourists visiting New York. She is currently acting as executive producer on *Doom Raider IV: Cindy Anna Jones, The Early Years*.

Detective Inspector Martin Jenkins married **Kim Marjorie Schofield** at Marylebone Registry Office. DI Jenkins transferred from Borders Policing Command to the Shetland Coastguard where he is now the Orkney Sector Manager based in Kirkwall. Kim works part-time providing marketing support for Orkney.com, a website run by Orkney Islands Council promoting tourism in the area. They are expecting their first child.

Paul "Big Paul" McInnes woke up on 3rd January to find a large basket outside his van containing two Jack Russell puppies and a brand new nail gun. Also inside the basket was a folded piece of A4 paper. One side was a copy of an email from the DVLA confirming his van was now taxed for twelve months; on the other side was an address written in a clear hand.

Mungo James Cullen lives alone. He has never owned a nailgun and is still not fond of salmon.

AUTHOR'S NOTE

I have used my own experience of working for a salmon company to inform the story and describe real facilities and features of the salmon farming industry. I am, however, no expert. Any mistakes are all my own and I apologise for them. Please don't write in.

I'd like to thank Emma, for reading early drafts and suggesting amendments – almost all of which I took on board (sometimes through gritted teeth) – and Ruth for her attentive feedback and eye for detail. I think their suggestions all improved the finished version.

Many of the places depicted in the book are based on actual locations, although some have been moved or merged together (to aid the story). For example, there is a bothy between West Linton and Peebles and it does look a bit as I have described. But not much.
There is also a location in Manor Valley which could be used for a salmon containment site. Probably.
There is no office building as described in Kirkwall, although it might look quite nice if there was.

All characters are completely fictitious, apart from Big Paul. He is based on someone real, who is sometimes called Big Paul, but who is nothing like the Big Paul in this book. Honest.
Cullen is not based on anyone and does not exist. He told me to tell you that.

mjf
19.08.2015

Tell others what you thought…

If you enjoyed this book, please leave a review on Amazon or Goodreads.

You can leave a review on Amazon here and on Goodreads here.

Cullen and Big Paul are back!

Follow their adventures in A Fistful of Collars. Available on Amazon here

About the Author

You can learn more about Mark Farrer at www.markfarrer.com, like him on Facebook here or follow him on Twitter @mark_farrer

Printed in Great Britain
by Amazon